NICE GUYS
FINISH DEAD

T0101988

*Look for these exciting Western series
from bestselling authors
William W. Johnstone and J.A. Johnstone*

The Mountain Man

Luke Jensen: Bounty Hunter

Brannigan's Land

The Jensen Brand

Smoke Jensen: The Early Years

Preacher and MacCallister

Fort Misery

The Fighting O'Neils

Perley Gates

MacCoole and Boone

Guns of the Vigilantes

Shotgun Johnny

The Chuckwagon Trail

The Jackals

The Slash and Pecos Westerns

The Texas Moonshiners

Stoneface Finnegan Westerns

Ben Savage: Saloon Ranger

The Buck Trammel Westerns

The Death and Texas Westerns

The Hunter Buchanon Westerns

Will Tanner, Deputy US Marshal

Old Cowboys Never Die

Go West, Young Man

NICE GUYS FINISH DEAD

WILLIAM W. JOHNSTONE

and

J.A. JOHNSTONE

KENSINGTON
PUBLISHING CORP.

www.kensingtonbooks.com

KENSINGTON BOOKS are published by
Kensington Publishing Corp.
119 West 40th Street
New York, NY 10018

Copyright © 2023 by J.A. Johnstone

All rights reserved. No part of this book may be reproduced in any form or by any means without the prior written consent of the Publisher, excepting brief quotes used in reviews.

All Kensington titles, imprints, and distributed lines are available at special quantity discounts for bulk purchases for sales promotion, premiums, fund-raising, educational, or institutional use.

Special book excerpts or customized printings can also be created to fit specific needs. For details, write or phone the office of the Kensington Sales Manager: Kensington Publishing Corp., 119 West 40th Street, New York, NY 10018. Attn. Sales Department. Phone: 1-800-221-2647.

This book is a work of fiction. Names, characters, businesses, organizations, places, events, and incidents either are the product of the author's imagination or are used fictitiously. Any resemblance to actual persons, living or dead, events, or locales is entirely coincidental.

To the extent that the image or images on the cover of this book depict a person or persons, such person or persons are merely models, and are not intended to portray any character or characters featured in the book.

PUBLISHER'S NOTE: Following the death of William W. Johnstone, the Johnstone family is working with a carefully selected writer to organize and complete Mr. Johnstone's outlines and many unfinished manuscripts to create additional novels in all of his series like the Last Gunfighter, Mountain Man, and Eagles, among others. This novel was inspired by Mr. Johnstone's superb storytelling.

KENSINGTON BOOKS and the WWJ steer head logo are trademarks of Kensington Publishing Corp.

ISBN: 978-0-7860-4905-9 (ebook)

ISBN: 978-1-4967-4067-0

First Kensington Hardcover Printing: February 2023

First Kensington Trade Paperback Printing: November 2023

10 9 8 7 6 5 4 3 2 1

Printed in the United States of America

NICE GUYS
FINISH DEAD

Chapter 1

"I don't believe I've ever heard of the D and T Ranch," Birch Bradshaw, of Bradshaw and Lane, commented to the two typical-looking cattlemen who had sought a few minutes of his time.

"I ain't surprised," Casey Tubbs remarked in return. "We never heard of Bradshaw and Lane before we rode into Fort Worth this mornin', did we, Eli?"

"That's a fact," Eli Doolin answered. "We thought it'd be a good idea to talk to you, since Fort Worth is a lot closer to Lampasas County than Abilene, Kansas, is."

"That's an important point for anyone selling cattle now," Bradshaw said. "Two of the biggest meat packers in the country have opened up here this year. We represent one of them."

"There's talk that the cattle market has finally gotten back up to reasonable prices for cows, so we thought we'd check with you folks to see what you're payin' these days."

Bradshaw took a hard look at the two leather-faced cowhands, then glanced again at the clock on the wall of his office and decided he'd wasted enough time with them. "You fellows didn't have to bother coming to my office to find out what the market for cattle is today. If you've got a few cows to sell, you can just drive them to our cattle pens, and they'll give you a dollar and a half apiece for them."

Casey looked at Eli and shrugged. Then back to Bradshaw, he said, "So you folks ain't payin' no more than you paid last year."

"Well, that is a price increase of fifty cents a cow," Bradshaw said.

"Reckon that's so," Casey admitted. "We thank you for your time. I reckon we'll be drivin' that herd up to Abilene, like we figured, Eli. It ain't back to what it used to be, but it's a helluva lot better'n a dollar and a half."

"How many cows have you got to sell?" Bradshaw asked.

"Three thousand head," Casey answered.

"'Three thousand'?" Bradshaw repeated. "For that many, we can pay five dollars a head for good cattle. That's the most anyone here in Fort Worth will offer you. You drive that herd into our pens, and we'll pay you cash money the day you deliver them. No fooling around with banks or anybody else. There's enough money in that safe right there to buy your whole herd." When both of the cattlemen looked skeptical, he said, "Abilene's not paying forty dollars a head, like it was two years ago."

"I reckon you're right about that," Casey agreed, "but they're payin' twenty-five."

"That's just a rumor," Bradshaw replied. "I'm offering you a solid price. You'd be crazy to drive them all the way to Kansas, when you could save money selling them to me. Tell you what, I'll go out on a limb and offer you six dollars a head."

"We'll think on it," Eli said, "and get back in touch."

"Don't wait too long, boys," Bradshaw said. "There's other ranches looking to get rid of their cows."

"That smug son of a gun," Eli remarked when they left Bradshaw's office. "Him and his kind are gettin' fat on the poor little ranches that are tryin' to sell their cattle to keep the banks from takin' over their land. He said he's got enough money right there in his safe to give us cash money for our three thousand cows at six dollars a head. How much is that?"

Casey paused to work it out in his head, then replied, "Eighteen thousand dollars, if I figured right. Three times five is fifteen, right?"

"That's right," Eli said. "And some say they're payin' twenty-five a head in Abilene and Wichita. How much is that?"

"A lot more," Casey answered. "I wonder how hard it would be to get that little safe of his open? I expect he's got a lot more than that in that safe. Wouldn't you expect that he's got more, Oscar?"

"I think he might, Elmer," Eli responded, using the other alias they had adopted for their lawless activities. About to jump on the idea, he hesitated when another thought struck him. "He's a dad-blamed thief, but if we was to put him outta business, these poor small ranches wouldn't have no place to get even a dollar and a half for their cows."

"I reckon that's right," Casey said. "I didn't consider that." It then occurred to him: "When you think about it, we're just doin' the same thing he is. We're buyin' up all the cows we can at a price way below their market value."

"That's so, but at least we're payin' a lot more than he is. We've been payin' 'em enough to pay off their bank loans, so they don't lose their land. So if we was to get the money Bradshaw has in that safe, we could buy more cattle from the ranchers. And we could give them a better price than what they'd get from Bradshaw. Everybody wins, but Bradshaw."

Casey grinned while he considered what Eli just said. "I declare, Oscar," he stated, "sometimes I think you coulda been the brains of this partnership, instead of me."

"Whoever said you was the brains?" Eli responded.

"Why, I think it was just automatically understood, weren't it?" Casey responded. "We need to figure out a way to get into that office of his one night."

"Even if we did, what are we gonna do with that iron safe he says his money's in. We can't hardly carry it outta there. It ain't a great big safe, but did you look at it? It's bolted to the floor. Even if it weren't, it'd be a job for Elmer and Oscar to carry it outta there, down the steps, and put it on a horse."

"Yeah, I took a good look at it," Casey said. "First thing I noticed was that old safe was built before 1861."

"How the hell do you know that?" Eli interrupted.

"'Cause it's got a keylock on it," Casey answered. "Every safe made after 1861 has a combination lock on it. So all we'd have to do is fill that keyhole with gunpowder and blow the door off."

"Well, I'll be . . ." Eli started, then paused to see if Casey was serious. "Do you know what you're talking about? Can you do that with gunpowder?" Casey said they could. "You know," Eli went on, "me and you have been workin' cattle for quite a few years. I ain't ever asked you before, but what was you doin' before we started workin' together?"

Casey chuckled and replied, "Workin' cattle. Before I run into you, I was an honest man," he joked.

Eli was thinking hard on the idea of taking the money out of that old safe. He looked back at the cattle buyer's office they had just left, considering how much trouble it might be to break into it. The office was actually a small two-room house built on poles that raised it so Birch Bradshaw could look out over the entire cattle pen area from his desk. "You reckon he stays up there all the time? There was a door to another room. You reckon that's where he sleeps?"

"I don't know," Casey replied. "He didn't look the kind to cook and do for himself. I bet he goes home at night. The only outhouse I saw was back yonder between the pens where we first came in here." He thought for a minute. "His name's Bradshaw. His partner, Lane, might usually be in the office, but just wasn't there right now." He paused to stroke his chin as another thought came to mind. "If they ain't worried about leavin' all that money in that old safe while they go home at night, then there must be some guards watchin' this place at night."

"Most likely have guards that watch all the pens and everything. I reckon we need to find all that out," Eli said. "You got any gunpowder in your pocket?"

Casey chuckled. "Not right now, but I reckon we could buy a pound of black powder at Hasting's," he suggested, referring to Hasting's Supply, a large supply house they passed on the way into Fort Worth. He waited for Eli to say more, but when he didn't, he asked, "Whaddaya think? You wanna do it?"

"I reckon it's about time we had another payday," Eli answered. "And that money would do a lot more good in our hands than his. Let's give it a try."

"As you and me, or as Elmer and Oscar?" Casey asked.

"I expect you're thinkin' about hittin' that office after dark and hopin' nobody sees us comin' or goin'. That'ud be all right for you and me. But I don't think we ought to take a chance on anybody seein' us near that office. So I think we oughta leave all the outlaw business to those two little old men."

"I reckon that's the reason we packed their outfits, just in case they showed up," Casey said. "Let's go get some supper and come back to take a walk around the pens after that. See what it's like around here in the evening."

After a supper of chicken and dumplings at a little restaurant named The Potluck Kitchen, Casey and Eli felt like they needed to take a walk. Chicken and dumplings were not an entrée they often had a chance to sample. It was not a dish that Juanita Garcia, their cook back at the D&T Ranch, was familiar with. As a result, they both found themselves uncomfortably full.

"I noticed that woman that does the cookin' back there was payin' kinda close attention to you," Casey said as they walked away. "You weren't makin' eyes at her, were you? She was a pretty good-sized woman. You sure you could handle her?"

"I didn't notice," Eli claimed. "She was just being friendly, most likely."

The hotel they were staying in that night was only a few doors down from the restaurant, and it was only a short stretch of the legs from the stable where they had left their horses. Everything in this little part of Fort Worth was built for the convenience of the cattle sales, so everything was close at hand. Even the cattle pens were within close walking distance. So that was where Casey and Eli planned to walk off their supper.

The sun was already in the process of finding a comfortable spot to drop below the horizon when they walked between the pens on their way to the Bradshaw and Lane office. They had gone only halfway to the office when a man on horseback met them. He pulled up before them and asked, "You gentlemen lost?"

"Why, no, we ain't," Casey answered at once. "Why do you ask?"

"'Cause the pens are closed for the day, and the owners don't generally want people in here at night."

"I swear," Casey continued, "we never even thought about that possibility. We just ate so doggone much at the Potluck Kitchen we decided to take a walk. And I think I left my watch on Birch Bradshaw's desk this afternoon. So we decided this was the best place to walk, and we'd go get my watch."

"Mr. Bradshaw ain't in his office this late," the man on the horse said. "There ain't nobody in that office after five o'clock any day."

"Now, ain't that something, Eli? That's gonna put us late

startin' for home in the mornin'." He smiled at the man then
and asked, "Are you some kinda guard or something?"

"That's right," he said, "but I'm just one of four riders who
will be patrolling these pens all night long."

"Well, I expect we'd best turn around and start back for the
hotel," Casey said to Eli. "Best not try to rustle any cattle
tonight."

"It'd be kinda hard on foot, anyway," the guard said with a
chuckle. "You fellers have a nice evenin'." He rode on past
them.

"Much obliged," Eli called after him.

"'Much obliged'?" Casey questioned after the guard had
ridden on. "I kept waitin' for you to jump in there and help
me out with that fellow, and you acted like your lips grew together."

"You was doin' all right," Eli remarked. "I was ready to
jump in there to bail you out if you got in too much trouble.
While you was makin' chatty talk with that feller, I was noticing the Roundup Saloon over yonder, next to the Potluck
Kitchen. If I can see the chairs on that porch, we could sit on
the porch of that saloon and see over here where we're
walkin'."

"And we could get an idea of about how much time we'd
have between them guards ridin' around," Casey finished for
him. "Damn, that's a good idea, Eli. Let's go buy a bottle of
whiskey and sit on the porch. It'll be a little while before it
gets hard dark."

So that's what they did. They went into the saloon and
bought a bottle of rye whiskey, that being Eli's favorite drink.
Casey preferred corn whiskey, because that's what he was raised
on, but he would drink rye on occasion, and this seemed to be
one such occasion. They told the bartender they wanted to
sit on the porch and enjoy it and promised to bring the two
glasses back to the bar. There were only two chairs on the

porch and there was a drunk in one of them. "I'll buy you a couple of shots of likker for that chair," Eli told him, and the drunk came out of the chair immediately, staggering as he did. Casey grabbed his elbow to steady him, while Eli pressed a couple of coins in his hand. Then Casey headed him toward the door. They sat down and poured themselves a drink.

It was a pleasant evening to sit on the porch and enjoy an after-supper drink. As they had speculated, they could see Bradshaw's office sitting above the fences of the cattle pens. They could also see the spot in the alleyway where they had been stopped by the guard. It was probably no more than fifty yards from where they sat. The drunk came back to the porch before they caught sight of a guard. His last two drinks evidently having erased his short memory, he asked if they could spare a quarter to buy him a drink. He went over and slumped down against the wall of the saloon after Casey told him they didn't have any money, while keeping their bottle out of sight.

It was forty-five minutes by Casey's watch before they sighted a guard passing the spot where they had encountered the man who stopped them. By that time, the light of day was already heading for the barn. If it was that long again before he made his next round, it might be dark enough to make it hard to see him. "Whaddaya think, partner?" Casey asked. "You wanna sit here for another hour to see if we can catch sight of him again?"

"Hell, I don't know if it's any use or not," Eli said. "There's a lotta cattle pens out there, but if there's four riders, like he said, they oughta be around a lot sooner than that. Maybe there's four of 'em, but there's just two of 'em ridin', while the other two are sleepin'. Let's give 'em a little bit longer, until it gets too dark to see from here."

As they suspected, after another thirty minutes had passed with no sign of a rider, they determined it too dark to see anymore. "I'm still thinkin' we could get in that office without anybody seein' us. Then watch for the night guard to pass by before we blow the door off that old safe," Casey declared.

"That suits me," Eli said. "We've got a big outfit to support, and I can't think of anybody I'd rather have some financial help from than Bradshaw and Lane. We'll get what we need at Hasting's tomorrow and get ready to go to work tomorrow night. Gimme your glass and I'll take 'em back to the bar."

While Eli returned their glasses, Casey walked over to the drunk slumped against the wall. "Hey," he said, "wake up."

"Huh?" the drunk blurted, not really asleep. Then he uttered "Huh?" once more when Casey dropped the half-full bottle of rye whiskey in his lap. Realizing what it was, he clutched it with both hands. Then, with no word of thanks, he scrambled off the porch and disappeared into the darkness of the alley between the saloon and the Potluck Kitchen. Casey was reminded of a stray dog that was thrown a scrap of meat.

"What'd you say to him?" Eli asked when he came back in time to see the drunk's exit.

"I didn't say anything to him," Casey replied. "I just dropped that whiskey bottle in his lap and he took off."

"What'd you do that for? That bottle wasn't half-empty."

"I figured you could afford it, and it would make that fellow's day," Casey said.

"Or be just enough to kill him," Eli declared.

"Either way, he'll be a whole lot happier."

Chapter 2

After breakfast the next morning, Casey and Eli checked out of the hotel, then went to the stable to get their horses. Raymond Rakestraw, the owner of the stable, offered a helping hand as they saddled their horses. "We've got a few places we've got some business to clean up," Casey told him. "So we'll leave our packhorses and packs here till this afternoon. Then we'll be headin' for home."

"That so?" Raymond asked. "Where's home?"

"About a hundred miles south of here on the Lampasas River," Casey answered.

"I reckon it's a good thing I gave them horses some grain last night," Raymond said.

"Reckon so," Eli said. "They got a pretty good ride ahead of 'em."

They rode out on the same road they had come into Fort Worth on, but now with two objectives in mind. First, a stop at Hasting's Supply to buy some black powder. But secondly, they were looking for likely places to leave their packhorses while they made their visit to Bradshaw and Lane. They had talked it over again last night, but still decided it best to make the visit as Elmer and Oscar, the two elderly bandits. Consequently, they would need a place to change into their "working clothes," a place where the horses would not likely be found. And that might take some time.

"Howdy, what can I help you fellows with this mornin'?" Floyd Hasting greeted them when they walked into his store. It was a large building with long rows of racks displaying many different tools and implements.

"Howdy," Casey returned his greeting. "My partner and I are headin' back home to Lampasas County. And we've been havin' this argument for two days. Maybe you can help us."

"Well, I'll be happy to try," Floyd said.

"Here's the thing," Casey went on. "Back at the ranch house, we've got a jim-dandy oak tree about yea-big." He demonstrated by making a circle with his arms. "It's growing right up beside the back porch, makes a wondrous amount of shade. The only problem is, it's got a big hole in the trunk, right there at eye level. And that ain't a problem because that hole is big, but it ain't nowhere near as big as the trunk. The problem is a bunch of yellow jackets have found that hole. And they've run us off the porch." He paused to make sure Floyd was following. He was, but he had a look like he wondered if it was ever going to lead anywhere useful.

"All right," Casey continued. "Here's what I'm thinkin'. You sell black powder for guns, right?" He paused again for an answer. Floyd nodded, so Casey continued. "I'm thinkin' a small amount of black powder in that hole would clean that nest outta there without hurtin' the tree trunk a whole lot. What do you think? Think that would work?"

"I expect it might," Hasting answered. "You ever use black powder before?" Casey and Eli both shook their heads. "Well, you gotta be careful how you handle it. That hole you described might be big enough to where the powder would just make a big ball of fire when you lit it. That sounds like it would get rid of your yellow jackets. But you wanna make sure you just dump the powder in the hole loose. 'Cause if you've got it closed up in a small container, it'll explode and tear hell outta your hole. It don't like confinement." Casey glanced at Eli and winked.

"That sounds like what I need," Casey said. "Probably don't need but a few pounds, you reckon?"

"I can sell you the smallest container it's sold in," Hasting said. "And that's a five-pound cannister. You have to keep it dry."

"We'll take a cannister of it, and we sure appreciate you tellin' us all about it. We'll be careful, won't we, Eli?"

"Just remember, don't let this stuff get down into any tight places, 'cause if fire touches it then, it explodes instead of makin' a big splash of fire."

"We're gonna remember that part, all right," Eli assured him.

"How are you gonna light it?" Hasting thought to ask.

"I don't know," Casey said. "I hadn't thought about that. I reckon to be safe, maybe tie a match to a broom or something so I ain't too close to it."

"I think it'd be a better idea to use some dynamite fuse," Hasting suggested. "That way, you can just cut the length you need to give you time to light it and walk away from the tree. I can fix you up with that, too."

"We 'preciate your help, Mr. Hasting. I believe you've solved our yellow-jacket problem for sure."

When they walked outside the store, Eli asked, "You got that idea about the tree from those yellow jackets in that little tree behind the bunkhouse, didn't ya?"

"Matter of fact," Casey said. "Brilliant, weren't it?"

They left Hasting's with their metal cannister of black powder and fuses, and rode on out the road leading south out of Fort Worth. They remembered a creek that ran right across the road, when they rode into the town, and they thought it might be the place for them to make their secret camp. As they recalled, it was about a mile short of Hasting's. It turned out to be less than that, when they struck it this morning, but everything else they had recalled about it was accurate. It was wide, but it wasn't deep enough to have to have a bridge to cross it, about axle deep on a standard farm wagon, they figured. The road passed through a heavily wooded area built up around the creek, so it looked to be the perfect spot for their camp. The first thing they checked for was hoofprints on either bank of the creek that might indicate others had camped there. They didn't want to leave their horses and packs in a popular campground.

To make sure they didn't leave any hoofprints now, they kept their horses on the road until entering the water. Then they turned them upstream and remained in the water until they reached the spot they thought was perfect for their needs, before leaving the water. "We ain't gonna find a much better place than this," Eli declared. Casey agreed, so they took a little time to picture the setup for their camp. After they decided where they would tie their packhorses with enough lead rope to let them reach water, they gathered enough dead limbs to build a fire. It would be late at night when they came from the cattle pens, and it would be awful dark back in those trees. Finally Eli said, "I'm satisfied. You?"

"Yep," Casey answered. "This oughta do just fine. I'm tempted to go get the packhorses and leave 'em here now, but I don't wanna dare bad luck to happen."

"Me neither," Eli agreed. "We better wait till it's time to come back here to get ready for tonight." He looked straight up through the trees at the sun almost directly overhead. "Accordin' to my belly, it's about time to eat some dinner. You wanna ride on back to that place we ate supper at yesterday?"

"The Potluck Kitchen," Casey reminded him. "Well, we ain't been hurt there so far. We've got plenty of time to kill before dark, if you wanna ride on in closer to town and try something different, though."

"It suits me to go back to the Potluck," Eli said. "Like you said, we ain't been hurt there yet. Besides, after them chicken and dumplin's, I'd like to see what that woman comes up with today. What was her name?"

"Joy," Casey replied.

"Right, Joy," Eli remarked. "I swear, if there was ever a woman that got stuck with the wrong name, it has to be her. I wonder who she's so mad at. When she set that plate down in front of me, she gimme a look like she dared me to eat it. Well, I didn't touch it till I saw you start eatin' yours. She didn't do nothin' to you, so I went ahead and ate mine."

Casey chuckled. "I saw her eyeballin' you. Hell, she weren't mad at you. You got worst things to worry about. She was lookin' at you like she was measurin' you for a weddin' outfit."

"I'll be damned," Eli protested. "That'ud be like matin' with a gorilla."

"So I reckon you're tellin' me you don't want to go back to the Potluck for dinner, right?"

"No, I ain't sayin' that," Eli answered meekly. "We wanna eat where the food's good, and we don't know nothin' about any of the other places here."

"Well, that's to my likin'," Casey said with a chuckle. "Let's go see what Joy's servin' today. We need a good dinner. We're workin' tonight."

They climbed back on their horses and entered the water again to ride back downstream to the road, then headed back to the cattle pens and the short strip of businesses that were close by. After tying Smoke and Biscuit up at the hitching rail in front of the Potluck Kitchen, they walked inside and took a seat at one end of the long table in the center of the dining room. When Joy Black came out of the kitchen and saw them, she broke out a crooked smile that was purposefully adapted to hide the missing teeth on one side of her mouth. "Well, look who's come back to see us, Roy."

"Howdy boys," Roy Black greeted them from his usual position by the cash register. "You musta liked Joy's chicken and dumplin's."

"We sure did," Casey said. "We're fixin' to head back home today, but we decided we had to stick around to see what Joy cooked for dinner."

"Somethin' you ain't likely to get nowhere around here," Roy told them, "especially if you folks are in the cattle business."

"What's that?" Eli asked.

"Lamb," Roy said. "And even if you've et it before, you ain't never had it like Joy fixes it with rice and gravy."

Both Casey and Eli were astonished to hear that. "Why, that's the same as sayin' a cussword to a cattleman," Eli said. "I ain't never ate no lamb, but I've ate rattlesnake on occasion, so I reckon I'll risk lamb, as long as Joy's cookin' it."

"I've never tried lamb before, either," Casey said, "but I'll try it, too. It'll be something to tell the boys at the ranch when we get back home."

"I remember you both wanted coffee," Joy said when she came to the table with two cups and placed them before the two men. She winked at Eli and said, "I remember you liked a little sugar with yours, too." She favored him with her lopsided smile.

Eli took a quick look to see if Roy was watching her closely, but he seemed oblivious to her attention to him. "Yes, ma'am," he said. "I like a little sugar when I can get it, but that's not very often."

"Well, you can get it here whenever you want it," Joy told him. Eli and Casey both swallowed hard at that point. Although her main focus was on Eli, she flashed a smile at Casey as well.

"I expect your husband likes a little sugar in his coffee, too," Eli suggested.

"Husband? Who, Roy?" She offered up a hearty laugh. "Roy ain't my husband. He's my brother."

"Well, thank the Lord for that," Casey uttered in relief, for Roy looked to be a sizable man, even sitting behind the counter. He flashed Joy a smile and asked, "How can we get some of this lamb you've fixed? I'm anxious to try it."

"I'll get you some right now, honey," Joy answered. She gave Eli a playful tweak on the cheek, and went to the kitchen to make up two plates of food.

Casey looked at Eli then and said, "Roy and Joy, you have my blessing, my son. Just remember we have work to do tonight."

Joy came out of the kitchen, carrying the two plates, piled high with lamb, rice, and beans, just as two men walked in the door. "Just set them two plates right down here," one of the men ordered, and pointed to the other end of the table. A heavyset man, with rough features accented by a thick black mustache, he and his friend appeared to have just come from the cattle pens. Their clothes were covered with the dust stirred up by the confused cows they had been transferring from one pen to another.

"I'll be right with you," Joy told him. "These fellows have already ordered their dinner."

"Maybe so," the burly-looking man insisted, "but we're in a hurry. So set 'em down right here, or I'm gonna turn this table upside down." He and his partner sat down on the bench, his hands placed under the edge of the big table as if ready to turn it over.

"Now, Jed," Roy Black finally spoke up, still seated behind the counter. "There ain't no call for you and Sam to come in here and act like that. You can see those two fellers at the other end of the table have already ordered their dinner, and Joy will bring yours right away."

Jed scowled in Casey and Eli's direction. "They don't look

to me like they mind a-tall. Do you, gents? If you did, I expect you'da opened your mouth by now, wouldn't you?" His look indicated he hoped they might. Casey and Eli exchanged questioning glances; then both of them shrugged, waiting to see if Roy was going to handle the rude bully.

With no intention of being intimidated by them, Joy started to place the plates before Casey and Eli, but Jed started to lift the table up from the floor. "Do like he said, Joy!" Roy blurted. "If you don't, they're gonna make a mess in here again." Joy stopped, still holding the plates; then she reluctantly put the plates in front of Jed and his companion. She looked at Eli and said, "I'll fix you fellers up another plate."

"After you get me and Sam some coffee," Jed said. Then he looked at Casey and Eli. "That's all right with you, too, ain't it, gents?"

"Whatever Joy wants," Eli said. "Ain't that what you say, Casey?"

"It don't matter what that whore wants," Jed declared.

Casey looked at Eli and shrugged. Then he slowly got to his feet and stood there for a few seconds, watching Jed and Sam dig into the food before them. Jed paused, his mouth full of lamb, when Casey walked down to that end of the long table and stood by his shoulder. "Don't let me disturb your eatin'," Casey said. "I was just curious. I ain't ever had no lamb before, and I was wonderin' what it tastes like." He reached down with his left hand, and using two fingers, he scooped up a blob of the stewed meat and rice and put it in his mouth. "That tastes pretty good, don't it?" He licked his fingers and repeated the sampling. "Yes, sir, that's good eatin'. I think you're gonna like this stuff, Eli." He reached over and wiped his fingers on Jed's shirt.

Captured in a long moment of shocked disbelief, Jed's brain suddenly began working again. "Why, you son of a . . ." was as far as he got before Casey's right hand came up and caught him beside his eye with the barrel of his Colt .45. He slumped forward onto the table, his face in his plate. His partner, Sam, equally frozen for a few seconds, realized too late what was happening. Sam reached for his gun, but Eli already had his Colt in hand and aimed at him.

"Take that piece of trash and get outta here," Eli told him. "I'm a U.S. deputy marshal, and the next time I catch you in here, you're under arrest. Now, git, before I decide to shoot you and be done with you." Sam was impressed enough to grab one of Jed's arms and pull him off the bench, then out the door. Casey and Eli went out with him and helped him throw Jed across the saddle of his horse.

Sam climbed on his horse and took the reins of Jed's in his hand. In one feeble act of defiance, he said, "I told him I didn't wanna eat at this dump again." He rode off toward town then, leading Jed's horse.

"That lamb stew did taste pretty good," Casey said, "and I've worked up a little appetite for it now."

So they went back inside, just as a couple more customers came into the Potluck, a man and a woman. The woman looked back at the man leading a horse with a body across the saddle and said, "I hope that wasn't from a case of food poisoning."

Overhearing her, Casey said, "No, ma'am. I think they came from the saloon next door."

When they went back to their places at the table, Joy was waiting for them with two fresh plates of lamb stew. "I'm awful sorry about that," she said. "Roy is also." While they were outside, she had picked up the first two plates and taken them back to the kitchen. In a gesture of respect for what Casey and Eli had done, she dipped out their stew before she dumped the other back in the pot.

"No real harm done, except you lost a couple of customers," Eli said. "We might not have caused such a fuss if he hadn't called you a name he shouldn't have." Actually, he and Casey were both wondering why Roy had been reluctant to take a role that should have been his.

"That's such a sweet thing for you to say," Joy replied. "But he weren't all wrong. I have to pick up a little extra money lookin' at the ceiling from time to time."

Eli almost choked on a mouthful of food when she said it. Flustered for a proper response, he said, "Of course, you do. Ain't nothin' wrong with that." He purposefully avoided Casey's eye, knowing he was grinning from ear to ear.

"I heard what you said to those two outside," Joy went on. "I didn't have no idea you was U.S. deputy marshals. Maybe we ought to let you eat for free today, especially after you got rid of those two."

"I wouldn't wanna be untruthful with you, ma'am," Eli confessed. "Me and Casey ain't deputy marshals. Casey just said that to try to make them stay away from here from now on. We're from a ranch about a hundred miles from here on the Lampasas River."

That brought a chuckle out of Joy. "Well, I hope it works. Those two have been in here a few times before, and they always act like a couple of jackasses." She refilled their cups with coffee and asked, "Are you gonna come back to supper with us?"

"That's hard to say," Eli said. "We've got a couple of people we've got to see before we leave Fort Worth. So it depends on how long that takes. But I know we'll surely try." Again he could feel Casey's grin without having to look at him.

They finished their dinner and went to the end of the counter, where Roy was still parked behind the register. "I feel like I ought to let you have your dinner on the house, after what you did. I feel bad that I didn't help you with those two losers, but I'm stuck here on this stool till I can get a chance to work on my chair." Casey looked around the end of the counter to discover Roy had no legs. He was seated on a stool with two stumps where his legs once were. The chair he was referring to was a wheelchair against the wall with a wheel missing. When he saw the look of surprise on Casey's face, he said, "You didn't know. I thought everybody did." He laughed then. "I bet you wondered why I didn't come over to that table and handle that problem."

"Well, I'll be . . ." Casey started. "We'll sure as hell pay for our dinner and pay for the two dinners we cost you to boot." When Roy started to protest, Casey put the money on the counter and said, "Done. Let's go, Eli, we're runnin' late."

Chapter 3

The afternoon passed slowly, with a good deal of time spent at the Roundup Saloon, a lot of it spent on the porch, watching the activity at the pens across the way. They realized there was a chance Joy might come out of the Potluck Kitchen right next door and see them sitting on the saloon porch, but there was no sign of her. Eli was really the only one worried about the possibility. Casey wasn't that concerned. He figured they owed her no explanation. When it got to be about suppertime, instead of eating, they went to the stable and got their packhorses and headed for their camping spot. Supper would be some beef jerky, until after the visit to Bradshaw and Lane, depending on whether or not they were able to get away without being followed.

Just as they had when they discovered their camping spot, they rode in the creek until reaching the spot where they had left the water. With still light enough to see, they checked the creek bank to make sure there were no tracks in addition to the ones they had left before. They checked the pile of wood they had gathered for their fire they hoped to build after they returned from the pens that night. A rope line was stretched between two trees to tie the packhorses to. When they were satisfied that they had prepared their camp as best they could, they opened the packs that held their costumes. By this time, after the successful ruses they had accomplished, they were both quite adept at duplicating the likenesses of Elmer and Oscar. As far as the makeup that worked so well to make their skin appear old and wrinkled, they used it quite sparingly, for they weren't sure where they could get more. It was so much better than the dirt and water they mixed up for their first job that they always looked for places to get more whenever in a new town. As Casey said, "There just ain't a market for it along the Brazos."

When they were ready to go, they held their final inspection of each other to make sure they looked like the two originals. Satisfied, they pulled on their oversized coats that gave them their familiar baggy look, and also hid their guns and holsters. "Ready, Elmer?"

"Ready, Oscar," Casey replied.

Out where the creek crossed the road to the south Fort Worth cattle pens, two old men rode out of the water and turned to the north. By the time they reached the pens, darkness was beginning to settle down into the divided fenced areas, so they decided the time was right. Thinking the best place to leave their horses was at the hitching rail at the Roundup Saloon, they tied them there and walked across the fifty-odd yards to the edge of the closest fence, carrying the cannister of black powder and fuses, plus a coil of rope and a crowbar. Their plan was to wait there in a ditch just outside the lane where the guards rode their rounds until a guard came by. If they were riding the same schedule as the day before, when Casey timed them from the porch of the saloon, the two partners should have plenty of time to go over the fence and go the short distance to Bradshaw and Lane's office. Prepared to sit down in the ditch and wait, they were surprised by the arrival of a guard at almost the same time they reached the ditch. They were forced to hurry to jump in the ditch before he was opposite them. "Damn if that ain't just about perfect timin'," Eli whispered. They hustled up out of the ditch and ran to the fence to peer into the darkness from which the guard had ridden. Seeing nothing, they climbed over the fence and hurried along the lane until coming to the steps that led up to the two-room office.

When almost up to the top of the steps, Eli reached up ahead of him and grabbed Casey's arm. "What?" Casey whispered.

Eli said nothing, but pointed to one of the windows in the room next to Bradshaw's office. There was a light in the room. "What the . . ." Casey started before he caught himself. It was a small lamp somewhere in the room. They sat down on the steps to decide what to do. "They wouldn't go home and leave a lamp burnin'."

"Not on purpose," Eli whispered. "That ain't the office, anyway. Maybe they just forgot about it when they quit and went home."

"Yeah, but you heard that guard yesterday," Casey countered. "Bradshaw ain't never in that office after five o'clock. They wouldn't even have had a lamp lit. There's somebody in there."

"Whaddaya think we oughta do?" Eli asked. "Call it off and get the hell outta here? Or try to take 'em by surprise, just like we would if we was robbin' a bank?"

"You know, we keep thinkin' there's at least two fellows in there, 'cause there's two names on the business. There might not be but one. Ol' Bradshaw might be all by himself. As long as we've come this far, let's see how hard it is to open the door. If there's somebody in that other room, he might not hear us at the door."

"Why don't we go on up on the porch and sneak over by

that window," Eli suggested, "and see if we can see anybody in there." Casey nodded at once, thinking that a better idea. So they climbed up the rest of the steps and tiptoed across the porch to the window, being careful not to be silhouetted in the glass. The windows were barred and the curtains drawn tight. They didn't hear anything from inside the room for quite some time. Eli shook his head and started to withdraw from the window, when they heard a sound. It sounded like a woman's giggle. They looked at each other, then quickly pressed their ears against the wall of the room again. A few seconds later, they heard it again and definitely identified the noise to be a woman's giggle. A picture was rapidly beginning to form in both their minds of Birch Bradshaw getting in a little extra work after office hours. That picture was embellished when they heard a growling voice, like that of a wolf. It was enough to cause them both to quickly retreat to keep from laughing.

"You reckon Mrs. Bradshaw knows about ol' Birch's extra work?" Casey asked.

"Maybe that's Mrs. Bradshaw in the room with him," Eli said.

"I got a feelin' it ain't," Casey said. "But I say, we might as well go on in there and blow that safe apart. They're so busy, they might not even hear it." When Eli gave him a questioning look, Casey said, "But first we'll take care of those two in the other room. It's a good thing we brought some rope. You can't never go wrong bringin' some rope."

They went back to the door then to look it over. They had not really paid a great deal of attention to it when they were there to talk to Bradshaw about selling cattle. At that time, there were no thoughts of breaking in. Now they considered themselves lucky to find Bradshaw was still inside, because there was a heavy padlock hanging on a hasp beside the door. It would no doubt be used to lock the door from the outside when he left for the day. It would have been much more difficult to open the door, had that been in place. As it now was, however, it was not a great deal of trouble to pry the simple door lock open with their crowbar. Once they were inside, they went at once to the door to the second room. There was a keylock on the door, but the key was on the inside of the room. "Ain't no use to disturb 'em till we're ready to go," Casey whispered. Eli agreed. So they tied one end of their rope around the doorknob and knotted the rest of it around a post that supported one end of a roof beam.

Eager to try the gunpowder on the door of the safe, Casey went to the little iron safe in the corner by Bradshaw's desk. Using rolling papers for making cigarettes, he patiently sifted black powder into the keyhole of the safe, filling the empty space around the lock with the powder until he could get no more inside. Then he stuck a twelve-inch fuse in the keyhole, and when Eli was outside the door on the porch, he lit it and hustled out there to join him. With absolutely no idea what was going to happen, they peeked through the door at the fuse spewing sparks as it ate its way to the keyhole. It did not disappoint them, startling them both when it produced one whopping bang. They hurried back inside to see if it worked, while keeping a wary eye on the door to the other room. There was no sound of any kind from the other room for a long time, the occupants having been shocked and confused. So Casey and Eli went to the safe, afraid the explosion may have set the money on fire.

They couldn't help chuckling when they saw the door of the safe torn free of the hinges on one side as black smoke rolled up out of the safe. Eli took the crowbar and forced the door open. They were in a hurry now, not sure if there might be mounted guards galloping their way already. It was difficult to speculate how loud the explosion really was, how far away it could have been heard, and if it could be assumed it came from here. "There's a lot more than that eighteen thousand we were talking about," Eli said as he pulled stacks of cash out of the smoking safe.

"We forgot to bring a sack to put it in," Casey blurted.

"Take the tablecloth off that table," Eli said, pointing toward a round table in the corner of the office with some dishes on it.

Casey fetched it at once and spread it on the floor for Eli to stack the money on it. "We're gonna have to do something about those two in that other room," he said. Judging by the strain he could see on the rope knotted around the post, it was obvious there was definitely more than one person in there and they were desperate to get out. "I don't know how long that doorknob is gonna hold up. It's already looser than it was. We'd best tie them up while we can get the jump on 'em. Tie 'em up so we'll have time to get away from here."

"I reckon you're right," Eli said as he tied the tablecloth corners to make a bag of it. "Let me put this on the porch so we can grab it when we run outta here, and then we'll take care of the lovebirds. I hope he ain't got a gun in there."

Eli put the money on the porch and came back with his weapon drawn. "Wait till they take a breath," Casey said. "Then untie it." Eli understood, holstered his weapon, and nodded. He stood close beside the doorknob, watching the rope. And when the tension suddenly went slack, he quickly untied the rope around the knob. They waited; then after a few seconds more, the door went flying open, sending Bradshaw and the woman sprawling, while Casey and Eli stepped inside the room with guns drawn.

Panic stricken and desperate moments before, Bradshaw and the woman now lay on the floor, staring in disbelief at the two ancient old men standing before them with weapons threatening. As for the two old men, the moment was equally shocking, for the woman staring back at them was Joy Black. No one on either side could speak for a few long moments before Bradshaw summoned the courage to demand, "Who the hell are you?"

Casey recovered first. "Well, we ain't your fairy god-mothers," he said, doing his best to talk like a ninety-year-old man. "Your missus was worried about you workin' late. She sent us to find you. It looks like you've been workin' pretty hard. You ain't got half your clothes on." Bradshaw started to get up, but Casey cocked his pistol and pointed it at his head. "Ain't nobody told you to get up!" Casey warned.

Bradshaw immediately sank back down on the floor. "What was that loud bang in the office?"

"What loud bang?" Casey replied. "I didn't hear no loud bang. Did you, Oscar?"

"I ain't heard no bang," Eli answered, "'course my hearin' ain't like it used to be. We gonna shoot 'em, or what?"

"I ain't made up my mind yet," Casey said.

"You ain't got no cause to shoot me," Joy spoke up then. "I'm just here to make a little money. I ain't got no part in any trouble between him and his wife."

"If it's money you old fellows are looking for," Bradshaw said, "there isn't any here in the office."

"You got that right," Eli declared, thinking of the tablecloth full of money outside on the porch. "What about it, Elmer, we gonna shoot 'em or not? His wife acted like she didn't care one way or the other."

"Now hold on a minute!" Bradshaw pleaded. "You gentle-men look too old to start what's left of your life runnin' from the law. And you don't want to have the killing of this inno-cent woman on your conscience."

"I hadn't thought about that," Casey said. "Whadda you think, Oscar? Maybe we'll just shoot him and let the woman go."

"That might do it," Eli replied. "His wife most likely ain't got nothin' against her, anyway."

"Wait!" Bradshaw exclaimed. "I'm a changed man! I've already told this woman that I won't do this anymore, because it isn't fair to my wife. Isn't that so, Joy?" She didn't answer, but looked at him as if it was news to her. Bradshaw continued his plea. "If it's money you're after, I can give you money."

"We've already been paid," Casey said. He gave Eli a look then that Eli interpreted as meaning they'd spent enough time tormenting Bradshaw and had best be on their way before one or more of the guards showed up. When Eli answered with a nod, Casey delivered the verdict. "This might be a mistake, but we're not gonna shoot you. We'll tie you up, instead."

"You don't have to tie us up," Bradshaw immediately protested. "We won't leave this room till you're gone."

"Damn you!" Casey responded. "I'm tired of foolin' with you. You rather have a hole blowed in the back of your head, it'll be a lot easier for us." He took dead aim with his pistol again.

"No!" Bradshaw blurted, and rolled over on his belly and placed his hands behind his back. Eli untied the rope from the post in the office and quickly tied him hand and foot. He picked up Bradshaw's shirt off a chair and used it for a gag, stuffing the body of the shirt into Bradshaw's mouth and tying it with the sleeves.

He then cut the rest of the rope and used it to bind Joy's hands together, but he didn't pull them behind her back. Then he tied her ankles together and tied them to her hands. When he finished, he spoke softly to her. "We'll just slow you down a little bit. There's a butcher knife on that table in the other room. I'll bet a young lady like you can most likely find a way to get hold of it and cut yourself loose. Can I trust you not to make a lot of noise until you get loose?" She nodded. "Then I won't gag you. When I was a younger man, I mighta just carried you off with me." She smiled at him, and he made a show of struggling to get to his feet again. "I'm gettin' too old for this. Let's go, Elmer!"

They went out the front door and cautiously looked out over the darkened cattle pens from the porch. With no sign of any movement from any direction, they went down the steps and hurried along the lane until they reached the place where they had climbed the fence. Casey tossed the bag of money over the fence; then they climbed over. "It sure is a lot more trouble with these oversized coats and trousers," he said. "I swear, I almost feel as old as we look."

"That was a pretty good test for these disguises," Eli commented. "I liked to croaked when that door flung open and I saw Joy Black layin' on the floor. But she didn't even know it was me when I was tyin' her up."

"Least, if she did, she had enough sense not to say anything about it," Casey suggested. "I reckon we'll know for sure if the rangers or the marshals come knockin' on the door of the D and T Ranch, wanting to speak to us."

They hurried across the fifty-odd yards of open ground between the pens and the road to their horses waiting at the hitching rail in front of the Roundup Saloon. Without seeing anyone on the short street of businesses, they walked their horses out the south road. Not a great distance past Hasting's Supply, which was closed for the night, they reached the creek and turned their horses upstream. They heard the welcome sound of their packhorses acknowledging their arrival before reaching the spot where they left the water. Everything was exactly how they had left it, so they took care of the horses first, then built a fire to cook some bacon and make some coffee. When they got that started, they decided it was time to find out what their night's work was worth moneywise. Casey untied the tablecloth and spread it on the ground and began the count. They counted it twice to make sure it was accurate, because it added up to twenty-eight thousand dollars, even more than it looked when Eli raked it out of the smoking safe. That was enough to carry the expenses of the ranch for a good while, and even some extra to buy more cattle, should the opportunity arise. Once the money was packed away with their other packs, and a few cups of coffee were downed, they decided it was time to remove all traces of Oscar and Elmer. So they took to the creek after they shucked the baggy clothes, mustaches, and wigs for a midnight frolic in the altogether.

Afterward, when they were warming by the fire, they talked again of the ease with which the job had been accomplished. All in all, they were highly satisfied with themselves. By this time, the hour was rapidly approaching the rising of the sun on a new day, and they had not yet gone to bed. It was Eli who first raised the subject. "You know, I ain't in such a hurry to get away from here that I couldn't be talked into crawlin' in my bedroll and goin' after some of that sleep we lost last night."

"You won't get no argument outta me," Casey replied. "We ain't got anybody chasin' us. Might be some people lookin' for Oscar and Elmer, but there ain't nobody lookin' for you and me. Nobody even knows what kind of horses those two gentlemen are ridin'."

Totally convinced that they were in no danger of being chased by anyone, they decided to get some sleep before starting back to the D&T Ranch. With nothing to bother them, they slept peacefully, awakened by the morning sun filtering through the branches of the trees overhead. "I swear," Eli declared, "I ain't used to wakin' up this late in the morning. You awake, Casey?" Casey said that he was. "Well, what time is it, anyway?"

Casey looked at his railroad pocket watch and answered, "Quarter to seven. We're sleepin' like the rich folks we are."

"Let's get the horses ready to go and ride on back to the Potluck Kitchen and eat like the rich folks, too," Eli said. "It ain't that far back there. We oughta be able to make it, if we don't lollygag around here."

"Are you crazy?" That was Casey's first reaction. "Are you just trying to get us caught with that twenty-eight thousand?"

"We ain't got nothin' to worry about. They ain't lookin' for us. I told you, they're lookin' for Oscar and Elmer."

Casey thought it over for a minute. Eli was probably right. And Joy and Roy would most likely make a fuss over them after the little tussle over the lamb stew. "All right, let's do it, but if we don't make it in time for breakfast, I ain't waitin' around there for dinner. So let's get the horses packed up and put this fire out."

They held the horses to a steady lope all the way back to the Potluck in an effort to get there before Joy shut the kitchen down after breakfast. They figured the horses could rest while they were eating, and they would take it easy on them when they started for home. After tying the horses out front, they walked in the dining room to be greeted loudly by Roy. "Howdy, boys! I didn't expect to see you fellers back here so soon. Joy," he called, "come see who's back."

Joy came to the kitchen door and reacted just as her brother had. "Well, I'll be . . ." she started. "I thought you two headed back south yesterday. You lookin' for some breakfast?"

"That's what we're looking for," Eli answered. "Are we too late?"

"No sirree," she said. "We quit servin' everybody else twenty minutes ago, but I'll cook breakfast for you two anytime. My stove's still hot and there's grease in the pan. Just tell me how many eggs you want." She took their requests and went back to the kitchen to cook it.

Although sitting on his stool behind the register, Roy still carried on the conversation with them while they were seated at the table. "Like Joy said, we thought you boys had already headed back home yesterday."

"We had some business in Fort Worth that took longer than we thought it would," Eli said. "It ended up in drinks in some saloon I can't even remember the name of. We was thinkin' maybe we could make it back here for supper, but we didn't. Ended up makin' camp on the road north of here and had to settle for bacon and coffee for supper. Right, Casey?"

"That's right," Casey said, "and we're headin' home right after breakfast." He had listened carefully to Eli's explanation, in case he had to comment on any part of it.

Joy came in with the two plates and set them down on the table. Then she went back to the kitchen for the coffeepot and three cups. She filled Roy's cup on the counter, filled the other three on the table, and sat down to have coffee with them. Noticing a bandage wrapped around the forefinger of her left hand, Eli asked, "How'd you hurt your finger?"

She looked at him with a coy smile and answered, "I cut it on a butcher knife."

"I asked her that this mornin'," Roy said. "And she said it was none of my business."

"No, I never said that," Joy responded. "I told him it wasn't nothin' for him to worry about. I can take care of myself. He's always wanted to protect me from all the bad people out there." She looked over at him and grinned. "It's kinda hard to kick somebody's behind when you ain't got no legs. Before that accident, he was hell on wheels when he was working on the railroad, though."

"I'm still hell on wheels when my blame wheelchair ain't broke down," Roy insisted. He reached under the counter and pulled out a sawed-off, double-barrel shotgun and held it up for them to see. "I thought I was gonna have to use my friend here yesterday before you boys took care of that trouble."

"I'm glad he didn't," Joy remarked, " 'cause I'da had to drag those two big bodies outta here and bury 'em."

They didn't linger long after they finished their breakfast, since they had a long ride ahead of them. There was a brief argument over the bill when Joy insisted there was no charge. But Casey and Eli wouldn't hear of it and laid the money on the counter. They both shook hands with Roy, and Joy walked outside with them to watch them mount up. "You boys take care of yourselves," she said. "And be sure you come back to see us when you're back up this way."

"We'll sure do that," Eli said, and reached down to take her hand. She was surprised when she felt the five-dollar bill in her hand. "I figure that's what I owe you when we didn't make it back here last night, like I planned."

She favored him with a wide grin. "You didn't have no cause to do that, but I reckon you can afford it. I 'preciate it. You boys take care of yourselves," she repeated, and stepped back from his horse.

Leading their packhorses, they started out the south road, with no words spoken between them until out of sight of the Potluck Kitchen. "She knew!" Eli exclaimed.

"I don't know," Casey replied. "I ain't so sure."

"I gave her five dollars 'cause I figured Bradshaw didn't pay her. And she said I could afford it. Why would she say that?

And how 'bout when she gimme that smile when she said she cut her finger on a butcher knife? She thinks that was us in that office last night."

"You're just addin' two and two and coming up with five," Casey said. "Even if she did suspect it, she ain't sure enough to come right out and say it." They rode a little farther down the road before he said, "But maybe it woulda been better not to give her that five dollars."

Chapter 4

Because of their late start from Fort Worth, Casey and Eli didn't arrive home to the Doolin and Tubbs Ranch until after supper two days after leaving the Potluck Kitchen. The first member of their crew to spot them was "Smiley" George, the bunkhouse cook, who was out beside the cookshack washing out some pots. Catching sight of the two riders approaching the barnyard, leading packhorses, Smiley paused with the pots until he recognized them. He walked down to the barn and called out, "Monroe! The bosses are back."

In a few seconds, Monroe Kelly and Davey Springer came out of the barn to join Smiley as they waited for Casey and Eli to ride up to the barn. "Welcome home," Monroe greeted the two owners. "Are we goin' to Abilene?"

"Looks that way," Casey answered him, "unless something happens in the Fort Worth market in the next few weeks. Best we could get outta Bradshaw and Lane was six dollars." He and Eli stepped down from the saddle and Davey took the reins for Biscuit and Smoke. "Set those packs in the barn, Davey," Casey said. "We need to get a few things out of 'em."

"Have you had any supper?" Monroe asked.

"No," Eli answered. "We were so close to home when it was gettin' time to rest the horses, so we decided to ride on in." He followed Davey in after the horses with the intention of helping take care of them. Casey and Monroe did the same. When they got inside, Monroe told Davey to run up to the house and tell Juanita that Casey and Eli were back, and they hadn't had any supper. Davey did so immediately. Both Casey and Eli took notice of Davey's response. It looked like Monroe had been successful in establishing himself in the position of foreman. It was a good sign to the two new ranch owners. Before they resurrected the old Whitmore Brothers Cattle Company under the name of the D&T Cattle Company, they were the two oldest cowhands on a crew of younger men. Now Monroe Kelly and Corey Johnson were the older hands, with Monroe at twenty-one and Corey at twenty. The rest of the crew were all in their teens, with Davey the youngest at fifteen. Smiley George, the chuck wagon cook, was the father figure at age thirty-three. They were going to get a chance to see what kind of crew they commanded when they started the drive of three thousand cattle north to Abilene, Kansas, in about a month from now.

There was only one problem left to deal with. After their last cattle drive to Abilene, which resulted in their becoming train robbers, they had decided whatever happened next, they were never going back to driving cattle. They had found it too easy to play the game using other people's money. They had, in effect, retired from the hard life of the cowhand, to enjoy the cattle business from the owner's perspective. In keeping with that, they did not plan to spend a single day driving a herd of cattle to the railroad. They had discussed the issue to some extent while sitting beside the campfire on the way back from Fort Worth. And they were both agreed that Monroe Kelly was the best choice for foreman. But to drive a herd as big as theirs, it was necessary to have an experienced trail boss to head the drive, a man who had done it before. They were convinced that they knew of a man who would fit the bill, so they decided to talk to Smiley about it tomorrow.

Once the horses were taken care of, Casey asked Monroe if there was anything he needed to talk about before he and Eli went to the house. "Nothin' that can't wait till mornin'," Monroe said. So they each took a couple of packs, holding their disguises and the cash profit for the trip, and walked to the ranch house. When they got there, they were warmly welcomed by Juanita and Miguel. Juanita had revived the fire in her cookstove and put on a pot of coffee.

She apologized that she had nothing but scrambled eggs and bacon she could fix in a hurry to go with half a cake of cornbread left from hers and Miguel's supper. "I sorry you have to eat breakfast tonight, but in the morning, I make you pancakes."

Casey looked at Eli and grinned. "It's good to be home, ain't it?"

Back in the comfort of a bed with a mattress, they both slept a little later than usual the next morning. Still, it was a little before seven when Casey woke up and went to Eli's room next door to see if he was awake. "I'm up," Eli called out, "but I was debatin' with myself whether or not to catch another forty winks." The money they came back with was put in the safe with the money already in there, and their working clothes were locked in a trunk. Satisfied there was nothing to awaken Juanita's curiosity when she was cleaning up, they went to breakfast.

In keeping with her respect for the owners, Juanita had set their places in the dining room. Casey noticed it when walking past the open door on their way to the kitchen. So he grabbed Eli by the arm and pulled him in the door after him. Then they both picked up their plates, cups, and silverware and carried them to the kitchen. "Good morning," Juanita greeted them, immediately concerned. "Is something wrong with the dishes?"

"Good mornin'," Casey returned. "No, there ain't nothin'

wrong with the dishes." He set them down on the kitchen table; then he and Eli sat down at the table. "If you and Miguel don't mind, we thought we'd eat with you this morning. That's just extra trouble for you to have to take everything to the dinin' room, and Miguel has to keep a fire goin' in the dinin'-room stove. Then you have two rooms to clean up. We're closer to the coffeepot here in the kitchen, and I have somebody to eat breakfast with besides Eli." Juanita looked astonished, so he asked, "Is that all right with you, or would you rather have Eli and me stay in the dinin' room?"

She looked at her husband and they both laughed. "No, no," she said. "You are welcome in my kitchen. I will fix you some pancakes and eggs."

The four of them enjoyed a pleasant breakfast, and when it was finished, they decided to eat breakfast every morning in the kitchen. After leaving the kitchen, they went down to the cookshack to have that talk with Smiley they had planned the night before. They found him cleaning out his breakfast pans. "You're too late for breakfast, if that's what you're looking for," he said.

"We ate already," Eli said. "Need to talk to you about something else. You gettin' your chuck wagon ready to go to Kansas?"

"Sure, I am," Smiley answered. "I'll be ready when you're ready."

"Good," Casey said. "You know we made Monroe foreman. You reckon he's ready to take that herd to Abilene?"

"You mean as trail boss?" Smiley asked. Casey nodded. "Ain't you two goin' on the drive?"

"Nope," Casey answered. "As owners of the ranch, Eli and I are gonna have to line up the financin' to make sure the ranch keeps raisin' more cattle. We'll come along after you, to be up there for the sale of the cattle, but we ain't gonna be on the drive."

Smiley hesitated for a minute while he thought about that. "Well, Monroe's a good man. He ain't got no experience leadin' a herd like that before. Maybe he'll work it out on the way."

"We've been thinkin' he could learn a lot if he had an older, more experienced man to show him the ropes," Casey said. "We were thinkin' about Gary Corbett. Whadda you think?"

Smiley was obviously surprised. Gary Corbett owned the ranch that Smiley went to work for when the Whitmore Brothers went out of business. Corbett had been glad to get Smiley back because he had worked for him before. But Corbett had gone under, like so many others, when the cattle market went bad, making Smiley available for the D&T. "Well, there ain't no doubt he's as good at it as anybody out there. He sure knows the way and I can tell you he knows what he's doin'. But I ain't sure he'd wanna take somebody else's cattle to market."

"Well, that's what we're gonna find out this mornin'," Eli said. "Me and Casey are gonna take a ride over there and see what he thinks about it. If we go right now, we oughta be back here by dinnertime." It was only about twelve miles, so he figured they could let the horses lope for most of the way, changing off and on to a walk.

"Tell him I recommended him," Smiley said.

"I will," Casey said. "We figure he'll probably wanna come, 'cause he knows you'll be doin' the cookin'." They saddled Smoke and Biscuit and headed out right away, having decided it best not to discuss it with Monroe until they knew if Corbett would take the deal.

"Pa," young Wayne Corbett called down from the hayloft to his father in the barn below. "There's a couple of riders comin' in."

"You know who it is?" Gary called back.

"No, sir. I've seen 'em here before, but I don't remember who they are." He remembered the occasion then. "I think they're the two men who came to get Smiley that time."

"The D and T," Corbett mumbled to himself. "I don't have any cattle to sell." He propped his pitchfork against the wall and walked out of the barn to meet them. "D and T," he said again, this time loud enough to serve as a greeting. "You still lookin' for cattle?"

"Nope," Casey answered him. "We're gettin' ready to drive about three thousand head to Kansas pretty soon and we thought we'd see if you wanted to go along with 'em."

"If you're just needin' some extra hands, I know a couple of good men who are lookin' for a job."

"We were more interested in you," Eli said. Corbett started shaking his head before Eli finished. "We was thinkin' more along the idea of guide and trail boss."

"We wanted to know if you were interested in takin' our cattle to Abilene or Wichita. We'd be willing to pay you a flat fee of five hundred dollars if you get a respectable number of 'em to the pens."

"You want me to take your cattle to market and sell 'em?"

"We want you to get the cattle to the market," Casey said. "We'll meet you there to sell 'em and pay you your full fee as soon as we have the money for 'em. While you and the men are drivin' 'em, we're gonna ride on up ahead of the herd so we can find out who's payin' the best price. Then we'll meet you somewhere along the trail and decide which market we're goin' to." He paused to wait for his reaction. "Whaddaya say?"

"I could sure use the money," Corbett confessed. "If you'da asked me a month ago, I'da had to tell you I couldn't leave my wife and my boy here to take care of the place. Since then, my brother sold his land about six miles from here, and him and his wife and two boys have come to live here. We're gonna see if we can make this piece of ground pay off. Five hundred dollars could buy us some things we need. And Jack can take care of the place while I'm gone, so I reckon I'm your man."

"Good," Casey said, and offered his hand. Then Eli shook Corbett's hand as well. "We could use those other two men you mentioned, too. If they're interested in a job, send 'em to the D and T. If they find the ranch, they've passed the first test. I expect we'll be ready to start out for the market in about a month, so that oughta give you plenty of time to see what kind of crew you're workin' with."

"Casey, Eli," Corbett said, "I 'preciate it."

They rode away, confident that their cattle were going to be well taken care of. They only had Smiley's word that Corbett was a reliable trail boss, but they trusted Smiley's opinion. Corbett most likely would still be in the business if he had not had to sell his cattle for a dollar and a half when the market bottomed out. He had not been as fortunate as they were. He didn't have the cash to hold on to his stock until the market came back. They could not, however, recommend their method of financing.

U.S. Marshal John Timmons sat at his desk reading a telegram for the second time. He looked up when his clerk, Ron Wilde, walked into the office. "Colton Gray just came back from delivering a summons. You wanna see him for anything?"

"As a matter of fact, I do," Timmons answered. "Send him in here."

Wilde walked back in the outer office. "The boss wants to see you, Colton."

"What about? Did he say?" Colton asked.

"He didn't say," Wilde said, which was the truth, but he was pretty sure it had to do with the telegram he had been reading. "He just said he wanted to see you."

Colton was afraid the marshal had some other little pain-in-the-ass job he wanted to send him on. He guessed the reason he was assigned to the least important jobs was the simple fact that he was the youngest deputy marshal in the company. He was sure he had been given the job of arresting the two old men who robbed a bank because Timmons thought that would be an easy job, even for the youngest deputy. Then the two old coots became the biggest crime story in Texas when they started knocking over trains and other banks. Two of the most harmless-looking old men, according to descriptions given by victims of their robberies, they were becoming nothing short of folk heroes. They would just suddenly appear at the scene of the robbery, take the cash, then disappear just as suddenly. Timmons had given him free rein on the pursuit of the two outlaws, with instructions to try to pick up their trail and stay on it until he ran them down. The problem was, they never left a trail that led him anywhere. And that was where the case was at this point, nowhere.

"You wanna see me?" Colton asked when he stuck his head inside the marshal's office.

"Yeah, Colton, come on in," Timmons replied. When Colton came in, Timmons slid the telegram toward him on the desk. "Your two old grandpas have come out of hiding again. This time, they blew open a safe in a cattle buyer's office in Fort Worth."

"Damn," Colton responded, "I was hopin' they had retired, or passed away from old age." He made the comment in jest, for he was still halfway convinced that the two old men were, in fact, two younger men in disguises. He was alone in that conviction, however, primarily because of the eyewitness reports from their victims. Everyone who was confronted by Elmer and Oscar, as they were now identified, swore they were the genuine articles. Colton speculated that if they were wearing disguises, the victim of the robbery was likely too shocked to see anything other than what they were told they saw.

"You might as well ride on up to Fort Worth and see what you can find out," Timmons said. "The name of the office is on the telegram, Bradshaw and Lane. They're most likely in the new section of the stockyards, south of town."

"That's about eighty-five or ninety miles up there," Colton said. "I'da thought that marshal up there mighta sent one of his deputies to check on that robbery."

"I expect they think we're more familiar with those two, since you've been following behind them for a helluva long time now," Timmons replied, not without a hint of sarcasm for Colton's progress to this point. "Besides, I think you kinda want to make this arrest, after the time you've spent eating their dust. Am I right?"

"I reckon you are," Colton answered. "I'll do my best to catch up with 'em."

"I know you will," Timmons said. "Just report back whenever you can, and I'll carry you on the rolls as special assignment."

"Yes, sir, I'll head up that way this afternoon." He turned and left the office, nodding to Ron Wilde on his way through the outer office. Ron smiled in return. He felt some sympathy for the young deputy. He knew that Timmons did not hold a high opinion for Colton Gray's potential as a tough-as-nails Texas deputy marshal. And he also suspected that Colton knew it as well. That's why he sincerely wished him luck.

Colton rode back to the stable on the bay gelding he affectionately called Scrappy, loaded his packsaddle on a grungy-looking gray, and struck out on the road to Fort Worth. His first stop would be at the Williams Brothers at the edge of Waco to buy the supplies he knew he would need for three days.

Colton actually made the trip to Fort Worth in a little over two and a half days. But he waited until the next morning before going to the sheriff to ask where the office of Bradshaw and Lane was located. The sheriff passed along all the information he had gotten from Birch Bradshaw about the robbery. Then, following the directions given him, he went to the lower cattle pens and found him at his desk. Bradshaw looked up at him when he walked in, and before Colton could speak, he said, "We're not buying any cattle now and won't be till sometime next month."

"I expect I know the reason why," Colton said. "I'm U.S. Deputy Marshal Colton Gray, and I'd like to talk to you about the robbery you recently suffered."

Bradshaw was obviously not in a receptive mood to talk about that particular subject. "I've already talked to the local law enforcement people about that night. The sheriff was out here. I told them everything I know about it. Those two old crooks made a mess of my office. They completely destroyed my safe and cleaned me out of every cent I had. Why don't you go talk to the sheriff about it?"

"I've already talked to the sheriff," Colton replied. He went on to explain that he was on special assignment by the U.S. Marshal Service to track down the two men who had robbed Bradshaw. "I've been trying to catch up with them for quite a while now, so I'm looking for any little piece of information that would give me a clue as to where I might head them off." When Bradshaw still looked impatient, Colton continued. "Listen, Mr. Bradshaw, I'm not working with the local law enforcement on this case. Anything I find will not be shared with local law enforcement. The marshal service is interested in putting the two men who robbed you behind bars and returning any part of the money you lost. So, how 'bout it? Can you walk me through that night?"

Bradshaw hesitated, still furious at having been taken by the two old men, but reluctant to give many of the details of that night. "All right," he finally agreed, "but only if you keep this information in the marshal's office. I don't trust that sheriff and his deputies."

"You have my word on it," Colton said. "Sheriff Courtright said you were in the office late that night, long after you usually quit for the day. He said you were working on something in the other room, there." He motioned toward the door to the second room. Bradshaw said that was right. That was what he told Courtright. "It must have been something important you were working on. You musta been really concentrating on it, if you didn't hear them come in your front door."

"I reckon I was concentrating pretty hard on what I was doing," Bradshaw allowed.

"Do you think it was just luck the two robbers were passin' by your office and saw your light on? Or did they come to the cattle pens because they knew you would be there that night, workin' on this important thing in the other room?"

"How do I know?" Bradshaw exclaimed. "I was here, and they broke in and blew up my safe!"

"And you didn't know they were in your office until you heard the safe bein' blown up?" Colton was trying to picture the scene in his mind, and it just didn't seem right. He began to suspect that there was more to this story than Bradshaw was willing to share. "How much money was stolen out of the safe?"

"Twenty-eight thousand dollars," Bradshaw replied.

"Your money?"

"Hell no," Bradshaw answered, "the company's money. That's why I need to get it back."

"What was that special thing you stayed so late to work on?" Colton asked. He was beginning to see other possible reasons for Bradshaw's late night at the office. Suddenly it hit him, Bradshaw stayed late so he could do the black-powder job on the safe, himself. Then he blamed it on the two elderly bandits that were rapidly becoming well known.

"It was just some pricing policies that needed working on," Bradshaw said, answering Colton's question. "Nothing important."

"And while you were working on it, those two old men happened to be at the cattle pens, when everybody had closed up and gone home, and came in and blew up your safe, and stole the company's money? Are you gonna stick with that story? Nobody else saw those two old men. You know, this is a helluva long way from where they've been workin' before this."

"Whoa!" Bradshaw blurted, just then realizing the implications of the picture Colton was creating. "You're talking like I stole the money! And that ain't what happened at all!"

"Did anyone else see these mysterious two old men?" Colton asked. "That would help your story a whole lot, if there was someone else who saw them."

"Damn, damn, damn," Bradshaw muttered as he stared into the face of a trap he hadn't seen coming. "You've got it all wrong, Deputy. You've painted yourself a picture that ain't anywhere close to accurate. I did not steal my own company's money. If I'd wanted the money, I could have just taken it. I wouldn't have to make up a wild story about it."

"I don't know," Colton hedged, unconvinced.

"All right," Bradshaw finally caved in. "There is one other person who saw the two old men, and knows it happened exactly the way I told you. But doggone it, you've got to give me your word none of this gets out locally."

"I told you that already," Colton said.

"There happened to be a woman here at the time," Bradshaw confessed.

"And that's the business you were workin' on? And the reason you didn't hear them break into your office?"

"Deputy," Bradshaw pleaded, "I'm a married man. I can't afford to have this get out in Fort Worth. You can understand that, can't you?"

Colton was not as convinced as he had been moments before that Bradshaw had taken the money himself. Maybe it actually was another holdup committed by Oscar and Elmer.

"Anything I learn here will stay with me," he finally promised. "But I'll need the name of the lady you were entertaining, to verify your story. You don't have to worry, I'll be discreet about contactin' her, so her name will not be made public."

At this point, Bradshaw saw no use in trying to maintain his dignity any longer. "You don't have to worry about the woman's reputation. She gets paid for her favors. Her name's Joy Black. She and her brother run the Potluck Kitchen behind the cattle pens."

"I 'preciate your help, Mr. Bradshaw," Colton said, ending the interview. "I'll check with Miss Black to confirm what you've told me. Let me assure you that my interest in this is to strike the trail of these two bandits, if they were, in fact, Oscar and Elmer. I can only wish you luck in recoverin' the money." He walked out of the office, leaving a somewhat-uncertain victim.

Chapter 5

Colton tied Scrappy and his packhorse at the hitching rail in front of the Potluck Kitchen. He gently stroked the bay gelding's face while he paused to take a look at the Roundup Saloon right next door. Since it was dinnertime, he had decided to take a chance on the food at the Potluck Kitchen. He hoped he wouldn't need to visit the saloon next door to kill the taste of the food afterward. He walked inside the dining room to find several people seated at a long table in the center of the room. There were three small tables against the sidewall, however, so he chose to sit at one of them, thinking that might be better for a more private talk with Joy Black.

He hadn't been seated more than a few seconds when she popped out of the kitchen carrying three plates of food for the customers at the big table. He was not sure this was the woman Bradshaw had risked his marriage for. She was not an ugly woman. "Plain" would be a better description of her, with a broad face and a heavy body, with arms that looked almost muscular. When she saw him, a grin spread across her broad face and she said, "I'll be right with you, cowboy." After she placed the plates on the table, she came to his small table. "You decide you wanna eat by yourself, huh?"

He nodded, then asked, "What's the potluck today?"

"Baked ham and beans and rice," she answered. "You gonna risk it?" He said he would, so she asked, "Coffee or water?" He picked coffee. "I figured," she said, and returned to the kitchen. He scanned the small eating place, from the large man seated behind the cash register on the counter, to the kitchen door. He looked to see if there was another woman in the kitchen. If there was, she never came out. He concluded the one bringing his coffee and plate to him now was the one he sought.

"Are you, by any chance, Joy?" Colton asked when she placed them before him.

"That's right," she answered. "I'm Joy, but not by chance. My daddy knew what he was fixin' to do when he cornered my mama in the bedroom."

Colton smiled politely in recognition of her humor before announcing, "Joy, my name is Colton Gray, and I'd—"

"Colton Gray," she interrupted. "My name's Joy Black. We oughta get along just fine."

He paid her another polite smile for her humor before continuing. "I shoulda said, 'I'm a U.S. deputy marshal, and I'd like to talk to you about the robbery in the Bradshaw and Lane buyer's office.'"

That caused her to pause, but only for a moment. "I ain't supposed to know anything about that," she said. "Everybody knows he got robbed." A small grin broke out in the corner of her mouth. "Did his wife hire you to ask some questions?"

"No, like I told you, I'm a deputy marshal. I ain't out for hire by jealous wives. I'm interested in the person who robbed his safe. Bradshaw said you could tell me who it was, 'cause you were there when it happened."

She shrugged. "All right, if he told you that, I reckon he's changed his story to the sheriff. But it weren't just one person, it was two of 'em, and they were the damnedest robbers you've ever seen. Two little old men, looked like your grandpa, and

they meant business. I almost asked if they needed help totin'
that money outta there. They tied us up, but they left a
butcher knife on the table so I could get myself loose after
they left. And when I got loose, let me tell you, I left." She
paused to recall the picture to her mind. "They was a curious
pair. One of 'em reared up like he was fixin' to shoot ol' Birch
when he acted like he was gonna get up off the floor. But I
don't think they was mean like most outlaws. They didn't
make me put my hands behind my back when they tied 'em
together, and I know that was so I could get to that butcher
knife." She chuckled at the thought.

"Did you notice any other strangers around that day?"
Colton asked.

"There was another curious pair of fellers that came through
here that day. When they came back the next day, on their way
home, one of 'em gave me five dollars. He said he owed me
that because he didn't get back here in time to visit with me."

"That other two," Colton asked, "you're saying they were
strangers, too?"

"That's right," she said, "never been here before." She was
interrupted then when someone at the big table wanted more
coffee. "I'll be right back," she said, obviously enjoying her
role in his investigation. She got the coffeepot off the stove
and filled everybody's cup, including his. Then she was back
and immediately continued her story. "You can ask Roy about
those two fellers. They weren't nothin' like those two old
men. And when we had two fellers come in here and start
some trouble, those two strangers ended it right quick. You're
lettin' your dinner get cold," she said then. "You go ahead and
finish eatin' and then you can talk to Roy about the other two
strangers."

"That's a good idea," Colton said. "The few bites I've tried
tasted mighty good." She left him then to give her other customers some attention. He cleaned his plate and had one
more cup of coffee. Then he went to the register to pay for it.

"Joy said you was a U.S. deputy marshal," Roy said when Colton walked up to the counter. "She said you was on the trail of them two old grandpas."

"That's a fact," Colton replied.

Joy joined them then. "He was wonderin' about our other pair of strangers, Eli and Casey. I told him what we thought of them."

Roy proceeded to repeat the story of how Casey and Eli had settled with Jed and Sam the first time they ate at the Potluck Kitchen. When he had finished, Colton asked why Casey and Eli happened to be there at the new cattle pens. "I think they came up here to see if they could sell some cattle. Matter of fact, I believe they said they'd been to see Birch Bradshaw, but he wasn't willing to give 'em a decent price. Ain't that what they said, Joy?" She said that was what they said.

"Did they say where they were goin' when they left here?" Colton asked.

"If they did, I don't recall where it was," Roy answered. "Just said they had some other business to tend to before they went home. Then they showed up here for breakfast the next day. Said they was on their way home."

"Did they say where home was?"

"I don't know." He looked at Joy. "Did he say where it was?"

"No," she answered, "only that it was about a hundred miles south of here on the Lampasas River." They talked a little while longer about Eli and Casey. Colton asked for their last names, but Joy did not recall that they were ever given. She described them as best she could when he asked if she would. Then he thanked them both for their help, and thanked Joy individually for the fine dinner. Then he took his leave.

He was not quite sure what to think after talking to Birch Bradshaw and Joy and Roy Black. This trip to Fort Worth left him in the same predicament he found himself in after every robbery by the two old men. They left no trail for anyone to follow. And now, with the entrance of two more strangers showing up at the same time, he couldn't help considering the possibility that they might be the same two men. That was a theory that no one believed except him, but he was not ready to abandon it. So now, he was undecided about what he should do. He knew he was not looking forward to riding back to Waco and reporting his failure to find anything that might lead him to the old bandits. He climbed up into the saddle and sat there for a couple of minutes, trying to decide what to do. He looked toward the road that led to the south. He knew that if you followed it all the way to its end, it would take you to San Antonio. Roy said that was the road Eli and Casey left town on. About a hundred miles, they told Joy, would take them home. He wondered if that was true. *Maybe I should wire my boss and tell him I want to track down Eli and Casey,* he thought. He knew that if he did, Timmons would likely tell him to forget it and come on back to Waco. *I don't have any other leads to check on.* "So, to hell with it, I'll do it to satisfy myself." He wheeled the bay away from the rail and started out the south road.

As he rode away from the new cattle pens, his mind was replaying the robbery, as it was told to him. He shook his head when he thought about it. "The two old geezers took some gunpowder and blew the safe apart," he told Scrappy. He read the sign on the big store he was approaching: HASTING'S SUPPLY. "I bet you could buy black powder there." This time, Scrappy gave a grunt in reply. *I wonder if Elmer and Oscar brought black powder with them,* he thought. *Maybe they had to buy some after they got here.* "What the hell?" He decided to stop and ask some questions. He needed to buy some more supplies, anyway, if he was going to add another hundred miles to his trip.

"Howdy," Floyd Hasting greeted him. "Can I help you?"

"I hope so," Colton answered. "I'm gonna need some coffee and flour and sugar and some bacon. And I'd like to ask you a couple of questions, if you don't mind."

"Don't mind a-tall, if I've got some answers," Hasting replied.

"I'm a U.S. deputy marshal," Colton said, and pulled his coat aside to show his badge. "You most likely heard about the robbery at the cattle pens."

Hasting chuckled. "You mean the one where the 'Geezer Brothers' blew the door offa some buyer's safe?"

"Yes, sir, that's the one," Colton answered.

"Are you tryin' to track those two down?" Hasting asked. Colton nodded. "Well, I expect you've got a job on your hands. I understand those two old boys have done other holdups in the state. I know it's the first we've heard of 'em workin' in this part of Texas."

"That's a fact," Colton said, thinking that was another argument supporting his opinion, since it happened when the other two strangers were in this part of the state. "You sell black powder?" he asked then. Hasting said that he did. "Do you happen to remember sellin' a small amount of black powder to two strangers back around the time that safe was blown up?"

"No, I don't recall . . ." He stopped, then said, "Wait a minute. I forgot about them. I did sell a cannister of black powder to a couple of fellows. But it wasn't to any old men. These fellows wanted some gunpowder to get rid of a nest of yellow jackets. They were on their way home to some ranch south of here. They were right respectable. I had to tell 'em how to handle the black powder."

Colton could feel his heart beating faster. It was just too much coincidence to let the matter drop and go back to Waco. "And these fellows, you never saw them before?"

"Nope, they were strangers to me, but like I said, they

weren't the type of fellows you'd think would rob anybody, and they sure weren't old men."

"You're probably right," Colton said. "I'm much obliged for the information. I'll pick up those things I mentioned, and I'll be on my way."

He packed his purchases in his packs and started out once again on the road south, trying to picture in his mind the two strangers. If they were the two old bandits, as he suspected, they had to buy the black powder, and they had to find a place to get into their disguises. That last thought was triggered by the creek flowing across the road he was now approaching. Letting his mind go free to play with his suspicions, he paid close attention to the tracks on both sides of the creek. It was not easy to determine anything, because there were so many old tracks. But he was thinking that if his theory was correct, the two bandits would have been looking for a place to put on their disguises. And this creek looked ideal, so he decided to take a look in the trees back away from the road. *Upstream or downstream?* he thought. *If it was me, I'd go upstream so I wouldn't be drinking the water after it washed over the road.* So he turned his horse upstream and watched the bank on both sides for evidence of horses leaving the creek.

He couldn't help grinning when he found the tracks of several horses leaving the water about forty-five or fifty yards up the creek. He rode up out of the water and dismounted. As he suspected, he found the remains of a campfire, but little else. He had to remind himself that actually he had found nothing more than a campsite, left by someone. It still fit right in with his theory, however, so he resumed his search for Eli and Casey. Instead of going back to the road in the water, he made his way through the trees along the bank, just as the men who had camped there had done. When he reached the road again, he reined Scrappy to a stop and paused there a few seconds to once again consider what he was about to do. It might cost him his job as a deputy marshal to ride down to Lampasas County on no more than an unlikely hunch. Then he turned Scrappy's head to the south and began a three-day ride.

The farther he traveled on the road to San Antonio, the more he began to think it was leading him too much to the east of where he thought Lampasas County should be. *Only a fool would keep traveling in a direction he wasn't sure led to his destination*, he thought. But he was too far committed to stop now. On the afternoon of the third day, he came upon a river, and the road followed along beside it for a mile or more before he sighted a log building up ahead on the riverbank. As he came closer, he decided it might be a trading post, so he pulled in when he reached the path leading to it. There was an old man sitting in a rocking chair on the front porch. He remained seated while Colton dismounted, but greeted him with "Howdy."

"Howdy," Colton returned. "This is a store, ain't it?" It just occurred to him that it might be a dwelling.

"Indeed it is, young feller," the snowy-haired old man answered. "It's a store, started out as a tradin' post. How can I help you?"

"Are you the owner?" Colton asked.

"Sure am. Name's Travis. Folks around these parts call me 'Pappy' Travis. Been doin' it for so long that I done forgot what my given name was." He paused to give Colton a good looking-over before commenting, "Boy, you look like you're lost."

Colton chuckled at that. "You pretty much hit the nail on the head," he replied.

"Ain't nothin' wrong with bein' lost," Pappy said. "It's when you're lost and don't admit it. That's when you're in trouble. Are you hungry? 'Cause Miss Atha can fix you up with some biscuits and bacon. Would that help you out?"

Colton laughed, thinking he must look desperate. "That sounds like a good idea, but I can pay you for it. If I could get a cup of coffee with it, it'd even be better."

Pappy got up out of the rocking chair. "Come on inside and I'll tell Miss Atha to fix you somethin' to eat. If you ain't lost, where was you headin'?"

"I'm on my way to San Antonio," Colton said. "But I am lost in one respect. While I was passin' through this close to Lampasas County, I thought I'd like to see if I could find a couple of fellows I know down this way. Yes, sir, I'd like to see ol' Casey and Eli, but I don't reckon I've got much chance of findin' them."

"You talkin' about Casey Tubbs and Eli Doolin?" Pappy asked.

"Why, yes, I sure am," Colton replied. " 'Casey Tubbs and Eli Doolin,' " he repeated in an effort to memorize the last names. "Do you know them?"

"I sure do. Hell, I can tell you how to find them. They're cowhands at the old Whitmore cattle ranch. And they might be my wife's favorite people, next to our baby boy, Alex. Come on inside." He led him inside the store. "Atha!" he called out. "We got a friend of Eli and Casey's lookin' for somethin' to eat."

A fragile-looking little gray-haired woman came in from the rear of the store, followed by a giant of a man. Colton estimated him to be around fifty years old. He turned out to be Atha's "baby boy," Alex. "How do, young feller?" Atha greeted him. "You a friend of Casey and Eli's?"

"I don't know them real well," Colton replied honestly. "But I hooked up with them over in Waco and developed a real likin' for 'em. And I thought as long as I was gonna be ridin' this close to their ranch, I'd stop by and say howdy. But like I was tellin' your husband, I don't even know how to get to their ranch."

"Well, that's easy enough," Alex said, "but it's over a day's ride from here."

"Shoot, that don't matter," Colton said, making an effort to sound as casual as he could.

"Just get back on the road and go about a quarter of a mile farther where a trail crosses the road. That's the old Comanche Trail. It runs right across the old Whitmore Brothers Ranch, and you can see the gate from the trail."

"'Preciate it, Alex, that's what I'll do. Maybe I'll catch 'em at the ranch house." He found it hard to believe his luck. It had to be more than coincidence. "If they're out on the range somewhere, I'll just try to see 'em on my way back to Fort Worth."

"You lookin' for work tendin' cattle?" Alex asked.

"Nope," Colton said, thinking it best to be honest about it. He pulled his coat aside to show his badge. "I'm a U.S. deputy marshal. I'm on my way to San Antonio to transport a prisoner."

"You ain't lookin' to arrest Casey and Eli, are you?" Miss Atha asked.

"Why, no, I ain't," Colton japed. "Have they done something I need to arrest 'em for?"

She cackled with laughter. "Gracious, no, not those two angels." She went on to tell him about a time when Casey and Eli didn't have enough money to pay for something to eat, so she gave it to them. "It was a year before we saw them again, but they showed up here one day and paid what they owed, plus a lot extra. Didn't they, Pappy?" He nodded vigorously, grinning from ear to ear. "Ain't it just like them two to make friends with a peace officer? Come on in the kitchen. There's some biscuits still warm in the oven and I'll put on some coffee."

Atha threw some bacon in the frying pan to go with the biscuits and then cut him a slice of apple pie. Alex sat down and had a slice of pie with him. When Colton had finished, he insisted, over her protests, on paying her something for her efforts. When he left, they asked him to say hello to Casey and Eli for them, and he promised he would. He felt a little guilty for having used them for his ulterior motives, but he counted himself extremely lucky that he had the opportunity. To make up for it, he bought some coffee and flour, which he didn't really need, since he resupplied them at Hasting's.

As Alex had said he would, he came to the old Comanche Trail after riding about a quarter of a mile. He turned west and started the last segment of his trip to meet Casey and Eli. According to Pappy and Miss Atha, Casey and Eli were a couple of cowhands working for the Whitmore Brothers Ranch.

Chapter 6

It was getting close to dark before he came upon a suitable camping spot to spend the night. The trail led across a narrow valley with a stream running along the center of it. There were ample trees for cover and firewood, as well as grass for his horses. He was not surprised to find evidence of several old campfires by the stream. The trail showed no signs of much traffic, but he rode upstream, anyway, to make his camp. Going by what Alex had told him, he figured he should make it to the ranch by dinnertime the next day. So he took care of his horses, then gathered some wood for a fire to cook his supper, still not certain what he was going to do when he found Casey Tubbs and Eli Doolin. He had to come up with some reason for the long ride to visit them, and he hadn't thought of one yet. By the time he decided to go to sleep, he had come up with an excuse for being here—although admittedly, it was pretty flimsy.

Back on the old Comanche Trail early the next morning, he caught first sight of the buildings of the old Whitmore Brothers Ranch just before noon. A little farther and he saw the entrance gate to the ranch about a hundred yards off to his right, so he left the trail and headed straight for the gate. Instead of Whitmore Brothers, there was a new sign over the gate: D&T CATTLE COMPANY. *D&T,* he thought. *That had to be Doolin and*

Tubbs. So evidently, they were the owners. That fact alone tended to weaken his theory. It worked a lot better when Casey and Eli were simply cowhands. "We've come this far," he told Scrappy, "we might as well go the rest of the way." He nudged the bay and walked his horses to the front of the ranch house, where he dismounted and dropped Scrappy's reins on the ground.

He climbed the steps to the porch and rapped on the front door with the knocker fashioned from a horseshoe. When no one came to the door, he knocked again and waited. After a couple of minutes, the door opened and Miguel Garcia stood staring at him, a questioning look upon his face. It was as if no one had ever knocked on the door before. "*Sí?*"

"I'm here to see Mr. Casey Tubbs or Mr. Eli Doolin," Colton told him. "Am I in the right place?"

Miguel was obviously confused. He craned his neck to look behind Colton to see if there was anyone with him. "*Sí,*" he answered then. "You wait here. I go see." He closed the door, leaving Colton to stand on the porch.

It wasn't long, however, before the door opened again. This time, it was Casey. "Howdy," he said. "I'm Casey Tubbs. Miguel said you wanted to see me. What can I do for you?" He figured that maybe this was another small farmer wanting to sell his cattle. But when he saw how young the man was, he decided that maybe he was looking for work.

"I'm U.S. Deputy Marshal Colton Gray," he said. "I wanted to ask you some questions about a robbery in Fort Worth."

"Fort Worth?" Casey replied. "Did you ride all the way down here from Fort Worth?"

"Yes, sir, I did," Colton answered.

"And you think I had something to do with a robbery? What kind of robbery was it? A bank? A train?" He opened the door wide. "You'd best come on inside. You mighta been on the trail too long. Are you hungry? We're just fixin' to sit down to eat. You can join us and tell me all about this robbery I pulled and musta forgot about."

"I didn't mean to imply . . ." Colton started to say, but Casey didn't wait to hear it. He just turned and went back down the hall, leaving Colton no choice but to follow him.

Casey went straight to the kitchen, where Eli and Miguel were seated at the table and Juanita was bringing serving bowls to place on it. "Look here, Eli," Casey sang out as he went into the room. "This is Deputy Marshal . . ." He paused to look around at Colton. "What did you say your name was, young fellow?"

"Gray," he responded. "Colton Gray."

"Right," Casey said. "Well, Deputy Gray rode all the way from Fort Worth to arrest me and you for robbin' a bank when we were up that way last week."

"Is that a fact?" Eli responded, aware that Casey was putting on a performance for the deputy. "Is it okay if we eat before we go to jail?" He looked around at Juanita and said, "We've got plenty for another mouth, ain't we? Get him a plate and some tools."

"I didn't come here to charge you with anything," Colton said, finally finding room to speak. "I'm just hopin' you might help me in any way you can, since you two gentlemen were at the site of the robbery that mornin'."

"I know," Casey laughed. "We were just havin' fun with you. Where was the robbery?"

"At the cattle pens in Mr. Birch Bradshaw's office," Colton said. "They opened the safe and cleaned all the money out of it."

"Well, I'll be . . ." Casey started as he pulled a chair back for Colton to sit. "Serves him right is what I say. That cheap crook coulda give us some of that money that mornin' for our cattle. Now we've gotta drive 'em all the way up to Kansas to sell 'em."

"Well, let's eat now while the food's hot," Eli said. "We don't want to get Juanita riled up. Then we can tell you anything we can, to help you."

"This is all mighty gracious of you," Colton said, finding a vacant spot in the conversation. "I didn't intend to interrupt your dinner, ma'am." He looked at Casey then and said, "I really oughta take care of my horses, though. They need water. Then I could talk to you after you've had your dinner."

"Nonsense," Casey said. "Set yourself down and eat. Miguel, stick your head out the back door and holler for Davey to come take care of Colton's horses." Miguel got up at once and went out the back door.

In a few minutes, he was back. "Davey take your horses to the barn," he said. "I tell him take off saddle and packs and water them."

Colton was trying hard not to become completely overwhelmed by the reaction he was getting from the people at D&T Cattle Company. But he was forced to acknowledge the gracious reception he was receiving. "I reckon I need to thank you all for your kind reception. I didn't expect to be treated so royally. It's not typical treatment for a deputy when he interrupts your dinner."

"I don't see why not," Casey replied. "You're the folks that try to keep law and order for the rest of us." He dared not look in Eli's direction, for fear they might lock eyes.

They turned their attention to Juanita's fine dinner then and Casey explained why they preferred to eat in the kitchen instead of the dining room. "It's just homier. Eli nor I have any family, so we enjoy eatin' with Miguel and Juanita." He chuckled then and added, "Miguel and Juanita might like it better if me and Eli ate by ourselves in the dining room, though." When everyone was finished, Casey asked, "Now, what is it you wanna know from Eli and me?"

"There's a lot we don't know about this robbery," Colton

started. "I found out that you two were there in Bradshaw's office that day before the robbery happened. I just thought if there was anybody you saw hangin' around those pens who didn't look like they belonged, maybe you noticed them." Playing their parts, Casey and Eli looked inquiringly at each other and shook their heads. "We know who committed the robbery," Colton continued. "You may have heard of the two old men who have been robbing banks and trains."

"No foolin'!" Eli exclaimed. "That's who you're lookin' for?" He chuckled as if it was some joke. "So they've gone into robbin' cattle buyers now? Did they go in with their guns drawn and force ol' Bradshaw to open his safe?"

"No," Colton said, "they hit it at night when they thought no one was there. But Bradshaw was in the next room when they opened the safe."

"Reckon how they knew the combination to the safe?" Casey wondered.

"It was an old safe," Colton said. "It wasn't a combination lock. It was a keylock."

"And they got it open?" Eli joined in the charade. "Maybe they got hold of a key that fits any of 'em. I expect that's what they had."

"They blew the safe open with black powder," Colton said.

"*They what?*" Casey exclaimed in disbelief. "And Bradshaw didn't hear it in the next room?"

"He heard it," Colton said, then went on to explain how he and a woman were trapped in the room, ultimately bound and gagged, and left there while the two old men made their getaway.

"So ol' Bradshaw had him a woman in the room with him?" Eli pondered the thought. "She musta been one desperate soul."

"It was the woman who runs the Potluck Kitchen with her brother," Colton said. "I talked to the woman and her brother.

They said that you were in the restaurant to eat. I really got more information about you and Mr. Tubbs from the woman than I got from Mr. Bradshaw."

"You bet," Eli responded. "We ate there a couple of times, and if you ain't ever et there, I recommend it. That woman can cook." He looked over at Casey and crowed, "I declare, so Joy can do something besides cookin'. She never let on, did she?"

"Maybe you ain't as charmin' as Birch Bradshaw," Casey suggested.

Colton could see that he was getting nowhere with his casual comments and questions. The two men acted as if the whole thing was humorous. They were either innocent or playing a convincing game of innocence. He decided to pose a more direct question. "What did you use the cannister of black powder for?"

There was no hesitation on Casey's part. He had anticipated the question and answered it right away. "The gunpowder we bought at Hasting's? Knocked out a nest of yellow jackets in a tree behind the bunkhouse with it. Hasting showed us how to use it so it would make a big fireball. I could hardly wait to get home to try it out. A couple of the boys were in the bunkhouse when I dumped a little of that black powder on a dish and set it inside that hole. They thought I was gonna blow a hole in the back of the bunkhouse. It made the prettiest ball of fire you ever saw, and good-bye yellow jackets."

Colton didn't comment for a few seconds. It was evident that they had an answer for every question. He wondered if this last one was true. "I woulda liked to have seen that, myself," he said. "Did it kill the tree?"

"I don't think so," Casey answered. "Least it don't look like it did. You wanna take a look at it?"

"I'll take your word for it . . ." He hesitated. "Well, maybe I'll take a look at it when I go to get my horses."

"Whatever you say," Casey replied. He glanced at Eli and gave him a smug look. Eli told him he was crazy when he talked about using the black powder in the hole in the tree. Smiley had already taken care of the yellow-jacket nest when he poured kerosene in the hole, then struck a match and threw it in after the kerosene. Casey had actually put some powder in the hole and ignited it, in case the yellow jackets had come back. It was mainly to cover the reason for having bought it. And it didn't hurt to have Smiley, Davey, and Monroe witness it.

"I don't feel like we're makin' it worth the time you took to ride all the way down here," Eli commented. "I wish we knew something we saw or heard when we were up that way, but I reckon we don't pay much attention to anything but our own business. After your long ride to get here, I hope you ain't plannin' to go back right away. You might as well stay over as a guest of the D and T and head back tomorrow. Meet some of the boys that make this the fastest-growin' ranch in this part of Texas. Right now, we're gettin' ready to drive close to three thousand cattle to the railroad yards in either Wichita or Abilene in about a month. So we'll be on the trail for months. We're gonna miss these meals by Juanita. Ain't we, Casey? But Smiley George is about as good a chuck wagon cook as you'll find anywhere." Eli wanted to plant that idea in the young deputy's mind so he would figure they were going to be on the cattle trail for the next few months.

"I reckon you and Casey have been in the cattle business for most of your adult lives," Colton speculated, finally dropping the *Mister*.

"That's the only business we know," Eli answered. "It ain't like we had a choice. Started out as young as Davey. He's fifteen."

"Musta been kinda rough for the past couple of years, though, when the cattle market went down," Colton said.

"You got that right," Casey responded. "We were one of the lucky ranches that could afford to hang on and keep our crew workin'. And now that the market has come halfway back, we can afford to sell our cattle and still make a profit." He studied Colton's face as he talked, and he felt sure he was swaying the young deputy's opinion of him and Eli more toward cattle barons, instead of bank robbers. "So whaddaya say? Stay over tonight and start back tomorrow. Have supper with us instead of bacon and beans beside a creek somewhere and get you a good night's sleep on a good bed."

"I reckon I can't turn down that invitation, if you're sure I won't be interfering with your work," Colton said.

"Good," Casey said. "Come on, we'll walk down to the barn, and you can get your saddlebags, or whatever you need for tonight. I'll show you the yellow-jacket nest back of the bunkhouse."

When they walked down to the barn, Davey walked out to meet them. "I didn't know if he was headin' back out right away or not. Miguel didn't say. So I took his saddle off and put it and his packs in a stall and turned the horses out in the corral," Davey told Eli.

"Davey, say howdy to Deputy Marshal Colton Gray," Eli said.

"Howdy," Davey said, then took an awkward step backward when Colton suddenly stepped toward him and extended his hand.

"Davey," Colton acknowledged, and shook his hand. "Thanks for takin' care of my horses."

Since Davey could think of no response, Casey laughed and said, "Colton's gonna spend the night with us, so I expect he'd appreciate it if you give his horses a portion of oats."

"Yes, sir," Davey spoke up then, "I'll take care of it." He led them back in the stable then to show them which stall he had left the saddle and packs in. Colton took his saddlebags from his saddle, saying that was all he needed.

When they walked out of the barn, Colton pointed to the bunkhouse and asked, "Is that the tree you attacked with gunpowder?" The top branches could be seen over the roof of the long building.

"That's Casey's tree," Eli answered. "Wanna take a look at his handiwork?"

"Might as well," Colton said. If it was a bluff they were trying, he decided he was going to call it. Davey went with them when they walked around behind the bunkhouse, even though he was baffled as to why they would want to show the poor battered gum tree to a visitor, when there were a lot more things to see on the ranch. He was further surprised when Colton walked up to the mutilated tree and examined it closely. "I don't know, Casey," Colton said. "You mighta killed the tree."

"You don't see no yellow jackets, though," Casey replied. "And that was the complaint."

"Who's that comin' yonder with Monroe?" Davey asked. They turned and looked in the direction Davey was pointing, but neither Casey nor Eli recognized the rider beside their foreman. He was leading a packhorse, so he must not have come from close by. They walked back around to the front of the barn so Monroe would see them, and they waited for them to ride in.

Eli walked over next to Casey and whispered low, "Are you thinkin' what I'm thinkin'?"

"Yeah," Casey answered, "another rancher gettin' squeezed off his land by the bank." It was a situation they were very familiar with by now. Included in the herd of cattle they were preparing to drive to Kansas were a couple of herds from some small ranchers who no longer had a profitable number of cattle to make the trip worthwhile. By combining their small herds with D&T's large herd, they could get their cows to market. Casey and Eli agreed to take them with their herd and pay them whatever the market price. In return, D&T received the benefit of using their men to help drive the main herd. "Well, let's see what he's got to say."

Monroe and the stranger pulled up in the barnyard and dismounted. Casey and Eli waited for an introduction from Monroe, who, in turn, was wondering who Colton was. The stranger sensed some hesitation on Monroe's part so he didn't wait. "My name's Grover Morris. I own a ranch about eighty miles south of here. I reckon I'm in the same fix as a lot of small ranchers are right now. But I've heard some things down my way about the D and T outfit helping some of the ranches in bad shape with the bank. So I said, 'What the hell, I'll ride up and see if I can do any business with you.' I came up on your foreman, here, back down near the river, and he was kind enough to bring me here." A lean man, with streaks of gray in his beard and hair, he looked from one of them to the other. "Maybe I oughta apologize for droppin' in on you like this, but I didn't know how to get in touch with you beforehand."

"No," Casey said, "no need to apologize a-tall. We cattlemen have to stick together through this messed-up market. I'm Casey Tubbs and this is my partner, Eli Doolin. This young fellow here is Deputy Marshal Colton Gray. Colton, this young man is our foreman, Monroe Kelly." He looked at Eli and grinned. "Now that we got all the introductions done, let's see if we can decide what we're gonna do. Monroe, Colton is our guest tonight. Maybe you could show him around the ranch as Eli and I talk with Mr. Morris. Davey, I expect Mr. Morris's horses need takin' care of. And I'll tell Juanita she'll have two guests for supper tonight." He paused to think a second. "We ain't got but one spare room in the house, but we got extra beds in the bunkhouse."

"I can sleep in the bunkhouse," Morris volunteered. "I just appreciate the invite to stay here tonight."

"No, I insist," Colton said. "I'll take the bunkhouse, and to tell you the truth, I'd like to eat with the men at the cookhouse."

"I'll take care of him," Monroe said. "By the time he spends some time with some of our crew, he might decide to take up herdin' cattle, instead of outlaws."

"Then we can all meet for breakfast in the morning," Eli declared. "I'll tell Juanita to expect ya." They split up then. Monroe took Colton into the bunkhouse and showed him which beds were not being used, so he could pick one. Casey and Eli walked up to the house with Grover Morris, leaving Davey to take care of the horses.

"Take Mr. Morris into the study and give him a drink of likker," Casey said, "unless you druther have a cup of coffee. And I'll go tell Juanita how many she'll be cookin' for."

"Please," Morris said, "call me Grover. And all the same to you, I'd druther have the coffee."

"Grover it is, then," Eli said. "Grover, Casey, and Eli. You can talk business better on a first-name basis."

Casey went to the kitchen to give Juanita the plan and she immediately started a pot of fresh coffee. When he went back to the study, Grover was already telling Eli about his financial problems. "I didn't see that dead market comin'. I couldn't understand it could last this long. I went to talk to Bryan Dawkins at the bank, told him I was buildin' my herd again. But he said, 'Nothin' doin', you promised to pay by the first of next month, or the land belongs to us.' "

"How many head have you got that's fit for market?" Casey asked.

"I can make three hundred and fifty head," Grover answered. "I've heard reports that the Kansas markets are payin' from twenty to twenty-five dollars now. If my cows bring that much, I can pay the bank what I owe 'em."

"How much do you owe the bank?" Eli asked.

"I don't owe them but seventy-five hundred. If the cattle go for twenty-five, I'd have a little money left over to pay whatever you charge me to borrow the seventy-five from you. But the bank won't wait till after I sell the cattle." He paused then, searching their faces for their reaction. "I brought all my loan papers to show you how much I owe." He took an envelope from his inside coat pocket and pulled the papers out. "There it is," he said, "seven thousand and five hundred dollars, Cotton Growers Bank of Austin. And there's the due date, first of the month. I reckon I went to the worst bank to finance a cattle ranch. Growin' cotton is a bigger business around Austin."

Casey looked at the papers, then handed them to Eli, who looked them over as well. He handed them back to Grover and nodded his approval to Casey. "Have you got enough men left to drive your cows up on our range?" Grover said that he did, so Casey continued. "Well, me and Eli ain't in the bankin' business, so there won't be no charge to borrow the money to pay the bank off. Whatever we get for our cattle is the same you'll get for yours. What are you fixin' to do after you sell your cows and you own your land free and clear?"

Grover looked as if he didn't understand the question. "Why, I reckon I'm gonna start over and do what I have to do to feed my family and pay you your seventy-five hundred."

"All right, Grover, here's our offer," Casey said after a quick word with Eli. "We'll stake you for the seventy-five-hundred bank payment as soon as you show up on our range with your cattle. Eighty miles, that oughta take you about a week, right? We'll have your money for you then. We don't keep large sums of money here at the ranch." He made that statement just as a matter of caution. "That'll give you time to settle up with the bank before we start the drive north."

"I'll take it," Grover stated without hesitation. His body sagged a bit as if it had been suddenly released of all its tension, and he looked like he needed to sit down.

"You sure you don't want that drink of likker?" Eli asked. "Have a seat there at that little table," he said when Juanita came in the room carrying a large tray with cups and a coffeepot on it.

He sat down in the chair Eli indicated, seemingly drained of the starch that had kept him on his feet. "Thank you just the same," he said, "but the coffee will do just fine. I thought that what I'd heard about you gentlemen was just talk. You were the only hope my family had, and you'll have my eternal gratitude."

"I expect you'da done the same for us, if it was the other way around," Casey said.

Chapter 7

Juanita served a big supper that night in the dining room, since Casey and Eli had guests. They persuaded Colton to join them for the meal, even though he was going to sleep in the bunkhouse. They thought it a good idea to give the young deputy every opportunity to form a picture of them as honorable, law-abiding cattle barons. Grover Morris proved to be an excellent advocate for their integrity. It was becoming more and more difficult for Colton to suspect the apparently successful partners of the D&T Cattle Company to be the two quaint robbers known as Elmer and Oscar. He found he could not prove it more than pure coincidence that they were in Fort Worth, in the same office, earlier the same day the elderly bandits were there. He was still of the opinion that the old bandits were younger men in disguises, however. Casey apologized to him for having to send him to the bunkhouse at the end of the evening, but Colton assured him that he didn't mind. He said he planned to get an early start in the morning, so he thanked Juanita for the supper and said good night to them all.

"I feel kinda bad that you weren't able to pick up some of the clues you were hopin' Eli and I could help you with. But it was our pleasure to have the visit. You're a bright young man, and I'm sure you'll eventually run those two old birds down.

Hope you'll drop in to see us whenever you find yourself in this part of the country."

"I'll surely do that, Casey. I wanna thank you again for your hospitality. I hate to miss another meal at Juanita's table, but I think I'll get up and eat with the crew in the morning and get on the road to Waco."

After Colton left, they had coffee and cigars with Grover Morris and talked about the planned cattle drive ahead of them, and how fortunate they were to have enlisted Gary Corbett as the trail boss. This surprised Grover, since he had assumed that Casey and Eli would lead the drive. They explained that their role was to ride on ahead of the herd to negotiate the best price from the best buyer. That would make the decision on the final destination. Then they would meet the herd and guide them to the best market. Grover seemed impressed.

Morning brought another splendid meal from Juanita's kitchen before Grover climbed back on his horse and started out on his way back to his ranch to give his wife and sons the joyful news. Casey and Eli stood in the yard to watch him ride away. "There goes a happy man," Casey commented.

"He's gonna be even happier when he finds out he don't have to pay us that seventy-five hundred we're gonna give him to pay off the banknote," Eli said. Casey started to protest, but Eli continued. "Don't try to tell me you ain't already decided to give him the dang money."

"Well, hell, he's talkin' about startin' over, and how's he gonna do that if he has to pay us that money back?" Casey demanded, then asked, "What?" when Eli mumbled something half under his breath.

"Cotton Growers Bank of Austin, I said," Eli blurted. "That's the next place we're goin' to get Grover's money, ain't it?"

Casey laughed. "I reckon so. Kinda has a ring to it, don't it?"

* * *

"Miguel said you wanted to see me," Monroe said when he walked into the study, where Casey and Eli did all their planning. They had never been inside the room when they were simple cowhands working for the Whitmore Brothers. Back in those days, they had never been past the kitchen door. It was a disappointment for them when they found out it was just another room. Casey wondered if Monroe was as disappointed as he had been.

"Yeah, Monroe," Casey said. "Come on in. Me and Eli are gonna have to take a trip to Waco for a meeting of the Cattleman's Association to see what we can find out about pricin' in Wichita and Abilene. We'll be gone awhile, I expect, so you'll be in charge. Just keep movin' those cattle up to the northern part of our range, like you've been doin'.'"

"Yes, sir, anything else?"

"No, you know what to do," Casey answered, smiling at Monroe's respectful use of "yes, sir" and "no, sir" when he addressed him and Eli. These young boys that he and Eli had worked side by side with were now respectful ever since they talked of Cattleman's Associations and such. Casey didn't even know if there was a Cattleman's Association in Waco. He and Eli weren't going to Waco, anyway. They were going to Austin.

"How long do you figure on being gone?" Monroe asked.

"We always figure on takin' two and a half days to get to Waco. We could get there in two, if we was in a hurry, but there ain't no use in pushin' the horses that hard. So that's five days just to get there and back. And it's hard to say how long we'll be there. One day, I hope, maybe two. So count on at least a full week before we get back." He could use the same estimates of time, even though they were not really going to Waco, because Austin was almost exactly the same distance from the ranch as Waco.

"Davey said you was each takin' a packhorse," Monroe said. "Is that right?"

"Yep," Casey answered. "We have to take extra outfits depending on what kind of meetin's they're havin', and sometimes we even get invited to a formal dinner. So we don't take no chances on showin' up like the cow pushers we really are."

Monroe had to smile at the image that brought to mind. "I'd truly like to see you and ol' Eli all dressed up to go to a formal dinner."

Casey laughed with him. "It ain't no different than what we'd look like goin' to a funeral," he said. "I told Davey we'd be down to the barn to pack up what we need to make camp with. After that, we'll bring 'em up to the house to pack the extra clothes. Here comes Eli now."

Monroe turned to see Eli coming from the kitchen. "Casey said you and him had to tote a bunch of fancy clothes with you when you go to Waco," Monroe said.

Eli was startled for a moment, thinking Casey had told Monroe about their disguises. "You know," Casey said when he saw Eli's reaction, "in case we have to go to a formal supper or something."

"Right," Eli responded. "We gotta look like we know what we're talking about. You ready to start packin' up?"

"I was just fixin' to," Casey answered.

"We might as well get started," Eli remarked.

The D&T Ranch was only about twenty miles east of the Colorado River, the river the town of Austin was built on. It was not a direct route, however, for the river took many turns in its journey to that town. Since they really knew no other trail to Austin, it was tempting to follow it. But it would make no sense to anyone there at the ranch to see them start out to the west, when Waco was to the east. So, after loading the packs carrying everything they would need for Elmer and Oscar, they left the ranch house on the old Comanche Trail. This was in case someone back at the house might be watching them leave. This was the trail they would take when going to Waco, so they followed it until out of sight of the ranch. Then they cut back to the south to pick up a trail that followed the Lampasas River, planning to follow the river until it reached the point where it swung sharply to the east. From there, they hoped they could strike a trail that might lead them to the Colorado and on to Austin. Neither man had ever been to Austin, so they were not familiar with the trail they decided to follow. But it seemed to be going in the right direction, until they came to a fork in the trail that gave them pause. "Whaddaya think?" Casey asked Eli when they pulled up to study their options. "The one on the left heads a little more to the east, more in the direction we've been ridin'. That trail on the right wants to keep goin' straight south."

"All my natural instinct as an expert tracker tells me the trail on the left is the one we want," Eli declared after studying the two choices for a few seconds.

"In that case, we'd best use the scientific method to see for sure," Casey said, and reached in his pocket for a coin. "Heads or tails?" Eli called tails, and Casey flipped the coin. "Dang," he blurted, "tails it is. I reckon I never shoulda doubted you." They took the trail to the left.

About three-quarters of a mile down that trail, they came to a heavily wooded area with a creek running through it. "Too bad we just rested the horses at that little stream back up the trail," Eli said. "If we'da known about that creek up ahead, it'da been a lot better place, wouldn't it?" When they got closer, they discovered there was already someone taking advantage of the camping place. They could see a campfire a dozen yards or more upstream, and there appeared to be only one man beside it. He saw them at about the same time they saw him, and he stopped to stare until Casey threw his hand up as a howdy. The man acknowledged with a wave in return.

"You know," Casey said, "he seems friendly enough. He might know where he's goin'. Maybe he could tell us if we're on the right road to Austin."

"Couldn't hurt to ask," Eli agreed.

So they turned their horses upstream and approached the camp. The man watched them cautiously; then Casey called out, "Howdy, friend! Just wanna ask you a question if you know these parts. Is this the road to Austin? We ain't been down this way before, so we just took a guess back at that fork."

The man seemed to relax a bit. "Yes, sir," he answered. "This road will take you to Austin after a while. The other'n back at the fork'll take you there quicker and easier. It runs south till it strikes the Colorado River. Then you just follow the river east to Austin."

"I'm glad we asked you," Eli said. "I had a feelin' that other trail was the one we wanted. 'Preciate the information."

"Glad I could help," the man said. "I'd invite ya to step down, if I had some coffee to offer ya, but I'm plum out of a lot of things right now."

"'Preciate the offer," Casey replied, "but we just rested the horses a little while ago, and we had some then. How 'bout we leave you some coffee so you can have some later on tonight?"

"That would be mighty neighborly of you fellers, but I wouldn't wanna run you short."

"We've got enough for all of us," Casey said as he dismounted and went to his packhorse. "You got something to put some of this in? It's ground up and ready to put in the pot."

"Yes, sir, I sure do." He went to his packs and produced an empty can and handed it to Casey. "I really 'preciate this, mister." He watched as Casey poured enough out of the sack to make several cups of coffee. "Yes, sir, you fellers is real Christian gentlemen. You ain't got but about another hour and a half before dark. If you was thinkin' about makin' camp, you're welcome to camp right here, use my fire. I wouldn't bother you none."

"Thanks," Casey said, "but I reckon we'll go back to that other trail and maybe ride till dark. Make up as much time as we can. Much as I love coffee, though, I don't like to see anybody go without it." He tied the sack up and climbed up into the saddle. They turned their horses around and headed back to the fork. Taking the right fork then, they set out for Austin again. After about a mile, they came to the same creek they had just left. They figured they might, so they pulled up to talk about it.

"We've got a little daylight left," Eli said. "And the horses aren't really tired yet. We can take a chance on findin' another water hole. Whaddaya think?"

"Shoulda asked that fellow back yonder how far it is to the river, I reckon," Casey remarked. "Hell, it ain't gonna make that much difference. Let's just go ahead and make camp here where we know we've got everything we need."

"Suits me," Eli responded. "I'm ready to eat right now." So they left the trail and rode up the creek until they found a spot where there was good grass for the horses and plenty of firewood. "I might wanna stay right here and build me a cabin," Eli joked.

"Bang, you're dead," Willy Brinker said when he sneaked up behind "Squirrel" Pelley.

"Like hell I am," Squirrel countered. "I heard you stompin' through the bushes like a bunch of wild hogs, ever since you left your horse at the road. Where you been? What was you doin' all that time?"

"What I told you I was gonna do," Willy answered. "I went down the creek to see if anybody took over that old fool's cabin."

"Have they?"

"Nope. Least there weren't no sign of anybody in there since we was there. Everything looked just like we left it."

"Any sign of anythin' diggin' up that body?" Squirrel asked. "We sure as hell didn't dig that hole very deep."

"Nope, no sign," Willy said. "I looked all around there to see if that old dog of his ever come back to the cabin. Didn't see no sign of it. I was hopin' to roast that old hound over that fire, there." He started to ramble on, but stopped suddenly. "What's that I smell?" He noticed the cup sitting on the ground beside Squirrel's foot then. "Is that coffee?" He looked at the fire then and saw the coffeepot sitting at the edge of it. "Where the . . . ?" He glared at his partner. "Where did you . . . ? You've been holdin' out on me, you son of a—"

"Shut up, you dang fool, and I'll tell you where I got the blame coffee," Squirrel interrupted. "Might even let you have a cup. While you was pokin' around in the woods, I found me a place where we can help ourselves to a real score. I had me some company while you was gone, two fellers that ain't got no idea how to get where they're wantin' to go." He had Willy's undivided attention now, so he went on to tell him of the opportunity just dropped into their laps. "Ridin' fine-lookin' horses, they was, and they both was leadin' pack-horses, loaded down. I sent 'em on the back trail to the river, and I'm willin' to bet they don't go very far before they camp. So we'll pay 'em a little visit tonight."

Willy didn't have to say anything. The grin on his wide, homely face spoke of the pleasure he anticipated. "Doggone, that sure come along at the right time, didn't it? What was they? Young fellers? Old fellers?"

"I don't know," Squirrel hesitated. "They wasn't young, and they wasn't old, just somewhere in the middle, I reckon, like me and you. They looked like they might could handle theirselves, if you give 'em a chance. So we won't give 'em a chance. We'll let 'em go to sleep before we pay 'em a visit."

"I hope they're totin' plenty of grub, 'cause I'm hungry enough to eat one of the horses. You say they was ridin' pretty good horses?"

"Yep, they was both good horses. One of 'em was ridin' a bay, and the other'n was ridin' a gray. And that's the one I'm claimin'."

"Whaddaya mean, the one you're claimin'?"

"I'm just sayin', I seen 'em first and I'm claimin' the gray."

"You ain't got no right to claim the gray," Willy immediately reacted. "We'll flip for it. Winner gets to take his pick. I might not even want the gray after I get a chance to look 'em both over, but I wanna look 'em over."

"Don't matter," Squirrel said. "I saw 'em first and I pick the gray."

"The hell you say. You ain't got no claim on nothin'. We're partners, and if I wanted to, I'd just kick your scrawny butt anytime I decided I wanted my pick of somethin'. You ever think about that?"

"Yeah, I think about that," Squirrel replied. "And the reason you don't ever try that is because you know I'd stick my knife in your belly and walk clean around you."

"Is that so? You mean like you did with that poor old feller in the cabin? He was so poorly, he could hardly stand up. You knifed him and he still told you what you was before he finally keeled over dead. Hell, I coulda killed him with one lick with my fist. It might take two for you, but not much more." They continued their verbal battle, as they had often fought before, and as before, they ended it in a stalemate; then it was easily forgotten, usually by some distraction. On this occasion, the distraction was the pot of coffee on the fire. "Did you ask 'em for some coffee?"

"No, I tried to get 'em to camp right here with us, but they didn't wanna. I told 'em I didn't have no coffee, or I'da offered 'em some. One of 'em poured me some ground beans outta a sack that looked like it was pretty full. It's damn good coffee."

"Well, gimme some of it, and we'll go find those boys tonight and get the rest of it."

"You think there's any chance that fellow back there might show up at our camp before the night's over?" Casey asked Eli. "He was pretty shabby-lookin', and those two horses by the creek looked in worse shape than he was."

"I don't know," Eli said, scratchin' his head in an effort to help him think better. "He sure seemed thankful enough when you gave him that coffee. He might show up lookin' for a donation of some food. Maybe we shoulda left him some more supplies, but I sure don't wanna adopt a drifter on our way to rob a bank."

"He didn't look like much of a threat, but that don't mean he wouldn't try to sneak in here tonight and run off with our horses." He looked at Eli and chuckled. "I swear, ever since we turned into outlaws, I don't trust anybody."

"It's always better if you can make your camp where nobody knows where it is, so you ain't likely to get bothered during the night," Eli said. "I kinda had a funny feelin' about that fellow. His eyes were set a little too close together or something."

Eli's comments were enough to make Casey's decision for him. "Might be kinda silly, but I'm sleepin' with my horse tonight. I ain't takin' a chance on havin' some little rat rummage through my packs, then run off with my horse. Smoke is just ornery enough to go with him."

It was enough to sway Eli. "We might as well play it safe. No sense in makin' it easy for anybody that wants to jump us to just walk right in."

So they fried some bacon and hardtack to go with their coffee and promised each other that tomorrow night's supper was going to be a far sight better. They figured to reach Austin by suppertime tomorrow, barring any unforeseen delays.

Chapter 8

After cleaning up the frying pan and rinsing out the coffeepot in the creek, they sat by the fire for a little while before Eli started yawning, and they both decided to turn in for the night. They arranged their saddles and rain slickers at the edge of the firelight to look like beds, just in case they had the wrong kind of visitors. But with their assailants in mind, they didn't bother to make elaborate decoys. They figured him more for a beggar, but one who would steal your horse, if given the opportunity. With the campfire scene set, they took their bedrolls over by the creek, where the horses were grazing. Both Smoke and Biscuit were free of restraints, since there were no worries that they would wander off. The two packhorses were hobbled to keep them from wandering. Eli joked that maybe they should hobble Smoke and Biscuit so they couldn't run, and let Squirrel run the packhorses off.

Eli was asleep as soon as he crawled in his bedroll, a knack that stood him well during his many nights herding cattle. Casey envied him that ability. He, on the other hand, seemed to bring back things to mind that he needed to check on. He was in the midst of thinking whether or not he and Eli should change their approach to the robbery. Their frequent routine—wanting to deposit a large sum of money so they wouldn't be carrying that much on their person—might have become a warning to banks. Especially when it was from two obviously ancient men. He decided to discuss it with Eli in the morning, because the low hum of Eli's snoring told him his partner had already passed out. He tried to quiet his mind in hopes of joining him. It was then that he heard the first sound. He couldn't identify it right away. It sounded like the wind ruffling the leaves of the trees. It occurred to him that the wind was calm.

He eased his hand slowly down to grasp his Henry rifle, then raised his head enough to see over the lump of blanket in his bedroll. Looking in the direction from which the noise had come, he peered at the darkened trunks of the trees. He could see nothing at first, but then, a dark form separated from those of the tree trunks. *Well, I'll be,* he thought. *The little rat did come after the horses.* He started to roll out of his bedroll, but stopped when a second form separated from the trees to follow the first one. He waited then to see if there were any more to follow the first two. He glanced over toward Eli, who was still humming peacefully, so softly that the two intruders obviously could not hear him. He thought to wake him, then decided against it. Eli was prone to awaken with a loud start when suddenly disturbed from a deep sleep. And at this point, he felt he was in control of the visit and had the advantage on the two visitors.

Now that they were well past the horses, Casey got up and positioned himself behind the two men. He had to concede the fact that they were a gutsy pair; having passed up the horses, they were obviously intent upon sneaking in close enough to the fire to steal the packs. He wondered if they thought they would have the time to saddle and pack up the horses before he and Eli finally woke up. When they got closer to the dying fire, they would see the saddles there; then they would have to do a quick about-face and head back for the horses. *But they're going to find me waiting for them,* he thought.

"Any minute now," he murmured to himself as they contin-ued to sneak closer and closer to the fire. Suddenly it was as if the dark forest exploded with gunfire, for both men opened up on what they thought were sleeping victims. "Whoa!" Casey blurted before he could catch himself. They had come with killing in mind! Eli came roaring out of his bedroll, his rifle in hand, with no idea where the trouble was coming from. "The camp!" Casey yelled at him. "They're shootin' up the camp!" Squirrel and Willy both heard him and turned in a panic to start shooting back toward the way they had come. "Cut 'em down before they shoot the horses," Casey cried. They dropped both of them with two well-placed shots.

Eli and Casey stood for a long moment after, somewhat in a mild state of shock, scarcely able to believe they had just shot down two men. They exchanged confused glances. In their short careers as armed robbers, they had never shot anyone, only threatened with no intention of following through, if pos-sible. They walked up to the campfire to look at their victims. Standing there, staring down at them, Casey said, "That's the one we gave the coffee to, all right." He pointed to Squirrel.

"His partner's a big'un, ain't he?" Eli remarked. "I don't know what else we coulda done. They didn't give us no choice. It was them or us."

"That's right," Casey said. "They called the play. Wasn't nothin' else we could do. Didn't make no sense to stand there and get shot."

"I reckon we coulda said, 'Hey! Let's set down and divide our goods up between us,'" Eli said.

"Well, let's drag 'em outta our camp. You wanna search 'em, see if they've got anything valuable?"

"I don't want nothin' they've got," Eli said. "Let's just get 'em to hell outta here. I wanna see how bad they tore my sad-dle up with all that shootin'."

"We need to see if any of our horses got hit," Casey said. The horses got excited when all the shooting happened, so they weren't sure if it was just fright, or if some of them got shot. He took another look at Squirrel. "I swear, I sure had that little fellow wrong. I'da never figured him for a gunman."

"Well, it don't take much to pull a trigger," Eli declared.

They went first to check on the welfare of their horses and were relieved to find they were all right. They decided to wait until morning before searching for their victims' horses. Then they returned to the fire and dragged the two bodies back deep into the woods. They were without tools to dig graves and without the desire to dig them. So they just dragged them far away from the campfire. When they checked their saddles afterward, they found they were going to have to dig some slugs out of the leather. "I reckon that was a good idea to sleep with the horses," Eli said. "I expect we'd best try to get a little bit of sleep outta what's left of the night, but I don't know if I can after all that." So, with nothing else to stay up for, they returned to their bedrolls. And just as before, Eli was peacefully humming within minutes.

Morning found them anxious to get started, but they had to take the time to search for the outlaws' horses. Willy and Squirrel were the outlaws' names Eli and Casey learned later. Willy and Squirrel's horses were tied up not far away, close enough, in fact, that one of them, a packhorse, was lying on the ground, shot dead by a stray bullet from one of the intruders. "From the look of that poor horse, I expect it was a blessin'," Eli declared. The two saddle horses didn't look a lot better, so they took the saddles off, removed their bridles, and set them free. Like the horses they rode on, the saddles weren't worth keeping, either. "I reckon those boys were havin' a pretty rough time of it," Eli said. "But I can't bring myself to feel sorry for 'em, considerin' the way they were goin' about improvin' their lives."

"I hope this trail goes where that fellow said it does," Casey remarked. "After the night we just had, I'm wonderin' if that other trail is really the quickest way to Austin."

They both paused to give that some thought. Then they both started to speak at the same time. "You go ahead," Eli said.

"I was gonna say, I'd bet on that other trail," Casey said.

"Me too," Eli declared. "Let's saddle up and get the hell away from this place. We'll eat breakfast when we rest the horses."

There was no way of knowing if the left fork was better than the one Squirrel had sent them on, but it seemed fairly direct, heading in a more southeastern direction before turning straight south to strike the Colorado River. Then they followed the river into the town of Austin, arriving at about suppertime. Their first priority was supper after having to cook their own for the last couple of days. "How 'bout that one?" Eli asked, pointing to a sign near the middle of the busy street. " 'Hardwick's Restaurant,' " he read. "That looks like it might be fancy enough for two gents like me and you."

"Might be at that," Casey said, his eye having been caught by the building on the corner across from it. "A nice view to boot," he added, causing Eli to follow his gaze. " 'Cotton Growers Bank of Austin,' " he read aloud. "Maybe you're right. Maybe we'd best test Hardwick's cookin'." That decided, they pulled over to the restaurant and tied their horses out front.

They were met by Edward Hardwick when they walked in the door. Standing by a desk with a cash register, he greeted them politely. "Good evening, gentlemen. Welcome to Hardwick's. Are you new in town, or just passing through?"

"Good evenin'," Casey returned. "We're just passin' through town, and we thought we'd see what kind of cookin' you do here."

"We're glad you did," Hardwick said. "We'll do our best to

give you your money's worth. Can I ask you to leave your guns with me here at the desk while you're enjoying your supper?"

"No problem a-tall," Casey answered, and he and Eli immediately unbuckled their gun belts. Casey looked around the half-filled room, then asked, "How about one of those tables by the front windows so we can see the people passin' by?"

"As you wish," Hardwick replied, and led them to a table. "How's this?" he asked, and they both said it was fine. "Your waiter will be right with you," Hardwick said, and returned to his desk by the door.

"Is this place fancy enough for you?" Eli asked when Hardwick had left. He looked around the restaurant and noticed that there were nothing but men waiting the tables. "Uh-oh, try to look dignified. Here comes one headin' for us."

"Howdy, fellows, my name's Steve. I'll be waiting on you tonight—"

"Well, you ain't gonna be waitin' long," Eli interrupted, "'cause I'm ready to eat."

Steve laughed politely and asked, "What are we drinking?"

On a roll now, Eli said, "Nothin' yet. We're hopin' for some coffee, though."

Steve smiled patiently, then looked at Casey. "I'll have coffee, too," Casey said. "What's on the menu tonight?" When told he had a choice between pork chops and a steak, he chose the chop.

"Cattlemen, right?" Steve asked. Casey said that was a fact, and Steve said, "Cattlemen always order the pork chop. I'll put your order in and get you some coffee." He hustled away to the kitchen.

"I wonder if the cook's a man," Eli mused aloud.

"What difference does it make?" Casey asked. "I just hope he or she is a good cook."

"It makes a lotta difference," Eli begged to differ. "It

brightens the place up when you've got women waitin' on you. They make you forget about whatever's been naggin' at you before you came in to eat. Makes it better for your digestion. Walk out of a place like this, where there ain't nobody but men bringin' your food and fillin' your cup, you feel like you just been to a cattle auction."

"I swear," Casey said. "All this time, I've been ridin' with you, and I never knew you were such a filla . . . fillosofu . . . deep thinker," he said when he couldn't think of the word. "It musta been a real hardship for you when we were on a cattle drive, and there weren't nobody to cook for you but Smiley."

"Hell, you know what I mean. It just seems homier when you've got the women bouncin' all around the room. I reckon a lot of them politicians over at the Capitol Buildin' come here to eat. Then I reckon they expect us to give 'em some money for waitin' on us. They'll most likely charge us more for the supper than the hotel at the other end of the street would."

"I was lookin' forward to eatin' that pork chop," Casey said. "But after listening to all your bellyachin', I ain't sure I can enjoy it."

Steve brought the coffee, and it was good. Just a few minutes later, he came back with their supper, and it was excellent. He gave them a few minutes to eat before he came again to see if everything was acceptable. "More than acceptable," Casey told him. "Tell the cook we've never had better."

Steve gave them a big smile and said, "I'll tell Mabel that. She'll be tickled."

When he went back to the kitchen, Casey grinned at Eli and said, "Mabel, now does that make you happy?" He was answered with an indifferent grunt.

They lingered awhile over coffee and apple pie studying the building that housed the bank across the street. It was located on a corner of the main street and a narrow side street that led out of town. The bank was already closed for the day, but there was still ample daylight to see what was around it. They decided they had best leave before they lost that remaining daylight, so they left a couple of quarters on the table and paid Hardwick for their supper when they collected their guns. Having already decided to make as little impression on the town of Austin as possible, they didn't go to the hotel. They would camp with their horses for the two nights they planned to be there. A hotel room would not be to their advantage, anyway, when it came to changing into their disguises, or their working clothes, as they preferred to call them.

They decided it a good idea to ride out of town on the narrow side street beside the bank. By doing that, they would have an opportunity to get a look at the side and back of the bank and see what was behind it. They walked the horses slowly along the side street, but they saw nothing that would help them one way or another. Still, it looked like the best route to get away from the center of town as quickly as possible. And if that side street provided a way out, then they wouldn't run the danger of galloping away down the main street with people shooting at them. They would normally go in the front door and come out the front door. What concerned them was the possibility of someone getting to the back door in time to get a shot at them as they rode away. "So we leave the horses behind the bank and come out the back door," Casey said.

"Makes sense," Eli agreed.

That settled, they continued on out the side street, concerned now about resting their horses and finding a place to camp. There were a few houses close to the main street, but then the road turned into little more than a trail, leading to who knew where. From the appearance of the trail, it was obvious that it was seldom used. They kept going, hoping to come to a stream or a creek. After about three-quarters of a mile, they saw what appeared to be a clearing in the rapidly fading light. It turned out to be a cemetery. "Well, damned if that ain't a dead end for ya," Eli declared. "We picked the road to the cemetery."

The trail continued on around the cemetery, so they kept following it, since it was leading toward a ridge with a heavy growth of trees beyond it. About ready to turn around at that point, they decided they might as well see what was beyond the ridge. The heavy growth of trees they had spotted beyond the ridge was, to their surprise, on both sides of a healthy creek. "Well, I'll be . . ." Casey declared. "Danged if this ain't the perfect campsite." They both dismounted and began to set up a camp. They unloaded the horses and let them go to water, then searched around in the heavy darkness of the trees for wood for a fire. In a short time, they had a fire going and were settled down for the night.

"In the mornin', when we can see, we can check all around this place and make sure we ain't campin' right next to somebody's backyard," Eli said. "We need to see if we can get outta here without goin' back through town. But if it looks as good in the morning as it does right now, then I think we're all set."

"I agree," Casey said. "If nobody bothers us tonight, we can take a look at that bank tomorrow. Then if nobody bothers us tomorrow night, I think we can leave our packhorses here, and Elmer and Oscar can go make the withdrawal and come right back here to get outta their workin' clothes." He paused to think a moment before continuing. "There's one thing that bothers me, though."

"Runnin' from the bank on that side street," Eli finished for him.

"That's right. Even if we go out the back door, there's those houses down that street. If just one person sees us gallop past, we're in for it." He scratched his chin to think about it. "When we look around here in the mornin', maybe we can find us an emergency escape route." They continued to talk on, into the night, until Casey realized he was doing all the talking, Eli having dropped off into sleep. Instead of bothering him, Casey got up to check the horses one last time. He hobbled the packhorses and then he turned in.

Casey awoke the next morning to the sound of Smoke nibbling on some skinny blades of grass growing next to his sleeping bag. "There ain't a lot of grass here, is there, boy? Too many trees. I'll buy you some corn when we go into town." He looked over to see if Eli was awake. He wasn't moving, so Casey got up and got the fire started again. He figured they might want to eat breakfast in town, but it wouldn't hurt to have a little coffee before they got started. So he picked up the coffeepot and walked down to the edge of the creek to fill it. After it was filled, he stood there and listened to the sounds of the creek waking up. There was not a sound that didn't belong, testament that he and Eli were the only intruders.

When he walked back up to the fire, he found Eli encouraging it. "I thought we'd have a little coffee while we're deciding what to do for breakfast," he said.

"Good idea," Eli said. "While you're makin' it, I'm gonna climb up that ridge behind us and see if there's anybody around this spot."

"That sounds like a good idea, too," Casey said, and went to the packs to get the ground coffee. The coffee was ready long before Eli returned. When he finally appeared from the trees, Casey said, "I thought for a while there that you musta stepped in a hole somewhere. And I was gonna have to drink this whole pot before I went lookin' for you."

"You can see pretty far up on that ridge, and I didn't see any sign of any houses in these woods. So I walked on, along the ridge a good ways, and you know what? I could see that cemetery from there. And you know what else? That trail we came in on ain't the only trail to that cemetery. There's an even smaller trail on the other side of it that leads out to town."

"Is that a fact?" Casey replied. "So we could go to town that way, if we wanted to."

"We could come here from the bank that way," Eli explained. "So we wouldn't have to ride by those houses after we rob the bank."

"Damn! That's right!" Casey said. "I didn't even think about that. We'll go into town that way and see where it comes out. There might be some people who could see us take that road. This is a dang good spot to do what we gotta do, but it's awful close to that town. You still think we oughta stick with it?"

"Yeah, I do," Eli said after a short pause to think about it. "If we can head right back here after we leave that bank, without anybody seein' which way we went, we oughta have time to get outta our work clothes. Then, even if they got up a posse and came lookin' back here, they wouldn't find nobody but you and me. Elmer and Oscar would be long gone." He paused again to let Casey think that over. "Besides," he continued, "when we started this business, we said we would most likely get caught pretty quick, and then we'd just retire in prison and talk about the good times we had."

"Yep," Casey laughed. "That is what we figured, ain't it? And now, we'll be famous when they do catch us. Maybe that Huntsville Unit has some special rooms for famous folks. That wouldn't be bad, would it?" He took a moment to visualize it, then nodded his head once to dismiss it. "But that ain't gonna happen on this trip. We've still got places to spend the bank's money. You ready to go into town?"

The decision to be made at this point was whether or not they were willing to gamble on leaving their packhorses, along with all their disguises and supplies, at their camp. "I don't know," Eli hedged. "We'd be up a creek for sure if somebody happened to stumble on 'em."

Casey was thinking the same thing, so he said, "Hell, let's load 'em up. We can't take the chance. We're gonna leave 'em here tomorrow morning while we're at the bank, but that ain't gonna be for long." So they loaded the packhorses again, and while they were doing that, Casey thought of one more thing. "You know what? It might be a smart thing to just ride back to town the same way we came in. That way, if somebody in one of those houses did see us come back here last night, they might see us leavin' with our packhorses and everything. They'd figure we'd gone for good after campin' overnight."

Chapter 9

They decided that Casey's idea about letting anyone see they were obviously leaving for good was a smart one. But there was still the possibility of being seen returning on the alternate path that Eli saw from the ridge. So they decided to first check that trail before they took the packhorses out. "Why don't you let me do that, while you stay here with the packhorses," Eli said. Casey was agreeable, so he sat waiting at the back corner of the graveyard while Eli rode around it to pick up the back trail to town. It wasn't long before he returned to report his findings. "I swear," he beamed, "it just keeps gittin' better. It comes out at the railroad tracks behind some kinda warehouse or something. And it ain't that far from the bank. We'd have to be awful unlucky for somebody to see us cut in behind that buildin'. You'll see what I mean when we come back that way tonight."

So they took a casual ride back past the houses on the side street and came out beside the bank. They noted the business hours painted on the glass of the front door. Like almost every bank, they opened at nine. That gave them plenty of time to buy themselves a big breakfast. They considered a return visit to Hardwick's Restaurant to try one of Mabel's breakfasts, but decided it wise not to become too well known in one place in town. So they rode toward the other end of the street until a small place, squeezed in between a barber's and a dry-goods store, caught their eye. " 'Mona Bell's,' " Casey read the simple sign, then the line below it, " 'Country Cooking.' " She seemed to be quite busy, so they decided to give it a try. There wasn't room to tie their horses up in front of Mona Bell's, but a passerby told them to tie them in front of the barber's. "Harry don't even open up for another hour and a half," the passerby said.

"Much obliged," Eli said, and he and Casey tied the horses up at the barber's.

It was as crowded inside the eating establishment as it was at the hitching rail. Casey and Eli concluded right away that it was awfully good, or awfully cheap. They were hoping it was the former. "Come on in, boys," Dudley Bell sang out when they walked in and stepped aside to allow two customers walking out to pass. "Two holes just opened up." He walked over to the one long table and picked up the two dirty dishes and set them on a high counter that separated the dining room from the kitchen. In a moment, a young girl came to the counter and took the dirty plates away to be washed. Beyond her, on the outside wall, they could see a rather stumpy-looking woman working over a hot stove—Mona, they presumed.

They both squeezed in a hole big enough to suit one person, since that was where Dudley indicated. Their intrusion appeared not to bother the customers on either side of them as they concentrated on their breakfasts. Dudley placed a cup of coffee down before each of them and asked, "How you want your eggs?" They told him and he took two forks and two spoons from a pocket in the apron he was wearing and placed them beside their cups. "Link sausage this mornin'. You won't need no knife," he said, and left to go behind the counter before they had time to tell him what they wanted with their eggs.

A young man sitting across the table from them read the

question on Casey's face and said, "I reckon this must be your first time here. Either Dudley or Sarah will bring the rest of your breakfast."

"Oh," Casey responded. "Well, much obliged. This is our first time."

In short order, Dudley returned to set their plates with eggs and sausage down before them. As the young man had said, Sarah came behind him with one arm wrapped around two large bowls, her opposite hand holding a large serving spoon. She stood behind them and asked, "Potatoes, grits, or both?" And when they chose, she left no vacant space on the plate.

Mona yelled, "Biscuits!" And she put a large platter of fresh baked biscuits on the counter. Dudley reached over and took the platter off the counter and brought them to Casey and Eli first. After they took a couple each, he moved it down the table for anyone else to have another one.

When new customers came in, they witnessed the same procedure a couple more times before they finished eating. The food was good, and due to the pace, they were not inclined to linger at the table. So they promptly got up and paid Dudley on their way out the door. They figured the price was probably about half what they might have paid for the same breakfast at Hardwick's. Outside, Eli commented, "Now I know how a hog feels when the farmer comes to the trough with the slops. But it was damn good."

There was still plenty of time left before the bank opened, so they rode back up the street to a stable they had passed. "Howdy," Casey said when a bowlegged old fellow walked out to meet them. "We're just gonna be in town for the day. Like to see about leavin' our packhorses with you and pick 'em up when you close. Like to see about givin' all four of 'em a portion of grain, corn, if you've got that. But we'll just leave the packhorses with you while we do a few things here in town. Can we do that?"

"Yes, sir, you sure can. You can pile your packs in an empty stall, and I'll take care of your horses. Name's Ernie Williams and I'll be here till six o'clock tonight."

"Proud to meetcha, Ernie. I'm Bob White and this is my brother, Tom. We won't be that late gettin' back here to pick 'em up."

While Ernie was feeding Smoke and Biscuit, Casey and Eli pulled the packs off the horses again and stacked them in a corner of one of the stalls. "Bob White, huh?" Eli muttered.

"That was the first thing I could think of," Casey said. "But I bet you don't forget it. Just remember, I'm Bob, you're Tom." Ernie walked in then with the feed bucket, so Casey asked, "You want us to pay you now, or wait till we pick up our horses?"

"Anytime we're talkin' about money, now is always better than later," Ernie said, then chuckled at his humor.

They paid Ernie, then climbed back into their saddles and rode down toward the train station, with Eli leading the way. Just before reaching the station, they came to a row of hedge plants that hid the storehouse from the station. Instead of continuing on to the platform, Eli left the street and went between the hedges and the storehouse. When he got to the end of the storehouse, he wheeled Biscuit to the right, around the end of the building, and pulled him to a stop. Casey pulled up beside him and Eli pointed to a weedy path running behind the building. "There she is," he said. "That's the path to the graveyard."

Casey stood up in his stirrups and looked all around him. Then he peered down the overgrown path that appeared to go well behind the buildings on the street. He turned then to look at Eli, and Eli answered his question before he asked it. "There ain't nothin' between here and that graveyard."

"You were right, it just keeps gittin' better and better. Now there ain't nothin' left to do but go to the bank and see if we can get something worth escaping with."

They talked it over and had already decided it was better for just one of them to go in the bank to see what they would have to deal with. Thinking about their young deputy marshal friend, Colton, it might not be wise to have witnesses remember two men visiting the bank before the two old bandits showed up the next day. They were under no impression that Colton rode away from the ranch completely convinced that he was wrong about them. So one man to the bank today was the right decision, and that one man had to be Casey by Eli's insistence. For he knew, of the two of them, Casey was the talker. "Well, they oughta be opened up by now," Casey said. "What are you gonna do while I'm in the bank?"

"I was wonderin' that, myself," Eli answered. "It's too early to go to a saloon for a drink of whiskey, and I can't hold any more coffee on top of that big breakfast I just ate." He looked around him, then said, "I think I'll go over there and set down on that bench and wait till I see you come out." He pointed to a bench at the corner of the capitol's ground. So they split up, and Casey rode Smoke over to the bank, dismounted, and looped his reins over the hitching rail.

When he walked inside, the first thing he saw was a bank guard. He hadn't expected that. No bank they had robbed so far had a security guard. He was talking to a man in a business suit, and they were standing in front of the three teller cages, one of which was vacant. There were no other customers in the bank. The guard and the man stopped talking when he walked in, and both turned to look at him. When he didn't go past them, the man in the business suit asked, "Can I help you, sir?"

Fighting an urge to do an about-face and leave, Casey decided he might as well case the bank. They couldn't arrest him if he didn't try to rob it. The guard didn't look like a very bright individual. In fact, he was dozing by the safe.

Casey would try to set it up, then talk it over with Eli to decide whether to go through with the robbery or not. "I'm on my way to a meeting at the Capitol Building and I just thought I'd stop in to inquire about the bank's loan and mortgage policies."

"I can help you with that," the man said, obviously an official of the bank. And when the guard, just awakened, stood there, he motioned, with a nod of his head, for him to leave. When the guard went back to his post by the front door, the banker said, "I'm Bryan Dawkins. I'm the owner and president of the bank. What can I do for you?"

"Excuse my trail clothes," Casey said. "I've come from Dallas on horseback. My preferred form of travel for this trip would have been the railroad, but there were a couple of ranches I wanted to look over on my way down." He extended his hand and Dawkins shook it. "My name's Robert White, and I'm in the business of developing cattle ranches that have failed through some fault of mismanagement or lack of proper funding. My company has been quite successful north and west of here, and I'm interested to see the potential for this part of Texas. A key part of our business is the availability of banking for our clients. I noticed there is another bank here in town, which I believe was the first bank in Austin. I haven't talked to them yet, but I do have a meeting scheduled. I'll admit, I was just curious, since you call yourself the Cotton Growers Bank. I wondered if you catered to the cattle industry at all, or do you specialize in making small loans to small farms?"

"That's just a name, Mr. White," Dawkins responded quickly. "Let me assure you, we make more loans to small cattle ranches than we do to cotton farms. Excuse my manners. Please come into my office. We'll be more comfortable there."

"I don't want to inconvenience you," Casey replied. "I just popped in on you like this when your day is just getting started."

"I have nothing more important to do than tell a potential customer what my bank can do for them. I insist, please come in and I'll answer any questions you have." Dawkins wasn't sure, but it sounded like an opportunity to work with a large company might have just walked in. He thought about offering coffee, but decided to wait until they had talked more.

Casey followed him into his office and sat down in the big leather-covered chair Dawkins offered. "I notice you have a security guard," Casey said. "Is there a problem with bank robbers here in Austin?"

"Heavens no," Dawkins replied, "here in the state capital? Not much risk of that. That guard you saw out there is mainly for show." He paused to chuckle. "And to give him some kind of job. That's Roscoe Crowder. He's my wife's nephew. We're kinda helping out the relatives by giving Roscoe a job. He earns what we pay him by doing all the cleanup. You don't have to worry about the safety of your money in this bank. It's protected in a safe with a time lock. Even I can't open it till it's time. We open every morning at nine o'clock, and that's when most bank robberies occur, right at opening time. So I set the time lock on our safe for ten o'clock. If someone tried to hit us at opening time, there's nothing I can do for them. But I don't expect that to happen here in Austin. Now let's talk about what your needs will be and what Cotton Growers can do to meet them."

"I assume you normally have sufficient funds available in the case of a quick transaction," Casey said. "Because we would basically handle all our financial plans through one bank."

"I understand," Dawkins said. "Of course, I would have to see a guarantee of your company's ability to cover any of the bank's losses due to failure of a loan recipient's failure to pay, as well as an option to take the land involved as payment."

"That seems reasonable," Casey told him. "Why don't we do this. As I said, I dropped in on you just on the spur of the moment. Why don't we make an appointment tomorrow afternoon sometime and I'll bring some more complete data on my company, including our forecast for next year. That should give you a complete picture of who we are."

"Excellent," Dawkins responded. "Sometime after dinner, say two o'clock?"

"That fits my schedule," Casey said. "Tomorrow at two, then." He got up to leave.

Dawkins got up with him to walk him out. "Would you like to see our safe?" He was evidently proud of it, because he didn't wait for Casey to answer. "Right through this door."

"Why, I suppose so," Casey answered, and followed him into the room right off the lobby.

When they walked in, a startled bank guard, caught taking a nap, jumped up from the chair he had tilted back against the wall. "I was guardin' the safe, Uncle Bryan," he blurted, unable to think of anything better. "I'll go back and guard the door now." He hurried out the door, and Dawkins looked at Casey, not sure what to say.

"That's the safe over there," Casey said, and walked over to it as if Roscoe had never happened. "That's a good idea, built right into the wall. They'd play the devil tryin' to take this outta the bank."

"I thought you'd appreciate that," Dawkins said, happy that Casey apparently hadn't been negatively influenced by his bank guard's laziness. "We keep it locked and only I have the combination. But even I can't open it before ten o'clock tomorrow morning, once I set the time lock on tonight."

"If the bank opens at nine, what do your tellers do if they can't get to the cash until ten?" Casey had to ask.

"I wouldn't tell everybody this," Dawkins admitted, "but I gamble with three hundred and fifty dollars in each of the tellers' cash trays. If they need more than that, they have to wait till ten."

"Well, then," Casey said, "I look forward to meeting with you at two tomorrow afternoon. I'll have all the legal information on the status of our company so you can decide if it's worth your while."

"Fine, fine," Dawkins said. "I look forward to it." He walked to the front door with Robert White. When he had gone, Dawkins looked at Roscoe standing there, leaning against the other side of the door. "I swear, Roscoe, if you cost me a big business deal, I think I may hang you."

"I just had to rest my feet for a spell, Uncle Bryan, then I was goin' back to my place by the door."

"I ain't your damn relative," Dawkins fumed, and marched to his office.

"Whadja find out?" Eli asked when Casey rode up to the corner of the capitol's ground.

Casey didn't answer until he stepped down from the saddle and parked himself beside Eli on the bench. "Well, I had a nice little visit with Mr. Bryan Dawkins, who is the president of the bank. It went so well that I have an appointment to meet with him again at two o'clock tomorrow afternoon."

"Is that a fact? I kinda thought at two o'clock tomorrow afternoon that you just might be shinin' your saddle with the seat of your britches. What changed your plans?"

"Oh, my plans ain't been changed, although I considered it when I first went in the bank and saw the bank guard."

" 'Bank guard'?" Eli reacted as he had. "They got a bank guard?"

"Well, they have, and they haven't. They've got an idiot dressed up like a bank guard. I don't think he'll be much of a problem. His name's Roscoe, and he's Mr. Dawkins's wife's nephew. There is more of a problem than Roscoe, though."

"What's that?" Eli asked, not sure he wanted to hear it.

"They've got a time lock on their safe." Eli just looked at him and waited, so he continued. "It opens at ten o'clock."

"I thought the bank opened at nine," Eli said. "Whadda they do for an hour?"

Casey told him about the money they left in the tellers' cash drawers. "That's the bank's way of stopping robberies. Dawkins says most bank robberies happen first thing when the bank opens. Then when the safe won't open, he thinks they won't wait around for an hour, and all they'll get is seven hundred dollars."

"This fellow, Dawkins," Eli said, "maybe he oughta be wearin' the guard's uniform."

"Well, I've told you what's goin' on inside that bank," Casey said. "So, whaddaya think? You wanna just forget about the Cotton Growers Bank?"

"I think I wanna wait till ten o'clock before we do it. Why? Are you thinkin' we can't take this one? Because, so far, I ain't heard nothin' that makes me think Oscar and Elmer ain't gonna be able to take 'em by surprise. Tell me if you've got a bad feelin' about this."

"I reckon we're gonna do it then," Casey said. "We better decide how we're gonna do it this time."

"Well, the first thing is to take care of Roscoe," Eli declared. "A fool with a gun will shoot you quicker'n a wise man. I think that ought to be my job, like I did it before. There ain't nothin' that gets faster action than an old man with loose bowels. So I need to go to the store and buy some rope. I'll hide it somewhere back of that outhouse behind the bank after it gets dark. You can't never have too much rope. We'll need it for that fellow, Dawkins, and the two tellers, so I'll buy plenty. Talkin' is what you're good at, so you'll have to take care of

Dawkins with your deposit. Then if it works, it works. If it don't, we'll get three meals a day and a cot to sleep on, as long as we don't shoot nobody."

"After we buy what we need and have us a nice dinner somewhere, we oughta go back to our camp and take a look around through those woods to see if we can find an easy way to leave that camp and strike that road we came into the town on. A mile or two north of town would be nice," Casey speculated. "Hell, we got things to do. And you thought this would be a long afternoon."

Chapter 10

In keeping with their intention not to become too familiar to any business owners in town, they decided to try the hotel dining room for their noontime meal. They were not disappointed with the food and decided they would return for supper that night. After dinner, they stopped in at Carlen's General Store to buy three coils of rope before returning to their camp by the creek. The first thing they did upon arriving at the camp was to look the area over to see if there were any signs of visitors since they had left that morning. They were satisfied that no one had discovered it yet. Next on the list was to plan their escape route after the bank was held up. They felt there was a good chance the creek they camped beside would lead them to the Colorado River, hopefully a good distance from town, and they could just continue to follow the trail they first rode into town. So they started out along the creek bank, weaving in and out of the trees that lined the creek until it came out on some open pastureland. From there, they could see the river, and when they reached it, they recognized the trail they had originally followed into town. Looking back toward the east, they could see the buildings of Austin approximately a mile and a half away. "I'd say that turned out to be just what we wanted," Eli felt inspired to comment.

"I can't think of nothin' else we need to do," Casey said, "except maybe have ourselves a drink of likker before we pick up our packhorses and eat supper. Whadda you think?"

"I was thinkin' pretty much along the same lines," Eli said. "We need to drink to our success in the mornin', anyway."

With that agreed upon, they followed the river trail back into Austin. Of the several saloons to choose from, they decided on one called Dillard's Saloon for no reason other than it was the first one they came to. There were a couple of horses tied out front, so they figured somebody must like it. Inside, they found a long bar running almost the length of the room on one side, and some small tables along the opposite side. They walked up to the bar, and the bartender broke off his conversation with two regular customers to wait on them. "Afternoon, gents. Whaddle it be?"

"Have you got some good rye whiskey?" Casey asked.

"Sure have," the bartender answered.

"Well, pour one for my partner," Casey said, "and I'll take a shot of corn." They watched as the bartender poured the two drinks. "You can always tell a first-class saloon when the bartender don't pour our whiskey outta the same bottle."

The bartender laughed and said, "Don't recall ever seein' you boys in here before."

"Then there ain't nothin' wrong with your memory," Eli said, "'cause we ain't ever been in here before."

The bartender laughed again. A heavyset fellow, his head completely bald except for heavy gray sideburns, and arms that resembled hams, he said, "Well, welcome to Dillard's. My name's Pete, Pete Devine. You just passin' through town?"

"Glad to meetcha, Pete," Casey answered. Then, remembering the alias he had used before, he said, "I'm Bob White, and this is my brother, Tom. Yep, we're just passin' through on the way to San Antonio."

"You two sure don't look like brothers," Pete remarked.

"Ma says we don't look like either one of our fathers, neither," Eli said. "Hit this one again, Pete." He pushed his empty shot glass over toward him. Pete filled it, set the bottle down, picked up the bottle of corn, and waited for Casey's signal, which he got right away.

Casey picked up his drink and turned to face Eli. Then he held the glass up toward him and said, "Here's to whatever." They clicked their glasses together and tossed the shots back.

"I declare," Pete remarked, "you boys are gittin' in the spirit of it. You ready for another shot?"

Casey held up his hand. "Nope, that's all the celebratin' we can afford to do before supper. Ain't it, Tom?"

"I s'pect you're right," Eli answered. Back to Pete then, he asked, "Where's the best place in town for two hungry brothers to get some supper?"

"That depends," Pete said. "You lookin' for somethin' real fancy, or just some good homestyle cookin'?"

"Homestyle cookin'," they both answered at the same time.

"Then you don't wanna go to Hardwick's," Pete said. "The hotel dinin' room is about as good as anybody else in town, and their prices are reasonable."

"Then we'll take your advice and go to the hotel," Eli said. He didn't tell him that they had already decided that was where they would eat supper.

They paid Pete for their whiskey and thanked him for his advice. Then they went to the stable after deciding they'd rather take as long as they wanted at supper and not have the worry of not catching Ernie Williams before he closed up. There was a hitching rail near the outside entrance to the hotel dining room, so they tied their horses there. And when they went inside, they asked for a table by the window so they could keep an eye on them. After they shed their guns, the manager, Marvin Waters, showed them to a table right up front by the window. When he seated them, he said, "Now, if you see anybody trying to run off with your horses, it won't take you no time a-tall to grab your guns right off the table and be out the door."

"'Preciate it," Eli told him.

In less than two minutes time, they were approached by a waitress, and she was the same one who had waited on them at noontime. "Well, hello, boys," she greeted them. "Your dinner must notta made you sick. I thought you were passing through town, but here you are again. Was your dinner that good?"

"You know, it was good," Eli answered her. "But to tell you the truth, we really came back to see you."

She responded with a throaty chuckle. "Now you're telling a tale," she said. "I bet you don't even remember my name."

"What if I was to tell you your name's Daisy?" Eli asked.

"Well, I'll be!" she exclaimed. "Did Marvin tell you?"

"Now you're hurtin' my feelin's," Eli said. "I won't never forget that name."

"You're making me blush," she said. "Are you wanting coffee?"

"Yes, we do," Casey answered her impatiently. "What are you servin' tonight? I remembered your name, too," he said, although he hadn't.

"Lamb chop or beef stew," Daisy replied.

"Lamb chop?" Casey questioned. "You can sure tell we ain't in cattle country. I'll take the beef stew."

"Me too, Miss Daisy," Eli said.

"I wonder if Daisy's husband is a jealous-type fellow," Casey said after she went back to the kitchen. "In case you're wonderin', you're on your own in that fight."

"Ah, she ain't married," Eli insisted. "She'da said so if she was. Besides, I was just funnin' with her. She knows that."

"Is that a fact?" Casey asked. "Kinda reminds me of another waitress in that hotel in Waco. I remember her name. Frances, weren't it? And I remember lookin' all over that hotel for you in the middle of the night, thinkin' something bad had happened to ya. If I remember correctly, when I finally found you, she was in the process of kickin' you out the door. Told us not to come back if we was ever in Waco again." He paused to point his finger at him. "And that was after you gave her a hundred dollars. Some lover boy you are."

Eli grinned when he thought about it. "Best hundred dollars I ever spent."

"You'd best get your mind to thinkin' more like Oscar, because that's who you're gonna be when the sun comes up in the mornin'."

"I was just funnin' with her," Eli insisted. "She's a little too young for my likin', anyway."

Daisy arrived at the table again, this time with coffee. "Here you go, boys. I'll be back with your beef stew in two shakes of a lamb's tail."

"Most likely the last two shakes of that lamb's tail before they made lamb chops out of him," Eli remarked.

Their supper proved to be worthy of Pete Devine's recommendation, and since they were in no hurry now that they had already picked up their packhorses, they took their time to enjoy it. Daisy kept their coffee cups filled, but didn't spend any more time gabbing. Casey had an idea that she was reluctant to give Eli any encouragement. And that increased Casey's respect for the young waitress.

By the time they finally left the dining room, it was beginning to grow dark outside. So they climbed on their horses and rode off toward the railroad station. There was no activity at the railway station, so they felt secure in thinking that no one noticed when they turned in behind the storehouse onto the deserted path to the graveyard. When they figured they were approximately somewhere behind the bank, they stopped. And Casey held the horses while Eli made his way on foot through the patch of trees between the backs of the buildings on the main street and the path. Once he got through the trees, he saw the bank and made his way to the outhouse behind it. Positive it was the bank's outhouse, he hid one of the coils of rope down in the bushes growing against the back of the outhouse. Then he returned to Casey and the horses, and they continued along the path, until reaching the cemetery, and from there they went on to their camp.

It was too dark by then to look closely, but it appeared that their camp had still not been discovered. They felt no need for any additional coffee, but they built a fire, anyway, just for a little light and warmth. While they sat by the fire, they rehearsed their intended plan of attack on the Cotton Growers Bank. They had used it successfully before, and they were confident it was their best chance of being successful again. Satisfied that they were ready, they retired to their sleeping bags.

They were in no great hurry when they woke up the next morning, since they knew the bank's safe was not set to open until ten o'clock. They considered a quick breakfast at Mona Bell's, but decided it was a good idea not to be seen in town this morning. "It's best if everybody who saw us thinks we left town last night or early this morning," Casey said. So breakfast consisted of coffee, some fried bacon, and some hardtack fried in the bacon grease. They took a little longer checking over their horses, making sure they were in good shape to make a run for it, if that became necessary. Satisfied that the horses were ready, they began the process of turning into two ancient bandits, a process they knew well by now. Keeping track of the time by Casey's railroad watch, they pulled on the baggy oversized old clothes, then started working on their wigs and beards. The two old hats, which Oscar and Elmer always wore, had gotten flattened when they were tied down in the packs. They tried to straighten the crowns out as best they could, but had to admit their condition only added to the effect they wanted.

"I wonder how long it's gonna be before somebody back at the ranch gets curious enough to ask what we're carryin' in these packs every time we go anywhere," Eli remarked.

"I told 'em we have to take a change of clothes to be ready to go to a cattleman's meetin' on short notice," Casey said.

"Yeah, but I'm wonderin' about Juanita and Miguel," Eli said. "Don't you reckon they might wonder why our extra clothes don't ever need a cleanin'?"

"Maybe they just think we don't have to wear 'em that often. I hadn't thought about that. Thanks for givin' me something more to worry about."

After the wigs and beards were stuck firmly in place, they turned to work on each other, to apply the aging creams and darkening around the eyes. "This stuff ain't gonna last forever," Eli commented. "We're gonna have to find a place to get some more." That was an issue they had talked about previously. There was no place they knew of to buy actors' supplies. When they both received the final okay from their partner, they strapped on their gun belts and settled them on their hips. As the final touch, they pulled on their oversized dusters, which almost reached the ground and were roomy enough to hide the rope, as well as the Colt six-shooter each man wore. The right-hand pocket of each duster had been cut out, so they could reach in and pull their pistols out, as well as the rope, without opening the coat.

When they were satisfied with themselves, they returned to a discussion about their horses that they had had earlier. They had talked about leaving Smoke and Biscuit there in the camp with their packs and riding their packhorses to the bank. It made a lot of sense for witnesses to their getaway to see them gallop off on two plain-looking sorrels. But to do that, it would be necessary to take the risk of someone stumbling upon their camp, causing them to lose two horses they didn't want to lose. They were taking a big enough risk by returning to this camp right after the holdup to get out of their disguises. "Why don't we just ride Biscuit and Smoke to the bank?" Eli asked. "Then, when we come back here, instead of gittin' out of our disguises, we can just pick up our packhorses and follow that escape route along the creek. Just get outta here quick as we can. We can find us a place to clean this mess off up the river somewhere. Then we wouldn't have to worry about somebody stealin' Biscuit and Smoke."

"That oughta work as well as the other way," Casey said. "And that way, if we was to get shot or arrested at the bank, they'd take our horses to the stable where that fellow, Ernie, would take care of 'em." He looked at his pocket watch again. "It's gettin' about time to ride, we'd best decide." Eli responded by picking up his saddle and throwing it on Biscuit's back. "Reckon so," Casey replied, and saddled Smoke. Then they loaded the packsaddles on the two sorrels, so they would be ready to go as soon as Oscar and Elmer showed up. "You ready?" Casey asked.

"As I'll ever be," Eli answered. "You got your money?"

"Yep," Casey answered. "Stuck it in the side that still has a pocket."

At nine o'clock, by the big clock on the wall over the teller cages, Bryan Dawkins went to the front door of the bank, raised the curtain on the glass panel, and turned the CLOSED sign around to the OPEN side. There was no one waiting outside for the bank to open, but he opened the door, anyway. He walked out and picked up a piece of a paper bag someone had carelessly dropped on the boardwalk. "Pigs," he uttered in disgust. He took a moment to decide what kind of day it would be. And taking the bright sun rising in a cloudless sky as a sign, he decided it was going to be an eventful one.

Back inside, Dawkins, still pinching the piece of the paper bag between his thumb and forefinger, looked left and right in the empty lobby before he asked, "Where's Roscoe?"

Emmett Hunter, the teller in the near cage, looked up from counting the cash in his drawer and said, "I think he's in the back room, Mr. Dawkins." Seeing the piece of trash in Dawkins's hand, he said, "Here, let me take that for you." He came out of his cage and took the piece of trash from him, and Dawkins went straight to the back room to find his guard. Emmett went back to his cage and dropped the piece of paper in his trashcan. When he looked up, he saw Dylan Jordan, the teller in the next cage, grinning at him. Emmett grinned back and whispered, "Roscoe's gonna catch hell if he's into that coffeepot again when the boss finds him." They were very familiar with their boss's fetish for neatness, and one of Roscoe's responsibilities was to spot things like trash on the walk or on the floor inside.

As the two tellers suspected, Roscoe was having himself another cup of coffee in the back room. "It's after nine o'clock, Roscoe. The bank is open. The guard's place is near the front door. I didn't hire you to guard the coffeepot."

"Yes, sir, I was just fixin' to go to the front door. I had to go to the outhouse. While I was back here, though, I thought I'd keep my eye on the safe. Make sure ain't nobody foolin' around back here."

"They'd be wasting their time if they did," Dawkins said. "I thought I'd explained to you that nobody can open that safe, not even me, until the time lock unlocks it. Button your shirt. You're representing the Cotton Growers Bank, and our customers like to think that you're guarding the money they deposit with us. In addition to that, your job is to be helpful to our customers when they come in, so they feel welcome. And your job is also to make sure our bank is neat and clean. I had to pick up some trash right at our front door when I opened up this morning. How many people have walked past our door already this morning and have associated that trash with our bank?"

"Probably not so many," Roscoe answered foolishly. "It's still pretty early in the mornin'."

Dawkins bit his lower lip to keep from swearing out loud. *Damn Crowders*, he thought. *There's not an intelligent one in the entire family, except my wife, and the brightest thing she ever did was marry me.* "Leave that sink like you found it," he said, and went back into the lobby. He greeted the two customers who came in at that point and paused to make some polite conversation before retreating to his office.

When the clock struck ten, he came out of his office again, and since there were no customers there, he went into the back room to oversee the opening of the safe. First Emmett, and then Dylan, brought their cash trays into the back to bring them up to the normal amount to handle most transactions. Then Dawkins closed the safe again and went back to his office. "These next ones coming in the door are yours," Dylan said to Emmett.

Emmett looked toward the front door and replied, "Uh-uh, you saw 'em first." What appeared to be two old men had just stepped inside the front door and seemed to be arguing with the guard.

It may have appeared to be an argument, but Roscoe was trying his best to explain to the agitated old man that he couldn't accept his money, he had to take it to the teller cage. "You work here, don'tcha?" Casey asked. "You're wearin' a gun, ain'tcha? Ain't you supposed to protect my money?" He stayed up in Roscoe's face so that no one noticed that the old man behind him quickly flipped the OPEN side around to the CLOSED side again.

"I'm just the guard," Roscoe tried to explain. "I don't take no money."

Casey pulled a fat wad of paper money out of his pocket and stuck it up in Roscoe's face. "I want you to put this money in your safe. I can't carry this much money around in this town. Somebody will knock me in the head to get my money."

Surprised by the size of the roll, Roscoe told him, "You ought not be wavin' it around like that, else somebody sure will."

"I tried to tell him that," Eli said. "The old fool, he don't even know how much he's totin'."

"The hell I don't!" Casey insisted. "I got five hundred and forty-five dollars right here, ever cent to my name. And I don't figure on gittin' it stole from me, neither." He turned around to face Roscoe again. "Here, put it in that safe of your'n."

"Dagnabbit," Roscoe complained. "Go give it to the teller, like I told you. You keep stickin' it in my face and I'm gonna take it."

Finally alert to trouble of some kind, Bryan Dawkins came out of his office. He checked up at once when he saw the two bedraggled-looking old men standing on either side of his bank guard, and all three of them yammering at the same time. "Is there some problem here?" he finally asked, trying to remain as calm as possible.

"Yes, sir," Roscoe said, relieved to see someone taking charge. "These two old . . ." He caught himself in time. "These gentlemen is trying to give me their money to put in the safe—"

Before he could finish, Eli interrupted him. "Just that one old fool," he said. "I weren't tryin' to give nobody no money."

"'Cause he ain't got no more money!" Casey blurted gleefully. "He done got his money stole when he was asleep by the crick. But I ain't gonna git my money stole. I'm gonna put it in the bank."

"Maybe I can help you," Dawkins said, anxious to do just about anything to get rid of the obviously senile old men. "I can help you open an account."

Casey drew back as if he had been tricked. "I don't want no account. I want you to put my money in your big ol' safe, where nobody can touch it."

Rapidly losing his patience, Dawkins asked, "How much money do you want to put in the bank?" When Casey reached into his pocket again and pulled the big roll of money out to hold up before Dawkins's face, Dawkins was struck speechless for a moment. "Do you know how much you've got there?" Casey told him the exact amount. "Well, we certainly don't want you to take a chance on losing your money," Dawkins said.

Casey drew his hand back. "I don't want no account," he repeated. "I want you to keep my money in your big ol' safe till I want it."

Even better, Dawkins thought. The man was obviously deranged. His friend was not that much better, it appeared. Dawkins was not above taking advantage of a weaker mind, especially one holding over five hundred dollars in a feeble hand. "If that's what you want, I think the bank can accommodate you." He was suddenly interrupted by the other old man. He couldn't help but notice the old man starting to fidget and rock from one foot to the other until finally he made a statement.

"We gotta come back later, Elmer," Eli mumbled.

"No, I wanna put my money in the bank," Casey insisted. "You just hold on till I see it in the safe."

"I can't hold on much longer," Eli implored. "I feel like I'm gonna lose it any second now."

"Damn you, Oscar!" Casey swore. He looked regretfully at Dawkins and said, "The old fool's got loose bowels. If he cuts loose, it'll be all over the floor. If you've got a thunder mug, I'd advise you to let him use it, or he's gonna run us all outta here."

"We don't have a thunder mug, as you call it," Dawkins said, even though he kept one in his office.

"I ain't foolin', Elmer, we better get outta here," Eli whined. "I gotta find an outhouse."

"We've got an outhouse," Dawkins quickly replied. "Roscoe, take the gentleman out to our outhouse and unlock it for him." He turned back toward Casey and said, "And I'll take you back and show you our safe. You can watch me put your money in the safe. This way, you'll know it's closed up." Casey grinned and nodded his head childlike in appreciation, while Eli gave his best impression of trying to walk rapidly while clinching everything as tight as he could.

Roscoe might have picked up the old man straining to hold everything together and rushed to the outhouse with him. But he was afraid that, like a balloon, the old man's bowels would burst and cover him with their contents. His keys in his hand, and his eyes focused on the back door lock, he didn't notice the old man's interest in a pile of bank sacks close to the door. "Almost there," he said, encouraging Eli. Then he ran ahead on the path to unlock the padlock, which ensured its personal use for the bank employees only. Roscoe had the lock open and was holding the door for him.

Eli stopped at the door and said, "Snakes." When Roscoe looked at him, puzzled, Eli said, "I'm skeered of snakes. Is there any in there?"

"No, there ain't no snakes in there," he answered, afraid they were wasting valuable time.

Still, Eli hung back. "Take a look," he pleaded.

"All right, I'll take a look," Roscoe said, and stepped into the outhouse. He was already inside when he realized Eli had pulled the pistol out of his holster, slammed the door shut, and was in the process of closing the padlock on the hasp. "What the . . . ? Are you crazy, you old coot?"

"I ain't gotta go no more," Eli said as he went behind the outhouse to get the rope he had left there. Then he wrapped it around the outhouse as many times as the length of rope permitted before tying a knot. "Good thing it were a single seater," he remarked, and hurried back to the bank.

As he ran down the path, he could hear Roscoe shouting, "This ain't funny, old man!" He stepped inside the bank to find Casey and Dawkins beside the safe, so he picked up some of the canvas bags he had seen by the door and brought them with him.

Dawkins opened the safe and stood back so Casey could see. "Now give me your money and you can watch me put it in with all the rest." He turned then when he heard Eli approaching and was puzzled that Roscoe wasn't with him. "Where's the guard?"

"Oh, him?" Eli answered. "When I got through, he said he had to go. Said I inspired him. Here you go," he said, and handed him one of the bags. Dawkins took the bag, still astonished, and turned back to face Casey, who was now holding a Colt .45 aimed at his belly. Now in complete shock, Dawkins just stood there, unable to move. "That bag's for you," Eli said. "Start filling it with money just as fast as you can."

Dawkins dropped to his knees. "You're out of your minds. You can't do this. You'll be hunted for the rest of your lives."

"If you had any sense, you'd see we're already at the end of our lives," Casey said, trying to maintain his attempt to talk like an old man. "So it don't make no difference to Oscar and me if we have to shoot you to get what we came for. So get busy and fill them bags. While you're doin' it, think of them poor people you foreclose on when they've had a little hard luck."

"He's wastin' our time, Elmer," Eli said. "Think we oughta shoot him so we can finish up here sometime today?"

"Nah, gag him and tie him up, and I'll finish fillin' these bags," Casey replied. "It ain't gonna take but two bags." Eli reached in the pocket of his duster and untied the rope hooked at his waist. He pushed Dawkins over on the floor, took his bandana off and stuffed it in Dawkins's mouth. Then he snatched Dawkins's necktie off his collar and used it to tie the gag in. Then he pulled the rope from the pocket of his duster and tied a dazed Bryan Dawkins, hand and foot, to lie there and wonder why his tellers didn't come to his rescue.

There was enough money in the safe to fill two of the large bags, so Casey poked Dawkins's foot with the toe of his boot and said, "You've been so cooperative, we ain't gonna clean you out. We're gonna leave you the money in the tellers' drawers to operate on. You ready, Oscar?"

"Yep, I'm ready, Elmer. Let's go and we'll get to San Antonio by suppertime tomorrow." They walked back out into the lobby and went to the teller cages. "Mr. Dawkins will be out in a little while to tell you what's goin' on."

"All right," Emmett replied. "We've been wondering why those people were standing in front of the door and didn't come on in."

"Mr. Dawkins will explain all that when he comes out of the back," Casey said.

When they went to the front door, Dylan asked, "Why didn't you ask him what was in those two bags?"

"Why didn't you?" Emmett returned.

There were several people standing at the front door when they went out. One of them, a matronly woman, asked, "What are they doing in there? When are they gonna open up?"

"Any minute now," Casey answered. Then remembering a time before, he said, "Don't worry, we got all the snakes." It caused the same reaction as before.

Chapter 11

Resisting the urge to run for the horses, they walked casually up the street to the post office, two doors up from the bank. They had thought it best not to tie their horses anywhere near the bank, in case they might be identified as the robbers' horses. They felt sure they would have plenty of time to get to the horses due to the time it should take inside the bank for everyone to realize what had happened. Even so, it was still hard to maintain their casual air as they walked to the horses, hung the large sacks on the saddle horns, then stepped up into the saddle for an unhurried ride toward the railroad station. After taking a good look around them to make sure there was no one watching them, they cut behind the storehouse and loped along the back path to the cemetery and their camp beyond it.

Their packhorses were waiting there, just as they expected. The camp had not been discovered the entire time they had been there. They even thought about the possibility of getting out of their disguises and cleaning up right there, as they had originally planned to do. But the desire to escape from the scene of the crime was too strong at that point, so they grabbed the reins of the packhorses and took off, following the creek away from Austin.

After riding for approximately a mile along the thickly wooded bank of the creek, they could see up ahead where the creek came out on the open pastureland. So Eli, who was in the lead, pulled up and waited for Casey to come alongside. "This is as good a place as we'll find," he said, "unless you wanna get a little farther from town."

"I think we oughta get out of our workin' clothes right here, where we've got plenty of cover," Casey said. "I'd rather not be ridin' out in the open dressed up like the two old men, especially since you told ol' Dawkins we were headin' south to San Antonio. I doubt he'll even remember you sayin' that. He was pretty shook up. But if he repeated that to a sharp young lawman, like Colton Gray, he'd most likely suspect we went north instead."

"So you're sayin' I shoulda said, 'We was headin' north,' so the law would think we went south?" Eli asked. Casey just shrugged. Eli was not willing to let it go at that. "I didn't tell Dawkins we were goin' to San Antonio. I told you we'd be there tomorrow night. I just let him hear me tell you that."

"I'm sayin' that it don't make no difference, 'cause he ain't gonna remember it, anyway. But it ain't gonna help us if somebody reports two old men ridin' north outta Austin. So let's get outta these clothes."

So they stripped off the baggy old clothes and carefully put away their wigs and facial hair and the makeup, then washed away all the evidence from their faces in the creek. Back in their regular clothes then, they started home to the D&T Ranch, a long ride ahead of them. They didn't take the time to count the money, deciding to count it when they camped for the night. But they split it up in smaller bundles and packed it among their supplies on the packhorses. The two bank sacks were left behind them, buried under the bank of the creek.

Due to their late start leaving Austin, their first stop to rest their horses left them short of the camp near the fork in the trail that led them to meet Squirrel and Willy. And when they came to the fork, it was too early to make camp for the night. It was an excellent spot to camp, but they were happy to pass it up. As Eli put it, "That spot is tainted. It's an unlucky place for me and you."

"Well, we'll sure as hell quit campin' there from now on," Casey said. He joked about it, but he was just as superstitious about the spot as Eli was. It was the first time they had been forced to kill someone on one of their jobs. True, it was not done during the actual robbery, but they were on their way to the robbery. There was no way to predict how long their lucky streak would last, but they hoped never to have to take a life during a robbery.

When they came to a good spring to camp by for the night, they counted their money. And after Casey took out the roll of money he had used as bait, they came up with a total of eighty-two thousand and fifty dollars. "I reckon it was worth the trip down there," Eli said. "I was wonderin' if we shoulda took those cash drawers outta the teller cages. But I reckon eighty-two thousand is a right nice-soundin' number. Besides, things mighta got a little out of hand if we had decided to rob those two bright boys of their trays. This way, it was much slicker."

"It don't pay to get too greedy, anyway," Casey said in agreement. "And look at it this way, Grover Morris is gonna give ol' Dawkins seventy-five hundred back to him."

The trip back to the ranch was uneventful, which was just what they hoped for when they were carrying that great a sum of money. The downside was the lack of anyplace to buy a decent plate of food. So they were looking forward to reaching the D&T by suppertime. They didn't quite make it, however. Juanita and Miguel had finished the supper she had made for the two of them, and Smiley was already cleaning up after the cowhands. But Davey spotted Casey and Eli approaching the entrance gate to the ranch and spread the word. As soon as he was sure the two riders were who Davey said they were, Monroe hurried up to the house to alert Juanita. Her stove was still hot, so she fired it up again and threw together what she could find to fill their bellies.

Monroe was waiting near the front porch when they rode into the yard, knowing they always unloaded their packs at the house before they took the horses to the barn. "Welcome back," Monroe greeted them. "Did you have a good trip?"

"Yeah, I reckon," Casey responded. "Typical, I guess you could call it. Wouldn't you say, Eli?"

"Yeah, I expect so," Eli said. "Everything all right here?"

"Yes, sir, we're gettin' ready to move these cows up the trail to Kansas. Grover Morris brought his herd onto our lower range this morning."

"When are you gonna stop 'sir-ing' me, Monroe?" Eli asked. "Wasn't long ago we was pushing cows together. You callin' me 'sir' makes me feel like an old man." He looked at Casey and winked.

"Don't seem right not to," Monroe said. "You're the boss— you and Casey."

"Did you get a count on his cows?" Casey asked.

"As near as we could," Monroe answered. "He's got three hundred and fifty, maybe a few more."

"Where is Morris?" Casey asked.

"He's with the rest of the men roundin' up strays," Monroe said. "They oughta be comin' back in pretty soon, everybody but the ones ridin' night herd."

"When he comes back to the bunkhouse, tell him we need

to talk to him," Casey said. "We're gonna empty these packs, and then we'll take care of the horses."

"If you want to take your saddlebags and what you'll need outta your packs, and put it on the porch, I'll take care of your horses and put your packsaddles in the barn," Monroe said.

"Good idea," Eli declared. "But there's some things I know I put in them packs, and I ain't been able to find 'em. I wanna look one more time. So you go ahead and take Biscuit and Smoke to the barn and get their saddles off 'em. We'll bring the packhorses down to the barn. Then me and Casey will see if Juanita's got any scraps left over from supper. Just tell Morris to come on up to the house."

"Okay, bosses," Monroe said with a chuckle. "I'll tell him." He untied the reins of the packhorses from the two saddles and led the saddled horses away.

Casey and Eli both jumped at once to open the packs and pull out the sacks they needed to keep in the house. "Just put 'em all in your room," Casey said, since Eli's room was the first one in the hall. "We'll sort 'em out later." They both gathered up a load under each arm, only to find the door locked. "Damn," Casey swore, afraid he was going to drop a bundle of money out of the load under his arm any second. He knocked on the door with the toe of his boot until it finally opened.

"Oh, Señor Casey, I forgot to unlock the door," Juanita declared. "Welcome home. I fix you supper."

"Thanks, Juanita," Casey said. "We're sorry to pop in on you after supper. You don't need to go to a lot of trouble. Me and Eli will settle for just about anything. Ain't that right, Eli?"

"That's a fact, Juanita, we don't want to put you to a lot of trouble."

"No trouble," she insisted. "I already put biscuits in the oven. Pretty soon I feed you."

"I declare, Juanita, you're the best," Eli told her. "We appreciate it. We'll go put this stuff away. We need to take those horses down to the barn, and then we'll be back to eat."

They went back to Eli's room and pulled all the money out of the packs. Casey counted out seventy-five hundred and set it aside for Grover Morris, then put the rest of the money in the safe. After taking the few personal items out of the packs, they returned them to the horses and took them down to the stable. The packs were piled in a corner of the tack room in the barn, their usual resting place. They were still partially filled with supplies and cooking pans and pots, plus a coffeepot, the ordinary things that everyone needed for camping. Had anyone been nosey enough to look through the packs, they might have been puzzled by the shabby old clothes packed inside.

When they came out of the tack room, they were met by Smiley George. "Hey, boys," Smiley greeted them. "Heard you got back. How are things in Waco?"

"Ah, you know Waco, Smiley. It's always the same. Don't never seem to change," Eli said. "We never thought about havin' to go to business meetin's and such as that when we became owners of a ranch. Did we, Casey?"

"That's a fact," Casey said. "Most of the time we were there, we were stuck in the hotel."

"Which hotel was you in?" Smiley asked.

"The big one, the McClellan House," Casey answered.

"Come on," Smiley persisted, "two old hound dogs like you. You tellin' me you didn't get over to the Reservation just once? That's what the town is famous for." He looked at young Davey Springer. "For you young boys that never been to Waco, the Reservation is, I expect, the biggest bordello district in the State of Texas."

"What's a bordello?" Davey asked.

Smiley chortled to think he was too young to know. "Whores!"

he blurted. "And everythin' else to turn a boy your age into a real man overnight."

"He's right, Davey," Casey said. "And, no, Smiley, me and Eli didn't go to the Reservation even one time. We were too busy seein' about makin' money for this ranch. That took all our time."

"You didn't get back in time for supper," Smiley said. "You want me to see if I've got some crackers or something you can gnaw on?"

"No, thanks just the same," Eli said. "Juanita's cookin' something for us." He gave Casey a quick look and said, "I expect we'd best get back to the house 'cause it oughta be about ready."

"Good," Juanita said when they walked in the kitchen door. "I was going to send Miguel to get you. Biscuits just come out of the oven. I fry you ham to eat with them. I no have time to fix much else."

"That'll be plenty," Casey told her. "It'll be like a banquet after what we had to eat the last two days. I could get full just on the smell of those biscuits." She looked at her husband and smiled. Miguel smiled back at her, knowing she was very proud.

They sat down at the kitchen table as usual, and she poured their coffee from the fresh pot she had made. They invited Miguel to have some, too, but he declined, saying he was still full from supper. They had not sat there long before hearing a knock on the back door. "I expect that'll be Grover Morris," Eli said. "Tell him to come on in, Miguel."

Grover walked in the kitchen and hesitated for a moment. "Maybe I'd better come back later. Looks like I'm interruptin' your supper."

"No, come on in," Casey said. "Juanita just fixed up a little something because we were too late for supper. She cooked too much, though. Come on in and help us eat it."

"Thank you kindly, but I'm still full from Smiley's beans, so I don't need any biscuits and ham. I could enjoy a cup of that coffee."

Juanita didn't wait to be told, but got another cup and filled it right away. "Thank you, ma'am," Morris said. He turned back to Casey. "Monroe said you wanted to see me."

"That's right, we do," Casey said. "Let's finish up eatin', then go in the study to talk business. So you might as well have a ham biscuit with that coffee."

Morris shrugged and replied, "Maybe just one. They do look mighty good." Miguel noticed the smile his comment brought to Juanita's face, which, in turn, brought one to his. While they sat there eating, Juanita lit a candle, then went to the study and lit the lamp on the desk.

While they enjoyed the quick repast that Juanita had fixed, they talked about the cattle drive that was almost ready to begin. "Now that you have had a good chance to look at our cattle, do you think they're ready to make the drive?" Casey asked because he was genuinely interested in hearing another cattleman's assessment of the stock.

"What I've seen of your cattle," Morris replied, "is first-class condition. They're ready for the market, but that's just my opinion."

Casey had to laugh. "Well, I'm glad you agree with us. Right, Eli?" Eli chuckled in answer. "Who helped you drive your three hundred and fifty cows up here?"

"Two hands that I had laid off, two brothers, Ray and Jay Moore, and my son, Billy, whose not but fourteen, but he's a good hand."

"Are all four of you goin' to stay with the drive?" Eli asked.

"Yep, that was my plan, but, of course, that's up to you, since you're payin' the wages." When Eli just nodded thoughtfully, Morris reminded him, "You remember that I agreed to ride at your regular cowhand wage. I ain't lookin' for no special treatment."

"Oh, that's understood," Eli was quick to assure him. "We need the men, and you must think Ray and Jay are good men." He had to pause. "Are they twins?"

"No, they're two years apart," Morris answered.

"You say your son is a good hand, too. I expect he'll work the remuda with Davey," Casey said. "Davey oughta like that. He won't be the youngest on this drive. I think we're gonna have the men we need for the number of cows we're movin'."

When they finished eating, they headed to the study to talk about a few more things to do before the drive actually started out for Kansas. When they got in the hall, Eli left them and went to his bedroom. "I expect you'll be wantin' to head back home right now so you can ride over to Austin to pay off that loan," Casey said to Grover when they went into the study.

"Well, yeah, I reckon so," Grover replied, "after we get it all wrote up." He had been given no idea what the requirements were going to be in his agreement with the two owners of D&T.

"You're gonna need this when you go," Eli said as he came into the room. He handed a small bag to Grover. "There's seventy-five hundred dollars in there. You might wanna count it, to make sure I got it all."

"That's a damn good idea to count it," Casey said with a chuckle, "just to make sure."

Grover was almost overcome with emotion. He knew they had agreed to loan him the money to pay off his debt, but he didn't really know Casey and Eli but a couple of weeks. Now with the money in his hand, he knew they had the advantage of asking almost anything in return, and it would be hard for him to refuse. He had even considered the fact that they might want him to put up his land as collateral, just as the bank had. Since they said nothing about their terms now, it was left for him to ask. "You want me to sign some kinda paper, promising to pay the money back?"

"No, a handshake will do," Casey answered. "We trust your word."

Grover immediately stuck his hand out and shook with each of them. "I swear," he choked out, "you fellows don't know how much this means to me and my family."

"I think maybe we do," Casey said. "But we'd better count that money again, just to be sure it's all there."

So they did another counting of the money; then Grover put it back in the bag and tied the string. "I'll be leavin' for home first thing in the morning. I'll take Billy with me, if that's all right with you fellows. I know his ma would like to see him before he's gone for so long a time."

"Your wife gonna be alone while you are workin' these cattle?" Eli wondered.

"No," Grover answered. "She'll have Billy's two younger brothers for her protection, and her brother and his wife for her company. She ain't gonna have to leave her home, and that's what's most important to her."

"Good, then we're all set then," Casey said. "You and Billy keep a sharp eye on your way home and make sure that bank gives you the papers that show you paid your debt. By the time you get back here, we oughta be just about ready to head 'em out."

Grover was still a little choked up when he thanked them again for saving his little ranch. "I'll say good night now. Billy and I'll be gone right after breakfast in the bunkhouse. So thanks, and God bless you."

They walked him to the front door, then locked the door again before returning to the study. "I swear, Casey, he 'God blessed' us. That's the first time I've ever been blessed. I've been 'damned' a heap of times, but I don't never recall bein' 'blessed' before. Feels kinda good, don't it?"

"Don't get to thinkin' too much about it," Casey said. "You'll get the big head. Think about what Bryan Dawkins is thinkin' about us."

Chapter 12

"You wanted to see me, boss?" Deputy Marshal Colton Gray asked when he walked into Marshal John Timmons's office in Waco.

"Yes, I do, Colton," Timmons replied. "I've just received a telegraph from U.S. Marshal Quincy Thomas that you might be interested in."

"Is that a fact?" Colton asked. "From the headquarters office in Austin?" He knew right away that it wasn't going to be anything he wanted to hear.

"That's right. It seems that *our two old men* have robbed the Cotton Growers Bank there in Austin, to the tune of over eighty-two thousand dollars. And that's their term for the robbers, 'our two old men.' They'd like to have me send 'our people' who've been working on the case to lend a hand down there. You are *our people* who have been following these two jolly old codgers."

"Why do they want me to go down there?" Colton couldn't help asking. "Why don't they go after them with their own men? That's the headquarters for the Western District Marshal Service, and they want help chasin' two decrepit old bank robbers?"

Timmons gazed at the young deputy, seemingly amused by

Colton's objections. He formed his familiar sarcastic smile when dispensing orders to him. "You talk like you don't want to go down to Austin to help your fellow deputies."

"You're my boss," Colton said, "and I go where you send me. It just doesn't sound like good sense for me to ride all the way down to Austin because the bank got robbed. They already know as much about those two old bandits as we do. Why don't they get on their trail and track 'em down? How do we know it's the same two that's been doin' the robberies? It might be somebody trying to look like them."

"You say it doesn't make sense to ride all the way down to Austin to try to get on their trail. That's kinda like saying it doesn't make sense to ride all the way from Fort Worth to Lampasas County on a wild hunch, isn't it?"

Colton cringed. He knew it was a mistake confessing to that ride he took over to the D&T Ranch. But he thought it just too much to be coincidence that Casey Tubbs and Eli Doolin were in that cattle buyer's office the very afternoon before he was robbed, and they had recently purchased black powder. After spending time with the two cattlemen, he was ninety percent convinced he had been wrong in suspecting them. There was still that ten percent of suspicion, however, that he couldn't seem to let go of. To Colton, this business just the other day in Austin didn't seem to point to Casey and Eli, because he had just left their ranch. And they were very busy getting ready to drive three thousand cows to the Kansas market. Their ranch was eighty or ninety miles from Austin. It just didn't seem likely. "Whatever you say, boss. I'll get down there right away. I don't know what help I could possibly be. Somebody's gonna have to catch those old boys in the act. They always get away without anybody seein' them."

"Colton," Timmons ordered politely, "please try to impress those people that you know what you're doing. This is the big boss, Quincy Thomas, himself, who asked for you."

"I'll do my best, boss," Colton said, and turned and walked out of the office. Outside the building, he climbed up on the bay gelding and rode down the street to the stable.

"Howdy, Colton," Horace Temple called to him from the barn. "You leavin' Scrappy for the night?"

"Yep, I'm gonna pick him up, and my packhorse, too, first thing in the mornin'," he said when Horace came out to meet him. He led Scrappy as they walked back into the stable and asked Horace to feed the horse some grain. "He's gotta go a long way in the next couple of days." He pulled Scrappy's saddle off and threw it in the corner of his stall.

"I'll take care of him," Horace said. "I'll turn him out in the corral for a while before dark."

"Much obliged," Colton said. "See ya in the mornin'." He walked back down the street toward the boardinghouse where he rented a small room.

He rode into Austin around suppertime on the second day of travel and went straight to the U.S. Marshal's Office near the Capitol Building. Marshal Thomas had already left for the day, but his clerk, Earl Dutton, was still there, in the process of closing the office. "How you doing, Colton? You just missed Marshal Thomas. He's already gone to supper. He always eats at Manning's Restaurant, so you can try to catch him there, if you need to see him tonight."

"I'll just wait and see him in the mornin'," Colton said. "No need to interrupt his supper. I'll see if I can get a room in that hotel right down the street and take care of my horses." Dutton said that was fine. He was obviously in a hurry to get out of the office.

He was able to get a room at the hotel, and the desk clerk told him where the nearest stable was. "Tell Ernie you're stayin' in the hotel, and he'll give you a better rate," the clerk told him.

"'Preciate it," Colton said. "How 'bout supper in the dinin' room? Is it still open?" The clerk told him he had another hour before closing, so he knew he had time to take care of his horses before eating. He left his saddlebags and his rifle in his room, then went to the stable.

"Are you Ernie?" Colton asked when he stepped down from the saddle in front of the stable. Price said that he was. "Clerk at the hotel said to tell you I'm stayin' there and I'd get your best rate."

"That's a fact," Ernie Williams replied. "How long you thinkin' about stayin' here?"

"I'm not sure," Colton told him honestly, "a day or two, maybe more. I'm a deputy marshal from Waco, and it depends on whether or not I'm any help to the marshal's office, I reckon."

Ernie looked at him and grinned. "Got anything to do with the bank robbery we just had, and them two old fellers Bryan Dawkins said did it?"

"As a matter of fact, it does. Did you happen to see those two old men ride outta town?"

"Nah," Ernie replied. "I never saw 'em. Nobody saw which way they rode outta town. But it was them two old men that's been doin' all them other robberies. Katie Moffit saw 'em when they came out the front door with the money in a couple of sacks. She said they was both old enough to be her granddaddy." He had to pause to chortle. "Katie said one of 'em told her they cleaned all the snakes outta the bank, and she thought that was what they had in the bags."

Colton remembered a witness at one of the earlier holdups saying the same thing about the snakes in that bank. It was already beginning to sound like it really was Elmer and Oscar, whoever they really were. A cattle buyer's office in Fort Worth, now a bank all the way down here in Austin. It seemed they were on the move all the time. If they were really as old as they appeared to be, he couldn't imagine how much longer they could keep it up. *Because they're not really that old*, he thought. "How's the food in the hotel dinin' room?" he asked. "Can you get a decent meal there?"

"You bet," Ernie answered. "You'll get as good a meal there as anyplace in town."

"All right, then. I reckon I'll see you tomorrow sometime. I don't expect I'll need my horses right away. I'll go to get some supper before the dinin' room closes."

He checked in at the marshal's office first thing after break-fast the next morning and spent an hour telling the marshal everything he had learned about the two bandits. Marshal Thomas was quick to inform him that it was not a great deal more than they already knew, except for Colton's suspicion that the bandits were younger men in disguise. "That's inter-esting," he said. "The same thought had occurred to me."

Well, now you know everything I know, Colton thought. To Thomas, he said, "I'm sorry I don't have more to tell you. But as long as I've ridden all the way down here, I'd like to go to the bank and talk to them, myself."

"You might as well. Maybe you'll pick up something that'll give you a connection with somebody who could be in dis-guise."

"Did the sheriff get involved, or was it all handled by the marshal's office?"

"Dawkins called the sheriff at first," Thomas replied. "There wasn't much he could do. He thought about a posse, but no-body knew which direction to start out in, so he asked us to get involved in it. And then he was satisfied to drop it in our laps. So good luck with Dawkins and that crew at the bank." Colton got up to leave, but Thomas stopped him. "One more thing, Gray. I have to apologize for having you ride down here for this. We thought you people up in Waco knew a lot more about these two bandits."

"I'm just awful sorry we don't, sir," Colton said, and took his leave.

When he got to the Cotton Growers Bank, he found a CLOSED sign on the front door. He tried the handle and found the door unlocked, so he opened it and walked in. There were two men standing in front of the teller cages talking. They stopped to stare at him when the door opened. "I'm sorry, sir, the bank is closed," Emmett Hunter said.

"I know. I'm Deputy Marshal Colton Gray. I was called down here from Waco to see what I could find out about your robbery."

"Oh, well, you want to talk to Mr. Dawkins, I expect. I'll get him for you." He started to walk away, but paused when Colton asked if he was there during the robbery. "Yes, I'm Emmett Hunter, and this is Dylan Jordan. We're the tellers."

"Did you get a close look at the two robbers?" Colton asked.

"Oh, we certainly did," Emmett replied.

"Well, not real close," Dylan corrected, "except that one time when they were leaving and one of them came up to the cage and told us Mr. Dawkins would be right out to explain everything."

"When he came up close to the cage that one time, did you notice anything odd or unusual about the way he looked?" Colton was hoping somebody would notice a fake mustache or something out of place.

"No, he was just an old, old man," Emmett said. "I'll go get Mr. Dawkins. He spent more time with them, and I'm sure he saw them up close."

In a few seconds, Dawkins came out of his office, with Emmett in his wake. "I'm Bryan Dawkins," he said. "I've already gone over that robbery I don't know how many times with the sheriff and the marshals." He could not see what good it would do to talk to another deputy marshal, especially one who looked as young as this one.

Colton assumed as much. "I understand and I apologize for havin' to question you again on the robbery. I was called down here from Waco because I've put in more time trying to track these two bandits than anyone else. The marshal is hopin' I can find some clue in your story that they might have missed."

"All right," Dawkins said with a sigh. He began his story again from the beginning, with one of the old codgers yelling about wanting his money in the bank. Colton listened to the whole report, interrupting occasionally to ask questions about one thing or another.

When Dawkins got to the part where one of the robbers had to be taken to the outhouse, Colton asked, "Where is your bank guard now? Is he here?"

Dawkins looked around him, and not seeing Roscoe, he said, "He's most likely in the back room drinking coffee. That seems to be what he's best at."

"How did he manage to get locked in the outhouse?" Colton asked.

"I'll be damned if I know," Dawkins answered. "That's something we all wonder about. He wasn't just locked in, he was tied in with a rope wrapped around the outhouse." He paused and shook his head. "And his gun was missing. He's not sure what happened to it."

Colton caught himself wanting to laugh, in spite of his duty to bring them to justice. He was afraid that he was even admiring their ingenuity. "During the whole time they were in the bank, did they ever become violent or use force?"

"They didn't have to," Dawkins said. "They were holding their guns on me, and I'm convinced they would not have hes-

itated to shoot, had I resisted. They were so old they didn't
care if they lived or died."

"But they never really laid hands on you, to rough you up,
or anything?"

"Except the one who tied me up, hand and foot," Dawkins
said. "That was unpleasant."

"Where did he get the rope?" Colton asked, thinking it
strange they would walk in the bank carrying a coil of rope.

"He was wearing it!" Dawkins exclaimed.

" 'Wearin' it'?" Colton responded.

"I told you they both were wearing these big dusters. He
had it inside his duster somehow. He didn't even unbutton it.
Just reached in his pocket and pulled the rope out through the
pocket." Colton tried to picture that, when they were suddenly interrupted by an issue at the front door. "Let me go
and take care of this," Dawkins said. "People just don't
understand that we're closed because we've been wiped out."
He hurried to the door where Emmett and Dylan were trying
to tell a man they were closed.

"Sir, the bank is closed until we receive operating capital
from our corporate bank in New Orleans. We'll be glad to take
care of your problem at that time."

"Damn it," the man swore. "I'm trying to give you some
operatin' capital, and you've gotta take it right now and give
me my mortgage back."

It just struck Dawkins who the man was. He hesitated, not
sure of the name. "Morris?"

"Right."

"How much have you got, Mr. Morris?"

"Every damn cent of the amount owed," Grover answered.
"Seven thousand and five hundred dollars, and it's ahead of the
due date. So I want the deed to my property back right now."

"And you shall have it," Dawkins replied, immediately assuming the friendly attitude he used when selling the loan. In

his present catastrophe, he needed every penny he could get his hands on. And seventy-five hundred walking in off the street was a blessing he didn't expect. "We'll go to my office and complete this transaction immediately." He extended his hand toward his office door to point the way. Only then did he remember Colton. "I'll be with you in a minute, Deputy. This is something I have to take care of for a customer." He was surprised by Colton's reaction. He just stood there grinning.

Grover was struck at the same time. "Deputy Gray," he asked, amazed, "what are you doin' here?"

"Howdy, Mr. Morris," Colton returned. "You go ahead and take care of business. I'll see you when you're done." He walked into the back room, where he found Roscoe Crowder, drinking coffee as Dawkins had predicted. "Are you the bank guard?"

"I sure am," Roscoe replied. "What can I do for ya?"

"I'm a deputy marshal investigatin' the bank robbery. I understand you somehow got tied up in the outhouse. How'd that happen?" He wasn't expecting to gain anything by questioning Roscoe. He was just interested to hear the story.

"Well, that one old feller's bowels was about to cut loose and Mr. Dawkins told me to take him to the outhouse. So I took him out back to the outhouse, but he wouldn't go in 'cause he was afraid there was snakes in there. He told me to go inside and see if there was any. Well, I ain't a-scared of snakes, so I went in to see and he slammed the door on me and stuck the lock back on it."

"Is that when you lost your gun?"

"Yeah. How'd you know that?"

"Just guessed," Colton said. "Go on."

"He musta found some rope in the bushes behind the outhouse and tied the whole outhouse up so I couldn't kick the door open."

"He was mighty lucky to find enough rope to tie that door

shut, wasn't he?" Colton asked, knowing he was having a conversation with a moron.

"I'll say he was, 'cause, if he hadn't, I bet I coulda kicked that door till the hasp came off. I'll tell you what I can't figure out, though."

"What's that, Roscoe?"

"When we was doin' the quickstep up the path to that outhouse, it was all he could do to keep from fillin' up his britches. But after he got me locked up, he said he didn't have to go no more. You don't reckon he filled his boots with it, do ya?"

"You ever figure he mighta been japin' ya? He might notta had to go in the first place."

"You know, he coulda been at that," Roscoe said, as if it was the first time he had considered that possibility.

"Thank you for your time, Roscoe, you've been a big help," Colton said. "I'll get back out there and wait for Mr. Dawkins." *You were the answer to Oscar and Elmer's prayers*, he thought.

He talked awhile to the two tellers until Dawkins and Grover came out of the office. There was not much more he could get from Dawkins. He was really waiting to talk to Grover Morris, finding it the rarest of coincidences that they bumped into each other in Austin, of all places. As far as the robbery, he had concluded it to be a typical holdup by Oscar and Elmer. Daring and clever, with no loose ends left untied, that was their trademark. One thing he was convinced of was, if they were, in fact, played by younger men, their makeup was superior. It made him wonder if they might actually be actors, escaped from the stage.

"I don't know how much more I can tell you, Deputy," Dawkins said when he walked Grover out to the front door.

"Thank you very much for your time and cooperation, Mr. Dawkins. I think I've heard enough about the robbery to know it's an authentic holdup by the two old bandits." He turned to Grover then and said, "Mr. Morris, I'll walk out with you." He followed him out the door.

"Colton Gray," Grover exclaimed, "fancy meetin' you here. I declare, I didn't know it was you till I took another look. You down here about this bank robbery business?"

"That's right," Colton replied. "I wasn't expecting to run into you in Austin. Last time I saw you, you were talkin' to the D and T about sellin' some cattle."

"That's right, I sure was. That's why I came to the bank today." He held a sheaf of papers up. "To get my ranch back, free and clear. Imagine my surprise when I got here and found the bank closed. And the bank had been robbed. I gotta admit, when they told me that, I thought about turnin' around and leavin', figurin' I might not have to pay 'em the money I owed. But they woulda still had the deed to my land, so I had to make sure they took care of the loan." He paused to take a breath. "And then, here you are down here. Do you know who stole the money?"

"Yep, we're pretty sure who it was," Colton said. "On the other hand, we don't really know who it was." He could see by the expression of confusion on Grover's face that he didn't really know anything about the robbery. "I know that sounds pretty crazy. Tell you what, why don't we go find us a place to get some dinner and I'll tell you all about it. I'm buyin'. Are you in a hurry to get back home?"

"No, no big hurry. That sounds like a good idea, but you don't need to buy mine. I know a good little place to get a good dinner, too. My ranch ain't but two and a half hours from here. I'm goin' back there tonight, then I'll start back to the D and T in the mornin'."

"The D and T?" Colton asked. "You goin' back to the D and T?"

"Sure am," Grover replied. "We're gettin' ready to push a

big herd of cattle up to Kansas. My little ol' herd of three hundred and fifty cows is right in with Casey and Eli's cattle and we're goin' to market."

"They sure gave you a good price for your cows. I heard you tell Dawkins you brought seventy-five hundred dollars to pay the debt."

"Oh, they didn't buy my cattle," Grover was quick to explain. "My cows are just goin' to the market with theirs, and whatever price they bring, that's what I'll get. No, that seventy-five hundred was a loan Casey and Eli made outta the kindness of their hearts. And I mean that. There weren't no paper to sign or anything like that. They just said a handshake will do, and that's all we did. I swear, Colton, I reckon you know those two boys better than I do, but in my book, there ain't no finer men in Texas. They sure helped me out when I got myself in a hole."

Grover untied his horse from the hitching rail and led it while he walked with Colton a couple of blocks down the street to a tiny restaurant called Aunt Molly's. "The food's good in here and you get your money's worth," Grover said as he held the door for Colton. Inside, there was one large table, with only a couple of empty places. There were two tables against the back wall, one of which was taken, each set with two places. Since the places at the big table were not close together, they quickly claimed the empty two-place table. A stocky, middle-aged woman wearing a bored expression came to the table and asked what they wanted to drink. They both chose coffee, and she turned around to go back for it. "That's Aunt Molly," Grover said.

"Does she do the cookin' and wait the tables, too?" Colton asked.

"She just waits the tables," Grover answered. "Her husband, Wilbur, does the cookin'. I reckon they musta figured more folks would try 'em out if they called the place Aunt Molly's."

"I think you're right," Colton said. "Has a better ring to it than Uncle Wilbur's. I take it there ain't no choice of what you wanna eat."

"That's right, but it's usually pretty good grub. I think Wilbur used to drive a chuck wagon quite a few years ago." It was no surprise to Colton when Aunt Molly brought their plates, it was beef stew. But Grover was right, it was pretty good grub.

After they took a little time to accommodate their hunger pangs, they leisurely finished cleaning their plates. Then it was time for talk over another cup of coffee, and Colton's curiosity had been awakened by the part Casey and Eli played in Grover's debt settlement. He casually asked, "Were Casey and Eli down here in Austin durin' the last week?"

"Lord, no," Grover responded. "They were too busy gettin' those cows ready to drive north. That's why I've gotta head back up there tomorrow mornin'. Me and my boy Billy are goin' on the drive with 'em. I'm goin' along just as another hand, but when they're sold, I'm gonna get the full price for my cows, same as theirs."

Colton felt a small sense of relief upon hearing that. If Grover had said Eli and Casey had come down to Austin for some reason, he would have been tempted to charge them with the bank robbery. Even so, it seemed that lately those two characters had some connection to the two old men who were pulling all the holdups. Although it was hard to find something to do with this latest robbery, if the two were at their ranch in Lampasas County when the bank was robbed. The two owners of the D&T were getting a reputation for generosity around their county. And not too long ago, they were both working cowhands at forty dollars a month. He couldn't help but ask, "Where do you reckon Casey and Eli got the money to build that ranch back the way it was?"

"I ain't got no idea," Grover said. "I figure it ain't none of my business. I'm just glad they don't mind lendin' a little of it to folks like me, who damn sure need help from somebody."

"How'd they find out you needed help?" Colton asked. "Did they know you?"

"I came beggin', with my hat in my hand. They didn't know me, but they didn't treat me like a beggar. Hell, you were there. They treated me like a neighborin' ranch owner."

"You're right, they did," Colton agreed. *And they treated me like a friend*, he thought.

Chapter 13

The beef stew had been good, and as Grover had promised, the price was very reasonable. They took the time to tell Aunt Molly as much. She thanked them graciously while maintaining her expression of boredom. "Well, thank you for the dinner," Grover said when they walked outside. "I expect I'd best get started back for home now, while I can make it before dark. It sure was a surprise seein' you again so soon after I first met you."

"Yep, it was a pleasure," Colton said. "Tell Casey and Eli that I said howdy."

"I'll tell 'em," Grover said as he climbed up into the saddle. "They'll be surprised to hear about the bank gettin' robbed."

"I expect they will," Colton said. *But will they?* he wondered.

He stood there for about a minute, watching Grover ride away, thinking about what a waste of time it had been to ride down from Waco. There was nothing he could tell Marshal Thomas, other than the fact that the bank had been hit by the infamous old codgers. He decided that as long as he was here, he'd check around to see if he could turn up any information that might be useful. Going on the assumption that the two old men didn't just ride into town that day, and seeing a bank, decide to go in and rob it, he figured they had to be there before to scout it. In his opinion, the robbers could not come in dressed as the two old men. Based on the many times he had heard descriptions of them, they would have been far too conspicuous. So he concluded that he was looking for an eyewitness to two strangers asking questions maybe. That raised a question right away, so he turned around and went back to the bank.

He caught Bryan Dawkins about to leave the bank. "Oh, Deputy, I thought we were finished. I'm on my way to dinner. Can this wait?"

"I won't delay you but a minute," Colton said. "I just want to ask you one question."

"Very well." Dawkins sighed heavily. "But please make it brief."

"Right," Colton said. "I remember the time lock on your safe is set for an hour after the bank opens. On the day before the robbery, did anyone ask what time the lock opened?"

"No, I don't recall anyone asking that."

"This would have been a stranger, someone who had not been in your bank before," Colton prompted.

"No, no one asked that question. The only new person in the bank that day was a man who was the developer of cattle ranches. He didn't ask what time the safe opened. He was a potential customer who made an appointment to meet with me the next day to establish an account. I'm sure the reason he never showed up might have had something to do with the bank being robbed that morning," Dawkins said with heavy sarcasm.

Colton smiled. "Did you show him your safe?"

Dawkins hesitated. "Yes, I showed him the safe. He was very impressed."

"You think you might have mentioned what time the time lock opened?" Dawkins didn't answer. "Mr. Dawkins, I think

that was your bank robber you were talking to." Dawkins
could not speak. His face began to take on a shade of crimson.
"Did he give you his name?" Colton continued.

"Robert White," Dawkins choked out.

"Bob White," Colton said, "like the bobwhite bird. Well,
I'm sorry to have delayed you. Thank you for your time." He
walked out of the bank, aware that he had just spoiled Dawkins's dinner. He would have questioned him further about
Bob White's description, but he felt pretty sure it would be of
a man well past his youth. Like Casey Tubbs or Eli Doolin, he
couldn't help thinking. He could picture Casey, especially, in
the role.

Next he decided to see if he could find any of the mer-
chants or businessmen who might have seen Bob White, and
possibly with another bird. He would check the hotel, but first
he decided to check the stable to see if they left their horses
there. He found Ernie Williams out in the corral. "Howdy,
Deputy. You wantin' your horses now?" Scrappy saw him and
came over to meet him. Colton reached over the rail and took
the bay gelding's head between his hands.

"Nope, I'm thinkin' about stayin' another night here," he
said as he scratched Scrappy's ears. "I just wanted to ask you a
question. That bank holdup was on the twenty-eighth, do you
remember doin' business with a couple of strangers on the day
before that?" Ernie scratched his head, trying to recall. "Was
one of 'em named Bob White?"

"Bob White," Ernie remembered right away then. "Sure
did, Bob White and his brother, Tom. They just left their
packhorses here. Didn't leave 'em overnight, just while they
was ridin' around doin' something. I don't know what."

"So they probably didn't check into the hotel, if they didn't
leave their horses here," Colton thought aloud.

"Reckon not," Ernie answered his thought. "I expect they
made camp with their horses somewhere."

"All right, much obliged. I'll see you later." He gave Scrappy a final pat and walked back down the street. There were several saloons on this side of town, and it occurred to him that they might have been in the mood for a drink. He planned to check the general store next to see if they might have bought all the rope they used here in Austin. But he came to a saloon first. It was called Dillard's Saloon. "What the hell? Won't hurt to ask." So he went inside. There was a long bar running almost the length of the room and it was manned by a heavyset fellow with a bald head and bushy sideburns.

"What can I pour ya?" Pete Devine asked when Colton walked up to the bar.

"I'd like to ask you a question, if you don't mind. I'm a deputy marshal lookin' into the bank robbery on the twenty-eighth." He pulled his coat aside to show his badge.

"The one by the little old grandpas?" Pete responded with a deep chuckle. "If you're gonna ask me if I saw 'em in here, I'll have to say no. I'da sure remembered two fellers like that."

"I don't expect they did stop for a drink on their way outta town," Colton said. "I wanted to ask you if you saw a couple of strangers in here the day before the robbery."

"I don't know. I probably did. There's strangers comin' and goin' here all the time. It's kinda hard for me to remember 'em all."

"What if their names were Bob White and his brother, Tom?" Colton asked.

"Oh, Bob White. Hell yeah, I remember them two boys. They were passin' through on their way to San Antonio. Yeah, they were quite talkative. One of 'em likes rye, and the other one likes corn. Said this was a classic saloon because I didn't pour both drinks outta the same bottle." He chuckled at the thought. "They asked me where to eat supper and I sent 'em to the hotel dinin' room."

He thanked Pete for his information and headed for the hotel. He was not on the trail of the two bandits, but he was satisfied that he was forming a complete picture of the robbery. And he was thinking that if nothing else he was confirming the fact that the two old men were younger men in disguise. Whether they were who he suspected or not, he couldn't prove. On his way to the hotel, he passed Carlen's General Store and debated whether or not to ask about the rope. It was not an important issue—but he wanted to paint the whole picture. So Colton stopped in and introduced himself to the owner; he learned his name was Jim Carlen.

"Yes, I do remember two men coming in the store and buying rope. I'm not sure, but I believe it mighta been the day before that bank robbery. I guess I remember it because they bought three coils of rope."

"Much obliged," Colton said, and didn't tarry. Back on his way to the hotel, he wondered about the storekeeper's memory. He claimed they bought three coils of rope. According to what he learned at the bank, there was one coil used at the outhouse, probably placed there earlier. And another at the safe was pulled from inside one robber's duster. Maybe the other one had a rope, too, and they just overestimated their need for rope.

His next stop was the hotel dining room, and it was closed. He could see a little bit between the shade and the side of the glass door panel, enough to see that people were moving around inside. So he tapped on the glass until someone finally raised the shade and pointed to the CLOSED sign. He pulled his coat aside and showed his badge, so she opened the door. Daisy turned and called, "Mr. Waters!"

In a few seconds, Marvin Waters came from the kitchen. "What is it, Daisy?" Then he saw Colton stepping inside. "Can I help you?"

"Yes, sir," Colton replied. "I see you're busy cleanin' up, so

I won't take much of your time. I'm Deputy Marshal Colton Gray and I'm doin' some follow-up investigation of the bank robbery on the twenty-eighth."

"I'm afraid there's nothing I can tell you about that robbery," Waters replied.

"I'm more interested in what you might remember about two strangers who came here to supper the night before the robbery."

"You think the robbers might have eaten here the night before?" Waters asked, surprised. He looked at Daisy, who was listening as hard as she could. "You remember serving two old men that night?" She shook her head.

"They wouldn't have looked like two old men that night," Colton told him. "They would have had their ridin' horses and a couple of packhorses with 'em."

"I know who you're talking about now," Waters said. "I remember them." He looked at Daisy and said, "You remember those two fellows. One of 'em was kinda taken by you." Back to Colton then, he said, "They asked me to seat 'em by the front window so they could keep an eye on their horses."

"Did you hear them talkin' about campin' anywhere?" Colton asked. "I know they didn't stay in the hotel."

"No, sorry, I didn't really hear what they talked about," Waters said. "I remember they didn't seem to be in any hurry. In fact, they sat there for quite a while after they finished eating. It was already gettin' dark by the time they walked out of here, so I doubt they were planning to go very far before makin' camp."

"I doubt it, myself. Are there any favorite campin' spots around the town where most folks camp?"

Waters scratched his head while he thought. "I don't know of any special places. Most drifters and everybody else camp along the river."

Daisy spoke up then. "My daddy said he saw a couple of

riders, leading packhorses, go past the house toward the cemetery, and they musta camped back there, 'cause they rode
back out early the next morning. But it wasn't two old men,
like the sheriff and everybody's been talking about."

"Who is your daddy?" Colton asked.

"John Skinner," Daisy replied. "He's a carpenter. Him and
Mama and my two brothers live in a house he built on Bank
Street."

"Bank Street?" Colton asked.

"That's that little side street that runs back beside the Cotton Growers Bank," Waters said. "It ends at the cemetery. Nobody goes back there anymore. There's a new cemetery on
the other end of town."

"Did your daddy tell the sheriff or one of the deputy marshals about those two fellows goin' back there to the cemetery?" Colton asked.

"No," Daisy answered. "He didn't think it had anything to
do with that bank robbery, and like I said, it wasn't two old
men, anyway."

"There wouldn't be any reason to think they were up to
anything," Colton said, but he had a strong feeling it might
have been the two bank robbers. "Bank Street, huh? Well, I'll
get outta your way now. Thank you for your help, and I apologize for interruptin' you."

"No problem a-tall, Deputy," Waters said. "Come on back
and have supper with us."

"I expect I might surely do that," Colton replied.

Daisy unlocked the door to let him out again and stood
watching him as he walked away. "He's kinda cute, ain't he?"
She looked at Waters and giggled.

From the hotel, he went straight back to the bank on the
corner of the main street and a side street that was called Bank
Street, confirmed by a sign nailed on the side of the bank. He
peered down the narrow street and wondered if he should

have kept Scrappy with him. He should have asked how far it was to the old cemetery. He could see a handful of houses farther down, but the road looked as if it continued a long way beyond them. It couldn't be all that far, he decided, and started walking down the street.

Past the last house, the road turned into little more than a lane, and a seldom-used one at that. Behind him, he could still hear the chorus of barking dogs he had set off at the houses he had walked past. At the end, he could see the graveyard, and there were recent hoofprints on the road, as well as on the narrow lane that continued after the road ended. When he reached the cemetery, it was obvious that there had recently been horses there and there were tracks beyond it toward a ridge and a thick growth of trees beyond. He suddenly became more excited by the second as he followed the trail beyond the ridge and down to the creek. He was sure he had found their campsite! There were the ashes of a recent campfire and the remains of a pile of collected firewood, plus the signs left by bedrolls and saddles and such. They had camped right in town. But the young lady in the hotel dining room said her father saw them ride out early that morning, and they were not in disguise as the two old men. They had to have come back, so they must have found another way to this camp.

It was not hard to find, for two men riding horses and leading two packhorses could not easily hide the trail they left through the bushes and weeds along the creek bank. He walked for what he figured to be a quarter of a mile before he decided the creek was not going to lead him back to town. So he began to search the ground more carefully. And when the trail led across a sandy wash, it told him what he had begun to suspect. The clear hoofprints in the sand were all going in one direction. There were none heading back toward the camp. This had to be their escape route after they robbed the bank. He turned around and went back to the camp.

He took another close look around the perimeter of the camp, but could find no entry evidence except where he originally came in from the graveyard. So he went back to the cemetery and discovered tracks around the back of it that led him to the overgrown path leading in the direction of town. He followed the path until it came out near the railroad station. "Damn!" he exclaimed when he saw the buildings of the center of town. "I didn't nail you this time, Oscar and Elmer, but I got the whole picture of how you robbed that bank, and how you got away. And I might not track you down, but when I leave here, I'm goin' to go back to that getaway route you took along that creek and see where it leads me."

He pulled out his pocket watch and checked the time. It was still an hour before the dining room at the hotel would open for supper, so he had plenty of time to check in with Marshal Thomas. He suddenly realized he was tired. "I ain't walked that far in I don't know when," he confessed aloud as he set out for the Capitol Building and the marshal's office behind it.

Earl Dutton looked up in surprise when Colton walked into the outer office. "Deputy Gray," he said. "We figured you were likely on your way back to Waco by now. Is everything all right?"

"Yes, sir," Colton replied. "I didn't think I could go back before I made my report to the marshal."

"Your report?" Dutton asked. "I don't really think the marshal was expecting one."

"You folks wired Waco for help, and they sent me down here. Granted, it wasn't in time to catch the men who robbed the bank, but I felt I owed the marshal an investigation of the crime. So that's what I did this afternoon, and I'm ready to give the marshal a complete picture of the way this robbery was committed. That is, if he's interested in what I found out."

"I see," Dutton responded, partially amused at what he

identified as a typical naïve young deputy. "I'll go and give Marshal Thomas your message. He's just getting ready to leave the office, so maybe you won't be too long."

When Dutton told Thomas that Deputy Gray was waiting to give him the report of his investigation, Thomas's reaction was the same as Dutton's had been. "His investigation? I thought he was already on his way back to Waco."

Dutton told him that was his thought as well. "Shall I tell him you don't need to see him, and he should just write it down and mail it to us?"

Thomas hesitated. "No," he said then, "it's not his fault we called him down here for no reason at all. It sounds like he's trying to justify his presence here. I'll talk to him." He got up from his desk then and walked to the door with Dutton. "Deputy Gray," he greeted Colton. "Come on in." When Colton walked in, Thomas waved him to a chair. "Dutton tells me you've been investigating the bank robbery."

"Yes, sir," Colton replied. "Since I was no help in catching the robbers, I felt I, at least, owed you my complete findings on exactly how the two robbers pulled the holdup, so you could have a complete picture of the crime. I've only just now finished my investigation, so I haven't written it down. But I thought I would bring you a verbal report now. And if you want the written report, I can send it later."

"I'm sure that will be interesting to have later, so go ahead and tell me what you've found in your investigation."

He started by saying the two felons arrived in Austin at suppertime on the evening of the twenty-sixth, set up a camp on the creek behind the old cemetery. Then on the morning of the twenty-seventh, they scouted the bank. One of them, using the alias of Robert White, cased the bank with Bryan Dawkins telling him what time the safe opened. After identifying the obstacles to their intended crime, they purchased enough rope to tie Dawkins up and tie the guard in the outhouse. Then they returned to their camp using the deserted old lane behind the railroad building. On the morning of the twenty-eighth, they put on their disguises as the two old men and went to the bank and committed the robbery. After an unhurried exit, they rode away from the bank, took the path behind the railroad building to their camp, picked up their packhorses, and escaped along the creek behind the ridge. He filled in every detail he had discovered regarding when they stabled their packhorses and for how long, where they ate, and where they drank whiskey. He finished by advising Thomas that he intended to follow that escape route along the creek on the odd chance he might be able to track them.

Thomas was astonished by the completeness of the young deputy's report. "That's one helluva complete report. That's twice as much as we put together on those two old birds. I believe you've convinced me that you're right about them being younger men dressed up like old men. I'd appreciate it if you would write all that down for me. Can you do that?"

"Yes, sir, I'd be happy to. I'll do it tonight and leave it with you in the mornin'. I want to get on that trail by the creek to see if it leads anywhere helpful."

"Fine," Thomas said. "And thanks for your help on this." He got up and walked with him into the outer office. When Colton left the office, Thomas looked at Dutton and said, "I might see if I can pull a few whiskers and get that boy transferred down here. He's got the right attitude."

Since he still had plenty of time left before the dining room would be closing, he went to the telegraph office and sent a wire to Marshal John Timmons, his boss in the Waco office. It was to advise him that he had finished working with the Austin marshal and tomorrow he was going to follow an escape trail he had uncovered and hoped would provide some results.

When he walked into the dining room, he was met by Marvin Waters, who welcomed him back. "Sit anywhere you like," Waters told him, "and Daisy will take care of you."

So he went over and sat at a table against the wall, and in a few minutes, Daisy appeared holding a cup of coffee. "Deputy Gray," she greeted him cheerfully. "You came back, just like you said you would."

"I guess I did," he answered, not sure what else he could say.

"I'm standing here holding this cup of hot coffee because I bet myself that coffee is what you want right now." When he didn't say anything for a few seconds, she said, "Or I can go back and get you a glass of water, if that's what you want."

"No, coffee is what I'd rather have. I need a cup of coffee tonight," he said. He was reacting a little slow because he was feeling the results of walking several miles in a pair of boots made for riding a horse. He hoped coffee would fix that problem.

"Good," she said coyly. "Want me to put some sugar in it for you?"

"No, thanks, I take it without," he answered. "What are you servin' tonight?"

"You mean, to eat?" she asked, smiling sweetly and fluttering her eyelashes.

"Yeah," he answered, oblivious to the flirtation.

Perplexed, she dropped the coy attitude and asked, "Have you got a sweetheart?"

He looked astonished. "'A sweetheart'? No, I don't have a sweetheart."

"Well, you do now. I'm your sweetheart. I'm claimin' you. Now, what do you want to eat? A steak or Mexican-style beans and rice over pork?"

"I guess I'll stick with a steak. That Mexican style might be a little too hot for me to handle." He paused, then added, *"Sweetheart."*

"Right," she declared. "That might not be all that's too hot for you to handle. How do you want your steak, burnt dry or still alive in the center?"

"Alive in the center, I reckon. I would like it warm all over, though."

"You got it, sweetie. I'll see to it, myself." She went to the kitchen to find Edna, the cook, grinning at her.

"Damned if you ain't been throwed offa that horse," Edna said. "You ready to give up, or are you gonna try to get back on?"

Daisy shook her head, exasperated. "I swear, he's cute, but he ain't but about six years old inside his head. Either that or he's dumb as a stump."

"Or just maybe he's one of the rare lawmen, cowboys, and drifters who are actually gentlemen in the presence of ladies, or maybe he does have someone he's promised his loyalty," Edna said.

Daisy shook her head. "You know, you're right. I'm afraid I've made him uncomfortable. I ought to apologize. Marvin will get after me for running the customers off." When she went back to his table, she said, "Your steak oughta be out in a couple of minutes. I hope you know I was just teasing you a little bit before. I'm sorry if I made you feel uncomfortable."

"Oh?" he responded. "I didn't even notice. No need to apologize."

She decided that what she had told Edna was right. Dumb as a stump, he wasn't even as developed as a six-year-old. But he was kinda cute. "Are you gonna be in town for a while?" she asked in an effort to make polite conversation, just to show him she could.

"No, ma'am. I'll be leavin' in the mornin'. I've gotta write a report tonight, and then I'll be done here in Austin."

"All work and no play, huh?"

"I suppose you could say that," he replied.

She went to the kitchen to get his supper. Then checked on him frequently to keep his cup filled with coffee. When he had finished eating and refused the last offer to fill his cup, he said, "Tell the cook I enjoyed my supper. The steak was cooked just like I like 'em."

She smiled and said, "I'll tell her. She'll be pleased. Will we see you at breakfast?"

"Most likely I'll be leavin' before the dinin' room opens," he replied.

"Going to work writing your report now, I suppose."

"Yes, ma'am. I'll be up in my room writing my report all evenin'. That's room number two hundred and eight, first room at the top of the back stairs." He gave her a polite smile, plopped his hat on his head, and walked out the door leading to the hotel, leaving her standing by the table with her jaw hanging open.

Edna came out of the kitchen to stand beside her. "I believe you just had your bluff called," she said. "Maybe that young man ain't as dumb as you thought."

Chapter 14

As he had intended, Colton left his hotel room at first light the next morning. He walked to Marshal Thomas's office and slid his report under the door. Written on hotel stationery and sealed in a matching envelope, it outlined an almost hourly schedule the two bank robbers kept up to—during and after the robbery. Leaving the marshal's office, he then walked to the stable and was there waiting for Ernie Williams when the colorful little man arrived to open up. "Looks like you're anxious to get an early start," Ernie said.

"Yep," Colton replied. "I'm gonna try to see if I can pick up a trail that's gettin' older by the second."

"I'll help you get saddled up," Ernie said as he unlocked the big padlock on the chain holding the stable doors closed. "I bet you ain't had no coffee or nothin' yet, and I've got a fire already built in my stove. I'll strike a match to it, and we can have some coffee soon as that little stove heats up."

"I 'preciate it, Ernie, but I'll just make some coffee and some breakfast when I have to stop to rest my horses. I've got enough supplies to stop a couple of times before I have to find someplace to buy some more. You go ahead and get your fire goin' and get your coffee started. I'll get my horses ready to go."

"I'll get my fire started," Ernie decided, "that won't take but a minute." He hurried over to the stove and lit the kindling under his split firewood. He stayed with it only until it caught on well enough so he could leave it to come help Colton. "If you'da told me you was wantin' to get away this early, I mighta got here earlier."

"This is plenty early enough," Colton assured him, "just right, in fact. You got my bill figured up?" He paid him and led the horses outside the stable.

"You take care of yourself, young feller," Ernie told him as the deputy stepped up into the saddle.

"I'll do that. You do the same," Colton replied, and wheeled Scrappy away from the stable. He turned the bay gelding back toward the Cotton Growers Bank, and when he reached it, he turned down the side street toward the old cemetery. As he approached it, he formed a picture in his mind of the two bank robbers—not in disguise as two old men, but as the younger men who played the parts. And when he pictured them, he saw Casey and Eli riding past the back corner of the graveyard, leading their packhorses past the ridge and down to the creek. On this morning, it was still early enough that barely enough light penetrated the heavy ceiling of tree branches covering the creek bank to reveal the trail marked by broken bushes. He had enough light to follow the trail left by the four horses, plus his own footprint occasionally from the day before, for at least part of the way. A random thought interrupted his concentration on the trail ahead of him. And for a moment, he thought about Daisy. And he wondered if she had awakened early enough to return to her room back of the kitchen without being seen. He hoped so. She was a sweet young woman, so much more tender than the rough exterior she chose to display in public.

The sun was climbing a little more above the treetops when he reached the point where he had turned around the day before. There was no sign of an attempt to hide their trail, nor was there any sense in thinking they could. This changed, however, when he became aware of a clearing in the trees ahead of him. A short way more and the creek left the thick woods and came out to split an open pastureland. At least the light was better now, and he could still see the hoofprints continuing along the creek bank. Looking up ahead, he could see the river, and he knew there was bound to be a wagon road beside it. More than likely, there would be many tracks on a road to Austin. From the open pastureland, he could see the buildings of the town, approximately a mile and a half away. So there was no need to guess which way the two bandits headed when they struck the road. As if to make sure he saw which way they had gone, they had left tracks where they crossed the creek before they reached the river road and angled toward it.

He took a look at the sun, then figured the river was running in a slightly northwest direction. If the two men were Casey and Eli, that would be the direction they might travel to get back home. The thought raised a tiny glimmer of hope as he set out to follow the road. The hoofprints soon became mixed in with too many others for him to be sure they were the ones he started out following. Worse than that, after a short distance, the river took a sharp bend to the south. He suddenly concluded that he didn't really have a trail to follow, for the road continued to follow the river, and that was in the wrong direction. He had passed several small trails connecting to the river road in the short distance the river had been running northwest. They could have turned onto any one of them. He turned Scrappy around and looked back the way he had come. He had no idea which way they went. It was difficult to concede defeat, but it was foolishness to simply wander in hopes of lucking onto a clue. "They've whipped me again, Scrappy. We might as well find us a good place to take a rest and cook some breakfast."

So, when he found a good grassy patch near the river's edge, he unloaded his horses and let them water and graze while he made a fire to prepare some coffee and bacon. He wasn't inspired to cook more than that, still suffering from the frustration of losing the trail of the two robbers. While he sat on the bank, drinking his coffee, he thought back about the dinner conversation he'd had with Grover Morris, and Grover's high opinion of Casey and Eli. Small wonder, Colton thought. Didn't know the man from Adam. He rides up to their door and tells them the bank is putting the squeeze on him for money he owes, but ain't got. So they give him the money so he can pay the bank off. When Colton had asked Grover how he knew he could get help from Casey and Eli, he said another small rancher, named Nicholson, had suggested that he should go talk to the D&T. Then Nicholson told him about another rancher who sold some cows to D&T for a great deal more than he could get in Fort Worth. Colton shook his head violently, in an effort to get his brain straight. He almost felt guilty for trying to connect Casey and Eli to the old men robbing the banks. He decided to call this particular robbery a dead trail and go on back to Waco.

"Well, I see you two got here in time for supper," Monroe said when Grover and Billy rode into the yard. "I think Smiley's just about ready to bang on that dang triangle of his."

"That's what we were countin' on," Grover said. "We pushed our horses a little bit, just in case."

"Everything all right back home?" Monroe asked. "Casey said you had to go home to take care of some business about the title to your land."

Monroe didn't mention anything about a loan or money, so Grover figured Casey hadn't told anyone the real reason he had to go to Austin. "Yep," he answered, "got everything straightened out. We'd best put our horses away, if it's time for grub." They took their horses to the corral and pulled their saddles off, thinking to feed them some grain after a while.

"Is Casey or Eli here, or are they gone off somewhere?" Grover asked. He knew they'd want to hear about the big bank robbery in Austin.

"No, they're here," Monroe said. "Matter of fact, they're in the back of the stable watchin' a mare give birth to a colt."

"Is that a fact?"

"Yep, they're watchin' Corey Johnson help the mare with the birthin'," Monroe said.

"I'd like to see that, myself," Grover declared.

"Corey's pretty good at it," Monroe said. He walked back to the last stall with Grover, where they found Casey, Eli, and Davey watching Corey working with the mare to help her with a difficult delivery.

"Well, I see you got back in time for supper," Eli said when he saw Grover.

"Yep, and we're ready for it," Grover replied.

"Watch much more of this and you'll lose your appetite," Davey remarked.

Grover gave that a chuckle, then said to Eli, "Damnedest thing happened in Austin the other day." That got Eli and Casey's attention. "You know that bank I had to go to, to get my deed back, the Cotton Growers Bank?"

"Yeah," Casey asked, "what about it?"

"It got robbed by those two old men bandits a few days before I got there."

"You don't mean it," Casey replied. "Those two old coots? Did they get away with much money?"

"I reckon. I don't know how much, but they cleaned the bank's safe out," Grover said, then chuckled when he added, "They tied the bank guard up in the outhouse back of the bank. Then they walked right out the front door with the money, and the two tellers didn't even know they was bein' robbed till they found ol' Dawkins tied up in the back room."

"Well, I'll be . . ." Eli started. "If that ain't somethin'. Were you able to get your deed back?"

"Yep, I got it. They didn't wanna let me in at first, but there was a deputy marshal there that told 'em to let me in." He waited to see if they would ask about the deputy. When they failed to, he said, "His name was Colton Gray." Then he got the reaction he expected.

"Now I know you're japin'," Casey replied. "Colton was down there in Austin?"

"He sure was," Grover said. "It sure surprised me. Him and me ate dinner together before I headed back home. He said to tell you boys howdy." He figured he'd give Casey and Eli the straight of the story later when they didn't have an audience. And that was that they let him in the bank after he protested that he had seventy-five hundred dollars to give the bank. Colton didn't know he was there until they let him inside.

They heard the signal that dinner was ready, so that reduced Corey and the mare's audience to zero. "Tell Smiley to hold a plate for me," Corey said. Monroe said he would.

"I expect we'd best get back to the house to eat, too," Casey said. "Juanita will be sending Miguel down here to get us." They started filing out of the stable, and Casey said to Grover, "Come up to the house after you eat. I wanna hear some more about that bank robbery, and there's a couple of more things we need to talk about."

"Right," Grover said, wondering what the other things might be.

They parted ways with the rest of the men, then headed for Juanita's kitchen. "Damned if that ain't one helluva coincidence, ain't it?" Eli asked as they walked across the yard to the back door. "They sent Colton down to Austin to look into that robbery. I swear, Casey, we're bumpin' into that young man everywhere we go. I'm afraid he's liable to get lucky enough one day to catch us." He paused for a few seconds while he considered what he just said. "And I like that young fellow, so when he does catch us, you're gonna have to shoot him."

"We'll flip a coin for it," Casey said as they started up the back steps to the kitchen.

Grover gave them plenty of time to finish their supper before he knocked on the kitchen door. Juanita answered the door and told him to go on through to the study. "You want coffee?" she asked him as he stepped inside the kitchen.

"What?" he asked, confused. "No, ma'am, I've just et my supper."

"Señor Casey said you might want more coffee," she said.

"Uh, no, ma'am, I reckon I've had enough for now, but thank you kindly." He went on to the study, to find both Eli and Casey with cups of coffee.

"You want some coffee?" Casey asked.

"No, thanks. Juanita offered me some," Grover replied, wondering if the whole meeting was going to be about drinking coffee. "Is everything all right? I know I was thinkin' after I left the bank the other day, that after that robbery, maybe I coulda got away without givin' 'em that money you loaned me. They was closed up, and they mighta been goin' outta business, so maybe they woulda let me have my deed back, anyway."

Casey smiled. "No, they won't go outta business, and I'll bet they were glad to get that seventy-five hundred. It's best that you paid the loan off and got your deed back. Now you're in the clear. Not only that, if you need to get a loan again in the future, you've got a good record of payin' off your debts."

"Well, I still have the loan to pay off with you and Eli," Grover reminded him. "And I'm sure hopin' we get the price we talked about for those cattle. I expect one of the things we need to talk about is how long I've got before that loan is due." He paused, then said, "How long have I got?"

Before answering, Casey glanced at Eli, who met his glance

and shrugged. Back to Grover then, Casey said, "What you've got, Grover, is what they call a hundred-year loan."

"A what?"

"A hundred-year loan," Casey repeated. "You've got to pay it in full in a hundred years. If you can't pay it off in a hundred years, you'll have to renew it for another hundred years."

Grover's reaction was the opposite of the one they expected. "Oh, well, now, I don't know what's going on here." He was confused, to say the least. "You're talkin' like that loan was free, and I know better'n that. There ain't no free loans in this life. I 'preciate the loan, but I'd 'preciate it more if you boys would just be straight with me, and I'll do the best I can to work with you."

"I swear, Grover" was all Casey could say at the moment. "Eli, you wanna be straight with Grover?"

"I'll try," Eli said. "Grover, that weren't no loan we gave you. I mean it was a loan to be paid back, if you spent it on whiskey, wild women, and gamblin'. But you spent it to pay off a mortgage so your wife and family would still have their home. So you don't have to pay us back. The money you make when you sell your cattle is all yours. And we're hopin' you'll use it to start buildin' your ranch back. Now do you understand?"

Grover was in shock. He couldn't form words for a long period until he finally mumbled, "You *gave* me the money . . ." While he stared at them, a big tear in each eye bubbled up and slid slowly down his cheeks.

"Ah, hell! I'm gittin' outta here if you're gonna start that," Eli declared. "We gave you the money, done and done. Let's get on to other things."

Grover wiped his tears away with his shirtsleeves. "I'm sorry. I couldn't help it. You said somethin' about some other things you wanted to talk to me about." It was obvious that he was still fighting with his emotions.

"Oh, yeah," Casey said. "We're expectin' Gary Corbett to show up here any day now. I think we told you about Corbett. We've hired him to lead this cattle drive, since Eli and I will be ridin' on ahead. Like you, he owns a ranch that suffered from the market goin' upside down. But he's pushed a few big herds up that trail before, so we hired him to take ours to market. He's the trail boss, and you're goin' along as just another hand, even though some of the cattle on this drive belong to you. So he'll be givin' the orders. Are you okay with that?"

"Like I told you when we made this deal, I'm just another hand. I'll try not to do anything to cause him any problem. As long as he stays in his place as trail boss, I'll stay in mine as a cowhand. But I won't allow any man to lay his hands on me or my son Billy without makin' him pay for it."

"Understood," Casey said.

Grover couldn't suppress a grin then. "After what you've told me tonight, though, it would have to be somethin' really bad."

The two owners of the D&T Cattle Company returned to the everyday business of getting their cattle ready for the long drive to the Kansas market. As they expected, Gary Corbett showed up one evening, ready to go to work. The last information that Casey had on the cattle markets had persuaded him and Eli to pick Dodge City as their destination. Their plan was to start out with that intention. Corbett was well familiar with the route they picked. They would cross the Red River into Oklahoma Indian Territory at Red River Station and follow the old Chisholm Trail north, just like their last cattle drive. But instead of continuing on to Abilene or Wichita, they would leave the trail and drive west to Dodge City, which had become the more active market. They were handicapped by the fact that the D&T was not close to a town or a telegraph to provide them with up-to-date prices for cattle. For this reason, they planned to ride out ahead of the herd in an effort to find where their best market was, and then ride back to direct the herd to that market. They emphasized to Corbett the importance of following the established trails as near as possible, or they might never find them. "Don't worry," Corbett joked. "If we don't run into you by the time we get to Kansas, I'll go ahead and take 'em to Dodge City and sell 'em."

These were happy times for Frank Carter, the owner of Carter's Merchandise, for he was seeing a lot of the D&T crew, with the necessity for all the supplies needed for the cattle drive. Smiley George had to get his chuck wagon in shape to make the trip, with some work for the blacksmith as well. And then he had to purchase the supplies for the trip, to be carried in the wagon and the extra packhorses he took with it. There were several months' supplies purchased for Juanita and Miguel in addition. And it was all paid for with cash.

Finally the day came, and Gary Corbett led the point riders out and sent Smiley up ahead with his chuck wagon. After starting early that morning, it was later in the afternoon that the last of the big herd left the D&T Ranch. Casey and Eli remained at the ranch until after the young boys driving the remuda followed after the cattle. They planned to stay at the ranch that night and leave the next morning, knowing they could easily overtake the herd. The morale was high with all the men, with the possible exception of Monroe Kelly, their foreman. He commented to Casey that it didn't feel right to start another cattle drive without him and Eli along to set the standards. And Fort Worth was the place in Texas to find out what was going on in the cattle market. It was being referred to as "Cowtown" in recent years, with meatpacking companies having established processing plants there. But their prices were still inferior to the Kansas shippers who sent the cows east. Casey explained to him that it was necessary for him and Eli to scout the markets ahead of the herd. And in addition to that, they were required to meet with their unnamed politician investor to ensure the continuation of the money to operate the ranch. That would mean a trip to Fort Worth again, Casey told him. "We're damn lucky to have met with this fellow, and when he says come to see him, we don't wait."

"I understand," Monroe said. "It just don't seem right to start out with a big herd without you and Eli with us."

"Seems to me like the boys are takin' to you pretty good as foreman. Eli and I feel like we've got the best man for the job as foreman. You might learn a lot from Gary Corbett, enough to make you the trail boss next time."

"I 'preciate you sayin' that, Casey. I'll try not to let you down."

Chapter 15

They ate breakfast with Juanita and Miguel the next morning before starting out after the herd. After supper the night before, they had talked about the problem with Colton Gray, and the fact that the U.S. Marshal Service had evidently assigned him the exclusive duty of tracking them down. The young deputy seemed as tenacious as a bulldog. And even though they had come to be on a friendly basis with Colton, there were too many signs that he suspected the two of them as potential candidates for the roles of Elmer and Oscar. At this point, they had led him to believe that they were going to be on that cattle drive, which would mean they would be gone for three to four months, depending on conditions they met on the trail. On first thought, they felt secure in knowing they couldn't be suspected of anything unlawful in Texas that happened during that period. But on second thought, it might be worse for them when there were no robberies by Elmer and Oscar while they were absent. Worse still, if the old men pulled a robbery during that time in Oklahoma or Kansas. "Damned if we do, and damned if we don't," Eli had voiced it.

"What we need to do is commit a robbery in Texas while we're supposed to be in Kansas," Casey said.

They were still talking about it the next morning when

they started out after the herd. Up to now in their careers as a most successful team in surprise holdups, they had always targeted the businesses that preyed upon the helpless working man. They weren't comfortable picking on honest individual businesses, operated by fair-minded people. So, while they were supposedly out of the state, it was not going to be easy to target a business just for the sake of staging a robbery by the old men.

Riding at a leisurely pace, they caught up with the herd before the cattle were stopped for the second night. They rode along with them for the rest of the afternoon until the herd came to a creek and were stopped for the night. Corbett had scouted ahead and said there was no water ahead for ten miles and it would be dark by then, so best to stop at the creek. By the usual rule of the trail, the cows drank first, and the drovers drank any water they could find afterward. When no one was close enough to hear his sarcastic comment, Casey said to Eli, "I forgot how nice it was to drive cattle."

"Hey, Casey," young Davey Springer called to him when he rode by the creek where Casey was watering Smoke. "You and Eli gonna ride the rest of the way with us now?"

"'Fraid not, Davey. We'd sure like to, but we've gotta ride on up ahead to get to a meetin' in Fort Worth. We'll be seein' you farther up the trail."

They ate at the chuck wagon with the men and bedded down for the night after those men riding night herd rode out. Monroe came to the chuck wagon then, having taken a look at the herd to make sure everything was all right. He took a look at Casey and Eli's packs and commented, "Looks like you're carryin' everything you own in them packs."

"We need a lotta things," Eli answered him. "You'll find out when you own your ranch. Won't he, Casey?"

"I expect he will," Casey said. "It ain't the free and easy life of a cowhand. That's for sure."

When morning came, they didn't linger at the chuck wagon. They saddled their horses and rode out in front of the herd with Gary Corbett, and soon the point riders and the herd were out of sight. In answer to Eli's question, Corbett said everything looked to be coming along just fine. When they approached a ridge that appeared to have been struck by a lightning fire, Corbett said that he'd best go back and signal the point men to lead the cows more to the west to avoid the area of burned trees and shrubs. "Any idea when I can expect to see you two again?" he asked as he wheeled his horse around.

"That's hard to say," Casey answered him. "We're gonna ride on into Fort Worth for a meeting with the man who's backin' the D and T. Then we'll find out where to go to get some current pricing at the different railheads. Might be a while before we find out what we need to know. So you keep pointin' toward Dodge City, and we'll meet you before you get that far."

They watched him ride back to signal the herd, and just sat there for a few minutes, both men realizing they didn't know what their next move should be. Eli was the first to confess it. "I'll be doggoned if I know what the hell we oughta do next."

"Hell, I don't know, either," Casey said. "I expect the only way we're gonna find out how much we're gonna get for our cattle is to go to the railhead and find out."

"So I reckon we might just as well plan to sell 'em in Dodge City, like we told Corbett, for whatever their price is," Eli said. "It'll be better than what we could get in Fort Worth. That much we're sure of."

"While we've still got the time before the herd gets very far, I'd like to find out if anything has changed in the pricin' at Fort Worth," Casey said. "I ain't talkin' about goin' back to see ol' Bradshaw at the new south cattle pens. I think we oughta ride on into the old cattle pens at the central market. They mighta been payin' a higher price than that crook."

"That's a good idea," Eli said. "I'd like to go into Fort Worth, anyway. It's a lively town. You can find most anything you're looking for in Fort Worth."

"Whadda you really know about the town of Fort Worth?" Casey asked sarcastically. "I bet you ain't been in any part of it except Hell's Half Acre."

"I didn't know there was any other part of it besides *the Acre*," Eli said, referring to the third ward of the town, which was home to the biggest collection of saloons, dancehalls, and cathouses south of Dodge City, Kansas. It was an area designed to take the last cent a cowhand had before he started out with a herd to the Kansas market, as well as the last penny he might have managed to bring back home with him after the cattle were sold and he got his pay.

"Well, I expect we need to find something to do to occupy our time while we're waitin' for our cattle to be sold," Casey said. "But I would like to go into the civilized part of town, just in case there is some place to find out what cattle are sellin' for. Of course, I could go into town and do that by myself," he joked. "You're most likely wantin' to visit with Joy Black, as long as we're goin' right close to the Potluck Kitchen. Seems to me, I remember you was kinda sweet on her."

"I know you think you're bein' sarcastic," Eli replied. "But I have to admire a gal who knows when to keep her mouth shut. You know she knew that was us that blew up ol' Bradshaw's safe. She's a hefty little gal, but she ain't really fat. It's more muscle, and that little bit of hair on her upper lip ain't coarse like a man's. It's finer and more feminine."

"If you say so," Casey crowed. "Last time you talked about her, you said it'd be like matin' with a gorilla."

"We just hadn't looked close enough," Eli concluded. "But I reckon we'd best not stop and remind her and her brother we were there before."

"That's right. As sure as we did, Colton Gray would probably show up the next day and ask her what we was doin' there." So they decided to avoid the Potluck Kitchen and go into the town of Fort Worth.

They arrived at a quiet creek on the edge of the town two nights after leaving the herd in Gary Corbett's capable hands, and they decided to make camp there, and go into town in the morning. "One more night of beans and bacon," Casey said. "And in the mornin', we'll go find us a breakfast fittin' for two wealthy cattle ranchers."

The next morning found them saddled up and ready to go before any restaurants were open for breakfast, but they rode on into town, finding no trouble in locating the Union Stockyards Company. They decided they would go there and talk to someone about buying their cattle, just as they had done before with Birch Bradshaw. He might have been lying about other Fort Worth buyers. They were hoping they would also find out what the prices were in Dodge City, as well as in Abilene. Since it would be a while before the stockyards office would be open, the next order of business was breakfast. So they rode on into town. Neither man had been in the center of Fort Worth for quite some time, so they were rightfully surprised by the size of the town. There were now more streets running north and south. They remembered the Acre as mostly on the lower end of Rusk Street. But now, as they rode north toward the nicer part of town, it seemed the Acre had expanded greatly. They continued to pass saloons and obvious dancehalls, which were closed at this early time of the morning. The north boundary of the Acre appeared to be a large vacant lot, after which the businesses they passed seemed to be legitimate. They continued on until they came to a small building with a sign that said APPLETON'S. It was one of the few businesses that had a light on inside. They almost rode past, until they realized it was a restaurant. Casey pulled up and asked, "Whaddaya think?"

"Any of 'em we try is gonna be a gamble," Eli said. "And

they look like they're open." So they pulled their horses over to the hitching rail. After making sure their packhorses were far enough out of the street, they tried the door, for there was no OPEN or CLOSED sign on it. It was not locked, so they walked in. "You folks open for breakfast?" Eli asked a man standing in the kitchen doorway.

"We are now," he answered. "Come on in and take your pick of tables."

"We weren't sure," Casey said. "There ain't no sign on the door sayin' when you open."

Jim laughed. "We never have had a certain time to open. We just get here every morning and my wife, Doris, starts fixin' food. And when the first hungry customer shows up, we're open. My name's Jim Appleton and we're pleased to cook your breakfast. Yonder's the menu." He pointed to a blackboard on the wall.

"I'll try those two eggs with sausage and four pancakes," Casey said, and Eli ordered the same.

Jim went to get the coffeepot after they told him how they wanted their eggs. When he returned and filled their cups, he said, "This is your first time in Appleton's, so I told Doris to mind how she cooks those eggs. We want you to wanna come back."

"We just rode in this mornin'," Casey told him, "and this was the first place we saw. We're hopin' we'll wanna come back, too."

"If I had to guess, I'd say you boys are in the business of raising cattle," Jim said. "You waiting for the stockyard to open up?"

"As a matter of fact, we are," Casey answered. "You know what time they open up down there at the Union Stock Yards?"

"The office doesn't open for another hour, but there'll be men down at the cattle pens right now. If you've got cows waiting outside of town, you could drive them into the pens."

"It'll be a while before the herd catches up with us," Casey told him. "We need to talk to the man who does the buyin'."

"That'll be Joe Taylor," Jim said.

"You sure of that?"

"Pretty sure," Jim answered. "He oughta be showin' up any minute."

"At the office?"

"No, here," Jim said. "He eats breakfast here every day on his way to work." Doris came out of the kitchen with their breakfasts, placed them on the table, then pulled a bottle of syrup out of her apron pocket and put it on the table. "They're waiting to see Joe Taylor, hon," Jim said.

"Well, here he comes now," she said, and nodded toward the door. She looked at Casey and Eli and said, "Now don't you let your breakfast get cold." Responding to her voice of authority, they both immediately went to work with the salt and pepper and the butter from the dish she slid toward them on the table.

"Mornin'," Joe Taylor said when he walked inside, his greeting obviously aimed in Jim and Doris's direction.

"Good morning, Joe," they both returned, almost in unison.

Casey gave Eli a quick wink, then said, "Good mornin', Mr. Taylor."

Taylor was obviously surprised and more than a little curious as he looked from Casey to Eli, then back again to Casey. "Mornin'," he replied briefly, then walked past them to another table. "I'll have the usual, Doris," he said to her. She went at once to the kitchen.

"These two fellows are waiting to go to your office to see you this morning," Jim said as he filled a cup of coffee for him.

"Is that a fact?" Taylor replied, and turned his attention to them. "What about?"

"We were interested in what your company is payin' for cows now," Casey answered him. "We've got some to sell."

"Oh, I see, well, you don't have to come to my office for that. You can just take them to our pens and there's a fellow down there that'll pay you two dollars a head for them." Hoping that answered Casey's question, he turned his attention back to his coffee.

"I'm afraid it ain't gonna be as easy as that," Casey said.

"Why is that? How many have you got?"

"About three hundred and fifty better'n three thousand," Casey answered.

"Three thousand!" Taylor exclaimed. "Where are they?" He was afraid they were standing outside the stockyard somewhere. " 'Three thousand'!" he repeated. "Why didn't you say so?"

"I just did," Casey replied calmly. "They're a few days behind us. We wouldn't bring 'em in before we had an understanding. But we didn't have any intention of interruptin' your breakfast. In fact, we had no idea we'd meet you here. We can wait till you're ready to do business."

"No, not at all. Talkin' business never bothered my appetite. Why don't I join you at your table? Would you mind?" When they both said not at all, he brought his coffee over to sit with them. When he was settled, he said, "You know my name's Joe Taylor. Who am I talkin' to?"

"Casey Tubbs and Eli Doolin," Casey answered. "We are the owners of D and T Cattle Company down in Lampasas County." They all shook hands. "And we've got a herd already movin' this way. We're just talkin' to you to see if this is as far as they go, or if they keep movin' on up the Chisholm Trail."

"Well, that shouldn't be hard to decide," Taylor said. "For a herd the size of the one you're drivin', I'm authorized to give you eight dollars a head, which would save you a helluva lot of money over drivin' them all the way up there to a folding market."

"Maybe you haven't gotten the latest figures from up that way," Casey disagreed politely. "The figures I received from a contact up in Dodge City said the market had rebounded to the tune of thirty dollars a head. And that's gettin' back up toward that old price of forty dollars."

"I have to beg to differ with you on that," Taylor insisted. "I get the latest figures from all the markets. And as of yesterday, Dodge City paid twenty dollars a head for a herd of two thousand cows. So that's only half what they paid before the market went busted. And I know that sounds like a helluva lot more than the eight dollars I'm offerin'. But I can guarantee that price for your cattle as soon as you get 'em here. Who knows what Dodge City's price will be by the time you drive that herd up there? And maybe you heard, the farmers up in Kansas have gotten the government to close the upper part of that trail, so you'd have to go farther west, instead of goin' to Abilene or Wichita. That kinda leaves you with Dodge City as your only choice, for however long that holds up." He paused to let Doris put his plate on the table. He thanked her; then when she left, he concluded his pitch. "It's as simple as this. What I'm offering is a solid, guaranteed price for your cattle today that will save you the cost and the risk of driving them five hundred miles or more, with the possibility the prices might have dropped to what I'm offerin' right now."

"You make one helluva argument to sell our cows right here," Casey said when Taylor finally paused to start on his eggs. "You gave me and Eli something to think about. We 'preciate it and we'll talk it over, but if we don't let you eat your breakfast, I'm afraid Doris is gonna run us outta here."

Taylor chuckled and replied, "You might be right about that. You think it over." He returned his attention to his eggs, while Casey and Eli finished up their breakfast.

Casey glanced in Eli's direction when he had finished eating, and Eli nodded that he was finished as well. So they got up from the table and Casey said, "We'll let you finish your breakfast in peace, Mr. Taylor. It was a pleasure meetin' you, and we 'preciate the information you gave us."

"The pleasure was all mine," Taylor said. "You think about the time and money you could save right here with that herd."

"We'll do that," Casey said. Then he called back to Doris in the kitchen, "That was a mighty fine breakfast, ma'am!"

Eli was waiting for him at the cash register, where he was paying Jim for their breakfast. "We'd like to pay for Mr. Taylor's breakfast, too," Eli said, and handed him a dollar bill.

"I'm sure he'll appreciate that," Jim said, and gave him a quarter in change.

They walked outside just as a couple of men were coming in. "Look what we started," Casey cracked.

"You owe me a dollar," Eli replied.

"I'll leave it to ya in my will," Casey said. They untied their horses, but paused a moment before stepping up into the saddle. "I swear, that was a lucky coincidence that brought us here to eat. Not only the food was good, but we found out what the pricin' is in Dodge City. I was expectin' to have to search all over this town to find the place to find what the market was north of here."

"Reckon what we oughta do now?" Eli wondered. "We've got a couple of months to kill, and I can't think of something to do to kill the rest of this day."

"As long as we're already here, I think we might as well hang around for a day or two and see what's here now. We might find some place that could use a visit from Oscar and Elmer. Whaddaya say we check into the hotel and put these packhorses in a stable? Then we'll look the town over, and maybe go back down to the Acre to see how bad it really is."

"I swear," Eli commented, "knowin' you like I do, I'da thought you'd wanna go back and meet the herd and help drive 'em up to Dodge."

"Is that so?" Casey responded. "Well, I think I've earned a vacation, but you go on back to the herd if your conscience is hurtin' you."

"Hell, I have to keep my eye on you to keep you outta trouble, especially if we're plannin' to pay Hell's Half Acre a visit."

"Well, let's go check on that hotel on the corner and see if we can get a room for tonight," Casey said. They climbed on their horses and rode the short two blocks to a square two-story building with a sign over the door: WOODWARD HOUSE HOTEL. "It ain't a very big one, is it?" Casey remarked after they dismounted and tied their horses to a rail fence that went around the entire lot the hotel sat on.

"Looks more like a great big boardin'house," Eli said. "They might not rent rooms for one night or two."

"The sign says they're a hotel. Let's go in and find out." They walked the short walkway and climbed three steps to a wide porch, complete with several rocking chairs. "That suits my style right there," Casey said, referring to the rocking chairs.

"That don't sound like a man who was talkin' about goin' to the Acre later on," Eli said, and held the front door open for him. "After you, old man."

They walked in, expecting to find a parlor, instead of the small registration desk in the center of the hall, although there was a parlor of sorts set off behind the desk. There was a stairway leading up from the back of the parlor. Finding no one in attendance, Eli rang a tiny bell sitting on the desk, with a sign that said RING FOR SERVICE.

In a few minutes, a slender woman with dark hair, wearing an apron over her black dress, came down the stairs to greet them. "Good morning, gentlemen. I hope I didn't keep you waiting long. I was upstairs helping Rose clean up a bedroom at the back of the house, and it's hard to hear that little bell up there."

"No, ma'am," Casey responded. "We didn't wait long a-tall. "We're not in a hurry, anyway, are we, Eli?"

"If you've come to eat breakfast, we're not quite ready to serve it," she said, "but it won't be but about twenty minutes from now."

"Thank you, ma'am," Casey said, "but we've already had breakfast." She looked surprised, so he went on to explain that they had just ridden into town and saw Appleton's open, so they ate there.

"I hear the food there is very good," the woman said.

"Yes, ma'am, it was good. We saw your sign that said you were a hotel, and that's why we stopped in. We were lookin' for a room for one or two nights. But it looks like you're more of a boardin' house."

"Oh, no, we're a hotel," she quickly replied. "We have vacant rooms we rent by the night, but you're right, most of our customers stay on here at a monthly rate. It's just that we're more like a family than a large hotel. We have three vacant rooms right now. If you're interested, I'd be glad to show them to you."

Casey glanced at Eli, and Eli shrugged indifferently, so he said, "Yes, ma'am, let's take a look at 'em."

"Just follow me," she said, and started toward the stairs. "My name's Emma Woodward, I'm the owner," she spoke back over her shoulder.

"I'm Casey Tubbs and he's Eli Doolin. We're pleased to make your acquaintance. We ain't used to gettin' personal attention like this in a regular hotel."

"Every one of our rooms has a window," Emma told them as she led them down the hall, "except for the two small rooms at the end." She stopped at a door and opened it. "This is one of the rooms, and the room next door is just like it." As she said it, the door opened and a young girl came out, carrying a broom and a bucket filled with cleaning implements.

"This is Rose. She does most of the hard work around here. Rose, is that room ready to rent now?"

"Yes, ma'am," Rose answered, and scurried away.

"Rose is an excellent worker," Emma said. "I don't know what we'd do without her." She got back to business then. "These two rooms are just alike. The only difference is this one has a striped quilt on top. The other has a plaid one."

"What are you askin' for rent?" Eli asked, thinking Casey wasn't ever going to get around to it.

"For these rooms for a single night, we charge one dollar, single occupancy. For two people in the room, we charge an extra fifty cents."

"That bed ain't big enough to hold two grown men," Casey said at once. "We'll take both rooms, and we'll pay you for two nights, since we ain't sure how long we'll be here. Is that all right?"

"Oh, yes, sir," Emma replied. "That'll be just fine. We'll go back downstairs and I'll show you the dining room and the washroom." They followed her back down to the first floor and into the dining room, where a huge table was set for breakfast. She explained that meals could be singularly purchased, or you could pay a monthly rate for all three meals. They told her they would take the pay-as-you-go plan, since they had no idea where they might be at mealtime while they were in town. They paid her in advance for the two rooms and she gave them keys to the bedroom doors.

"We're gonna go ahead and take some things off our packhorses and leave them in our rooms," Casey told her. "Then we'll take 'em to the stable to keep while we're in town."

"That'll be just fine," she said.

"Where is the closest stable from here?" Eli asked.

"All the way out to the end of the street beside our hotel," Emma told him. "It's owned by Donald Plunket. He will take good care of your horses and treat you right on the price. He was a good friend of my late husband."

"That sounds like the place we want," Eli said. "You say it's all the way out to the end of that street. How long a walk is it after we leave him our saddle horses tonight?"

She laughed. "That street's not but three blocks long."

"What time do you serve dinner?" Casey asked. "If we're in this part of town at dinnertime, we might just come see what kind of cook you've got workin' for you."

Emma laughed again. "I think Pearl would welcome the challenge. She's been with us ever since my husband opened this place up. You see those little folded tables over in the corner? They're used to seat the extra supper customers that can't find a place at the table."

"Is that a fact?" Casey replied. "Now I know we're gonna have to eat here, Eli."

"Dinner's at twelve noon every day, but Sunday dinner's at one o'clock."

Chapter 16

With their makeup and disguises, as well as quite a quantity of cash money off their packhorses and stowed in their rooms, Casey and Eli rode to the stable at the end of the street. Seeing no one around, they dismounted and walked into the stable and looked around. Still seeing no one, Eli called out. "Mr. Plunket?"

"Be right with you," he answered the call.

"He's in the barn," Eli said, so they walked through the line of stalls and went into the barn. Seeing a pole extending from the floor joists of the hayloft to the floor of the barn, they walked over to it, thinking it had no useful purpose in the structure of the barn. Still, no Plunket. Eli started to call out again. But all of a sudden, he appeared between them, landing nimbly on two bowlegs with a thud, like some figure out of a fairy tale. Startled, both Eli and Casey jumped backward with hands reaching for their six-shooters.

"Hold on!" Plunket exclaimed. "I didn't go to scare ya!"

"What the hell . . . ?" Eli blurted. "You tryin' to get yourself shot?"

"I didn't look before I leaped," Plunket said with a grin. "But you fellers was standin' right under my trap. I was in the hayloft, and when I wanna get down real quick, I slide down this pole." He gave the pole a pat with his hands. "I saw you fellers ride up to the stable, so I wanted to get down as quick as I could. I'm sorry if I gave you a start. What can I do for you?"

"We're in town for a day or two," Casey explained. "We took rooms at Emma Woodward's hotel, and she said this was the best place to leave our horses. She didn't say nothin' about you jumpin' outta the hayloft like a June bug, though." He paused for the chuckle, then went on to say they wanted to leave their packhorses now and bring their saddle horses later for the night. "She said you and her late husband were good friends."

"She's right," Plunket said. "Jake Woodward was my best friend all my life. It was like losin' my brother when he took sick and died."

"How long ago was that?" Eli asked.

"Oh, Lord, lemme see." He took a couple of minutes to try to figure it out. "I don't remember exactly, but it's been about eight or nine years now." He shook his head slowly back and forth as he thought back. "Seemed like there weren't nobody straighter and stronger than Jake, and then he just took sick and died. Doc said it was the pneumonia that took him. It was right after he built that hotel."

"Musta been awful hard on his wife," Casey said.

"I'll say it was," Plunket declared. "But I'll tell you one thing. I ain't never admired anybody, man or woman, as much as I admire that lady for takin' that hotel and makin' it work, just like Robert wanted it to. And it's all them three women that's made a success out of it, Emma, Pearl, and Pearl's daughter, Rose. It still ain't easy for 'em. They're havin' some tough times, but there ain't no give-up in 'em."

"Whaddaya mean by 'tough times'?" Casey asked, finding the story interesting.

"Oh, you know, money problems, and the bank ain't really givin' her no help. She had to rebuild that whole back washroom behind the kitchen and have a deeper well dug, so she had to borrow money from the bank." As soon as Plunket said "bank," Eli immediately became alert. He tried to catch Casey's attention, but it was too late. Casey was already into the story too deep. *Now all we need to know is the name of the bank*, Eli thought.

"What's the name of the bank?" Casey asked right on schedule.

"Fort Worth Investment Bank," Plunket said. It was obvious to Eli that Plunket had become just as passionate in the relating of the story as Casey had become in hearing it. "You see, there's more goin' on with the bank and that loan than meets the eye," Plunket continued. "Emma told me that she's makin' her monthly payments on that loan right on time, just like she agreed to when they gave her the loan. That's a valuable piece of property on that corner, and there ain't no doubt there's some big businesses that would like to make a deal with the bank and tear that little hotel down."

"But if she would pay the loan off in full, that would make her problem go away. Is that right?"

"I reckon so," Plunket answered. "I ain't got no idea how much it would take to pay it off, though. Whatever it is, Emma ain't got it in a lump sum."

"The First Fort Worth Investment Bank," Casey pronounced.

"Yeah," Plunket replied. "The only reason she went there was because it's the closest one to her. Jake never did no bankin' with them."

"I expect we might as well leave our packhorses here, since that's the reason we rode over here," Eli finally interrupted the discussion about Emma Woodward's hard luck.

"Yes, sir," Plunket said at once. "I'll take care of 'em for ya. You can just leave your packs in a stall and we'll turn the horses out in the corral for now."

"That sounds like a good idea," Eli said, still trying to move Casey off the subject of bank loans. "I expect Mr. Plunket is anxious to get back to whatever he was doin' in the hayloft before we interrupted him." He met Casey's look of amusement and added, "Unless you wanna wait to see him slide back up that pole."

The remark brought a chuckle from Plunket, and he said, "I ain't got to where I can slide back up it. I still have to climb the ladder if I wanna go up to the hayloft."

After leaving the packhorses, they slow-walked Smoke and Biscuit side by side while they talked. "Looks like we've picked out the next place Elmer and Oscar are gonna make a visit," Eli remarked. "I expect we'd best go take a look at it."

"Yep," Casey replied, "I expect we'd better. I would have asked Plunket where it was, but I didn't want to seem too interested in it."

"Oh, I could see that," Eli remarked sarcastically.

"Well, we already decided we needed to have Elmer and Oscar pull another job while we're drivin' the herd north," Casey said in defense. "Plunket just made it a helluva lot easier to decide who deserves a visit."

"I reckon," Eli agreed. "I hope they ain't a big bank with a whole lotta people workin' there." He knew Casey was in agreement with that. The more people there were, the more the chance somebody might get shot.

"Plunket said it was the closest bank to Emma's hotel," Casey recalled. "The hotel's just one block over from the main street. Maybe that bank's on the main street." Eli agreed, so that's where they headed.

The Fort Worth Investment Bank was not hard to find. In

fact, it stood out with a gleaming white façade built to look like a Southern plantation house. In contrast, it dwarfed the businesses on either side of it, a barber's and a dress shop. "It looks kinda high-falutin', don't it?" Eli remarked. "You reckon it's too high class for the likes of Elmer and Oscar?"

"I reckon we'll find out when we go in and look around," Casey answered. "I'd like to know how much Emma owes. It can't be all that much, judgin' by the work Plunket said she had done to the hotel, and she's been payin' it off right regular, he said. It might be that we've got enough cash with us to pay off her debt. Then we could wait awhile before we hit that bank. That way, Colton and his fellow deputies will think we're in Oklahoma or Kansas somewhere." That made sense to Eli, and he was sure they had enough money to pay off any loan Emma might have for repair work on her hotel.

They tied the horses up in front of the bank and walked through the entrance door, which had narrow glass panels on each side of it. Inside, they found themselves in a large lobby with several groupings of easy chairs, which were unoccupied. They figured it must be because it was still morning, and the bank had just opened. "You reckon their customers come around later to sit around and visit?" Eli asked.

"I'll bet don't nobody ever set in 'em," Casey answered.

There were three cages for tellers, but there was only one of them occupied. He looked up when they walked in and smiled expectantly at them. So Casey walked on up to the cage and said, "Good mornin'."

"Good morning, sir," the teller returned. "How can I help you?"

"I just need to break a hundred," Casey replied.

"Do you have an account with us?"

"No. No, I don't," Casey said. "You see, me and my partner just rode into town this mornin', and I'm afraid I can't buy a blame thing with this hundred-dollar bill 'cause nobody's got change for it. I promised that nice fellow at Appleton's that I'd be right back to pay him for breakfast. Here you take a look at it. It's a real genuine hundred-dollar bill. Problem is, I can't spend it 'cause nobody's got any change for it," he repeated. While he talked to the teller, Eli looked around him to take in as much as he could.

"I'm sorry, sir," the teller told Casey. "We don't make change unless you have an account with us."

"Well, like I said," Casey went on, "we're just passin' through town, so it wouldn't make much sense to open an account. I ain't really askin' for nothin' but swappin' some real money for the same amount of real money in smaller bills. Don't see how the bank could lose on that deal."

"I'm not supposed to do that," the teller said. "Wait right here and I'll go ask Mr. Polk to talk to you."

"Much obliged," Casey said. The teller backed out of his cage and hurried across the lobby to the manager's office. While he was gone, a man walked in the front door and got in line behind Casey. Casey turned and said, "He'll be right back. He's gone to get Mr. Polk." The man nodded. Casey looked around to discover Eli sitting in one of the leather easy chairs. In a moment, the teller came out of the manager's office, with the manager behind him. The teller motioned for Casey to come to them.

"Mr. Polk will take care of you," the teller told him, then went back to his cage to accommodate the man waiting.

"I'm Edwin Polk. Julian said you had a problem."

"Robert White, Mr. Polk. First of all, let me say that Julian didn't cause me no problem. He was as polite as he could be. It's this hundred-dollar bill that's causin' the problem." He then repeated the story he had told the teller, and as he had with Julian, he handed the bill to Polk for him to examine.

Polk listened politely before he responded. "Julian was correct in telling you it's not the bank's policy to perform services for anyone who does not have an account with the bank. I know you say you are just passing through town today, but for an insignificant fee of five dollars you could open an account. And take advantage of these services anytime you're passing through Fort Worth."

Casey paused and nodded his head thoughtfully, as if he was giving it serious thought. After a few moments, he said, "We've never had to pay a bank to open an account. We've got bank accounts in Waco and San Antonio. I don't recall ever payin' to open 'em. They just all seemed happy to handle our money." He smiled and said, "I'll talk to my partner about it. Might be a good idea to have a bank right here to deposit the money for that herd of cattle we're bringing in next week. We talked about it before."

He turned to leave, but Polk stopped him. "Wait just a minute and I'll change that hundred for you." He held out his hand.

"Well, that's mighty neighborly of you," Casey said, and handed him the bill. "I'm obliged."

"When you make up your mind about a bank to work with in Fort Worth, I just hope you'll remember we'd be honored to serve you."

"I'll surely remember that," Casey said, and followed him back to the teller cage.

Polk handed the hundred to Julian. "Break this up for Mr. White." He looked at Casey and asked, "Tens and twenties okay?"

"That'll be perfect," Casey answered. Then while Julian was counting out the money, Casey said to Polk, "I reckon you have a good safe room with a time lock and everything."

"Yes, indeed," Polk replied. "We have a safe with a time

lock that doesn't open until twelve noon. And it's in our safe room, which was built with reinforced walls and a door of iron bars, just like those in the jailhouse."

"Is that a fact?" Casey responded. "How do you handle all your transactions if your safe don't open till noon?"

"We keep enough money to operate on in the safe room for ordinary business," Polk told him. "Would you like to see it?"

"I don't wanna take up any more of your time, but it would be kind of interestin'. You sure it wouldn't be too much trouble right now?"

"No trouble at all," Polk insisted. He took the little stack of bills from Julian and counted them out for Casey. "Now just follow me." He led him through a door to a back room and Casey could see the door to the safe room. As Polk had described it, it resembled a door to a jail cell. "You can see the big safe in the back of the room. I have the key to the door, but I can't open the safe until the time lock releases it."

Casey nodded his head and said, "You've convinced me. The money looks pretty safe in here to me."

Polk walked back to the lobby with Casey. Eli got up from his chair when he saw them coming. "Mr. Polk," Casey said, "this is my brother, Tom. Tom, meet Mr. Edwin Polk." Eli shook his hand.

"Oh," Polk said, "you didn't tell me your partner was your brother."

"He don't like the word to get around," Eli said, and chuckled. "Come on, Bob, and let's let the man get back to work."

Polk walked them to the door. "I hope you'll remember us when you bring that herd into the stockyard. We work with a lot of the larger companies in Fort Worth."

"I promise you, we'll remember Fort Worth Investment Bank," Casey said.

Polk stood at the door for a few seconds longer, watching

the two men get on their horses. "Bob White," he murmured to himself. "I wonder if he was putting me on . . . Nah, that would be too obvious. I bet he catches a lot of grief over his name."

They spent much of the remaining morning just taking a look at Fort Worth. It had grown so much since either man had been in the center of town that they couldn't find old places they had visited before. They realized that in years past, when they were on a cattle drive, Fort Worth to them was only Hell's Half Acre and the last chance to spend any money they had before starting on the Chisholm Trail. Now there was a dignified part of town that cut themselves off from the rowdy trash that frequented the Acre.

When it was approaching noon, they made it a point to start back to the Woodward House Hotel with the intention of having a good dinner, but also to find out more about Emma Woodward's loan to the bank. "Well, I'm glad to see you came back to eat with us, gentlemen," Emma greeted them when they walked in the door.

"No, ma'am," Eli said, "we had to come back here to call your bluff on Pearl's cookin'."

Emma laughed, delighted. "You're lucky I didn't wanna lay down any bets on it. Ain't that right, Walt?"

"She's right, boys," Walt said. "Ain't nobody in Fort Worth can touch Pearl Pigeon's cookin'." He walked on into the dining room. "That's why I'm always on time for dinner. I stopped here two years ago just to try out the cookin'. After that dinner, I left the boardin'house I'd been livin' at for eight years and moved in here." He stuck his hand out. "Walt Evans is my name. You boys movin' in?"

"Nope," Casey told him. "We're just here for a night or two to check out the market prices on cattle. We've got a herd a few days behind us, and we've gotta decide what's best to do, sell 'em here or drive 'em north."

"I hear the trails north, like the Chisholm, are gittin' pushed farther west," Walt said. "They say the Kansas farmers have protested so much that they got the government behind 'em to keep Texas cattle from ruinin' their crops and eatin' all the grass."

"You heard the truth," Casey said, "but right now, there are still some markets we can get to. So that's what we're gonna do this year. Next year, we'll just have to wait and see."

"What line of work are you in, Walt?" Eli asked. He had been studying the man, and decided he was a man who worked with his hands.

"I'm a farrier," Walt answered. "I shoe horses," he added, in case they didn't know the term, even though they were evidently cowhands.

"Now, ain't that something, Casey? Seems like everything we need we find at this hotel." He turned his attention back to Walt. "We got four horses with us that need lookin' at, and two of 'em, for sure, need new shoes."

They were interrupted briefly when Pearl and Rose came from the kitchen carrying serving bowls. "Set yourselves down," Emma said to those who were still standing around. Casey and Eli found places on either side of Walt Evans.

"You know where you took your packhorses to the stable," Walt continued, eager to get the business. "Well, my shop is on the same side of the road, just before you get to Plunket's. Be glad to take a look at your horses."

"How 'bout right after dinner?" Eli asked.

"That's as good a time as any," Walt answered. "We'll do it."

The dinner was every bit as good as Walt advertised, and Pearl was serving one of Casey's favorites, pork chops. He and Eli visited with some of the other regulars at the table, exchanging names and forgetting them immediately. For dessert, Pearl baked a dried-apple pie that Casey liked so much he asked for the recipe to give to Juanita. There was coffee enough to have another cup after all the food was gone. Casey promised himself he would make sure the bank never closed this little hotel down. When it was over, he and Eli were happy to pay the extremely fair price Emma was asking. They complimented Pearl on the cooking and told Emma she should raise her prices.

After dinner, they walked with Walt back to his shop, leading their horses. When they got there, they remembered passing it that morning and thinking it was a blacksmith's forge. They found out that Walt was a farrier by trade and a blacksmith by chance. They found him to be an honest man, for they knew their horses were not quite ready for new shoes. Walt told them as much after he looked at them. "They're showin' signs of wear, but they ain't really in bad shape. You can wait a while yet before they need 'em."

"I'll tell you what we were concerned about," Casey told him. "In a few days, that herd is gonna catch up with us, and we're gonna start on a five-hundred-mile drive to Dodge City. There ain't no tellin' when we'll come across a farrier on the Chisholm Trail."

"Ain't you got nobody on your crew who can shoe a horse?" Walt asked.

"Yeah, but not like I suspect you can do the job, and I'd like to at least start out with brand-new shoes on my horse." What he didn't tell him was that he and Eli wanted to have that time to talk about the bank loan on Emma's hotel. And they suspected that all of the old regulars at the hotel probably knew the exact amount to be paid off.

Walt got his tools and started right away on Smoke, and Casey threw out the bait. "Like we said at the table, we're findin' everything we need right there at Emma's place. We rode by a bank, just over on the next street from her hotel. What was the name of it, Eli?" They noticed a slight hesitation of Walt's hand, but he kept on working on Smoke's hoof.

"I think it was called the Fort Worth Investment Bank," Eli answered. That was enough to halt Walt's hand completely.

"Don't mess with that bank," he said. "There's a couple of other banks that ain't too far from here. You strike me as two honest fellows, so I wouldn't feel right if I didn't warn you to stay away from that bank. They'll cheat you any way they can."

"What makes you say that?" Casey asked. "We stopped in there and talked to a fellow named Edwin Polk. He seemed like a nice enough fellow."

"He's a snake," Walt said.

"Well, I'll be . . ." Casey started. "What makes you say that?"

"It ain't my place to talk about it, but he's the sorry dog that's tryin' to foreclose on Emma over a measly three thousand dollars, after she's been payin' it off right on the due date accordin' to her loan, except for one time when the date fell on a Sunday. The bank was closed, so she paid it on Monday. That snake, Polk, told her the bank is filing to take over the property if she don't pay them the final three thousand by the end of this month."

"*Three thousand*, huh?" Casey emphasized, and looked at Eli, who nodded in return. Back to Walt then, he asked, "You sure that would take it outta the bank's hands?"

"Yeah, Emma went to a lawyer with her copy of the loan agreement. That cost her twenty-five dollars. Anyway, the lawyer read through the whole agreement and said the bank could take the property. They wrote the agreement up to say, if she was late makin' her payments, they could demand the full balance in one payment, and if she didn't do that, they could take the property. He said she shoulda had a lawyer read it before she signed it." He picked up the file he had dropped in his exasperation and began working on Smoke's hoof again. "Listen, fellows, I had no business runnin' my mouth about Emma's private business. I reckon I can't help myself when it comes to what that snake is doin' to that fine lady. If I had the money, I'd give it to her."

"I can understand how you feel," Casey said. "You don't have to worry about me or Eli repeatin' what you've told us. And we need to thank you for tippin' us off about that bank. Believe me, we won't set foot in it again." *But Oscar and Elmer will pay them a visit*, he thought. "I can't believe that could be a legal agreement."

"Me neither," Walt replied. "But Emma didn't know no better and she signed it."

When Walt finished shoeing Smoke and Biscuit, Casey told him he could go over to the stable and take a look at their packhorses. "You want us to pay you for these two horses now?"

"You gonna be back at the hotel for supper?" Walt asked. Casey said they planned to, so Walt told him they could just wait and pay him for all four horses. He grinned and commented, "'Course, you'd have to trust me to tell you the truth about your packhorses."

"I reckon we'll have to trust you," Casey said. He wasn't sure what Eli wanted to do, but he didn't particularly want to hang around any longer watching Walt shoe their horses. "What time is supper?" he asked. "I don't wanna miss it." Walt told him they ate at five o'clock. "Good, we'll settle up then." Then remembering he had a partner, he asked, "Is that all right with you, Eli?"

"That suits me just fine," Eli answered. Like Casey, he

preferred to pass the time somewhere else, now that Walt had volunteered all the information they needed about Emma's debt. Maybe a saloon for a drink of rye whiskey would be one way to pass the time. "That'll give us a little time to see what Biscuit and Smoke think about their new shoes."

"You let me know if there's any problem and I'll fix it," Walt said.

Chapter 17

Eli's suggestion to drop by a saloon for a drink of whiskey was met with a favorable reception from Casey. They had plenty of money with them to take care of her problem, so they could now concentrate on the planning of the return visit to the Fort Worth Investment Bank. Just for the hell of it, they decided to ride back down into the Acre and pick a saloon there. Even though the area had expanded since their earlier days as cowhands, they wondered if they could still find one of the saloons they had visited during that time. They rode up one street, then down the next, passing several saloons and dancehalls, but none they remembered. "Hell, let's just pick one," Eli said. "We keep this up, we'll be late for supper."

"How 'bout the Wrangler's?" Casey suggested.

"How 'bout the one across the street from it?" Eli countered.

" 'The Ace Of Spades,' " Casey read the sign. "That ain't a saloon. That's a dancehall."

"That don't make no difference. They all sell whiskey, and we might as well have something to look at while we're havin' a drink."

"It's a little bit too early for much to be goin' on in a dancehall," Casey said. "I don't hear no music, so I doubt you're gonna have anything to look at."

"Least, they'll have some tables and chairs to set down on while we're havin' a drink," Eli persisted.

"All right, we'll try the Ace Of Spades," Casey said, knowing that Eli always liked to look at the women, fair or otherwise. So they tied their horses at the hitching rail and walked into the dark dancehall, pausing at the door to let their eyes adjust to the dim interior. There was a small platform near the center of the wall opposite the bar with a couple of chairs on it, but there were no musicians. At the end of the bar, there was a collection of tables with a few people sitting there. Two women, somewhat past the bloom of spring, were talking at the bar, but there was no bartender. "Hell, let's try the saloon across the street," Casey suggested.

Eli wasn't ready to abandon the dancehall yet. "As long as we're already here, let's see if we can get a drink of likker." He walked over to the bar, giving Casey no choice but to follow.

The two women at the bar stopped talking to look them over. Then one of them yelled, "Hey, 'Curly,' you got customers at the bar!"

A couple of minutes later, a small, bald man hurried out of a door near the tables and came behind the bar. "Yes, sir, gents, sorry to make you wait. Whaddle it be?"

"A shot of rye for me and a shot of corn for him," Eli answered. Curly poured the drinks, and Eli held his up to toast. "Here's to keepin' the snake outta Emma's hotel," he said.

"I'll drink to that," Casey said with a smile, and they tossed them back.

"I believe it's gonna take more than that one," Eli said as he slid his empty glass toward the bartender. "Come on, Casey, keep up." Casey followed suit.

The two women suspended their conversation while they watched the two strangers. And when Casey put a dollar on the bar to pay for the four drinks, one of the women moved up the bar to stand next to him. "How about buyin' a drink for a lady, handsome?"

"Why, sure," Casey replied. "I'd be proud to buy you a drink. Curly, pour the lady a drink. Pour her friend one, too." The other woman moved up to join them. "Rye or corn?" Casey asked her, but Curly didn't wait. He poured her a drink of corn whiskey, the same as he did for her friend.

"What time does the dancin' usually start?" Eli asked Curly.

"Just whenever there's enough people who wanna dance," Curly answered. "That don't usually happen till later on, closer to suppertime. But the two musicians are settin' at one of them tables in the corner. One of 'em's got a guitar, the other'n's got a fiddle. Was you fellers wantin' to dance?"

"No sirree," Eli said. "I was just wantin' to watch."

"I reckon for a little money, you could get them boys to tune up their instruments, and you could pay some of the gals to dance for ya."

"I don't wanna see 'em dance that bad," Eli said. "I reckon I'll just settle for the whiskey. How 'bout you, Casey? You ready to go?" Casey said that he was, so Eli paid for the drinks for the two women. While he did, Casey kept an eye on them. "Maybe we'll be back later when the dancin' starts," Eli told Curly; then he followed Casey out the door.

Outside, Eli found Casey standing beside Smoke, apparently getting something out of his saddlebags. He was about to ask what he was looking for, when Casey said, "Best get ready for some company." Responding to the urgency in Casey's warning, Eli stepped quickly to the hitching rail, but not before two men came out of the dancehall behind them.

"What's your hurry, friend?" one of them, a large man, with

a broad, unshaven face, wearing a black patch over one eye, asked. "I thought you wanted to see some dancin'. Whatcha fishin' in them saddlebags for?"

Casey turned to face him. "Nothin' you'd want, so if you'll back away, we'll be on our way."

"I don't think so, not till I see what you're totin' in them bags," "One Eye" said.

Casey pulled his hand out of the saddlebag. It was holding his Colt .45, which was now aimed at One Eye. "Is this what you're wantin'?" Startled, One Eye took a step backward and started to reach for his gun. "Please," Casey encouraged, "go for it." One Eye put his hands in the air, realizing the mistake it would have been. "You all set, Eli?" Casey asked.

"Yep," Eli said. "I'm waitin' for 'Wormy,' here, to decide if he's fast enough to beat a six-shooter that's already aimed at him. "Well, are you, Wormy?" Eli asked One Eye's skinny partner.

"All right," Casey said. "Here's what we're gonna do. I'd just as soon shoot both of you scum down, right here in the street. But since we don't want to make a disturbance on this quiet afternoon, we're gonna let you by and hope you learn something by it. Is that all right with you, partner, or you wanna just go ahead and shoot 'em?" He paused to hear Eli's answer.

"It don't matter that much to me whether we kill 'em or not," Eli said. "Let them make the decision."

"All right," Casey said. "My partner's willin' to let you decide whether you wanna live or die. So here's what we'll do. Both of ya take your left hand and pull that gun outta your holster with nothin' but your thumb and one finger and drop it on the ground. That's simple enough, ain't it? Now I got my eyes on you, One Eye. My partner's got his eyes on Wormy. So if one of us hears a gun go off, the other one will automatically shoot the one we're watchin'. You get the picture? So it's best to just pull the gun out and drop it, like I told you. Go ahead and do it."

They pulled their guns out and dropped them as instructed. "Now turn around and walk up to that wall," Casey said, and when they did, he hurriedly picked up their weapons. "Face the wall," he ordered. He and Eli climbed up into their saddles. "Get down on your knees and count to one hundred. Then you can get up." He and Eli galloped away up the street, and Casey dropped the two guns in the street a couple of blocks away.

Behind them, One Eye struggled to get up off his knees, while Wormy remained on his and continued counting. "Shut up and get up from there," One Eye growled.

"Yeah, but he said—" Wormy started, but One Eye cut him off.

"They've done gone, dummy. You heard 'em ride away, didn'tcha?"

"Oh, that's right," Wormy answered. "You ever see them fellers before?" One Eye said he had never seen them prior. Wormy thought about that for a moment, then asked, "Reckon how they knew your name?"

Out of sight of the Ace Of Spades, Casey and Eli reined their galloping horses back to a walk, and Eli came up beside Casey. "Biscuit ain't showin' any sign of trouble with his new shoes. How 'bout Smoke?"

"No trouble a-tall," Casey answered. "I reckon we'll have to pay Walt for the shoein'."

"How did you know about those two back there?" Eli asked. "I didn't notice when you drew your gun and stuck it in your saddlebag."

"When we were fixin' to leave, and you were payin' for the whiskey those two women drank, they musta saw that roll of bills you carry, 'cause I saw one of 'em make a little noddin' motion back toward that bunch in the corner."

"I figured it musta been something like that," Eli said. "So, whaddaya wanna do now? You wanna try another saloon, maybe not in the Acre, but in the civilized part of town?"

"Nah, those two drinks of whiskey was about all I needed. Tell you the truth, I'd just as soon go on back to the hotel and set down in one of those rockin' chairs on the front porch and wait for supper."

"I declare, Casey, sometimes I think you're gettin' old. Another year or two, and maybe you won't have to put on that makeup every time we go to the bank."

They rode straight back to the stable to leave their horses. Donald Plunket met them in front of the stable and informed them that Walt Evans had been there and put new shoes on their packhorses. They pulled their saddles off and told Plunket to feed both horses some grain, since they hadn't had any opportunity to graze anywhere. Then they took a look at the packhorses and decided everything looked fine. So, when they left the stable, they stopped by Walt's shop to settle up with him. He was pleased to hear that they thought he did a first-rate job on all four horses. They paid him for the job and told him they'd see him at supper, which was still an hour away.

"I see you got back in plenty of time for supper," Emma greeted them when they walked in. "It's still a little while before it's ready."

"That's quite all right," Casey told her. "I wanted to get back here a little early, anyway, so I could sit in one of those rockin' chairs on the porch."

"I reckon I'll have to set there with him," Eli said. "I think he's tryin' to get old on me."

"Well, it's a nice evening to sit on the porch," Emma said.

"You know what would be even nicer? If there was any coffee left on the stove. If there's not, I'll make a pot and bring you a cup."

"Now that would be nice," Casey said. "I don't know of any hotel that treats a person that nice."

"You just go and sit down on the porch, and I'll bring your coffee. If I remember from dinner, you take it black, and Eli likes a little sugar in his."

"Yes, ma'am, he still drinks it like a little young'un."

They retired to the porch then to await their supper, at peace with the world and the knowledge that they were going to block the bank's scheme to take this wonderful woman's hotel. While they sat there, they talked about what their immediate plans should be. They had pretty much decided that it was a good idea to wait before attempting the bank job. It would be much better to have anyone who suspected them, namely Colton Gray, to believe that the two of them were miles away up the Chisholm Trail when that bank was robbed.

"Here you are," Emma sang out sweetly, "coffee for you gentlemen."

"Thank you kindly, ma'am," Casey said. "You be sure and put this on our bill."

"Nonsense," she replied. "This was my idea. It's my pleasure."

"It's kinda hard to leave this kind of treatment, ain't it?" Eli asked when she went back inside the house.

"Yes, it is," Casey agreed. "But I'm thinkin' we've got no reason to stay here any longer. We've already done what we came here to do, and we've picked out a target for Oscar and Elmer. I suppose we might as well go on back and meet the herd and go back to workin' cows for a while. At least until we're up in Oklahoma somewhere. We don't wanna get too far, because we'll have to come back here, then turn around and get ahead of the herd again to get on up to Dodge City."

"I swear, when I hear you say it, it sounds like the craziest thing to even think we can do all that," Eli confessed. He looked at Casey and asked, "Do you think we're crazy to think we can get away with that?"

"Without a doubt," Casey answered him. "But we might as well go down swingin'."

Eli shook his head, amazed. "I reckon," he said. "So you wanna pack up and leave here in the mornin'?"

"After breakfast," Casey said.

"Right. After breakfast," Eli agreed.

Walt came up the steps then, so they knew it was just about suppertime. When he saw the coffee cups, he had to ask, "How'd you boys get special treatment like that?"

"They know how to treat important people here," Eli answered. The call that supper was ready was heard then, so they got up and followed Walt inside.

It was another enjoyable meal at the Woodward House supper table. Roast beef, mashed potatoes, and gravy with hot biscuits, it was a feast suitable for two cowhands who were contemplating eating at the chuck wagon for the next few weeks. After supper, it was back to the porch. This time, however, they had to share it with several other satisfied bellies. There were a lot of questions from the other guests who lived at the hotel, when they learned that Casey and Eli were owners of a large herd of cattle already under way on a drive to Dodge City, Kansas. For the two owners of the D&T, it was a chance to experience a completely different kind of existence than either of them had ever known. It was such a peaceful atmosphere, yet only blocks away from the world of One Eye and Wormy, the part of their town the civilized folks referred to as the "bloody third ward."

The next morning before breakfast, they walked down to

the stable and picked up their horses. They settled up with Plunket for what they owed him; then they took the horses back to the hotel and tied them in the backyard, while they went inside for breakfast. "I see you brought all your horses back this morning," Emma commented. "You're not leaving us this morning, are you?"

"Yes, ma'am, I think we'd best get back to the herd," Casey told her. "It's been a real pleasure stayin' here in your hotel."

"You paid in advance for tonight, too," she said. "See me after breakfast and I'll refund your money for tonight."

"Yes, ma'am," Casey said. "We'll stop by after breakfast and settle up then." He and Eli went into the dining room then for breakfast.

Emma went into her bedroom to get her cash box out of her dresser drawer to count the money she had left after buying groceries. She hated to have to refund the night's rate for two rooms with money she had already counted on to spend. But they were two fine men and she wanted them to remember her kindly. She wished they were going to stay in town a little longer, and not just for the room rent. There was a carefree nature about them that made her feel good. She was going to miss them. She sighed as she folded the money for their refund and tucked it in the pocket of her apron, then returned to the dining room.

There was no indication that Casey and Eli were in any particular hurry to leave, since they took their time to enjoy their breakfast, and stayed long enough to have a last cup of coffee. "I reckon we'd best get up from the table, if we're ever gonna get back to the herd," Eli finally said. "Enjoyed meetin' you folks. Maybe we'll see you again, if we're back in Fort Worth sometime."

Eli's little farewell speech surprised Casey. Eli wasn't much for parting sentiments. "What Eli said," Casey seconded. Several of the guests wished them success with their cattle drive, and Walt stood up to shake their hands. Emma got up to position herself at the dining-room door, so she could intercept them on their way out.

She walked with them into the parlor and the small registration desk, where she stopped. "I see you've gotten everything out of your rooms," she said. They nodded and said they had, so she reached in the pocket of her apron and drew out the folded bills. "This is your refund for the rent for your rooms tonight. And don't give me any argument."

Casey held up his hand. "No argument, Emma, we just ain't takin' it, and that's that."

She looked truly thankful when he said that and expressed it simply. "Thank you, both of you. I hope you'll come back sometime." They started to leave, but she stopped them again. "One more thing," she said. "I checked your rooms to make sure you didn't forget anything. Are you sure you got everything?" They both nodded in response. "Well, I have an idea we might have seen you two a lot sooner than you expected." She lifted the top of the registration desk and pulled out a large roll of money and handed it to Casey. "It was in your room. You need to be a lot more careful with your money, especially this much of it. I found it right on top of the dresser." She smiled, obviously very pleased to have found it before they left.

"That ain't my money," Casey said. "That's your money. If I'da had an envelope and a pencil, I'da wrote on it what it was. But I didn't, so we decided you'd figure it out." He looked at Eli, and Eli nodded in agreement. "Anyway, there's three thousand and one hundred and twenty-five dollars there. Three thousand is for the loan you owe, twenty-five is for what you had to pay that lawyer when he looked at the loan papers. We think maybe you oughta take that lawyer with you when you go to pay the bank off. He'll most likely charge you more than twenty-five for doing that, so that's what the extra hundred is for."

Her pleased smile remained on her face, but it was frozen there in a state of shock as she stared in disbelief for a few moments. Then her eyelids started to flutter, and her knees began to give away. Casey and Eli both caught her by an elbow before she dropped. They took her over to the sofa and sat her down. "Dang, I hope we ain't killed her," Eli blurted.

After a few minutes, her eyes stopped their fluttering and tears began forming in them. "Is it true?" she asked. "Why would you . . ." she started to say, several times, unable to find words to express her feelings. "You two men are the miracle I have prayed for," she decided. "How can I ever thank you? I'll pay you back every cent of it, just like I was paying the bank."

"You don't have to pay it back," Casey told her. "That money ain't no loan. That money is to pay for two chairs. Those two big rockin' chairs out there on the porch belong to me and Eli now. We have to leave 'em here 'cause we can't carry 'em with us on a cattle drive. But anytime we come back, nobody but me and Eli can sit in those two chairs. And that's the deal. Do you accept it?"

Totally recovered by then, and immersed in a state of bliss, she said, "I accept, Casey Tubbs and Eli Doolin, I accept." She got up from the sofa and kissed each one of them on the cheek. "And God bless you both."

"I reckon we oughta get outta here before we all start blubberin'," Eli declared.

"I think you're right," Casey agreed. So they both gave Emma a farewell nod and walked out of the Woodward House Hotel. Both of them doubted they'd ever have occasion to revisit. And both satisfied that it was a lucky thing they had picked the little hotel to stay overnight.

Back in the saddle, they rode out of Fort Worth by way of the newer cattle pens, where they had met up with Birch Bradshaw. They again avoided the Potluck Kitchen, but did stop at Hasting's Supply to make sure their supplies were adequate for what they might need. They would eat with the crew until they decided it time enough to return to Fort Worth, but they would need their packhorses and supplies after that.

Chapter 18

Floyd Hasting was in the front part of his supply house when Casey and Eli walked in. He recognized them immediately and broke out a wide smile. "Well, howdy, boys. There was a fellow in here the other day askin' me how to get rid of some yellow jackets, and I thought of you boys. Did you go after 'em with that black powder?"

"Sure did," Casey answered. "We used it just like you said to, and it worked like a charm, didn't it, Eli?"

"Yep," Eli said. "Got rid of the yellow jackets, but the tree's still tryin' to get over it."

That brought a chuckle out of Hasting. "Yep, that stuff ain't nothing to play with. What can I help you with? Did you come back for some more black powder?"

"Nope, don't need any more of that black powder, we just need some white powder, you know, the kind you call flour, that and a few other things."

"Be glad to fix you right up," Hasting said, but he was still thinking about the black powder. "You know, it was along about that same time those two old-geezer bandits robbed one of those cattle buyer's offices at the new stockyards. They blew the door off his safe with gunpowder. And it wasn't long after that when a young U.S. deputy marshal came in the store askin' me if I'd sold any black powder to two men recently."

"Is that a fact?" Casey laughed with him. "Did you tell him you sold some to me and Eli?"

"I told him I sold a little cannister of it to two fellows who wanted to get rid of some yellow jackets, but I hadn't sold none to two old men like he was talkin' about."

"You musta told him something about us 'cause damned if he didn't show up at our ranch way down in Lampasas County," Eli said. "We had to take him out and show him the hole we burnt up with that powder."

"I sure hope I didn't cause you fellows any trouble by tellin' him about you. I told him you fellows was honest cattle ranchers."

"It weren't no trouble for us," Casey said. "He's the one who went to some trouble to ride all the way down there to find us. It kinda tickled us, matter of fact. He was a nice enough young man. Ended up spendin' the night with us. We never heard, though, did they ever catch those old boys?"

"Not that I know of," Hasting said.

They called off a list of things they would need to sustain themselves for a while and said good day to Hasting. Now they were ready to find their herd of cattle, they didn't anticipate having to eat any of the supplies they just bought for more than a day or two. Surely, the herd would catch up to them by then. Having traveled the trail several times before, they had a fair idea where the cattle might be. So they picked out a draw they had driven a herd down before and made camp there. By noontime on the day after they made their camp, they had seen no sign of Corbett or the point men. It was cause for concern, if the herd was moving that slowly, so they tried to decide what was best to do. They could ride back until they met them or shift their camp east or west. The question would be which direction, east or west? It was only a few minutes after that they heard the faint bawling of the cows about a quarter of a mile to the west of them.

"Damn!" Eli swore. "We didn't exactly nail 'em dead center, did we?" They both hustled to strike their camp and load the horses up, then jumped on their horses.

Eli led out across the draw toward the northwest, causing Casey to yell, "Where the hell are you goin'?"

"To get ahead of 'em!" Eli shouted back at him. "I don't want Corbett to know we missed 'em by a quarter of a mile."

"That ain't hardly what I'd call a big miss on a trail as wide as the Chisholm," Casey grumbled.

"Yonder they are," Eli said, pointing toward the low-lying dust cloud they had been watching for the past thirty minutes. Now seeing a rider come into view, he said, "That's Corbett, and there's the point riders behind him." Then out even farther to the west of the herd, they saw Smiley's chuck wagon coming ahead of the cattle. Casey and Eli sat there on their horses and waited for the herd to come to them.

"Didn't expect to see you boys so soon," Gary Corbett said when he rode up between them. "Everything all right?"

"Yep," Casey answered, "everything's just dandy. We didn't have to spend as much time in Fort Worth as we expected. We went to breakfast with Joe Taylor. He's the head buyer for the Union Stock Yards Company. He was offerin' us eight dollars a head for our cows. But we were able to find out that we could get about ten or twelve dollars more than that if we drive 'em on up the trail to Dodge. And it looks like that's where you'll take 'em, 'cause the upper end of the Chisholm Trail to Abilene is shut down by the Kansas farmers."

Corbett shrugged and said, "Well, the last time we talked, you said Dodge City was gonna be our trail's end, so ain't nothin' changed for me. That's the reason we swung wide of Fort Worth to pick up the trail north of it."

"That's right," Eli said. "That's what we're sayin', but we'll be checkin' on the other markets again when you get a little farther up the trail. That's in case things change. We wanna get the best price we can for our cattle."

Casey could see from Corbett's facial expressions that he was a little bit confused by his and Eli's attempts to justify their odd behavior on this cattle drive. It was in further evidence when he said, "I scouted up ahead of here already. There's a sizable creek about a mile away, and that's where I'm plannin' on stoppin' 'em for the night. Is that all right with you?"

"Maybe I'd better say this again, so there ain't no misunderstandin'," Casey answered him. "You're the trail boss of this herd. We hired you because we've got every confidence in you that you know your job and you'll deliver our cattle to market in good shape. We're just taggin' along with the herd partway, because we've got other business we have to attend to before we go on out to Dodge City. And to tell you the truth, we're just gonna try to stay outta your way. We've got a couple of investors we have to get together with in Atoka— Oklahoma Indian Territory. So we'll most likely leave you when you cross over the Red, most likely won't see you again till you get to Dodge."

"Fair enough," Corbett said. "'Preciate you tellin' me. I was wonderin' if you was gettin' ready to fire me."

"Nope," Eli said. "We're satisfied that you're doin' the job. We'll drop back and ride with the swing riders, or maybe the lead riders. We don't wanna eat too much dust."

Corbett laughed. "Suit yourself. They're your cattle. You can ride wherever you want." He nudged his horse and rode on up ahead.

"That was a pretty good speech you made," Eli said when Corbett was gone. "It was gettin' downright impossible to explain what the heck we were doin'. I hope those two investors in Atoka have got plenty of money." They were distracted then by a call from a voice behind them.

"Hey! You fellows lost? You stay there, you're liable to get run over!" They looked back to see the smiling face of Monroe Kelly, riding point. They waited until he caught up with them, then rode along with him. "You come back to take this herd to Dodge?"

"Nope," Casey answered. "You and Corbett are takin' this herd to Dodge. We're just visitin'. We'll be leavin' you again after you cross the Red."

"What for?" Monroe asked.

"We have to tend to some business over in the Nations," Casey said. "It's all part of the financial arrangement we have to keep D and T in the cattle business." It was easy to tell that Monroe made no sense out of that, but he appeared to accept it. "Who's ridin' swing on this side?" Casey asked.

"Grover Morris," Monroe answered.

"We'll drop back a-ways, so Corbett won't think we're gettin' in the way," Eli said. "I think he's gonna bed 'em down for the night after about another mile."

"Well, look what wandered in with the cattle," Smiley George announced when he walked up from the creek, carrying two buckets of water to fill up his water barrel. It was a job of first priority whenever reaching a creek, to get fresh water before the cattle reached there. "Corbett rode by a little while ago. He said you boys was back, but you was only goin' with us till we crossed the Red. What did he mean by that?" It required another vague explanation from Casey and Eli, and they were already regretting their decision to join up with the herd.

"I swear, if this keeps on, I believe we might as well tell 'em where we really get the money to bankroll this operation," Eli told Casey when they were watering their horses, also to fill their canteens before the cattle moved in and turned the creek into a mudhole. "They wouldn't believe that, and then maybe they'd just let it be."

As it turned out, however, it was not as big a nuisance as they expected. For the most part, everybody was just glad to see them. For the next six days, they rode along with the herd during the day, leading their packhorses, and camped with the men at the chuck wagon at night. On the seventh day after leaving Fort Worth, they reached the Red River at the thriving settlement called Red River Station. It was really little more than a growing community, but there was a store closer to the river crossing, Blunt's Store. It had started life as a trading post and endured mostly on the claim that it was the last place to buy whiskey before entering Indian Territory, where the sale of whiskey was illegal. Casey and Eli made it a point to visit the store to purchase a couple of bottles of whiskey so the men could celebrate the crossing of the Red. Actually, the real point of their visit to the store was to establish the fact that they were with the cattle.

"Howdy," the shopkeeper greeted them when they walked in the store. "I reckon you boys are with that herd fixin' to cross the river."

"That's a fact," Casey said.

"It's the first big herd to make the crossin' in a pretty good while," Amos said. "Where you from?"

"D and T Cattle Company in Lampasas County," Casey answered. "We're the owners. He's *D* and I'm *T*. Eli Doolin and Casey Tubbs."

"Is that a fact? Well, I'm pleased to meet'cha. My name's Amos Blunt. This here's my store."

"The last time we crossed the river here, we were just cowhands, trying to get by," Eli said. "But this time, we're the owners, so we wanna make it a special occasion when our men get our cattle across. We thought we'd buy a couple of bottles of your best whiskey to celebrate a successful crossin'."

"That's right," Casey said. "We don't want enough to get 'em too drunk to work. And if we lose too many cows crossin' over, me and Eli will drink it all, ourselves, 'cause if that happens, we're gonna need to get drunk."

Amos threw his head back and laughed. "Well, I hope you don't have to drink it all by yourself." He pulled a couple of bottles out from under the counter. "This is the best I've got." He handed one to each of them.

"Ahh," Eli exhaled, "rye, that's my favorite."

They paid him for the whiskey and said so long. He wished them a safe crossin' and luck on the rest of the drive. "D and T Cattle Company," he called after them. "I'll remember that."

"See that you do," Eli said after they rode out of earshot. They went back to get their packhorses then. They had left them on the other side of the herd, thinking it better that Blunt didn't see that they were leading packhorses. It might possibly cause him to wonder.

Most of the seventh day was spent crossing the cattle over the river at Red River Station. After they saw the cattle safely across, they told Corbett about the two bottles of whiskey, and gave him the option of celebrating their successful crossing. He preferred them to keep it, saying he didn't want to reward the men for something they were supposed to do. So Eli and Casey said so long to the crew, and struck out along a trail on the Oklahoma side, following the Red River east. "We'll see you in Dodge City," Casey said in parting. "Try to have most of the cows with you when you get there," he japed.

They continued along the river trail for a distance of almost two miles, just to make sure there was no chance they might be seen crossing back over to Texas. Once they figured it far enough, they continued on, until finding what appeared to be an easy crossing place. It was a section of the river that had parted as it flowed around an island, so they crossed over to the island, finding the water shallow enough for the horses to walk on the bottom. They figured the remaining portion, between the island and Texas, had to be the channel. They were proven right when the bottom dropped off right after leaving the island and their horses started swimming. Smoke and Biscuit handled it all right, even though Casey and Eli both came out of the saddle when their packhorses began to panic when the ground disappeared under their hooves, and they began to drift with the current. "Hang on to them reins!" Eli yelled as Casey's packhorse bumped into his. They both looped the packhorses' reins around the saddle horns on their horses, while the two packhorses struggled against each other. Finally Biscuit, then Smoke, gained solid footing again and could pull the packhorses up to solid ground.

"I swear, that was fun, weren't it?" Eli joked when they led the horses up from the water's edge. "I wish to hell we had waited a little while and gone back to Red River Station to cross."

"Well, we can always cross back over and ride back there, if that's what you want," Casey suggested.

Eli ignored the sarcasm. "I reckon it ain't that much longer till suppertime, anyway, so we might as well go on up to that little patch of trees yonder and make us a good fire. I'm soaked to the skin."

"The sooner, the better," Casey said. "The only thing on me that ain't soaked is my hat. It's a good thing I put my watch and my money under my hat before we went in the river. We need to get them packs off the horses and see what's spoiled and what ain't."

After they gathered enough wood to maintain a healthy fire for a good while, they cut some limbs to hang their clothes on, then stripped down to nothing but their boots, while their clothes were draped on the drying rack of limbs they had constructed. They went into their packs then and found that most of the damage had been contained by the outer layers of the old men's coats, which had been rolled up in their rain slickers. Their large quantity of money, which they always carried whenever they were going to be away from the ranch for a long time, was protected by the oilskin bag that contained it. They hung their bedrolls and blankets, along with their saddle blankets, up in the trees. The flour they had just bought at Hasting's was ruined, so they threw it out. The bacon was unharmed, as was the hardtack, and the coffee was untouched. "Thank the Lord for that," Casey declared. "If we'da lost the coffee, I'da gone after the herd, or shot myself. I reckon there ain't much else we can do to dry out, so we might as well cook some supper."

"I reckon," Eli said. "But I'd appreciate it if you can find something to wrap around yourself while you're doin' your cookin'."

"I was gettin' ready to tell you the same thing."

They sat up later than usual that night, primarily because their things weren't drying as well as they had hoped. Finally they had to settle for mostly dry bedrolls used as blankets on top of them while they lay on dry rain slickers covering half-dry saddle blankets. They kept the fire going all night with one or the other waking during the night and putting more wood on it. The next morning, in dry underwear and clothes that still had damp collars and cuffs, they set out for Fort Worth, angling on a course to intercept the trail they had ridden out on. By the first time they stopped to rest the horses, all thoughts of their discomforts of the night before were forgotten. While the horses grazed and drank water, they fried bacon and hardtack to go with their coffee and discussed their mission at the Fort Worth Investment Bank. For all practical purposes, there was little to rehearse. Their approach was always the same with some little variation. And as long as it worked, they could see no reason to try anything drastically different. They made it a point to dry and oil their weapons and ammunition, even though they had yet to use them during a robbery. They even fired a couple of shots to make sure they were working properly. It took them two and a half days to make the trip back to Fort Worth, a trip that normally would have taken them just two days. But that was because of the delay caused by their swim in the river. They reached the northern edge of the town a little after twelve o'clock in the afternoon. So they decided to strike the bank the next day, right after the stroke of noon. There were two things of importance on their minds at this juncture: where to hide their packhorses after they changed into their disguises, and where to buy a good supper without leaving too much of a footprint.

Since there was plenty of daylight left, they began a search for the place to hide their packhorses first. This, however, turned out to be a problem. They rode out on several roads leading out of town, but found nothing they felt safe with. There were too many houses close in, and too many farms farther out. They were sure they could find someplace suitable if they continued out on any of the roads. The problem with that was, it would give them too long a ride to get to their packhorses and change out of their work clothes. "Hell, it's a shorter ride from that bank to the place we used last time than it is from this end of town," Eli said.

"You know, you're right," Casey replied. "There weren't any houses built on that road. There wasn't anything after you passed Hasting's."

"Let's go take a look at it and see if anybody's found it," Eli said.

"Might as well," Casey responded. So they turned their horses and rode across town to the west side. Then they rode south on one of the north-south streets until they passed the stockyards and turned on a road that led them to the San Antonio road, south of the Potluck Kitchen and just short of Hasting's. Trying to look as inconspicuous as possible, they rode quickly by Hasting's and proceeded to the creek that crossed the road. Just as they had before, they turned their horses into the water and rode upstream until they reached the spot where they had left the water before. They dismounted and began to search the ground for signs of other riders. They found old tracks, probably their own, but for certain, there were no recent tracks. When they had left this camp the last time, they had not taken the precaution of leaving it by way of the creek to hide their tracks. When they examined the bank now, they were not sure, but they thought there was a possibility there were tracks left by another horse. They were old tracks, like those that would be left by a single rider.

It occurred to them both at the same time, but it was Casey who spoke first. "Colton Gray!" he exclaimed.

"It had to be," Eli responded. "He was at the Potluck Kitchen, he was at Hasting's, and you know he had to go lookin' for the place we camped. He found this camp, and you know he had to go all the way to the D and T to talk to us."

"I swear, he's a piece of work, ain't he? He knows it's us, but he can't prove it." Casey laughed when he thought about it, but he was prompted to say, "And we'd best be damn careful we don't give him the proof he needs." Eli nodded his head in complete agreement. "So, whaddaya say?" Casey continued. "You think we oughta take a chance and use this camp again?"

"I say, why not?" Eli answered. "Look at this place. Ain't nobody been here since Colton Gray. And for a test, I think we could leave these packhorses here tonight while we find a place to eat a good supper."

"All right," Casey agreed. "But just in case, we'll take that sack of money with us. Then if we lose the bet, we'll just lose those old clothes and our disguises, and we'll have to go on a vacation for a while till we get new duds."

"We'd most likely lose the horses, and they'd leave that stuff," Eli said. "And we'd still be in business. But it's gonna be dark by the time we get back here tonight. So we'd best gather some wood and lay us a fire ready to light."

When they were ready to leave, they tied the packhorses on a rope close to the water. Then they rode in the creek back to the road, pausing cautiously before reaching the road, to be certain there was no one on it. Retracing the route they took to reach the creek, they went back to the north part of town with the intention of finding a place to eat that was nowhere near the bank or the Woodward House Hotel. They finally decided on the Cattleman, which was next to a small hotel. When they went in, they were met by the manager, Howard Kemp, who introduced himself and requested that they remove their weapons. After they hung their gun belts on a row of hooks behind Howard's desk, he showed them to a table. "Your server will be with you in a minute, gentlemen. I hope you enjoy your meal."

Eli looked around him at the other customers. Most of them married couples, he guessed, maybe guests of the hotel next door. They all looked fairly neat and clean; then he took a look at Casey in the clothes he had gone swimming in. "It's a wonder they didn't seat us on the back steps," he commented. "I didn't think about what a sight we might be to civilized folks. I hope they ain't got men waiters. He called 'em a server. You heard that, didn't you?"

"Yeah, I heard him," Casey said. "Relax, here comes a woman."

"Good evening, gents," she greeted them. "My name's Paula, and I'm gonna be your waitress tonight. So right away, you're probably wondering how you got so lucky, right? Well, once in a while, it don't hurt to give a break to a couple of old broken-down cowpokes like you two. When Howard came back to the kitchen and pointed you two out, I said, 'I'll take 'em. I was born on a ranch.' I don't have to ask, I know you want coffee to drink. How'd you two get in here, anyway? You look like you just had a rough river crossing."

They both sat wide-eyed, astonished by the rough woman's opening barrage of thinly veiled insults until she finally paused to take a breath. "I like her," Eli said, turning to face Casey. "What a relief," he added when he saw a male server come from the kitchen carrying a tray. Back to her then, he said, "Paula, honey, you're gonna make a little money tonight. Ain't she, partner?"

"I wouldn't be surprised," Casey said, "if the food's fit to eat."

Paula smiled. "I'll see that it is," she said. "I'll be happy to take care of you fellows tonight. I'm glad you came in. You have a choice between a steak or baked ham. I expect you eat your share of steak, so if you want something different, the baked ham is really good, and you can get a baked potato with it."

"I'll take the baked ham," Casey said.

"Me too," Eli followed. "And it was yesterday."

"Yesterday?" she asked, not understanding.

"Swimming," Eli said. "It was yesterday when we went swimming with four horses."

Paula threw her head back and cackled. "I'll get your coffee. Be right back."

When she left, Casey said, "I'm beginning to think you musta got some water on the brain when we went in that river."

"Why?"

"'Cause it was two and a half days ago when we went in that river. It weren't yesterday."

Eli shrugged. "It don't make no difference to her, and yesterday just sounds better. Why do you reckon she came out here talkin' so tough for? Then she turned into the sweetest little honey you ever saw."

"Lookin' around the room here, I don't see nobody as rough-lookin' as me and you. I kinda have an idea ol' Howard sent her out here to run us off, if possible. And when we didn't show no signs of gettin' offended and leavin', she gave up on the idea. 'Course, there was that one part where you said you liked her and told her she was gonna make some money tonight. That's been known to sweeten a woman up before."

Paula lived up to her word, whatever her true motivation might have been. She took excellent care of them, and the ham she recommended was excellent. She suggested a peach cobbler for dessert that neither of them had ever tried before, and that was excellent as well. And she kept them drowning in coffee all during supper. When they left, Eli pressed a fifty-dollar bill in her hand to make sure no one else got it off the table. She thanked them graciously and walked with them to the desk, where they paid Howard and collected their guns. Both she and Howard said good night. After they went out the door, Howard looked at her and said, "Some job you did getting rid of those drifters."

"I gave it my best shot," Paula said. "They were just determined to stay, no matter how much I insulted them."

Chapter 19

Feeling well satisfied with their supper at the Cattleman, they rode back to the south side of town, anxious now to see the results of their gamble with their packhorses. Now that it was getting dark, they were not so concerned about being spotted by anyone who might recognize them. They rode at a comfortable lope past Hasting's, which was now closed. When they reached the creek, they again rode up the creek in the water, for they were still concerned about leaving tracks that might be seen the next day. Before reaching the point where they would exit the creek, they were relieved to hear the welcome greeting from the packhorses, which Smoke and Biscuit answered.

When their horses climbed up on the bank, they dismounted and relieved them of their saddles and left them to graze, knowing they would not wander. They debated then on whether or not they wanted to start the fire they had ready to light. Since both of them were overly full of the meal they had just put away, they decided to save the fire for morning and get some sleep that night. Tomorrow was going to be another busy day.

With morning, a discussion came on whether or not they should ride into town and eat breakfast. Their planned visit to the bank was not going to be until noon, since that was when the time lock was set for. So there was plenty of time for breakfast. But after talking it over, they decided it was best not to risk another ride out of their camp before they rode out in costume. What was irritating was the fact that Hasting's Supply was so convenient to their camp, and they couldn't go there to replace the things that were ruined in the river crossing. They could imagine Colton Gray checking both places, the camp and Hasting's. The camp might only tell him that someone was there, but Hasting could tell him who it was. So they started their fire and prepared their meager breakfast there by the creek. There was time to spare, so they leisurely drank coffee and ate their bacon, and speculated on how many employees they might meet when they got to the bank.

"There wasn't nobody in that bank but Polk and one teller when we were there," Casey recalled. "You know there's gotta be more people workin' at that bank than that. They had three teller cages, and they must have somebody that does the cleanup and all that kinda stuff. I sure hope we don't go walkin' in there today and find a whole bunch of folks workin' there."

"And a whole bunch of customers in there, too," Eli finished for him. "I reckon we'd best try to get a look inside before we go in. We can maybe see what's goin' on through those little glass panels on each side of the door. We might decide not to go in today."

"I hope to hell that ain't the case," Casey remarked. "I'd like to get this one done with today and get on outta here."

It was not an especially good day for Edwin Polk at the Fort Worth Investment Bank. In fact, the last couple of weeks had been bad. It had all started when Emma Woodward marched into the bank one morning, accompanied by her lawyer, carrying three thousand dollars in cash to pay off her loan. He had been taken completely by surprise. Sweet, simple little Emma Woodward with a lawyer, he could not believe it until the lawyer turned that loan agreement inside out and threatened to take the bank to court if that loan was not marked "paid in full" with Emma's final payment of three thousand. He had been caught red-handed, and there had been no choice but to return her deed to her. He could not defend the language of the loan in a court of law and win.

Now, this morning, he was scheduled to meet with his business partner to explain to him how a prime property they had all but closed on had suddenly been jerked out from under them. He had already assured Brock Jennings that the Woodward House Hotel was theirs after Emma Woodward had told him she didn't have the money to pay the loan in full. And when at this final meeting he had asked her where she got the money, she had the gall to tell him it was none of his business. *That little witch*, he thought when the image of her telling him formed in his mind. He was still grimacing painfully when Julian stuck his head in the door.

"Mr. Jennings is here to see you, Mr. Polk," Julian announced.

"Very well, Julian." Polk got up from his desk and walked out into the lobby to greet him. "Good morning, Brock, come on back to my office. Would you like a cup of coffee or something stronger?"

"Coffee will be fine," Jennings said.

Polk called after Julian, who was walking back to his cage, "Julian, bring a couple of cups of coffee to my office."

"Yes, sir," Julian replied. "It might be a minute or two, if there isn't any made." He looked at Sidney in the teller cage next to his and winked. They knew Polk was not looking forward to the meeting.

Polk and Jennings went inside Polk's office and shut the door. It had no sooner closed when Jennings demanded, "Edwin, what the hell happened? I already had my architect draw up the floor plans for that building, specifically designed to make the most use out of that piece of property. You told me it was as good as done."

"It was, Brock. That woman sat right there in that chair and told me she couldn't pay the loan off in time when I read that paragraph to her. Now, somewhere between that meeting and this last one, she got hold of some money. And worse than that, she got herself a lawyer. What the hell could I do? I couldn't go to court." He shrugged and offered lamely, "At least the bank received full payment of the loan."

"Yeah, you saved three thousand dollars and gave up one that would likely have made you ten times that much, just your share," Jennings said in disgust. "Are you sure there isn't some way you could still claim that woman owes the bank money, late fees or something?"

"It's too late," Polk replied. "She's got her loan papers and her deed, and everything's certified and paid. Her damn lawyer saw to that." Brock started to ask another question, but was interrupted by a knock on the door.

"Yeah?" Polk responded loudly.

"Sorry to bother you," Julian said when he stuck his head in the door. "It's twelve o'clock and the safe's open."

"What do you need to get into the safe for?" Polk asked.

"I don't have to get in the safe," Julian answered, "but we need to get into the safe room, and you've got the key to that door. Both Sidney and I will need to replenish our cash drawers before long. We've had a lot of small withdrawals, it being Saturday. We do have a new account, though, and it looks like it's going to be a big one. I figure, since you are busy, you'll want me to go ahead and get it started. Then you can check it over and deposit the money."

"What are you talking about when you say it's 'going to be a big one'?" Polk asked.

"They're opening the account with a thousand dollars in cash," Julian answered.

"A thousand . . ." Polk started. "Maybe I'd better come out there and meet them. You say it's a couple, a man and his wife?"

"No, sir," Julian answered. "It's two old men, brothers. And from the look of them, you'd think they've saved every penny they ever came across."

Polk was intrigued immediately, thinking of a possible replacement for the pigeon he just lost in Emma Woodward. He turned to look at Jennings, but Jennings spoke first. "Go ahead and take care of them. I'll sit right here."

"This shouldn't take long," Polk assured him. "Saturdays are usually all withdrawal days. It'll be nice to get a sizable deposit for a change." He walked out and closed the door behind him. There were a few people in line at the tellers, but Julian had walked over to a table beside the cages, where he was talking with two old men. "Ancient" would be a better term, for Polk didn't believe he'd ever seen anyone that old before. And each one of them was carrying a large carpetbag. "Good afternoon, gentlemen. Julian tells me you wish to open an account." He took the paperwork from Julian and said, "Thank you, Julian. Looks like you've got people waiting." Then remembering, he said, "Take some coffee in for Mr. Jennings first."

"Yes, sir. This is Mr. Polk," Julian told the old men. "He'll take good care of you and your money."

"Julian told me you wanted to open your account with a deposit of one thousand dollars," Polk said. "Is that right?"

"We never said for sure," Casey answered. "We said we was thinkin' about it. Has this bank ever been held up?"

"No, it has not," Polk answered, "and I can assure you that it never will be."

"How can you say that?" Eli asked, using his best version of an old man's voice. "Every bank can be broke into."

"Not this one," Polk insisted. "Oh, they might break into

the bank, but our safe is in a safe room with iron bars on the door. And I'm the only one with the key to that door. Even if I unlocked the door, the safe won't open until the time lock opens it. They can't blow the safe open and they can't drag it out of the bank. So the money in it is safe."

"I swear," Eli said. "That is a wonderment . . . if it really is so."

Polk watched the two old men muttering to each other as if trying to make a decision, so he asked, "Would you like to see the safe room and the safe?"

Casey and Eli were careful not to jump at the chance. So, as they had rehearsed it before, they whispered back and forth as if undecided whether they wanted to see it or not. Finally Polk became impatient. "Have you two got a thousand dollars to put in the safe?"

"Show him some money, Oscar," Casey said.

Eli went into his act then. He put his carpetbag down and looked right and left, making sure no one was watching. Then he opened the bag, reached in, and pulled out a fat wad of money. He stuck it up in Polk's face so he could get a good look at it. Then he quickly threw it back in the bag and closed it, looking around nervously to see if anyone had seen. They could see that it had the effect on Polk that they hoped for. They could almost hear his brain working on the possibilities. "What else do you carry in your bags?" he asked.

"Just stuff," Casey answered him. "Stuff we need from time to time."

"Come with me and I'll show you where you can keep all your money safe," Polk said. He led them to the door to the back room. "You can leave your bags here by the door if you want, nobody will bother them."

Casey and Eli stopped immediately. "No, sir," Casey said, "this bag goes where I go. It don't leave my hand." They both backed away from the door, as if afraid to go through it.

"No problem at all, gentlemen," Polk quickly insisted. "You can keep your bags with you. I think you'll feel much better when you see where your money can be kept safe." He opened the door. "See, this is just the back room, where we keep supplies and things. Over in that end of the room is the safe room. See the door with the bars. That's to keep people from even getting in where the safe is." By this time, Polk was literally itching to see how much more money was in those carpetbags. He couldn't wait to tell Brock Jennings about the two old coots whose brains had evidently worn out, along with their bodies. They might not even remember they put their money in the bank. It was a dream come true. He decided to dazzle them. So he took out his key and inserted it in the safe room door and opened the door. "Now, what do you think?" he asked as he opened the door to the safe. "Is your money safer in those carpetbags than it would be in this safe?"

"You sold me," Casey said. "How 'bout you, Oscar?"

"I'm sold," Eli answered. "Let's get to work."

They both dropped their carpetbags and opened them, while Polk stood there with a broad smile on his face like a parent who had pleased his children. The smile froze, how-ever, when Casey reached into his bag and brought out his Colt .45 and stuck it against Polk's belly. At the same time, Eli pulled a rope out of his bag, grabbed Polk's wrists and pulled them behind his back to be quickly tied. Working rapidly, Casey tripped Polk so he landed on the floor, where Eli tied his ankles together, then tied them to his hands. While he was doing that, Casey pulled a hand towel out of his bag and used it to gag their victim. With Polk taken care of, they hurriedly started emptying the safe into their carpetbags. When the bags were full, Casey did his best to maintain his old-timer's way of talking when he said, "It was a downright pleasure doin' business with ya."

Everything had gone according to plan up to this point.

Neither one of the tellers had come back to the safe room, as they had intended. Casey and Eli had sweated that possibility, not sure how they would have handled it. But their luck held out, and when they walked back out to the lobby, they saw the reason why. Both tellers were busy with customers. The trick now was to leave the bank without arousing suspicion from tellers or customers. So they walked across the lobby unhurriedly. And when Julian looked their way, Casey raised his hand to acknowledge him. Julian waved back.

Outside the bank, they paused briefly to look down the busy street before going to their horses, which they had tied in front of the dress shop. Acting without haste, so as to cause no suspicion, they hooked their carpetbags over their saddle horns, climbed up into the saddle, and walked the horses down the street. They decided that it would be a bit too risky to ride back by Hasting's in the middle of a Saturday afternoon, dressed as they were. So they picked a road running out of town that appeared to run close to parallel to the San Antonio road. After they had ridden what they estimated to be far enough, they turned off the road and rode straight west. As they figured, they eventually struck the San Antonio road. So they turned back to the north and rode until they came to their creek. Once again riding up the creek, they found their pack-horses waiting and their camp undisturbed. So they started the process of changing Oscar and Elmer back into Eli and Casey, far enough from the center of town to be unaware of what might be happening at the scene of the robbery.

"What the hell is he doing?" Brock Jennings wondered aloud after an unusually long time after Edwin Polk left him in the office. He had finished the coffee Julian had brought him shortly after Polk left. Then out of a fit of boredom, he rifled through Polk's desk drawers until he found his box of cigars. That was good for a pretty long time, but now as he

looked at the clock on the wall, he realized he had been waiting for almost an hour. Indignant now to be ignored for this
long, he stormed out of the office and went to the teller cages.
"Where the hell is Edwin?"

"Wasn't he with you?" Julian asked.

"Would I be looking for him if he was with me?" Jennings
replied sarcastically.

Concerned now, Julian looked at Sidney, who shrugged in
return. "We thought he was with you because the two old gentlemen left a long time ago. Sid, I'm gonna close my window
and check in the back." He put his CLOSED sign in place and
went to the back room. Jennings followed him. They found
Polk trussed up and gagged, lying on the floor of the safe
room, the iron-barred door open and the almost-empty safe
gaping helplessly.

"Oh, my Lord. Oh, my Lord. Oh, my Lord," Julian kept re-
peating as he worked to untie the knot in Polk's gag.

As soon as it was free, Polk cried, "Did you stop them?"

"Who?" Julian responded, thinking it could not possibly be
the two elderly men.

"Those two old men!" Polk screamed. "Who do you think?"

"Did they do this to you?" Julian asked. "We saw them when
they walked out." He looked at the almost-empty safe. "Is that
what they had in those bags?"

"Yes, you moron, and you let them just stroll on out the
door with the bank's money."

"Worse than that," Jennings finally spoke, "they strolled
out with the people's money. This isn't going to reflect too
well on this bank's reputation. I expect you'll be looking for
new employment somewhere."

"Wait a minute, you can't lay all the blame for this on me,"
Polk said as Julian finally loosened his ropes. He looked at Julian then. "You came to get me to unlock the safe room door so
you and Sidney could restock your trays. Why didn't you go
there?"

"Because you told me to take care of the customers. I've been busy," Julian answered, wanting none of the blame.

"Well, you'd better put the CLOSED sign up and tell folks there'll be no more withdrawals, because you'll be handing out IOUs," Jennings said. "And don't you think somebody should send for the sheriff?"

"I'll go get him," Sidney volunteered, and headed for the door at once.

"Well, I believe my business is finished here for the day, so there's no need for me to hang around any longer. Good luck with your recovery, Edwin."

"Yeah, thanks," Polk replied sarcastically. "I appreciate all your support on this."

It was not long after Jennings's departure that Sidney returned with Sheriff "Longhair Jim" Courtright. He listened to everyone who was in contact with the two robbers and didn't hesitate to inform them that the bank had been visited by the notorious pair of old-geezer bandits. "These ain't local boys from the Acre. They've hit banks and trains all over the state. They're the pair that blew the door offa Birch Bradshaw's safe down in the cattle pens. And since they robbed the bank and walked out, without nobody in the bank knowing they'd been robbed, there ain't much use to talk about a posse. We ain't got the slightest idea which way to start. I'll notify the U.S. Marshal's Office. They've been tryin' to track those two down for quite some time now. They've even got one deputy marshal who's assigned to 'em full-time. He's been up here trying to track 'em, but he ain't had no luck a-tall. I expect he'll show up pretty soon. He's a right fine young man, but I believe those two old boys are a little too slick for him."

Courtright was honest in his opinion that there wasn't much he could do about the bank robbery. He was hired as sheriff with one job above all others, and that was to clamp down on the lawlessness going on in Hell's Half Acre. And to a great extent, he was doing just that. It was not good news to hear that the old-grandpa robbers had struck his town for the second time.

In contrast to the slowness with which it became known in the bank, itself, the news that the bank had been robbed spread across town very quickly. The residents and guests at Woodward House Hotel found out about it at suppertime that night from Walt Evans, who heard it from Donald Plunket. Everyone at the table turned to look at Emma, who was staring, wide-eyed and openmouthed at Walt, hardly able to believe what he was saying. "Pretty much wiped the bank out," Walt went on. "It was them two little old men they been talkin' about."

Pearl Pigeon walked in from the kitchen when she heard the excitement. "You can't tell me there ain't somebody on the Lord's payroll whose job is to take care of crooks like Edwin Polk."

Emma nodded in agreement with her cook. *And you can't tell me there aren't angels walking around on this earth to help folks who can't help themselves*, she thought.

Chapter 20

Back at their camp by the creek, Casey and Eli did a final inspection of each other to make sure all evidence of the facial paint was scrubbed off. All the work clothes were folded up in the packs, this time with packs of money folded up in them, and the packs loaded on the horses. They had not taken the time to count the money taken, but it was substantial, since they couldn't get any more into their carpetbags. When the horses were ready, they did take some time to try to put their campsite back as close as they could to the way they had originally found it. It had been a good camp for them, on two separate occasions, and who could say? They might have use for it again sometime. But for now, the priority was to disappear from the Fort Worth area. So they rode back in the creek again to strike the road, then turned to the south on the San Antonio road, leaving it after half a mile and following a stream west until they struck the trail left by the cattle herd. Then they headed for Oklahoma Territory, following the wide path left by three thousand–plus cows. "At least the dust has settled," Eli joked.

They had really made no plans for what they would do after the robbery. There was the option of simply catching up with the herd and continuing on to Dodge City with the cattle.

The problem with that was the story they had created for their men, and how difficult it would be to create a bigger lie to explain the change. "The part about meeting the investors in Atoka would be a sticky one to explain," Casey commented. "You know, we're gonna have to cross the Red somewhere different from where the herd crossed. We can't let Amos Blunt see us goin' across again."

"I swear," Eli replied. "And that's the only place we mighta been able to buy something to eat, too."

"We're gonna have to go huntin'," Casey said. "I need something besides bacon to carry me all the way to Kansas."

"Maybe not," Eli said, and pointed toward a little stream up ahead. "Correct me if I'm wrong, but I believe that's one of our cows down in that stream."

"Hallelujah! I believe you're right!" Casey exclaimed. "No bacon for supper tonight. Maybe we'd best follow the herd all the way to Dodge." They headed toward the stray cow, and Casey shook out some rope ready to throw. The stray didn't run, but stood in the stream watching them as they approached. When he was close enough, Casey threw his lasso and caught the cow around the neck. Then he played out enough rope to let the cow walk along beside the packhorses. "Welcome to the family," Casey joked. "The packhorses ain't got no names, but this is Smoke and that's Biscuit. We're gonna name you Supper. You like that?"

They continued on for another five or six miles, when they came to a creek and realized it was the creek where they had first caught up to the herd and spent the first night with the crew. The big herd had left plenty of evidence of their passing the creek. The banks were torn up, but the water had had time to clear up, especially near the center of the creek. They decided to stop there for the night, give their horses a good rest, and butcher their steer while there was plenty of daylight left. The unfortunate steer was mercifully dispatched by a bullet in its head, then hauled up with the rope to hang from a tree limb, skinned, gutted, and bled. Most of the butchering was done by Eli while Casey built a healthy fire. They took the choice cuts and cut them into strips they could manage on branches over the fire. Neither man claimed to be an expert on cooking or preserving meat, but they managed to figure out a way to smoke a quantity of it to eat later on. They did so by cutting it into thin strips, mashing the blood out of it, then laying the strips on a tree branch over the fire.

They ate fresh cooked meat that night until their bellies would hold no more. A sizable slab was wrapped in the cowskin, to be eaten the next day. Then, late into the night, they smoked their jerky over the fire, keeping the smoldering fire covered with leaves in order to make plenty of smoke. Before they retired to their bedrolls, they dropped what was left of the cow from the tree limb and dragged it away from the creek.

The next morning, they got under way again after they wrapped up their supply of smoked beef jerky, both men complaining of bellyaches. "It was damn good, though," Eli declared.

"We'll see when we start tryin' to eat that jerky," Casey commented. "It might be like trying to chew shoelaces. I don't think we woulda made it as Injuns."

When they came to the next place to rest the horses, they rode upstream, wide of the broad trail left by their cattle in an effort to find some grass that hadn't been grazed down. They decided to eat jerky and coffee for breakfast and save their slab of fresh beef to cook for their dinner. They figured it wouldn't turn before then. The weather was mild enough that they actually got two more meals out of the fresh beef, but that was as far as they dared test it. They left the rest of it for the buzzards on the bank of the Red River, about half a mile upstream of Red River Station. Fortunately, the crossing they picked turned out to be an easy one and they avoided the soaking they suffered before. They continued across a western Oklahoma wilderness, keeping a vigilant eye out for any more stray cows, but the boys from the D&T outfit were doing a good job of saving the beef.

Each day was pretty much like the one before it as their horses padded along in monotony, until one morning while preparing to leave their camp of the night before. "Casey, look," Eli called softly. When Casey looked at him, he pointed toward the stream they had camped beside. Casey followed the direction he was pointing in and discovered another cow standing in the creek, staring at them.

"Well, I'll be . . ." Casey whispered. "They come to us just like manna from Heaven. We might better start keepin' count so we know how much to charge Corbett for lost cows," he joked.

"Get your rope out," Eli said. "Maybe you can walk up to him without spookin' him."

Moving very slowly with no jerky motions, Casey walked over and got his rope from his saddle. Then slowly making his loop while he walked toward the cow, he began to twirl it around and around. The cow seemed puzzled, but interested, to see what came next. What came next was a lasso, and when it dropped over its wide horns, it panicked. Casey drew the loop up tight around the cow's neck, but the steer bolted, dragging Casey with him, his boots plowing two furrows in the ground. "Hang on to him, Casey!" Eli yelled, and ran to help him. The steer pulled the two of them until they passed close enough to a tree to loop the rope around the trunk.

"That there's our cow. We 'preciate you catchin' him for us. We been chasin' him for a long ways." Both Casey and Eli were startled by the voice behind them. So caught up were they in trying to stop the reluctant longhorn from dragging them across Oklahoma, they had not been aware of the two men approaching their camp. "Much obliged for your help," the voice continued. "We'll take him off your hands now."

Eli quickly tied the rope around the tree, and he and Casey scanned the stream in search of the owner of the voice. In a few seconds, a man appeared from the other side of the bushes by the stream. Carrying a rifle, he was followed by another man, also carrying rifle. They were a dirty-looking pair and obviously hunting strays from the D&T herd. Casey took a quick glance at the steer and saw the D&T brand. "I think you fellows have been chasin' the wrong cow. This one is wearin' the D and T brand. That's the brand we work for. Our job is to pick up the strays that got left behind."

"Well, now, that's a funny thing, ain't it?" the older one, doing all the talking, stated. "You boys are ridin' a helluva long ways behind that herd, and I don't see no other strays except that one that belongs to us. You see, the trail boss of that outfit sold us that there cow for four dollars. You're so far behind them, you didn't know that. No hard feelin's, though. We'll just take our cow and be on our way."

"I'm afraid we can't let you do that," Eli said. "We're responsible for all the strays we find."

"Is that a fact?" the older man replied. "Then maybe you're responsible for givin' me back my four dollars I paid for the cow."

"Sorry," Eli told him, "if somebody told you they could sell you this cow for four dollars, they was lyin' to ya. We ain't carryin' no cash, anyway."

"Sounds like you're callin' me a liar," the man said.

"It did sound that way, didn't it?" Eli glanced at Casey. "Did it sound to you like I called him a liar?"

"That's what it sounded like to me," Casey said. With a strong feeling that he knew what was coming next, he took another step away from the tree and softly said, "I'll take the young one."

"Right," Eli answered, never taking his eyes off the older man.

"Take it easy, Lige," the older man cautioned when it appeared Casey and Eli were ready to fight. "Little misunderstandin', I reckon," he said then. "Ain't worth gittin' hot about. Just a little misunderstandin'. Come on, Lige, let's be on our way." Lige looked undecided, but he did as he was told. They turned around and walked back on the other side of the stream. After a minute or two, they rode out of the trees and headed back toward the Red.

"I thought for a minute there, I was gonna have to see how much rust had gotten on my fast-draw action," Casey commented. "The last time I checked it, I timed it with a sundial."

"The young one he called Lige looked like he was disappointed when the older one called him off," Eli said. "I expect he didn't like a fast-draw contest when it was rifles against handguns."

"Reckon how long it'll be before they come back to see us?" Casey wondered.

"Hard to say," Eli replied. "Depends on how bad they want that cow. But we better be mighty particular where we pick to rest the horses, in case they ain't willin' to follow us till we make camp tonight."

"It's a damn shame, ain't it?" Casey said.

"What is?" Eli asked.

"Them fellows back there," Casey replied. "You know there ain't but one reason they wanted that cow, and that was to eat it. The same thing we're gonna do with it. If they'da come up to us and admitted they was just chasin' a stray that got left behind, we'da most likely just shared it with 'em. Now somebody's liable to get killed over this one dumb cow that ain't got enough sense to keep up."

"Whaddaya reckon they'd try if they knew what was in these saddlebags?" Eli posed the question.

The discussion was much the same between Rufus and Lige Coggins from the opposite side of the matter. "I don't know why we just didn't go ahead and cut them two fellers down," Lige complained. "Didn't neither one of 'em look very fast to me."

"You can't judge a man's speed with a gun just by lookin' at him," his older brother said. "If they was any good a-tall, they oughta beat our rifles with their handguns. Did you have a cartridge in the chamber and the hammer back?" Lige didn't answer. "I didn't think so," Rufus said. "Neither did I. So there weren't no use in takin' a chance when we can just wait till we get a better chance. I got a feelin' we can pick up somethin' a lot better'n a cow. Them packhorses was loaded pretty heavy."

"I reckon you're right," Lige agreed. "I sure got me a cravin' for some fresh beef, but it don't make no sense to take chances when you don't have to."

"Now you're talkin' smart. We'll get in behind these fellers and see what kinda shot they give us next time they stop to rest their horses. If we don't get a good shot at 'em then, we'll just wait till tonight and catch 'em when they're asleep."

They were already seeing signs that told them they were catching up with the herd of cattle moving across the flat terrain of western Oklahoma. Water was scarce in long stretches, and when they reached a small creek or stream, it was sometimes reduced to a small trickle of water. When they made their first stop after breaking camp that morning, it was beside a narrow stream that was struggling to recover from the passing of the cattle. They made their fire on the open bank of the stream. And while they sat and watched the prairie behind them, they were confident it would be difficult for the two would-be horse thieves to approach them without being seen a mile away.

When it was time to make their camp for the night, they were fortunate to find a narrow creek running parallel to the path of the cattle trail. Like the water opportunities before on this day's journey, it showed signs of the cattle's wear and tear, but there was water. Fortunately, the creek's course was traced by a belt of trees on each side, so there was protection. They set their camp up to take advantage of the trees and the banks of the creek. Fully expecting a visit, they made their supper with what was left of the smoked jerky, hardtack, and coffee. They thought about the men who worked for them, eating like kings at Smiley's chuck wagon compared to their humble repast. They had a cow, but they couldn't take the risk of killing and butchering it. The poor beast was already beginning to look in bad shape because it had to travel at the horses' speed and was not allowed to graze along the way. At nightfall, they pulled the horses and the cow in and tied them behind them in the creek bottom.

"You wanna try to get some sleep?" Eli asked when they let the fire die down. "We can take turns stayin' awake. I'll take the first watch."

"I'll get some sleep after we take care of these two birds," Casey answered. "You go ahead, if you want to."

"Maybe later," Eli said. Like Casey, he didn't trust himself to wake up, and he didn't trust Casey to wake him. So they stayed awake and talked about what they would do the next day. "I'll tell you one thing, after the last several days, I'm ready to ride around that herd and head straight for Dodge City. And when we get there, I'm gonna check into the hotel, get myself a bath and a shave. Then I'm going to a fancy restaurant and eat a decent meal. We've got the money to afford it, and we ain't even counted Edwin Polk's contribution yet."

Casey laughed. "That's right, we never got the chance to see what that visit to the Fort Worth Investment Bank brought in. And I don't reckon right now would be a good time to count it, either." So it was pretty much concluded that neither one of them was going to be able to sleep, and they decided where best to position themselves to wait for their guests.

Just in case the cow was really the only thing they planned to take, they moved the longhorn a little farther downstream from the horses to make it easier to steal. "You know, it mighta made a whole lot more sense to have just given them the damn cow in the first place. It mighta saved us all this trouble."

"I don't know, I kinda doubt it. Those two looked like they'd cut your throat just to see if you had anything in your pockets. If we had just given them the cow, they mighta thought it was because we'd rather give it up to keep them from wantin' to see what's in the packs."

It was well past midnight when Rufus and Lige tied their horses in the trees short of the glow of the smoldering campfire on the creek bank. "I can't see nobody settin' up near that fire, can you?" Rufus asked.

"No," Lige answered. "I don't see nobody. Looks like they stacked some of them packs on top of the bank so they could hide behind 'em. I think they're waitin' for us."

"Maybe so," Rufus said. Then a movement in the bushes near the water caught their attention. They both trained their rifles on the spot. "Don't shoot!" Rufus whispered. "It's the cow. They tied the cow down there. Left it as bait so we'd try to steal it. Then they'd cut loose on us." They waited several minutes longer. "I bet they went to sleep." They waited several minutes more. "I'm gonna slip down this bank and untie that cow. If that don't wake 'em up, I'm gonna lead the cow on up here. If one of 'em raises up to shoot, you cut him down."

"You sure that ain't a little too chancy?" Lige asked. "That's why they tied the cow back this way in the first place, to get one of us to try to steal it."

"I know that, damn it, but they're asleep. You just be ready in case they ain't." Rufus didn't wait to talk about it further, but slid over the edge of the bank and sneaked up to the tree and untied the cow's rope. Then he led the cow back to where he had left Lige and tied it to a tree there.

"I swear," Lige whispered, amazed to think that Rufus had been right.

"I told you," Rufus said, "they went to sleep. Let's go make sure they don't wake up." He moved quickly along the bank and Lige followed right behind him. When they were almost even with the packs that had been placed along the top of the bank, like breastworks, they slowed down and sneaked quietly up to the packs. With rifles ready to fire, they rose up over the packs to see two sleeping bodies halfway down the bank. They opened fire simultaneously, cranked another cartridge in and fired again, then once more to be certain.

They stood there, staring down at their slaughter, when they heard the voice behind them, "Hey." They both turned in time to catch a shot, dead center in their chests, fired by their intended victims, who were lying on the ground in the darkness of the road that ran along the creek.

They got up and walked over to the creek bank to make sure their would-be assassins were dead. "They didn't give us much choice, did they?" Eli asked.

"Reckon not," Casey replied. "We take no joy in killin'. Looks like we might be sewin' some patches on Elmer and Oscar's coats."

"Let's drag 'em outta here and find their horses in the mornin'. Maybe we can get a couple of hours' sleep."

"Maybe you can," Casey said. He wasn't quite sure he could go to sleep until he recovered from having to shoot a man down. "I'm gonna look for their horses now and cut 'em loose. You don't wanna keep 'em, do you?"

"Nah," Eli said. "I doubt they're worth much, anyway. Might as well let 'em go free."

"Go ahead and get some sleep, if you can," Casey said. "I'll take care of the bodies and the horses." He didn't wait for Eli to volunteer to help him, but turned and walked down the creek, figuring the horses had to be back that way somewhere. It wasn't fifteen minutes before he was back, leading the two horses. "You were right, they ain't worth a whole lot." He took a rope off the saddle of one of the horses and tied one end of it around Rufus's boots. When Eli saw what he was doing, he took the rope off the other horse and started tying Lige's boots together. "I thought you were gonna go to bed," Casey said.

"How the hell can I go to sleep with you doin' all this stuff?" Eli asked. "Let's take 'em over yonder on the other side of that little rise." He pointed out a low rise in the darkness about forty yards away. They each took the reins of one of the horses and led them to the rise, where they untied the ropes. Then they pulled the saddles and bridles off the horses and left them beside the bodies. Like the horses, the saddles were poor quality and not worth bothering with. Just for the hell of it, they did a quick check of Rufus's and Lige's pockets and found a dollar and a half in change. "We shoulda just let 'em have the damn cow," Eli repeated.

"What are we gonna do about that cow, anyway?" Casey asked. "If we don't butcher him pretty soon, we'll run the fat right off him. You know, we're gonna catch up with the herd tomorrow, so we're gonna have to swing wide around 'em to make sure we don't get spotted by any of the boys out lookin' for strays. Why don't we butcher that cow right here, we're gonna be runnin' outta food pretty damn quick. And there ain't no place to buy any between here and Kansas." He paused and waited for Eli's opinion.

"Hell, fine by me," Eli said. "We'll do it in the mornin'." That settled, they both climbed in their bedrolls and went to sleep.

Chapter 21

As they had planned the night before, they built their fire up the next morning and butchered the steer, feasting on freshly cooked beef while they worked. Using the same methods that had worked on the cow before this one, they cut strips of meat and smoked them to serve as jerky. In a hurry to go ahead of the herd of cattle, they spent half a day in the preparation of their meat, hoping it was enough to preserve it for a reasonable period of time. It was afternoon when they packed up again, and even though a short inspection of the old men's coats still showed signs of dampness, they decided they would eventually dry. And the bullet holes could be patched. "It'll just add to the disguise," Eli commented. They saddled up then and set out once again for Kansas.

After a ride of about fifteen or sixteen miles, they came to a sizable creek that was still muddy from the passing of the herd, so they knew they had almost caught up to them. They decided to stop there and rest the horses. They took the occasion to eat some of their fresh beef. Then when the horses were ready, they set out again. They had not ridden far when they saw the dust cloud ahead of them. Not willing to risk being seen, they veered off well to the west and started around the herd. Before long, the main body of the dust cloud was directly east of them, so they knew they had caught up. It was getting along late in the afternoon by then, but their horses had only traveled about twenty miles since leaving their last night's camp. So they would continue on. They knew the herd would be stopping pretty soon for the night, giving them the opportunity to put the cattle some distance behind them. They continued on after darkness descended upon the flat prairie, planning to ride until the horses tired or they came upon a campsite too good to pass up. The appearance of a full moon helped to avoid bad spots in their path. Finally they came to a healthy creek and decided to camp there for the night. After another meal of fresh beef, they were awarded a peaceful night's sleep.

They set out the next morning, confident that they had a sizable lead on the herd, and it was increasing by the hour. They had traveled only about fifteen miles when they spotted a ribbon of trees crossing their path in the distance, which would normally indicate a river. "The Canadian, I expect," Casey speculated. "I didn't think we were that close yet."

"That's the only river it could be," Eli said. "We're makin' pretty good time, I reckon. It's hard for me to tell. We started out, then went back, then started out again. Looks like we came to a river at a pretty good time to rest the horses and eat some breakfast."

They continued on for another mile when Eli suddenly exclaimed, "What's that? Look yonder!"

"Where?" Casey asked. He could see it was a river then, but couldn't spot whatever had gotten Eli's attention. He looked then in the direction Eli was pointing and saw what had caught his attention. "A cabin," he said. "Somebody built a cabin on the river."

"That weren't there the last time we drove a herd up this trail. Whoever it is built it right in the middle of the Chisholm Trail. Might be some trouble there."

"I don't see no crops of any kind," Casey said. "Maybe he ain't a farmer."

"This land ain't been opened to homesteaders, anyway," Eli remarked. "The government most likely don't even know he's here yet."

They continued to stare at the cabin on the north bank of the Canadian River, noticing as they drew closer that it was of new logs, a little larger than the typical log dwelling, with a sizable porch in front. "There's a sign on that porch post by the steps," Casey said. "I didn't see it at first. We'll have to get closer to read what it says."

"Most likely, 'Keep out or I'll shoot,'" Eli japed.

"It's a store," Casey said after a short distance closer. "'Britt's Store,'" he read.

"Well, I'll be . . ." Eli started. "The last place in the world you'd find one, and the only place in the world we need one right now. I hope he's got some of the supplies we need."

They guided their horses directly toward the store, forded the river, and pulled up in front of the store. A tall, gray-haired man walked out on the porch and watched them dismount. "Mornin'," he greeted them while looking them over carefully.

"Mornin'," Casey returned. "This your store?"

"Yes, sir, it is." He pointed to the sign on the post. "I'm Leonard Britt. What can I help you fellers with? I've got most general supplies, like lard and flour, bacon and coffee, sugar, beans. Whaddaya need?"

"Everything you just called off," Casey said. "We're down pretty low on most everything. How long have you been here? You weren't here the last time we came up this way."

"I've been here a little shy of ten months," Britt said.

"What made you decide to build a store out here?" Eli wondered aloud, finding it hard to believe.

Britt laughed. "Lack of sense would be my first answer, but if you really wanna know, I thought I would get the jump on everybody else. I had a little tradin' post east of here, back on the Blue River in the Nations. I got to thinkin' about all those folks drivin' cattle up the Chisholm Trail and nowhere all the way through Injun Territory to buy a pound of lard. So I came on out and built this place. Well, I got the jump on everybody, all right, just in time for the cattle market to go dead." He shook his head as if unable to believe it, himself. "That's my story. Where are you fellers headed?"

"Dodge City," Casey answered. "But I've got a little bit of news for you that might brighten your day. There's a great big herd of Texas longhorns about a day or two behind us." He glanced at Eli. "Wouldn't you say, Tom?" He asked it to alert him not to use their real names.

Eli snuffed a chuckle. "Yeah, Bob, about a day or two." He looked at Britt then and asked, "Where do you get your merchandise, way out here on the Canadian?"

"Same place you're goin'," Britt answered, "Dodge City. My son, Tucker, drives a wagon up there to get what we need. It ain't very handy, I'll say that. But I'm right glad to see you fellers. Come on in the store and I'll see if I can fix you up with everything you need."

When they followed him inside, Britt called out, "It's all right, hon, couple of fellers needin' some supplies." A woman, who had been standing just inside the door to a storeroom, came out to meet them. She was holding a shotgun, which she quickly placed behind the counter. "This is my wife, Peggy. We've had to take a few precautions lately. Had some trouble from two brothers who tried to break into the storeroom one night."

"Pleased to meet you, ma'am. We're Bob and Tom White," Casey said, then asked, "Was one of those two you're talkin' about named Lige?"

"That's a fact," Britt replied. "Lige and Rufus Coggins. Do you know 'em?"

"Know of 'em," Casey answered. "I don't think you'll be seein' them anymore. We heard they ran into some trouble and went south for good."

"Are you sure about that?" Britt asked.

"I think you can count on it," Casey said.

"Well, I hope so," Peggy said. "They were the two nastiest men I think I have ever seen."

Casey and Eli got down to business then and started calling out the things they needed. Peggy and Leonard both hustled to fetch the items as soon as they were called and placed them on the counter. When they could think of nothing else, Peggy began suggesting things, prompting Casey to tell her that neither one of them could cook. They did take the dried apples, though, since they would require no cooking. "We better save something for that outfit driving those cattle behind us," Casey said.

"I've got plenty on hand for them," Britt said. "Don't worry about them."

There was a moment of silence on the part of Britt and his wife when he added up the total bill and informed them of the total. It was immediately followed by a blossoming of smiles on their faces when Casey and Eli promptly pulled out some cash and each paid half of the bill. "I'll help you carry that out to put on your packhorses," Britt offered.

"Much obliged," Casey said. "We're gonna move down the bank a little way and build a fire to cook some breakfast and rest the horses. We'll arrange the packs then."

"You haven't had your breakfast yet?" Peggy asked.

"No, ma'am," Eli answered her. "We generally start out first thing in the morning and don't stop till the horses need a rest. And that's when we fix breakfast."

"After the nice order you gave us this mornin', I ought to fix your breakfast," Peggy said.

"Oh, no, ma'am," Casey responded. "No need for you to go to that trouble. We 'preciate the offer, though." He winked at Eli.

"Nonsense," Peggy replied. "My stove's still hot. I'll fire it up again and make you some pancakes and ham with real maple syrup and coffee. Will that do? I can make that real quick."

"It sure would," Casey replied, "but we can pay you for it."

"No, indeed, this is our way of sayin' thanks for the business," Peggy said. "You go ahead and take care of your horses and put your supplies away, and I'll call you when your breakfast is ready."

"Say 'yes, ma'am,' Bob," Eli directed.

"Yes, ma'am," Casey said, and they started carrying their sacks outside with Britt lending a hand. They pulled the saddles off and the packs as well. They left Biscuit and Smoke free to graze on the grass near the store, but hobbled the packhorses. After Britt went back in the store, they took the packs apart and repacked them with their new supplies, taking great care to protect the large sum of money they were carrying. In a short while, Peggy came out on the porch and told them that breakfast was ready. They hurried inside to find it set up for them on the kitchen table, complete with a pot of fresh coffee.

"I think I mighta died and gone to Heaven," Eli cracked.

"We were pretty desperate for a decent meal," Casey explained for him. "And we thought there wasn't anyplace to buy anything to eat before we got to Dodge City."

They lingered long after polishing off the pancakes to drink the pot dry. Then after trying to pay Peggy something for the breakfast, they thanked them profusely and rode off to the north. Their visit left Peggy and Leonard very happy to have met their new friends, Bob and Tom White.

* * *

When Casey and Eli were saying good-bye to their new friends, some two hundred and fifty miles south of the store on the Canadian River, another man who was treated like a friend was riding a bay horse named Scrappy down the street in Fort Worth. As he approached the sheriff's office, Colton Gray was fighting mixed emotions about the news that had brought him from Waco. They had robbed a bank in Fort Worth, the notorious old-men robbers. He intended to follow up with an investigation as thoroughly as he had with the bank in Austin. He had to talk to the eyewitnesses and hear their description of the two bandits. For surely, it was someone imitating the old men. The cattle herd from the D&T Ranch had started out weeks ago and they would have been somewhere up in the middle of the Oklahoma Territory at the time of this bank robbery in Fort Worth. The word he had was Casey and Eli were both with the cattle drive. His intention was to investigate this latest bank robbery as if they were still his prime suspects. And his hope was to find proof that they could not have been involved in it.

When he arrived at the sheriff's office, he tried to clear his mind to hear Sheriff Courtright's report. "Mornin', Colton," Longhair Jim Courtright greeted him when he walked in the door. "Figured I'd be seein' you. Looks like your old boys are still up to their mischief."

"Looks that way," Colton replied. "If it is the same old men and not somebody tryin' to copy them."

"There weren't nothin' I could do about that robbery," the sheriff said, intending to establish that fact at once. "It was already over, and the thieves had already left town before I was even notified. The crazy part about it is, they didn't even know it in the bank that they was bein' robbed, and the tellers carried right on with business. Edwin Polk was tied up and layin' on the floor of the safe room, while the two old bandits filled two carpetbags with money outta the safe." He had to pause to chuckle. Then he excused himself. "I know it ain't funny, but that's the way it happened. And the two old men strolled outta the bank as casual as you please, carrying their carpetbags full of money. Well, like I said, by the time they told me about it, the trail was stone cold. Nobody on the street paid any attention to the two old birds ridin' outta town. So there weren't nothin' I could do about it. They just disappeared."

"I understand that, Sheriff," Colton said. "My boss told me the same thing, so nobody in the marshal's office thinks there could have been any action on your part. Truth of the matter is, the only reason I'm up here is to cover the same ground as I did on the first robbery they pulled here. And maybe I'll find some of their footprints in the same places as the pair who robbed the cattle buyer's office. I'll try to stay out of your way while I'm in town."

"That won't be no problem," Courtright said. "If I can help you, just let me know."

"'Preciate it, Sheriff. I'll go on up to the bank now and talk to them."

He left the sheriff's office and rode back up the street to the bank, where he caught Edwin Polk coming from the back room, carrying a cup of coffee. "Are you Mr. Polk?" Colton asked, taking a guess.

"Yes, I am," Polk answered, a little irritated at having been caught out of his office. "How can I help you?"

Colton opened his coat to show his badge. "I'm U.S. Deputy Marshal Colton Gray," he said. "I'm following up on the robbery you had here. I'd appreciate a few minutes of your time, if you don't mind." He nodded toward his coffee cup. "Is this a bad time?"

"No, it's as good a time as any," Polk answered. "Would you

like a cup?" Colton declined, so Polk said, "Come on into my office," and led the way. Inside his office, Polk sat down at his desk and went through the robbery again, obviously weary of telling the story. At Colton's request, he described the two robbers as completely as he could remember them. "They didn't come when the bank opens in the morning, as you would expect," Polk pointed out. "They knew somehow that the time lock wouldn't open the safe until twelve, noon."

"Think back about the day before the robbery," Colton said. "Maybe you remember two men coming in to talk to you about opening an account, or something like that. And you mighta told them when the time lock opened. You remember anyone like that?"

Polk hesitated a moment to recall. "Well, not specifically two men like that, but I often talk to different people about the bank's policies."

"Did you show the safe to anyone that you'd never talked to before that day?"

Polk hesitated again. "I've showed our safe to many new customers, but I don't recall anyone near the time of the robbery."

"I think we're dealing with two very intelligent men who are staging their robberies in disguise as two older men," Colton said.

Polk wasn't so sure. "Maybe you're right, Deputy, but those two old men certainly looked, and talked, like the real thing."

Colton could see that he wasn't going to learn anything new or helpful from Edwin Polk, so he thanked him for his time and left him to finish his coffee. On the way out, Colton stopped to talk to the two tellers. He was told that Julian had the most contact with the two old men. Like Polk, the tellers were convinced they had been talking to two genuine old men. When he left the bank, Colton had an even higher appreciation for the genius of the two bank robbers, whoever they were. And he was still not convinced that his trail would not eventually lead to the D&T Cattle Company.

With no fresh leads to follow, he decided to check the old ones again, and that called for a trip out the San Antonio road to the camp they had used for the robbery of Birch Bradshaw's office. If they were the same two men who pulled that robbery off, chances were they used that hideout again. If nothing else, it would confirm the fact that they definitely were the same two men. When he came to Hasting's Supply, he decided to check with Hasting as well, so he asked him if he had seen the two men who bought black powder to get rid of some yellow jackets. Hasting hesitated before saying that they had been in since then, but it was obvious to him that Casey and Eli had nothing to do with any robberies. He suspected that the young deputy was full of wild ideas. So he said he had not seen them.

Colton continued on to the creek. As he suspected the two bandits would have done, he rode up the middle of the creek until he reached the campsite. Except for some old scarring of the creek bank where the horses had once left the water, there appeared to be no sign of anyone recently. Actually, it occurred to him that the campsite showed no sign that anyone had camped there before. So he dismounted and began a closer search of the small clearing, until he located the ashes of a campfire, covered by a dead tree limb. After its last use, the ashes were hidden under the dead leaves. He guessed that the wood that wasn't completely consumed by the fire was thrown into the water to float away down the creek.

He tried to envision the scene in his mind. "It's after the robbery," he said to himself. "We've gotten back to our hideout, and nobody's seen us. Do we take our packhorses and run? Or do we get out of our disguises first? It'll be a lot safer to get out of our disguises first. Everybody's looking for two old men. Nobody's looking for two younger men." That meant they would have to clean themselves up after taking off their wigs and beards and whatever, because all witnesses insisted that their skin was old man's skin. He looked around him for the best place to wash your face and hands and decided on a little section of the bank with no bushes in the way. So he went there and knelt next to a small oak tree.

"This would be my choice," he announced as he envisioned himself washing his face and hands. After a few moments, he started to get up again, but when he took hold of the tree to help himself, he felt something slimy. Thinking he had mashed a worm or a caterpillar, he was surprised to find a little smear of grease of some kind on the tree trunk. It was dark, like grease you might pack a gun in to ship it somewhere, he thought. "Or rub all over your face to make you look a hundred years old," he said, and rubbed some on the back of his hand. "They were here! And they didn't go to Kansas with the cattle! They robbed that bank and went right back to their ranch." He knew he was going to have to make the two-day ride to the D&T Ranch to prove it.

With no reason to stay there any longer, he rode back out to the road and headed back to Fort Worth, straight to the stable to get his packhorse. When he had first hit town that morning, he had dropped his packhorse·off at a stable, thinking he would be in town all day. Now he was regretting that decision for it meant just that much more lost time. It was not yet noon, so he could still arrive at D&T by suppertime in two days. He would just ride a little longer tonight.

After he picked up his packhorse, he wasted little time returning to the San Antonio road and starting out for the D&T. As he set a gait for Scrappy of walking, alternating with a gentle trot, he had to wonder what he was going to do when he confronted Casey and Eli with an accusation that he was not sure he could prove. He couldn't help what he suspected. His gut feeling was they had to be the two old men. The thing that complicated it for him was the fact that he wished he were wrong.

He rode through the gate at the ranch around suppertime after pushing Scrappy and the sorrel hard most of the day. Once through the gate, he went directly to the house, dismounted, and walked up to knock on the front door. After a short wait, the door was opened by Miguel Garcia. "Señor Gray!" Miguel exclaimed, surprised to see him again. He looked past him to see if he was alone.

"Howdy, Miguel," Colton said. "I need to see Casey or Eli."

"They are not here. Only my wife and I are here."

"When will they be back?" Colton asked, assuming they were somewhere on the ranch.

"I do not know," Miguel said.

"What is it, Miguel?" Juanita said, coming up the hall behind him. "Señor Gray!" she exclaimed as well. "Is something wrong?"

"He say he need to see Señor Tubbs or Señor Doolin," Miguel told her.

"They are not here," she said. "They take the cattle to be sold. They have been gone about four weeks. They not tell you?"

They told me, but I didn't believe them, he thought. To her, he said, "I knew the men were taking the cattle to Kansas, but I didn't know they were goin' with them."

"Yes, they have to go to make the price and take care of the money," Juanita said. "They will be sad they missed you."

"It's no problem," Colton said. "I was just on my way back to Waco, and as long as I was this close, I thought I'd stop by and say howdy."

"You must come in and I fix you some supper," Juanita said. "Is too late for you to go on tonight. You can stay here. Miguel will put your horses in the barn and you start out again in the morning after breakfast."

"I don't wanna put you to that trouble," Colton said. "I would like to sleep in the bunkhouse tonight, though. That would be real handy."

"I fix you supper. Then you sleep in bunkhouse. In the morning, I fix you breakfast. Casey and Eli be mad at me if I don't. They say you good friend."

How could he argue? He went with Miguel to take care of his horses; then they returned to the kitchen, where Juanita was adding to the supper she had already started for Miguel and herself.

Chapter 22

With no other goal in mind for the immediate future, Casey and Eli concentrated on getting to Dodge City as soon as possible without putting unnecessary stress on Smoke and Biscuit. As it turned out, it took them six days from the time they said so long to Leonard and Peggy Britt. They rode past the cattle pens near the railroad to see if there were cattle waiting to be loaded on a train, but the pens were empty. "That ain't a good sign, is it?" Eli remarked. There were several hundred cows in one of the holding pens, however.

"Probably just means they ain't really started yet," Casey said. "We'll wake 'em up when our cattle get here."

"That ain't gonna be for about another three weeks at the rate they're movin'," Eli said. "What the heck are we gonna do while we're waitin' for them to get here?"

"What we said we was gonna do back on that prairie when we didn't have nothin' to eat but that one bony cow and no place to buy food," Casey said. "We're gonna get us a room in that hotel we just passed and enjoy some of the fruits of our labor for a spell. We can dang sure afford it. This ain't a bad-lookin' little town. Looks like they got enough saloons for us to find one that suits us."

"Reckon how much money we have got?" Eli asked. "I

can't believe we ain't counted it yet." The money from the bank holdup had been packed so well in with their old clothes and blankets, they were reluctant to take it all out, afraid they'd never get it put away so well again. "I don't know about you, but I ain't feelin' real easy about all the cash money we've got with us. I hope that hotel back there has got some good locks on the doors. 'Cause I don't think I can sleep at night if we leave it in our packs in a stable."

"Maybe we could put some of it in the hotel safe, if they've got one. It looks like a brand-new hotel. They might have a good safe." It didn't help their problem when they each brought ten thousand dollars with them when they left the ranch. "Let's go check on that hotel right now and make sure we can get a room."

Eli agreed with that, so they turned their horses around and went back to the Dodge Railroad Hotel, where they were met by John Danbury, the desk clerk. "Can I help you, gentlemen?"

"We've just rode in across Oklahoma and part of Kansas," Casey said, "and we're gonna need a couple of rooms."

"How long will you be with us?" John asked.

"I'd say about twenty days," Casey answered. "Unless that herd gets in a day or two before that."

"'Twenty days'?" John repeated, in case he hadn't heard correctly.

"*Twenty days,*" Casey confirmed.

"For that length of time, we could let you have the weekly rate," John offered. "Six dollars a week. The usual rate is one dollar a night, so that is the same as giving you one night free."

"That sounds fair," Eli said. "We'll take that."

"We ask that you pay the first week in advance if you take that special rate," John said.

"That'll be fine," Casey said, pulling a roll of bills out and counting out six dollars. Eli did the same. "Now," Casey continued, "we're carryin' a little more cash than we're comfortable with when we're in a town that's new to us. Has the hotel got a safe that we could keep some of our money in?"

"Yes, sir, we do," John said, giving the dusty pair a closer inspection. "Let me get Mr. Pearson to talk to you. He's the manager of the hotel. I'll be right back." He stepped away from the desk and went into an office behind the check-in. In a few moments, he was back, followed by the manager.

"Good afternoon, gentlemen. I'm Richard Pearson. John tells me you'd like to keep some money in the hotel safe."

"That's a fact," Casey said. "We'd just feel more comfortable if it was in your safe, instead of our rooms."

"That's certainly understandable, although I'd like to assure you that our cleaning staff here at the hotel is highly trustworthy. How much do you want to put in the safe?"

"We ain't decided yet. We thought we'd unpack our things and see what we wanted to carry and how much we oughta put in safekeepin'."

"I understand you're plannin' to be with us for about three weeks. Is that right?"

"That's right," Casey said. "We'll bring you the money, and you can have a couple of folks stand by us when you open the safe. We're Casey Tubbs and Eli Doolin from the D and T Cattle Company in Lampasas County, Texas. We look pretty rough right now, 'cause we just got done ridin' across Oklahoma Territory and half of Kansas. We'll look a lot better to you after we get a bath and a shave and some clean clothes on."

Pearson had to laugh. "All right, Mr. Tubbs and Mr. Doolin, you just bring whatever amount you want to put in our safe and give it to John, here. And he'll give you a paper stating the amount you put in our safe and I'll sign it. Fair enough?"

"Fair enough," Casey said. "I don't blame John a bit for bein' careful, though. These days, you never know who might walk in off the prairie. The next question is, do you have a stable the hotel guests use, or do we just find one ourselves?"

"The hotel isn't affiliated with either of the two stables in town, but Louis Brown is the closest, and he has a fine reputation. You passed his stable when you rode in from the south. I take it you didn't happen to notice the sign just before you reached the stable that says no firearms are allowed in Dodge City."

That came as a surprise to them both. "No, we didn't notice that sign," Eli said. "Didn't expect to see one like that."

"I should warn you that it is not a casual warning. In reality, it applies in most part to this side of town, north of the railroad tracks. That's where Marshal Wyatt Earp drew his 'deadline.' Everything on the other side of that line is the brothel district and the wild part of town. And that's where he wants to keep the wild ones who wanna shoot up the town. So please take my word for it, on this side of the deadline, you will be arrested for carrying a gun."

"I reckon we'd best take our guns off then," Casey said.

"You can check them at the sheriff's office," Pearson said. "They'll give you a little check to redeem your gun when you leave." Then he nodded to both of them. "I hope you enjoy your stay with us. John will tell you where everything is." He chuckled and said, "The washroom and the dining room." He went back to his office then and John gave them their keys to two rooms on the second floor. When he left, John told them that most of their guests just left their firearms in their rooms.

They went outside and took bundles holding the money out of the packs and took them upstairs to their rooms. Then they made a second trip to get their saddlebags and war bags. Once everything they wanted to guard was in the room, they locked the doors and took their horses to Brown's Stable. After making their arrangements with Louis for the care of their horses, Casey said, "This is the first time we've ever brought a herd to Dodge City, so we don't know much about the way things are handled here. Where do you go to find the buyers at the stockyards?"

"Most of the buyers are stayin' at the same hotel that you are," Brown said. "How many cows are you boys bringin' in?"

"A few hundred over three thousand," Casey answered.

Brown looked surprised. "Oh," he said. "I expect when they find that out, they'll be comin' to talk to you."

They had a little time before the hotel dining room would be open for supper, so they went back to the hotel to take care of a few things. The first of these was to count their money. So they took the paper-wrapped bundles of bills out of the various articles of clothing and blankets they had been hidden in after they disposed of the carpetbags they had used to carry the money out of the bank. They were somewhat disappointed to find there was not as much money as they had expected. Most of the wrapped bundles held small bills, ones and fives, with a smaller proportion holding large bills. They counted forty-two thousand dollars, and with the few thousand dollars they each had left after paying Emma Woodward's debts, they had a grand sum of forty-eight thousand dollars. "I swear," Eli declared, "we don't never wanna get caught in a fix like this again, with so much money we can't hide it."

Casey had to agree. "We shoulda took the doggone money from the bank back home," he said, even though they knew that would have thrown too much light on what they were up to. All their work clothes and makeup paraphernalia took up too much room in their packsaddles, as it was. They discussed the money situation further, and finally decided to put twenty-five thousand in the hotel safe. That would leave them each with ten thousand and five hundred dollars to conceal the best way they could. They ended up carrying a thousand dollars pocket money and risking the rest in the stable. They figured that if Louis Brown was inclined to see what they had in their packs, he would most likely not wait long to find out. So, if they gave him a day or two to satisfy his curiosity, the risk would not be great if they slipped the balance into their packs.

After the money issue was decided, the next thing on the agenda was to visit the washroom. So they took their shaving kits and their one change of clothes, locked up their rooms, and went down the back stairs to the washroom. When they got there, they discovered there was an attendant present to fill a tub with hot water and provide them with towels and washcloths. His name was Vance, and he also provided them with a handled mirror so they could shave while they were in the tub. It was pure luxury, and to top it off, Vance offered to cut their hair for fifty cents each. By the time they were finished, they weren't sure anyone they knew would recognize them. They each paid Vance for the haircut and gave him a dollar for all the extra care he provided. They went back to their rooms then to get the money to put in the hotel's safe. When that had been taken care of, it was time for the dining room to open.

"Good evening, gentlemen," David Morgan, the dining-room manager, greeted them as they walked in. "You can sit anywhere you like." They looked beyond him at the nearly empty room and decided on a table beside a window. They had just gotten comfortable in their chairs when a young woman with a hard face approached their table.

"Evenin', fellows," she said. "My name's Ethel, and I'll be taking care of your supper. You want coffee?" They said yes. "I figured you would. The special tonight is venison. If you don't want venison, we can fry you a steak."

"I'll take the venison," Casey said.

"Me too," Eli declared.

"Cattlemen?" Ethel asked. When Eli said they were, and asked how did she know? She said, "'Cause you jumped on venison so quick. Tells me you eat beef most of the time. You come in with a herd today?"

"Not today," Eli answered. "We came in ahead of one that'll be here in a couple of weeks or more."

"I didn't think I heard any cattle come into town today," she said. "Where are your cattle coming from?"

"Texas," Eli said. "We came on ahead of the herd to get an idea of what the prices have been."

"Do you have many cows?"

"About three thousand," he answered.

"That's a big herd," she remarked. "I'll go get your coffee, and your supper will be out in a minute." She disappeared through the kitchen door.

When she left, Casey said, "Ethel sure must be interested in cattle. I thought if we were gonna get any coffee, we'd have to go get it, ourselves."

"I doubt it," Eli replied. "I think she was just trying to find something I was interested in so she could talk to me. That's what I get for gettin' so slicked up tonight."

"I reckon that musta been it," Casey said sarcastically as Ethel reappeared, carrying two cups of coffee. The dining room began to see more customers then as the supper hour grew older. Many of the diners were men, eating alone, dressed in business suits. Since it was called the Dodge Railroad Hotel, Casey and Eli figured those businessmen might work for the railroad. Soon Ethel brought their supper, and the venison was done very well, so they took their time to enjoy it. Afterward, Ethel brought fresh coffee and removed the dirty dishes. "That was good deer meat, Ethel, we enjoyed it," Casey told her, which seemed to please her.

"You just sit there and enjoy your coffee," she said as she walked away to wait on her other customers.

"I ain't sayin' a word," Eli said when she was gone. "I'm gonna make her come out and ask for it."

"What are you mumblin' about?" Casey asked. "Ask for what?"

"My room number," Eli answered.

"Ha!" Casey barked. "You might be right, and the next question she'd ask is, 'Would you like to meet my mother?'"

Eli was thinking of his retort when they were suddenly interrupted. "Pardon me, gentlemen, I hope I'm not interrupting. But Ethel was telling me that you're in the cattle business. My name's Marvin Fletcher, and I'm a representative for Chicago Meat Packers, Inc. I was just curious. Our spotters haven't caught any sign of a herd anywhere near Dodge at the present time. Mind if I sit down?"

"No, not at all," Casey responded. "Have a seat. I'm Casey Tubbs and this is my partner, Eli Doolin. We're the owners of D and T Cattle Company down in Lampasas County, Texas. And Ethel is right, we do have a herd that should get here in about nineteen or twenty days."

"That long, huh?"

"Yep, Eli and I decided to come on ahead of the cattle so we could hang around for a while to see what the prices are doin' and who's payin' the best prices." He grinned and said, "We thought we'd give ourselves a little vacation at the same time."

Fletcher chuckled. "I understand that. Sometimes Ethel doesn't get things straight. She thought you said you had three thousand cows in that herd."

"About three hundred and fifty more than three thousand, actually," Casey replied. "The last word we got before we left Texas was that the market is showing some life again and the folks back east are payin' reasonable prices again. Are you involved in the buyin' of cattle for your company?" Fletcher said that he would be bidding on their cattle. "Maybe you could tell us what the last herd went for, just so we know whether or not we wanna go back and turn our cattle toward Montana."

Fletcher chuckled again. "You won't have to do that. The last cattle loaded on the train here counted something around twelve hundred head, and they sold for twenty-seven dollars a head. Granted, that's not what the market once was, but it's a lot better than last year."

"I reckon you're right," Casey said. He wondered if Fletcher noticed the grin on Eli's face.

Fletcher got up and returned to his table, telling them he looked forward to bidding on their cattle, if they ever arrived. Casey looked at Eli and grinned back at him. "I think this calls for a slice of pie to finish off this coffee." They signaled for Ethel.

They got to know the folks at the hotel and the dining room very well during the following days. They even became accustomed to walking around town with no gun on their hips. They made it a point to exercise their horses every other day.

There was one problem that came to their attention once when they were checking their packsaddles in Louis Brown's stable. They had not checked their work clothes thoroughly since they had used them to bait Rufus and Lige Coggins on that creek bank. When Eli reached in and pulled a sleeve of his big coat out of the way, it tore as if it was rotten. He realized that it was still damp from the crossing of the Red River. They decided then that they would have to take the packs out of the stable somewhere so they could empty them without being seen. So one day, when they came to get Smoke and Biscuit, they loaded up their packhorses, too. When Louis showed some concern, they assured him that they'd be back before suppertime.

So they rode off into the prairie north of Dodge City until completely out of sight of the town, then rode until they found a stream. They stopped there to let the horses graze while they opened up all the packs and took everything out. What they found was what they suspected back at the stable. The wool garments they had been wearing as disguises were literally rotting. To demonstrate, Eli took hold of the sleeve he had accidentally ripped at the stable and gave it a sharp tug. It ripped halfway loose at the shoulder. Adding to their shabby condition, the bullet holes from Rufus and Lige's attack were very prominent. "We can't use these rags anymore," Eli declared. Even the hats were coming apart. They were afraid to open the canvas sack that held their wigs, beards, mustaches, and makeup. When they did, they were relieved to find they were not harmed. "What the hell are we gonna do now?" he asked.

"The same thing we did the first time," Casey told him. "We'll find us an undertaker in the poor part of town, maybe Hell's Half Acre in Fort Worth, and buy the cheapest stuff he's got. But for now, let's burn this stuff."

So they built a big fire and dumped all the old men's clothes on it. It burned, but the old damp clothing made so much smoke, they were afraid they would attract company. They continued to sweat it out for more than half an hour before the old clothes dried out enough to burn cleaner. When it was finished, they put the fire out and left a pile of ashes and scraps of wool, but nothing that told a story of any kind. "Let's go back to town and get some supper," Casey said. "I'm hungry."

They couldn't remember ever being happier than the day they finally saw Gary Corbett lead that herd of cattle into Dodge City. The men seemed as glad to see them as well. After the cattle were sold, they stampeded below the deadline to blow off the cobwebs gathered on the long trail drive and spent most of the money they received in bonus. A buyer for Swift Meat Company topped Marvin Fletcher's bid with one of twenty-nine dollars, so the D&T's risk to drive the cattle to Dodge City paid off. Each man received a bonus, and Grover Morris got the full price for his cattle, plus the bonus. When it was time to leave, Casey and Eli rode back with the men. The whole crew traveled at the pace of Smiley's chuck wagon. It was slower, but not as slow as when they had traveled at the cattle's pace. It was a celebration of sorts, for it was proof that the ranch was back in the business of raising cattle. And it appeared that, under the direction of Casey and Eli, it would be for a long time to come.

Chapter 23

It was a happy crew that returned to the D&T Ranch that summer, due mainly to the fact that they learned they would still be employed by the D&T permanently. There was a joyful parting for Grover Morris, as he once again thanked Casey and Eli for saving his family and his land. In spite of the recent recovery in the cattle market, Grover was not convinced that it would last. And because of that belief, he proposed to invest his money and efforts in crossbreeding the Texas longhorn with Hereford cattle to sell in the Fort Worth market. "I'm hopin' to have a cow that's a better quality of meat than these stringy, tough longhorns." Casey and Eli considered Grover a fairly intelligent fellow, so they told him they might have an interest in his crossbreeding, and they'd like to keep in touch. Their interest pleased Grover greatly and he told them so when he said good-bye and left to return to his ranch with his son, Billy, and Ray and Jay Moore.

"You know, that ain't a bad idea Grover's got," Eli said to Casey after they had gone. "That might be the way to go for us."

"Right now, I'm thinkin' about all the money we've got, but I'm also thinkin' about how fast it'll get sucked up with the cost of runnin' this ranch," Casey confessed. "I'm afraid we ain't gonna be able to let ol' Oscar and Elmer retire anytime real soon. So I think we'd best not wait too long before we buy those two old boys some new duds."

"You talkin' about goin' somewhere right away?" Eli asked. "Hell, we just got home."

"I was just thinking there ain't no use to put it off, in case we might suddenly need those two boys for something."

"I reckon you're right," Eli said. "You thinkin' about the Acre?"

"I was, but maybe we oughta go over to Waco, instead, go to the Reservation maybe. We've been seen around Fort Worth too much lately. We could go back to that fellow's barn, that undertaker. What was his name? Somethin' Pope, weren't it?" Eli shrugged and shook his head. "Carl," Casey said, "Carl Pope. We bought ourselves two pretty good outfits from ol' Carl." He paused for a moment when he thought of something else. "Did Miguel or Juanita tell you that Colton Gray came here to the ranch while we were gone?"

"Yeah, Miguel told me he showed up here. Wonder what that was about? Miguel said Juanita told him we were with the herd and had been gone about a month."

"Hell," Casey exclaimed. "You know why he was here, that bank holdup. He wanted to see if we had stayed here, instead of goin' with the herd. I swear, he's like a snappin' turtle. Maybe this time he'll think we really were up the Chisholm Trail when that bank got hit." He considered the possibility. "We'd better go pick up some new duds, though."

"Maybe we'd better," Eli agreed.

So they left early the next morning on a business trip to Waco, prompting Monroe to comment to Corey Johnson, "I swear, they don't even get time to rest after just gittin' back from Dodge before they gotta go see their business partners."

Casey and Eli were not the only travelers to return to Waco. After having spent another frustrating investigation of another bank robbery, Colton Gray returned to Waco. His trip to Fort Worth had included a long ride from there to the D&T head-quarters, once again to no avail. The two bandits had left him no trail from Fort Worth beyond a camp beside a creek that he was convinced was the place where they changed into and out of their disguises. He was afraid that his total lack of success was stacking up a record of incompetence for his job. He wondered now if he had been sent for today just to be told by Timmons that he was being reassigned to something more mundane. He almost welcomed it. They could assign one of the "old heads," as Timmons liked to refer to them, to the job of running two feeble old men to the ground. That turned out not to be the case, however, when he walked into Marshal Timmons's office.

The marshal was standing behind his desk, talking to two of the old heads that Colton recognized as Hank Penny and Cecil Stark. "Come on in, Colton," Timmons said when he saw him. "You know Hank and Cecil, right?"

"Yes, sir," Colton replied. "I rode in a posse with them and one other deputy when we went to capture Jack Garner and his brother in Mexia."

"Colton," Hank acknowledged with a nod. Cecil did the same. Colton returned the brief greeting with a nod of his own.

"That business with Jack Garner is the reason I called you in today," Timmons said. "Since Jack Garner was shot down that day, and Buck, his brother, captured, Buck ain't never quit tellin' everybody he's gonna get the man who shot Jack—"

"That was his own damn choice," Hank interrupted. "The sheriff weren't the only one put a bullet in Garner that day. He chose to put up a fight, so we obliged him."

"I know," Timmons said, "but his brother thinks the sheriff was the one that done it. He broke outta prison last month. Killed a guard, and last week he showed up in Mexia and shot the sheriff down right in front of the jailhouse. Fellow over there who knows Buck says he figures he came to Waco because he's sweet on a woman who works in one of the dancehalls over in the Reservation. So, Colton, I called you in to help look for him. He might have other friends besides that woman, so it won't hurt to have an extra gun to go after him."

"Do you know the woman's name?" Colton asked.

"Lyla's the name she's been using. That's what the fellow said," Timmons answered. "We don't have no idea which one of those dancehalls she works in, though."

"We only saw Buck Garner that one time," Colton remarked. "He might not look the same after bein' in prison that long."

"Hell, son, you wanna take all the fun outta the job," Cecil japed, causing Hank to crack up. Hank had a large gray mustache that wrapped around his mouth, down to his chin. And when he chuckled, he made a snorting noise, not unlike a bull about to charge.

"I'm putting Hank in charge of this detail," Timmons told them. "He'll be callin' all the shots, since he's the senior man here. Your orders are simple, go find the man. Capture him if possible."

"Right," Colton said. *I'm right back working with two old geezers*, he thought.

It was still fairly early in the morning, and not a time when you would expect to find any of the dancehalls open, but Hank decided they could visit the saloons and possibly talk to the bartenders as they prepared for the day ahead of them. So the three deputy marshals went to the section of town known as the Reservation. Colton was of the opinion that it was a total waste of time, this time of day, but he kept it to himself. "Might as well try the Dead Dog Saloon," Hank said. "It's right in the middle of the street where most of the action is." Neither Cecil nor Colton had any reason to object, or a better suggestion, so they went into the Dead Dog.

"Hank Penny!" Ned Barber blurted. "Where the hell have you been? I ain't seen you in a coon's age."

"Howdy, Ned, you ol' mule. I've been workin' north of here for over a year. I just came back to see if anybody'd shot you yet. Say howdy to Cecil and Colton."

"Howdy," Ned said; then back to Hank, he asked, "You still wearin' a deputy marshal's badge, or did you finally get tired of workin' for nothin'?"

"Still wearin' it," he said, and snorted a chuckle as he pulled his coat aside so Ned could see it.

"These two fellers with you," Ned asked, "are they deputies, too?" They both nodded and Hank said that they were. "I swear," Ned went on, "you still ain't particular about the company you keep." He waited for another snorting chuckle, then adopted a more serious tone. "Three deputy U.S. marshals at the Dead Dog. What's goin' on, Hank?" He wasn't aware of anything his boss was up to that might have attracted the attention of the law.

"Ain't nothin' wrong at the Dead Dog," Hank assured him. "We're huntin' a woman you might know, and a man that mighta come to see her. And I'm bettin' you know ever'body on the Reservation."

"Ah, come on, now, Hank," Ned pulled back. "The Reservation's a helluva big place now. I don't know nobody but them folks that's right around the Dead Dog, especially the women. There ain't no women that hang around this little ol' saloon. Who are you looking for?"

"Lyla," Hank answered.

"Lyla who?" Ned asked. Colton almost said it with him. He didn't expect him to say anything else.

"You know who," Hank charged. "She most likely don't even go by a last name. Lyla, she works in one of these dance-halls around you. She might come in here now with a feller named Buck."

Ned started shaking his head and kept shaking it until Hank finished his statement. "I swear," he said then, "I'd help you if I could, but I just don't know any Lyla or a feller named Buck. I'm sorry I can't help you, but I can offer you boys a drink of likker on the house."

In Colton's mind, that meant that he was lying and offering whiskey to make up for it. He refused the drink, saying it was too early for him.

Hank and Cecil both accepted the whiskey, and Cecil commented that what Colton really meant was he was too young to take a drink. It garnered a chuckle from Ned and Cecil, with a snort from Hank. They remained in the Dead Dog Saloon long enough for Cecil and Hank to enjoy their whiskeys before telling Ned they would see him later. Then they picked a dancehall at random to cast their unbaited hook into the water, as Colton saw it. The first dancehall they picked was called Minerva Mae's Social Club. When they walked in, they found a couple of men and half-a-dozen women sitting at a group of tables beyond the bar, eating breakfast. One of the men called out to them without getting up from the table. "The club ain't open yet, boys. We don't open till noon." When the three strangers continued to walk on back to the tables, he protested. "We're just eatin' our breakfast back here. We ain't open for business."

"We ain't gonna trouble you," Hank told him, and showed him his badge. "We just wanna have a word with Lyla."

His statement brought a lot of blank expressions to faces already holding inquisitive ones, and the man asked, "Who?" When Hank repeated the name, the man looked at a rather stout woman at one of the other little tables. "Mae, any of your girls named Lyla?"

"No," Mae said. "Whaddaya wanna talk to her about?"

"Well, I reckon that would be hers and our business," Hank told her. "You sayin' you don't know her?"

"That's what I'm sayin', Sheriff or Marshal or whatever you are."

"I'm a U.S. deputy marshal," Hank informed her, "and so are they."

"All three of ya, huh?" Mae responded. "She must be awful important."

"We think her life might be in danger, ma'am," Colton said. "That's why we're trying to find her."

"Why didn't you say that in the first place?" Mae responded.

"I think Deputy Penny was just gettin' ready to tell you," Colton said.

"That's right," Hank said. "I was just fixin' to tell you that."

"Lyla don't work here," Mae said. "She works at the Waco Waltz Palace. What kind of danger is she in?"

"There's a feller named Buck Garner just got outta prison," Hank said at once. "And we're pretty sure he's lookin' for her. That's why we need to find her real quick."

"Why do you figure Lyla's in danger? She ain't gonna be in any danger from him. She's been true-lovin' Buck ever since I've knowed her."

"I reckon it couldn't hurt to make sure she's all right," Colton told her. "We sure thank you for your help."

"Yeah, thanks for your help," Hank said. He turned around and headed for the door. When they got outside, he asked, "Where the hell is the Waco Waltz Palace? We shoulda asked them before we left."

"I know where it is," Colton said. "It's on the street that runs behind this one."

"I swear," Cecil declared, "it's a good thing Timmons called you in to help on this job. You know where everything is."

"I live in Waco," Colton said.

"That was a pretty smart thing you did back there when you told that woman we was afraid Lyla was in danger," Cecil said. "She opened right up then and told us everything."

"That's right," Hank said. "I was just fixin' to tell her that when you came out with it."

"So, whaddaya wanna do now?" Cecil asked. "You wanna go to the Waco Waltz Palace, or wait till these places start openin' up for the day? Whadda you think, Colton?"

"Hank's callin' the shots," Colton replied. "Whatever he says is fine by me. If we wait till they're open for business, it might be easier to do some lookin' without everybody noticin' what we're doin', though. It would help a little if we knew if Buck has anybody with him."

"I think we'd do better to wait till these places get cranked up, so we might as well go ahead and get some dinner somewhere, and then come back here," Hank said. "Since you live here, Colton, where's a good place to eat?"

"Well, you can't go wrong with the hotel dinin' room," Colton replied. That seemed to work for Hank and Cecil, so that's where they decided to go. They climbed on their horses and turned them back toward the center of town and the Mc-Clellan House Hotel. They turned the corner barely seconds before two riders passed Minerva Mae's on their way to the undertaker.

"There it is," Eli said, and pointed to the small barn where Carl Pope practiced his mortuary business. They pulled their horses up in front of the building and dismounted. "Don't look like anybody's there."

There was a big padlock on the front door, so Casey walked to the back double door to make sure. "Looks like we hit him at a bad time," he said. "Maybe he's just gone somewhere to eat dinner."

"I hope to hell so," Eli replied. "It is dinnertime. I'd like to go, myself."

"I bet I know where you wanna eat, too," Casey said. "Maybe

we oughta try someplace besides the hotel dinin' room, though. We ain't ever tried out any of the other places in town."

"I couldn't take a chance on Frances findin' out I was in town and went someplace else to eat dinner," Eli joked. "It might break her heart."

"Ha!" Casey barked. "Tough as that gal is, you couldn't break her heart with a sledgehammer." He tried the lock, even though he knew it wouldn't open. "We could wait around here for a little while to see if he shows up." So they waited for what seemed like a long time with still no sign of Carl Pope. "If I knew someplace else to get our clothes, I'd say let's go there, but I imagine this is the only place we can find the kind of clothes we need."

"We might as well go and get some dinner before the dinin' room closes," Eli said.

"Let's go by the Dead Dog Saloon," Casey suggested. "That was where we found him the first time we did business with him." Eli agreed, so they climbed back on their horses and rode the short distance to the Dead Dog.

"Howdy, boys," Ned greeted them when they walked in. "Haven't seen you in a while." This must be the day for it, he was thinking. Earlier, Hank Penny showed up, now these two. He was trying to recall who they said they were, some kind of lawmen or something like that. "Whaddalya have?"

"Nothin' right now," Casey said. "Ned, ain't it?" When Ned said that was correct, Casey continued. "We're looking for Carl Pope again. Has he been in this mornin'? We went by his place, but it was all locked up."

"Carl was here for a little while this mornin', but left earlier than usual. I expect he'll be back before long. He don't never go outta town. You want me to tell him you're lookin' for him?"

"Yeah, you can tell him that," Casey said. "We're gonna go

eat some dinner, and then we'll have that drink of likker."
When they walked back outside to the horses, Casey said,
"We're cuttin' it pretty close, we'd best get a move on, if
we're gonna make the dinin' room before they close." They
wasted no time climbing aboard and loping off toward the
hotel. As it turned out, Casey was not far off in his calcula-
tions.

"Well, look what the cat dragged in," Frances remarked
when they walked in the outside entrance to the hotel dining
room. "Thelma was just getting ready to put the Closed sign
on the door."

"We're delighted to see you again, too, Frances, darlin',"
Eli greeted her.

"Frances is right," Thelma Townsend, the dining-room
manager, said. "If it wasn't you two boys, I would have told
you it's too late to eat. But I'll make an exception for you. We
haven't seen you for a while."

"We appreciate it, Thelma," Casey replied. "We'll take
whatever's left over. We're used to eatin' table scraps, as long
as we can wash it down with some hot coffee."

"Here," Frances said, and led them to a table right by the
kitchen door. "Sit down here next to the kitchen so we don't
have to walk so far to feed you." Then when Thelma went to
put the sign in the door, Frances asked, "Are you stayin' in the
hotel tonight?"

"We ain't decided yet," Eli told her. "We was wonderin' if
there was any reason to stay over tonight, or just start for home
this afternoon." As he said it, he was thinking if she would
check with the desk in the hotel, she would know they already had a room. "You think there's any reason?"

"Why are you asking me?" Frances answered coyly.

"Last time I was here, you told me not to come back, so I
wouldn't wanna make you mad again."

"Well, that was a while back," she said demurely. "A person can't hold a grudge forever."

"I'm real glad to hear that 'cause we're stayin' here tonight, and I wouldn't wanna feel unwelcome." *Ain't nothing that'll melt a righteous woman's heart like a hundred-dollar bill,* he thought. He remembered telling Casey it was the best hundred dollars he had ever spent.

Chapter 24

"Hello, 'Reba.'" The gruff voice came from behind the open hallway door to suddenly startle her as she walked from the dressing room to the dance floor. She could not help but stumble as she tried to catch herself. "Did I scare ya?" He stepped out from behind the door. "Maybe I shoulda called you Lyla. Would you like that better?"

"What are you doin' here, Buck?"

"Ain't you glad to see me, Reba? I come a long way to see you. Went to a lotta trouble, too, 'cause you said you'd wait for me no matter how long I was in that prison. You remember that, don't you, Reba? I counted on that, and when I said I'd come for you, you knew I meant it. Didn't you, Reba?" He waited for her response, but she was too terrified to speak. "When I went to your pa's old place, there weren't nobody there but your brother, Cletus. You know what he told me? He told me you had left the home place and said not to tell me where you went." Tears began to well up in her eyes as a picture of the confrontation between Buck and her younger brother began to form in her mind. "I knew he had it wrong," Buck continued. "I knew you never told him that. I had to make him see he was wrong, and he finally told me where you were."

She sobbed then. "Did you hurt Cletus?"

"He don't hurt no more," Buck said. "I think he's really glad me and you can be together again."

"Tell me!" she demanded angrily. "Is Cletus all right?"

He smiled at her and replied, "He was feelin' kinda poorly before I got there, but now, he ain't feelin' no pain. He don't matter, anyway. It's me and you that matters. I killed a prison guard to get outta that hellhole. And I killed the man that killed my brother. And I'll kill anybody else who gets in our way."

Desperate now, for she could see that he was insane as well as evil, she tried to appeal to his common sense. "You've got to get away from here! You know they'll send an army of law officers after you. And they know you'll come here where I am." When he just continued to stare at her glassy-eyed, she pleaded, "They'll shoot you on sight. I can't go with you. I'd only slow you down."

"Ain't nobody knows where I am. I didn't tell nobody where I was headin', and Cletus sure as hell ain't told nobody. He can't." That caused her to sob again, thinking of her brother. He grabbed one of her wrists. "You can shut up that bawlin', or I'm gonna give you somethin' to bawl about. Now, Reba, where was you goin'?"

"I was goin' to the dancehall," she answered. "I have to go there."

"Why? I don't want you to be dancin' out there for everybody to be lookin' at you."

"I have to dance," she pleaded. "That's what they pay me to do. If I don't dance, I don't get paid. And nobody will be lookin' at me, anyway, just the fellow I'm dancin' with." She saw in his immediate change of expression that he had been under the impression that she was part of a chorus of dancers.

"You mean you been dancin' with other men, lettin' them

rub all over you and feelin' all of you?" She could see the anger boiling up inside his simple mind.

"It ain't like that at all," she pleaded. "They're all very polite. If they get outta hand, Troy takes care of 'em. Just a polite dance, that's all that it is." She didn't want him to see those times when the woman was interested in making it turn into something more than a dance. And that was where the woman earned a nicer payday.

He wasn't convinced. "I don't think you better dance no more."

"All right," she said, "if that'll make you feel better. You stay here, and I'll go in and tell the boss that I'm not dancin' anymore. Then we'll go back to my room." He didn't look as if he was confident in what she promised. "Just stay right here. I'll be right back." She very carefully pulled his fingers off her wrist. "I'll be right back," she said again. He looked like a panther just set to pounce, but he let her walk through the door into the noisy dancehall.

Safely through the door, her first thought was to run and hide. She ran past the three musicians, straight across the middle of the dance floor, trying to dodge the startled dancers. The floor was already moderately crowded with early customers. Behind her, the door to the hallway that led to the dressing room opened again and Buck looked out on the dance floor. Seeing her dodging, then bumping into couples dancing, and dodging again, he roared out, "Reba!" And he immediately went after her, making no effort to avoid the couples, and leaving a number of disgruntled dancers in his wake.

Standing at the bar, Troy, the Waltz Palace's massive protector of the peace, was quick to head him off, angling across the dance floor to intercept him. When confronted with the huge man, Buck drew the .44 he was wearing and put two rounds into Troy's belly. Then he walked around him and started running for the door again. Outside, he saw Reba running across the street toward the corner. "Reba!" Enraged, he roared at her again, which only made her run faster.

Little more than a couple of blocks away, Eli paused when he heard two shots fired. "That was petty close," he remarked as he continued to tie down his and Casey's purchases from Carl Pope's inventory. "Mighta come from that dancehall."

"Sounded like a forty-four," Casey said. "Might be some more business comin' your way, Carl."

"Could be at that," Pope replied. "I might have to get my handcart out of the shed. If I do, this'll turn out to be a good day, what with you boys showin' up again." Like the first time they came to his business, the government authorized them to pay him ten dollars just to look through the clothes he'd taken off of the bodies he buried. And like the first time, they didn't find the particular suit jacket they were looking for, although he had more than a few with bullet holes in them. Also like the first time, they purchased quite a bit from his inventory to contribute to an old folks' home somewhere near Austin. He had to admire them for that. "I sure appreciate the business."

"You bet, Carl," Casey said as he climbed up into the saddle. "Maybe we'll see you again sometime." He waited for Eli to mount up, then said, "We might as well ride on up this street to the corner so we won't ride in front of that dancehall, in case whoever's doin' the shootin' ain't finished yet." Eli nodded his okay. Carl Pope's business was one street over, but it was directly behind the dancehall. When they reached the corner, Casey started to guide Smoke onto the cross street, but suddenly pulled him back sharply. "Hold it!" he cautioned Eli. There were three riders coming toward them on the cross street. They had not reached the corner where the Dead Dog Saloon sat, but he thought he recognized one of them. When they got a little closer to the corner and the Dead Dog, Casey blurted, "Damn! That's Colton Gray!"

"You sure!" Eli exclaimed, already wondering how they

would explain their presence in Waco. "It is him!" he confirmed when the three riders got closer to the corner. "I wonder who that is with him?"

There wasn't time for Casey to answer, because at that moment, they saw a man on foot, running toward the Dead Dog. Both men with Colton drew their handguns and opened fire. The running man turned at once and fired back, hitting one of the riders, who jerked upright in his saddle before falling forward on his horse's neck.

"Cecil's hit!" Colton exclaimed, and pulled his Colt .45.

"Buck Garner!" Hank roared. "Drop your gun! You're under arrest!" Both deputy marshals were too busy to notice Casey and Eli watching, stunned, from a block away. Buck's answer to Hank's order was a couple more shots in their direction before he turned and ran to the saloon, with shots from Hank and Colton to spur his escape. "He's in the saloon!" Hank said. "We'll go in and get him."

"What about Cecil?" Colton came back. "We need to see how bad he's hit."

"Right," Hank replied. He looked at his fellow deputy lying on his horse's neck. "How bad are you hurt, Cecil?"

"I don't know," Cecil gasped. "He got me in the chest. I'm bleedin' pretty bad, and it hurts like hell."

"We're gonna have to go on in there and run him to ground," Hank told him. "You know we can't let him get outta that saloon. We'll get you off that horse and let you set comfortable right here on the corner. Then we'll be back to getcha."

"Damn, Hank," Cecil groaned. "I don't know how bad I'm hurt. I don't feel so good."

"You'll be all right," Hank told him. "We won't be gone long. Then I'll take you to the doctor. We don't wanna let this devil get away with this." He didn't wait for Colton to help, but pulled Cecil out of the saddle and set him on the ground.

When Colton started to go to Cecil's side to see how bad he was, Hank stopped him. "He's all right. He ain't bleedin' near as bad as he was. Just leave him be. Our job is to go in that saloon and get that killer outta there. I'll go in the back door, 'cause that's where he'll most likely try to run. You go in the front door, and we'll have him between us."

Yeah, you sneak in the back, and I'll walk in the front door, yelling, "Shoot me, shoot me, Buck Garner!" Colton thought, but he didn't express it. Instead, he said, "All right, Hank, I'll go in the front. Are you going to give him a chance to surrender?"

"Yeah," Hank said, "the same chance he gave Cecil. Let's go, we're wastin' time."

Still watching from the corner of the street that Carl's shop was on, Casey and Eli were captured by the attempt to stop the man on foot. "He's puttin' the wounded one on the ground," Eli said. "Looks like he's plannin' to leave him there." They had determined by then that the big man with the gray mustache was giving the orders.

"There they go," Casey said when they left Cecil on the ground. "It looks like he's sendin' Colton in the front door. This could be the end of our troubles with Colton Gray," he couldn't resist saying.

"I reckon we can get off this corner now, before somebody sees us," Eli said.

Colton left his horse at the corner of the saloon and waited until Hank disappeared around the back of the building. He gave him a few more seconds; then he went to the front door and eased up beside it to peek in before exposing himself to Buck's gunfire. There were a handful of customers, all seated at the tables. Ned was standing near the end of the bar. There was no noise of any kind, not even a whispered word. He knew his first step inside that door would likely be his last on earth, so he looked right and left to see if there was a window or some other way to enter. "You might as well come on in,

Deputy, and I might let you live," a coarse voice suddenly announced. "But if you don't come in," it continued, "I'm gonna put a bullet in the head of this double-dealin' whore who said she'd wait for me. Maybe you don't believe me. Reba, honey, say somethin' to the deputy." He twisted her arm until she couldn't help crying out.

"I believe you," Colton said. "But why would I think you'd let me live if I walked in there?"

"Because I'm willin' to trade her life and your life for a free ticket out of this town. I've got a horse tied at that dancehall. I'll need that horse and I'll take this lyin' little whore for a ride. And if there ain't nobody followin' me, I'll let her go at the edge of town. That's my deal. If you don't like it, then I'm just gonna start killin' people in here until there ain't no more to kill. Then you'll have to come in to get yours."

Would he do it? That was the question. How good is a man's word who's just killed two men and maybe a third, depending on how bad Cecil was hurt? He was about to decide when he was startled by two gunshots, so close together they sounded almost as one. "Here's your other deputy!" Buck sang out. "Hard for a man that big to sneak up on anybody. How 'bout it, Deputy? The woman's next. I'm sick of lookin' at her blubberin' face."

Colton couldn't understand the man's reasoning. What could he gain by having him in there with everybody else? "All right, I'm tired of waitin'," Buck said. "I'm killin' the whore."

"No, wait!" Colton yelled. "I'm comin' in!"

"Drop your gun on the floor first," Buck ordered.

Colton laid his gun on the floor. *Lord,* he thought, *I might be coming to see you real soon. I don't even know who the woman is he's talking about. I hope this ain't a mistake.* He stepped in front of the batwing doors and pushed on through them. Buck Garner was behind the bar, holding the woman by her wrist with one hand. His other hand was holding a .44 revolver propped on the bar and aimed at him. Hank Penny's body was laid out flat on its back beside the wall. Colton started to go to check for signs of life, but was stopped by Buck's command.

"Leave him be. He's dead. I remember him from that day. He was one of that posse that shot Jack down and sent me to that hellhole. He had it comin'. I woulda got him sooner or later." He stared hard at Colton. "I might remember you, too. There was a young feller with that posse. It was you, weren't it?"

"I was there," Colton said. "I was with the posse. I didn't shoot at you or your brother."

"You're lyin'," Buck snapped. "Every one of you coyotes shot at me and Jack. I've still got lead I'm totin' inside me. Maybe you put it there. You're lyin', just like she's lyin'." He gave her arm another hard twist, forcing her to cry out again. "You've both gotta pay for your lyin'." He cocked the hammer back and lifted the gun from the bar and aimed it at Colton. The sound of the shot startled everyone in the saloon. It seemed way too loud for the .44 he held. His eyes stared wide open beneath the black hole centered on his forehead just above them. He hung on the bar for a few moments, supported by his elbows, before he fell over backward to the floor.

Colton could not deny the feeling of weakness in his knees, having come within seconds of going to his grave. He turned then, scarcely able to believe his own eyes. "You?" he exclaimed, stunned to see Casey Tubbs, standing in the door, holding a Henry rifle in his hand. "Casey!" Colton exclaimed, astonished and overjoyed at the same time. "What are you . . . ? Boy, am I glad to see you!"

"I would like to think you have better sense than to let yourself be drawn into a situation like this," Casey scolded. "Where's your gun?"

Colton, still grinning from ear to ear, just then remembered it. "Right by the front door, where I dropped it." He went at once to retrieve it.

When he dropped his gun back in his holster, Casey asked him, "Who is the fellow I just shot?" Colton told him who Jack Garner was and that Buck was his brother. "So I ain't killed anybody the world needs, then?"

"That's right," Colton answered. Then he remembered something the moment of excitement had driven from his mind. "Cecil!" he exclaimed. "I've gotta check on Cecil!"

"Is he the fellow you left on the corner?" Casey asked. "Don't worry about him. Eli picked him up on Carl Pope's handcart and took him to the doctor. He'll tell you where when he gets back."

"I didn't like leavin' him there, but Hank was in charge, and he said he'd be all right till we got back."

Casey nodded toward the corpse on the floor. "Hank?"

"Yep," Colton replied. "Too bad. Hank had been a deputy marshal for a long time."

"Don't look like he learned a helluva lot," Casey remarked. "But I reckon we all blunder once in a while, and just hope it ain't too costly. This was one of the costly times for Hank."

"But what are you and Eli doin' over here in the Reservation? Who's Carl Pope?"

"Carl's an undertaker. Eli's bringin' him up here with him to pick up a body," he said to Ned when the bartender walked over to join them. "How's the woman?"

"Lyla?" Ned asked as if there were others. "She's all right. Just a little bruised up is all." He stepped on the footrail, so he could take a look over the bar at Buck's corpse on the floor. He chuckled. "Lyla said now we've finally got the name of the saloon right." Back to Casey then, he said, "You shot him with a rifle. Lucky that you had it with you."

"I brought it with me, just in case I had to take a shot like that one from the door. I knew I had to nail it. If I'da had to use my six-shooter, I'da probably shot Colton."

Colton was about to question Casey again about the coincidence of his being in Waco at this particular time. But Casey was spared when Eli walked in the door. "Howdy, Colton," he said. "Glad to see you're still alive."

"Cecil?" That was as far as Colton got before Eli answered.

"Took him to Dr. Payne," Eli said. "Carl can tell you where his office is, if you don't know." Eli gave Casey a slight nod of the head, motioning toward the door.

Casey was well aware of why he was signaling. Eli had a packhorse outside, loaded down with nothing but old clothes to be used as disguises. Casey had already been trying to detour Colton's questions as best he could, but he decided to give Colton a bigger push. "Well, this kinda leaves you with a lot to do right away, don't it? I expect you'll want to take Hank, there, back to the marshal's office when you report that you got the fellow you and the other two deputies went after. Me and Eli will help you load him on his horse. How 'bout the fellow you came after? Maybe you need to take the body behind the bar, too, since he is the one you came after. Carl can take care of the body in the dancehall that the fellow behind the bar shot. What's his name again? Right, Troy," he continued when Colton answered. "So I reckon you ain't wantin' to waste any time in reportin' back to your boss at marshal headquarters. Come on, Eli, we don't wanna hold him up. He's got a lot to do. I heard that fellow, Buck, say his horse was tied at the dancehall. We'll go over and get it before Carl claims it. We can tote his body out front on the way."

Colton stood speechless while Casey rattled off all his responsibilities. And when Casey listed them, they sounded like more than he normally would have thought. It did serve to inform him that he was left with the command of the original three-man detail, so it was up to him to bring his report, along with the casualties, to his boss. Finally he said, " 'Preciate it," when they went by him carrying Buck Garner's body out the door. He turned to the spectators standing around, gawking, and said, "One of you fellows wanna pick up his feet and give me a hand?" A volunteer stepped up, and they carried Hank Penny out to lay beside Buck Garner.

A few minutes later, Casey came riding back on Buck's horse. "Here you go, Colton. I see you already got Hank's body on his horse. Good idea. This warm weather, ain't no tellin' how long before they'll get stiff as a board. We won't hold you up." He looked at a husky young cowhand who had stopped to gawk. "Here, big'un, help me throw that body on this horse." The young man stepped forward and they loaded Buck on his horse. When Colton looked about to ask him a question, Casey said, "Eli's bringin' my horse, I won't hold you up." He stood back and watched Colton ride off with his bodies. Then he walked around the corner to the back of the saloon where Eli was waiting with the horses.

"Is he gone?" Eli asked when Casey appeared.

"Yep, he's on his way back to report to the marshal, and I thought he'd never leave. I'm wonderin' if maybe we might wanna go ahead and start back home right now."

"Oh, no, we ain't," Eli responded at once. "It ain't gonna be long before supper, and there ain't no place to buy supper on the way home. Besides, we've already paid for a hotel room."

"And Frances decided she could use a hundred bucks, right?"

"Oh, I forgot about that," Eli lied. "Anyway, she don't do it for the money."

"Right," Casey mocked.

*　*　*

As a result of the recent confrontation with the escaped prisoner, Buck Garner, Colton Gray found himself treading in a sea of confusion. It had been bad enough having to report that Garner was actually killed by cattle rancher Casey Tubbs, a man that Colton had suspected of having something to do with the old-men robberies. It was worse that he couldn't explain why Casey was there in the first place. Hank Penny was killed and that was a great loss, as far as Timmons was concerned. On the other hand, Cecil Stark was recovering nicely from his wound. In Colton's favor was the fact that Cecil spoke highly of his actions during the incident, and that Hank had given Colton the most dangerous job of going in the front of the saloon. Timmons learned that his young deputy was reasonably intelligent and not short of courage, but he was still permanently assigned to the old-men outlaws.

As far as Colton's personal bewilderment, he found himself at sea, mentally, with the conflicting facts and emotions that picked away at his common sense. Although he hoped he was wrong, he seemed always to be confronted with clues that might connect Casey and Eli to the robberies committed by two men dressed up in old men's clothes and wearing disguises. And now this to throw in the pot, he owed his life to them, for Casey shot Buck Garner to save his life. If he had been the victim, instead of Buck, the only person suspicious of Eli and Casey would have been eliminated. He shook his head, trying to clear it. "And yet, Casey saved my life. Damn it!"

As far as Casey and Eli were concerned, a day they had planned for some simple clothes shopping had unexpectedly been quite complicated. It all ended well for their young deputy friend, however, and that was good, they supposed. They looked forward now to a nice quiet supper at the hotel dining room, and as they slow-walked their horses in that direction, Casey made a comment. "You know, I think I'd like to go back to Fort Worth someday and visit the Woodward House Hotel for one of Pearl's fine meals."

"I expect Emma and the gang would be glad to see us," Eli said. If they had been there that night, they would have noticed the two rocking chairs on the porch—one with the name *Eli* painted on the headrest, the other with the name *Casey*.

Visit our website at
KensingtonBooks.com
to sign up for our newsletters, read
more from your favorite authors, see
books by series, view reading group
guides, and more!

Become a Part of Our
Between the Chapters Book Club
Community and Join the Conversation

Betweenthechapters.net

Submit your book review for a chance to win exclusive
Between the Chapters swag you can't get anywhere else!
https://www.kensingtonbooks.com/pages/review/